MARK CHRISTOPHER

By Stan Matthews

MARK CHRISTOPHER

iUniverse books may be ordered through booksellers or by contacting:

iUniverse
1663 Liberty Drive
Bloomington, IN 47403
www.iuniverse.com
1-800-Authors (1-800-288-4677)

ISBN: 978-1-4917-8564-5 (sc)
ISBN: 978-1-4917-8563-8 (e)

Library of Congress Control Number: 2016900395

Print information available on the last page.

iUniverse rev. date: 01/19/2016

DEDICATION

Edith Joan Matthews
1920-2002

CHAPTER ONE

It was the first time that Mark Christopher had been in a jail to minister to one of his church's members. He strode along a dim corridor toward the cell where Steve Roberts was waiting with both of his bruised arms thrust between the bars.

"Did they arrest you too?" Steve asked as he grasped Mark's hand. "Good God, you're bleeding, Pastor!"

"It doesn't matter, Steve. Here comes the guard. He will let me in."

A tall dark figure, accompanied by the rattle of a batch of keys, emerged from the gloom.

"Well there, Steve," the guard called out cheerfully. He snapped to attention, stretching to his full height. He stroked a fleck of dust from his blue uniform jacket. "And who do we have here?" he commanded. "Oh, sorry. You must be the pastor? I just came on duty. The desk sarge told me you were visiting Steve. What's it this time, Steve? Drunk again?"

"Open the blasted door," Steve cried out as he shook the iron bars. "I haven't got all night."

The guard stepped forward, grimacing. "Hasn't got all night, he says. What you think of that, Pastor?"

"Nothing, and I do have the privilege of the cell," Mark replied. He brushed aside a streak of blood on his pale white forehead. He wiped his hands on his tan trousers.

"Sure, Pastor. What happened to you?"

"Ask Sheriff Delaney."

"Sheriff Delaney! Must be serious." The guard turned a key in the door's lock. The door swung wide. "In you go. Yell when you want to leave, Pastor." Mark entered the cell. The guard turned the key and marched away.

Mark knew what they had done. They had jailed the wrong man. As injured as himself, Steve was bruised and broken but unconquered. Their cause had triumphed. The County Fair had been integrated.

Steve, sitting on the cot, his unruly black hair draped across his forehead, covering the bloody bruise suffered when he had fallen on the fair's concrete entrance road. He bent over, his reddened eyes scanning the floor. "They can't hold me without trial, can they?" he asked.

"You'll be out of here soon, Steve. We've got a lot to be thankful for."

Mark slowly and painfully began to take off his jacket.

"Don't tell me it's too hot in here for you!" Steve exclaimed.

Mark laughed, a noiseless chuckle. "I'm going to change places with you."

Steve gasped with pain as he stood up. "What did you say?"

"I said I'm going to change places with you ."

"Hah! Hah!" Steve's thin body shook. "Give me one good reason why."

Mark leaned toward him. "Because you're innocent," he said softly. "You've got to do it because I must do it."

"Why must you?"

"It's hard to put into words, Steve, but I'll try." Overhead a bare bulb dangled, emitting a pitiful glimmer of light. "I'm walking on glass. I'm going to be tried by the Presbytery. Don't ask me how I know. I can't ever tell you why, believe me. I wouldn't lie to you. But I've done more to hurt you than you will ever know, perhaps compromised your life. I want to take your place, not to make it up to you, I can't ever do that, but because I must, for my own sake." Mark handed his jacket to Steve, "I should be locked up instead of you."

Steve sprang to his feet. "Just a minute, Pastor Mark. I was a leader as well as you."

"No, you were not," Mark said. "Your sweater, please."

"Listen, Pastor Mark, I went with the Negroes of my own free will."

"Did you, Steve?" Mark placed his hand gently on Steve's shoulder. "Be honest. You went because I persuaded you."

"I would have gone regardless," Steve said.. He started to remove his sweater. "What am I doing? Pretty soon you'll have me believing you."

"Steve, I don't have much time, so listen to me carefully." Mark sat gingerly on a stool. It was never easy, he told himself. Why wasn't it clear to Steve? If he could make Steve believe, so might others. "When you come right down to it, Steve, I had only one thing to fight with-- this." He struck his chest, indicating his body. "All else is words. Well, I'm through with words. I don't know why you were taken here in my place. One of those accidents, I suppose. That first blow was meant for me, don't you see?"

"Doesn't make sense."

"In the world's view, yes. But not from my view. I must take your place, because that is why I have been sent."

"Sent! Sent?" Steve rose up. He flailed the air with both arms. "Now I see! You're putting yourself up as one of those guys who's got to be a martyr or something. But, darn it, don't you see? I'm no martyr, let alone any sort of saint. I didn't go to the fair looking for this, even though, as I can see it now, you did!"

"I admit it," Mark replied. The overhead light seemed to dim. "Confusing, isn't it? I guess I was looking for a cause. To be some sort of sacrificial lamb, perhaps. But not now. You aren't the sacrificial lamb type, Steve. If anyone's got to be sacrificed it's got to be me."

"I still don't get you," said Steve. He shaded his eyes against the suddenly brightening light. "What makes you so special?"

"That's a cruel thing to ask, but you have a right to ask it, I suppose. Most of my life I wanted to do something special. Well, I've failed miserably at that. Realistically, I set my sights too high. I have feet of clay, as the saying goes, which is a crazy thing to say, because it sounds pompous. But I mean it. I thought I was on a par with the angels, and acted like it." Mark laughed. "Don't tell me you haven't noticed."

Steve smiled. "Once in a while. Somebody said something about that."

"Believe me, Steve, I've done nothing that deserves being punished for. Perhaps, to some, it may appear I'm guilty, but I hope not to you."

"You've always been and okay guy with me, Pastor ."

"What's happened? You usually call me by my first name."

"But you're my pastor, aren't you? I mean, you're not like other guys."

3

"No, and I can't ever be," Mark said. He fought for breath. "O God, that's what I can't stand. Being set apart, being looked upon as something other than an ordinary man, with the same feelings."

"That may be the way you look at yourself, but that's not the way I see you, and certainly not the way anyone else I know sees you."

This was too much. Mark felt a throb scoring his mind. "Everybody has a certain view of me, Steve. Yes, even you. Don't you expect something from me that you don't expect of others? Honestly, tell me."

Steve wrung his hands. "Good Lord, Pastor, what do you want me to say?"

"I am sorry, Steve. Forget it. Let's get on with it. Not much time left before I have to call the guard."

They were silently efficient, swiftly exchanging their clothing. Steve, in the cell's enclosing gloom, gave Mark a thumb's up. "How do I look, Pastor?"

"Ridiculous," Mark said. "My jacket's too big for you." .

Mark took a last look around the darkening cell before he would be left alone in its stark stony grip. "Guard! Guard!" he shouted. He hastened to the cot and laid down, face to the wall. Steve covered his chilled body with a thin gray blanket.

Soon he heard the jingle-jangle of the guard's keys.

The burly dark figure arrived. The liberating key was turned. The door was unlocked and opened. Steve, head lowered, silently followed the guard down the corridor.

Mark lay still on the cot. Five minutes passed before he heard the cautious click of the key, then his shoulder was being shaken. "You alight, Steve?"

"Yes," Mark said quietly. He rose unsteadily. "Did Steve get away?"

"I thought it was you," the guard said. "You're the one that's in trouble now." He grasped Mark by the arm and guided him to the open cell doorway. "Going to take you to the sarge."

Mark grasped the bars on either side of the doorway. The guard tried to tug him away. Mark held on fiercely.

"Alright, Pastor," the guard said. "You want to stay? Stay!"

The guard slammed the door. Mark's horrific cry drained down the corridor.

"Oh, God," the guard cried out as he pushed the door open. Mark folded his bloodied hands together and stumbled to the cot.

Much later, Mark bent down to untie his shoes. But his shoes were gone, and his socks too. His hands were swollen and purple. The cell door banged open. "Now aren't you a pretty sight?" He recognized the voice of Dr. Cleland Roach, whose balding head lowered toward him. The doctor opened his case and took out a small bottle, poured a few drops on Mark's wounds, bandaged them and left noiselessly. Mark turned on his back and slept.

The door opened again. Miss Herkimer, a county nurse, adorned by a flowing cape. "Pastor Christopher," she exclaimed dryly. "Thought you'd like something to eat." She set a tray on the stool. She helped him sit up and placed the tray on his lap. Her wide face was very pale in the dim light from the corridor. For the first time he noticed that the overhead light bulb was out. He held a cup of soup in his padded hands and raised it to his lips. The acrid aroma of onion smote his nostrils. He felt tears swell in his eyes. "I do appreciate it," he said. "It's very good." His shoulders shuddered.

"You're cold," Miss Herkimer said. She removed her cape and placed it around his shoulders.

Sometime during the cool night Mark's wife, Laura, came in. She was wearing a tight-fitting white dress, the same one she wore regularly while working in their manse's kitchen. Her light red hair drifted over her brilliant blue eyes, her prominent nose and her square dimpled chin. She kissed his wounded hands one by one. "Mark, why?"

"I suppose you think I'm crazy."

"Darling, no. I don't think you're crazy. Hasty, perhaps."

"I don't like being here."

"Then come home."

"No!" He struck the metal cot's spring. The pain seared his wounded hand.

"But you can't do any good here," Laura protested. "I know what I'll do. I'll talk to Sam Bryson. He has influence."

"No!"

"They can't hold you against your will."

"No!"

Laura pressed his hurting hand softly to her pale cheek. "Why are you punishing yourself like this? What good can come of this?"

They hugged and kissed hungrily until it was time for Laura to leave. Mark laid down on the hard cot, his head on the rough pillow. Perhaps no good could come of this. Still, if he had failed as a preacher and as a pastor, the least he could do was to take the place of a man who was innocent. He folded his aching hands together, but no words of supplication that were sufficient to his need would come. He closed his eyes and prayed for sleep.

Sleep was denied him. He raised his stricken hands, opened his eyes slightly. Narrow shadow bars crossed the cell floor.

His mother's sweet voice came from far away.

"A little farther, Mark, just a little farther. Stretch. That's it, between the bars here. Good. Now, open it up. Pull the string. It's money, see. Golden money."

That was long, long ago---

CHAPTER TWO

Andrew and Mary Christopher took their three-year-old son, Mark, on the Transcontinental Chief to Attumwa, and every day they went to the hospital to see him. They were not permitted in Mark's room, because whatever was wrong with him it might be catching. That was why they had to climb the fire escape to see him through a barred window. A nurse turned Mark's face toward the window and whether he could see them or not they did not know. They waved to him and said kind words.

The days passed in a blind blur, melding into one another. Stiff, unyielding, the bed did not move, and the single light bulb overhead did not blink. The world stopped and Mark slept while his body wasted. His legs, his arms, always quick and sure, ceased to exist. Knowing nothing of prison cells, Mark did not fear the room, even in the night's stillness, alone, for day would come and love again.

Each afternoon his parents brought gifts. One day it was a stringed bag of golden coins that miraculously opened to reveal dark Dutch chocolate. Mark had recovered enough so that his nurse could hold him up to the window bars. Mark's father peeled off the gold paper, broke the chocolate and slipped bits into the boy's mouth. Mark's eyes spoke his pleasure and wonder of money that tasted so sweet.

"Polio," his father told Mark years later. "It must have been polio. What else could it have been? You unable to move, not a muscle." Andrew's eyes, blue as his boyhood home, Boston Bay, an hour after dawn, would open wide, as if they dared Mark to challenge his conclusion. Young Doctor White, who had brought his third child into the world—yes, and slapped his bottom to bring him hollering to life— could not diagnose the case. He called it a "strange disease" that left no effects, unless salvation can be called an effect. "It was a miracle, that's what," Andrew said. "And don't ever forget it."

Andrew would never let him forget, because on the day Mark was returned in his father's arms to Westminster from Attumwa, Mary received a telegram from her brother, John Goddard, telling her that their father, Samuel, had been lost at sea. Mark was still too weak for his mother to leave him to attend the memorial service in Springport, and she never let Mark forget that either. When she did get around to telling him about her father and his strange death, there was always a tinge of accusation in her voice, as if it had been Mark's fault that she had to miss the service. "Why did he have to go to sea again?" she asked Mark many times. "Men are such fools."

Mary could never admit that she herself was weak, not even when she was bearing Mark. She often protested to Andrew of an evening, while she knitted, "I'm as strong as a horse." Two days after Mark was born in her own Westminster bed, since it was Monday, she hung out the washing on the line in their shaded grassless yard. With perfect cycling motions of her tanned mottled hands dipping into an apron pocket, reaching up to the rope strung between two towering swamp maples, and with a fancy snapping of fist, thumb and stubby forefinger, hardly pausing to dip her hand for another pin and reaching up again.

Mark had never seen his mother dance, but his father told him she once fox-trotted with the best. That was how his father had met her at a dance at Boston's Railroad Y.M.C.A., where the girls came to entertain the soldiers and sailors during the First World War, except that Andrew wasn't a soldier. He was an apprentice telegrapher, like his father had been, with the Transcontinental Telegraph Company, which was run by the railway.

She was just another girl down from the Maine farms. She hated it at the Boston shirt factory where she ran a power sewing machine. That accounted for her flat thumbs, or so she said. Mark believed, following his years at Springport, that her hours pitching hay had more to do with it.

Mary and Andrew were married in Springport Baptist Church, because that was Mary's church. However, when the time came for Mark's baptism, they were living in Westminster, a small railroad town in the far Midwest, to which Andrew had been transferred by the telegraph company. Unfortunately, as far as Mary was concerned, there was no Baptist church in their new town. Since the only other mainline Protestant church was Methodist, and at Andrew's insistence, Mark was baptized there. Or, rather, "Christened," as the Methodists would have it. Mary held Mark firmly enough as she handed him over to the minister.

Her husband viewed the matter from an entirely different perspective. He came from a long line of Methodists, and their way to baptize was the right way. However, he and Mary had come to an early agreement, even before they were married, that they could "get along" alright if each of them could attend their preferred denomination when possible.

There had been little disagreement as they lent themselves to the task of choosing a name for their third child. They both followed family naming traditions. Mainly they were biblical traditions. Selecting Bible names was a law. For them, a proper Bible name signified their hope that their children would reflect their points of view, out of parental respect. Better still, the names would be memorials honoring ancestors and close family relatives, especially parents, brothers and sisters and, if necessary, beloved uncles and aunts.

As far as Andrew was concerned, choosing the name of one of the Disciples was the only choice, which was agreeable with Mary since those names were abundant on the Goddard family tree, as were the names of notable New Testament women. In the Christopher clan there had been Andrew's father, Thomas, and a Matthew, his grandfather.

They named their first born Peter Andrew and their daughter Martha Theresa, the second name being in honor of Mary's mother. Since there had never been a Mark in the Christopher line, as far as they knew, Andrew got his choice. Actually, there had been little choice, since Bartholomew was out of the question.

What was to be Mark's middle name was another matter. Mary was surprised when Andrew suggested Goddard. "Because," said Andrew, "we have to preserve the Goddard name." He pointed out that Mary's brother, John, was unmarried and wasn't likely to ever get married, by John's own vow. Since there were no other Goddard children, the end of John would be the end of the direct Goddard family.

As for the Christophers, Andrew stressed, perpetuation of that name depended upon their two sons, since he was the only child of his parents, who died in the great influenza epidemic of 1919. Mary herself had come down with the disease and been bedded four months. Peter and Andrew lived through it.

For several years Mary was barren. When she became pregnant at last Andrew prayed for a second son. Mark was born in their unpainted shingled company house in Westminster on a windy March night. Afterward Andrew read to Mary, from the thumb-indexed family Bible, the story of the calling of the twelve disciples.

During the thirties, whenever there was a baptism at the Methodist church on the waterfront road in Attumwa, Mary would smile down at Mark as if to say "Remember?" He had been only three months old, but he could picture what happened. Pastor Wilson (only a name, no face) held him on his left arm as he dipped two fingers into the basin of a granite baptismal font and held the fingers there for a moment. Then he touched Mark's forehead three times with those wet fingers as he proclaimed: "I baptize thee, Mark Goddard Christopher, in the name of the Father, and of the Son, and of the Holy Ghost, Amen." Then, smiling benignly: "And may the spirit of the Lord descend upon thee and be gracious unto thee, and dwell in thine heart forever." Surely baby Mark had waited politely for the words to end before letting out a joyous yell, to the delight of the congregation.

Mark was five when Andrew was transferred to the Transcontinental Telegraph office in Attumwa, the state capital. It was the beginning of the Great Depression in the nineteen-thirties, a period when houses he could afford to rent were hard to come by. After a long search he found one on Maple Street in a waterfront section called The Flats. Two rows of red brick houses butted against the street's dead-end cliff. Maple Street (no one knew why it was named that, since it bore no maple trees) actually went up a cut in the cliff toward Upper Maple, where a monstrous monastery seemed to touch the sky.

The Christopher family arrived at Maple Street after a long drive from Westminster. They came in their first automobile, a 1929 Graham Paige. Peter, now fifteen, was the first to express his dismay as he stood akimbo before the house, looking up at its dismal brick walls. "What a dump," he said. Andrew, just behind him, shook his head in protest. Because he felt the same way, he said nothing. He had loved the openness of the country around Westminster, where he drove freely to fish, rejoicing in the freedom to do as he pleased when he pleased. When he left the limitations of Boston he swore he would never return to city life. But he had no choice. His employment demanded that he accept a transfer and that was that. Andrew shrugged and led his family into the confines of its new home.

Shivering in the shut-up dark dampness, they toured the house together. Peter held his nose as they inspected the bathroom upstairs. Mark was assigned the smallest of four bedrooms adjacent to that of his parents. Mary looked carefully around. "I like it," she said quietly. "It will do." Peter and Martha, meanwhile, had flipped a coin to choose their rooms. The moving van arrived. By nightfall the family was settled in. A bright full moon rose from the east. Peter and Mary went to high school. Mark entered kindergarten.

For Mark, the Great Depression was a time for sitting on the sun-splashed curb waiting for the scrap man to arrive with his rickety wagon piled high with worn tires and rusted bedsprings. The wagon was pulled by a sway-backed horse attired in a filthy fedora in which holes had been cut out for its ears. Mark and his friend, Jack Strong, sold the scrap man tires that they found in vacant lots and pieces of iron that they stole from backyard porches. A tire brought one cent, the metal one cent a pound. The boys did not sell some pieces of metal such as iron hoops they pried off nail kegs. Using push-sticks made of two crossed pieces of wood, they rolled the hoops, guiding them along the sidewalk, down a curb, up a curb, around the block. Last one home was a rotten egg.

At other times there were cool evenings to while away on the front porch, sitting under a moth-covered bare light bulb, as traffic puttered far away on the waterfront road. The gang would gather to sit and talk, and occasionally to get up and play run-sheep-run in the twilight. Mark's favorite hiding place was under the stoop of a neighbor, Mrs. Creighton. It was his secret that the cross-hatched lath covering one end of the stoop swung aside to admit him. When he hid under Mrs. Creighton's stoop he was never found.

Then there was the scary night when the monastery burned. Mark became aware of it while Andrew was carrying him to Mrs. Creighton's, there to deposit him for safe keeping. A high hot wind funneled down the hill into Maple Street, carrying with it a shower of flaming bits of wood, which fell onto the tar-papered roofs of the row houses below. A screaming red fire engine, long ladders atop, buckled around the corner, scattering a crowd of gawking onlookers, most of whom, having been roused by police from their homes, were still in their sleeping apparel. At the end of the street black-coated firemen sprayed great streams of hissing water onto the housetops.

At mid-morning, after the sun rose on the smoking monastery, the people, faces taut, their eyes red with soot-drawn tears, shuffled silently back to their homes, husbands with arms around wives, girls and boys holding tight to their mothers and fathers.

Later, Mark stepped out of his home's kitchen into the backyard, looked back to check that his mother wasn't watching, drew open the gate slowly to minimize its creak, and slipped through to the muddy lane that paralleled Maple Street. Racing, he streaked toward the cliff, climbed a rock-strewn path up the cliff, pushed between the wall of the end house and some bushes. He entered Upper Maple Street.

High above lay the burned monastery, its great gray granite walls intact and gleaming in the bright light of the risen sun. To Mark it was the great castle of King Arthur and the courageous knights of the Round Table. Mark climbed a tortuous slope. Scraped and bleeding, he crept beneath a steel mesh barrier at the top. Beyond a smoking pile of loose stones and blackened timbers the Cape Cods of Upper Maple stood well back from the street lined with rows of stately elms.

Everywhere were snaking hoses tangled in black pools of water. Brown-robed monks, their shaved scalps shining, stood mutely gazing, transfixed by the solemn debris. Firemen in long black and yellow waterproofs passed silently to and fro behind the remnant walls. Each time they emerged they carried bundles of limp dripping books. These they laid, like offerings, at the feet of the mourning monks. Some monks only stared at pulpy pyramids, disbelieving, while others flipped through stained soggy pages. Mark politely clasped his hands behind his back. He studied a grieving monk fingering a long beaded chain hanging from his gray cloth belt. The monk's lips moved. Mark could hear no sound to break the silence of the steaming air.

CHAPTER THREE

Peter was in his fourth year of high school when Mark celebrated his tenth birthday. Peter was an athletic champion at Attumwa's Technical High School. He excelled in acrobatics, swimming and hockey. Mark attended many events in which his brother contended, his attendance made possible by his sister Martha's insistence that the "youngster" required a guardian almost anywhere outside the boundaries of home, school or church. Mark's mother termed this "mother instinct" and Mark relished it. He was forever publishing the news of Peter's fame to his gang, citing Attumwa Gazette reports of Peter's team and individual achievements.

While he wasn't tall enough to play basketball, Peter was proficient in so many sports that he won a few silver cups. One year he was crowned Attumwa high school athlete of the year. He was also a favorite with the girls. He was never without a date. His father praised him no end among his Kiwanis buddies. For his mother it was always "Handsome is as handsome does." She was always worried about his academic standing, clearly tut-tutting to his face over every report card with anything lower than a *B* on it.

On family car trips to Echo Lake he displayed his prowess as a diver, taking off the 20-foot springboard without a trace of "just showing off," as his greatest fan, his sister Martha, would say. He was best at long distance swims. He didn't have time for short-term anything. "Takes too much time," he would tell Martha. He muttered to Mark one day that Martha suffered from "hero worship" and he had no use for the term in athletics.

Sailing, or any kind of boating really, was another matter. Peter and his best friend, Ron Rutledge, shared crewing a small craft they would rent by the hour at a waterfront marina. Once Peter took Mark aboard for brief run. Mark threw up repeatedly and Peter never invited him aboard again.

Peter was still in his last high school year when Andrew decided it was time for his son to decide what college he should attend. It was therefore a shock, when the discussion was held, that Peter said he was thinking about joining the Navy. Peter never relented and shortly after graduation he signed up and was soon gone to San Francisco for training. It was six years before Pearl Harbor.

Martha had argued against Peter's ambitions, but it was useless, It was about then that Andrew realized how much Martha depended upon her Older Brother. For months she remained uncomforted. Peter, whom she actually adored, was gone. He had been her mentor, her patron and her guide. There had been few secrets between them. Family ties were the summit of achievement for them both. Now that Peter was gone she turned the spotlight upon Mark, the Younger Brother who needed her attention even more.

Like her mother, Martha was a skilled seamstress. For years they had labored together making dresses for themselves and sweaters for Peter and Mark. Although Andrew would have them make his workman shirts, he insisted on buying his office-style ones at a reasonable haberdashers. For Mark they also knitted socks and sewed black-and-orange clown costumes for his annual Halloween trick-or-treat expeditions.

For a time Andrew and Mary rented out Peter's vacant room. For a little while they debated the pros and cons. At first Mary insisted that the room remain vacant. "Peter will need it when he comes home on furlough," she said. "He can have Mark's room." Andrew countered: "So where do we put Mark?" They decided to rent Peter's room only on a weekly, short-term, basis.

The first boarder they had was Robert Anderson, a young bachelor who came knocking in response to a "Room For Let" sign Andrew had hung on the front door. An illustrator, he had lost his job with an Attumwa advertising agency. He was the thinnest man that Mark had ever seen, or at least that he could remember seeing. He was also the tallest. He was forever pushing a forelock of his brown hair out of his eyes. Mr. Anderson took his meals with the family. He was quite friendly. He talked a lot about his art career and showed the family a carton full of his fashion sketches. He helped Andrew to paper the walls of Steve's room. After the old paper was stripped, Mr. Anderson drew a charcoal sketch of Mark on the wall. Mark recognized himself by the flat brown hair falling over his right ear. "I wish I could draw like that," Mark said. Mr. Anderson gave him a set of charcoals and some drawing paper. For the two weeks that Mr. Anderson rented the room Mark filled the batch of paper with sketches of churches.

The depression worsened. Crowds of unemployed men began marching to Attumwa, to demand that the state government get them jobs. They came in along the waterfront road by the hundreds singing "I've been working on the railroad" and "I'm tired and I want to go home." They marched to the State Capitol building, a mile down river on the Promontory. After school was out Mark joined other Barker School boys to watch and wave, as if the marchers were a parade and their soiled workpants and overalls were resplendent uniforms. Sometimes the boys marched down the sidewalks, keeping pace, until they reached Veterans Town, a tent and shanty village set down in Memorial Park just below the Promontory where the Capitol's granite pile shone golden at dusk. Soldiers with rifles on their shoulders stood on guard around the town's perimeter as the marchers squatted in silence before their fires, forking beans from tin cans and glaring silently, intently, into the flames.

As the grim years of the Great Depression moved slowly on, Mark would often recall the tragedy of the great monastery, but more often he would think about the times he and Jack rode their tricycles from the top of the cliff down Maple Street. Sure, you would coast, but if you weren't careful you could catapult over the handlebars. From the cliff bottom you peddled furiously until you reached home. Last one home was a rotten egg.

Mark's club, as they called it then, since "gang" meant gangsters, easily found things to do. They dug holes in backyards. Three feet down a yard square and they didn't strike China, they struck water. They walked a mile Saturday mornings to the Attumwa Museum to watch movies about Indians and Eskimos. They hiked along Rayoodoo River to the dam, where they ate their sacked lunches. They walked back by way of the Transcontinental roundhouse where they watched the oilers working on a black engine, hauled up by four chains so you could see the many-wheeled trucks. Other times they returned through the hills back of the Duquesne Mansion where the cave was. They hiked part way into the cave where it was dark and cold and deep, where the echo of their halloos sounded like Tarzan's. They followed the girls to Barker School, taunting them with "Sally loves Jack," or throwing snowballs at them, and making out they didn't care a bean for them, when all the time they would give them their hearts on a silver cushion. They pretended they didn't like their teachers, except beautiful Miss Brown.

James W. Barton School was a brick two-story building with tall windows fronting on the waterfront road. A worn wooden staircase led to the double walnut doors under an arch. On the second floor were the windows of Miss Brown's room. Mark's desk was by a window five rows away from the first row. Looking through the window Mark could see the hundred-car freight trains rolling slowly to the north or south. One morning in December his view was suddenly obscured by Miss Brown as she stood beside his desk.

"See anything interesting?" she asked curtly.

Mark determined never again to cause her to find fault with him.

Miss Brown returned to her desk, took off her glasses and began to call the roll. Mark gazed at her with unquestionable adoration. Her light brown hair, parted far to the left, shone brilliantly in the soft window light. Her fair face bore three slight blemishes, one just to the right of her cherry-red lips, another to her small, quite slim, nose, and the third above her left eyebrow, almost on her high shining temple. For Mark they weren't blemishes: they were beauty marks.

Finished calling the roll, Miss Brown stood up. Mark and the entire class stood with her. Miss Brown folded her hands and closed her eyes. Chin down, she led the morning Lord's Prayer: "Our Father, who art in heaven …" Mark, eyes open, peered at Miss Brown, noted that her eyes were tightly closed. He sighed with resignation. He loved beautiful Miss Brown.

Later, he sat at her feet for a group story reading. Miss Brown, her soft voice stressing every nuance, unfolded the magic and mystery of the adventurous Persian youth who, fortunate one, unlocked the secret of the lamp. It seemed to Mark that there could never be another as good as she. In the tale of the poor Snowmaiden it was Miss Brown who assumed the role. She was Sleeping Beauty and Snow White. She was all the pure and beautiful women of the hundred stories she read, and all the heroic and untrammeled maidens of the books he devoured. In a thousand unmapped places he met her, on burning desert sands and storm-tossed waters, on India's golden plains and on the Spanish Main. By gunboat, man-o'-war, canoe and plane he rescued her a hundred times. From evil tribes and bearded cutthroats, from hated revolutionaries and enemy soldiers, he rescued her. She swooned in his arms in Tudor England, pledged him her troth in Napoleonic France, loaded his rifles in Georgian America, and waited his return from Czarist Russia.

Every Sunday afternoon, except in May and June when the family clambered into the Graham Paige for a trip to the Attumwa Hills or Echo Lake, Mark went to Sunday school with Peter and Martha. All classes met around chipped wooden tables in the center of the church's basement hall. Mark was usually the first of Mrs. Hopkins's class to arrive. He was always willing to help her set out lesson materials. After the opening exercises, in which the department superintendent gave a prayer and led a hymn, usually "Jesus Wants Me for a Sunbeam," the children turned their chairs to the tables. The quiet hum of the teachers' voices signaled the beginning of the lesson period.

"Our lesson for today," Mrs. Hopkins said in a peculiar way, as if she were ever on the verge of tears, "is about the calling of the disciples. Let's see how many disciples we can name." She looked about expectantly. A grandmother, she wore her white hair in small waves. Her pale skin was drawn tight over her sunken cheeks. Two of her students called out a name. She smiled and turned to Mark. Her rheumy eyes lit up. "Mark, can you recite the verse in which all of the disciples are named?"

Feeling proud, Mark launched into the verse he had memorized the week before: "Simon, whom he surnamed Peter; James the son of Zebedee and John the brother of James, whom he surnamed Boanerges, that is, son of thunder, Andrew, and Philip, and Bartholomew, and Matthew, and Thomas, and James the son of Alpheus, and Thaddeus, and Simon the Canaanite, and Judas Iscariot, who betrayed him."

Mark saw the green rolling hills of Galilee sweeping down to the sea. And Jesus, white-robed on the shore, calling Peter and Andrew to come to Him from their boats. And of them all Peter was his favorite, for it was he whose story he had read again and again, how he had been the first to say "Thou art the Christ, the son of the living God"; and it was he who, in his weakness, had betrayed Him, in the courtyard; and it was Peter who, in his strength, had been the disciples' leader ever after, even unto death.

It was Mary, Mark's mother, who attended the weekly Women's Bible Class with faithful regularity, having witnessed the intensity with which Mark memorized his Bible verses, once spoke to him about his future. "You have a certain way about you, Mark," she told him. She looked at him with deep-set dark eyes, those eyes so soft and transparent that they could peer into his very soul, as they often did when he told a lie. She always had translucent skin, but now it was paler than ever, pulled taut over her narrow chin and high cheekbones, giving her a gaunt, intense appearance. "I have just one hope," she said, "and that is, whatever you decide to devote your life to, that you will try to do good for others." She held him by his shoulders and turned him so that he looked into her burning, intense eyes. "And I want you to think some day, not now, of becoming a minister."

She had known well only three or four ministers in her life. The latest was John Wesley Woods of their Methodist Church, who had the unusual habit of repeating annually what he termed his most successful sermons. Mary's favorite was "God, Our Shield and Defender," which was scheduled for the following month. "That's one I'm not going to miss," she said.

She did miss it. She had leukemia. Mark learned about it later from his father. Mary had been spending ever longer periods in bed. One day Andrew told Mark he was taking his mother to City Hospital. Mark asked his father many questions. "Mom will have an operation," Andrew told him. To Mark she had always appeared strong enough. She even did the washing as usual the day before. When Andrew returned he told Mark not to worry. She's been working too hard," Andrew told him. "She needs a good rest."

Five days later Andrew opened the door to Mark's room before dawn. "Want to come to the hospital with me?" he asked his drowsy son. Although Andrew had taken Martha with him on his many previous visits he had held off taking Mark. Years later Martha told Mark that their father probably presumed Mark was too young.

City Hospital was a rambling brick structure, surrounded by wide lawns studded with elms. Andrew and Mark walked silently together down a long corridor to Mary's room. Propped up by pillows, following a hug from Andrew, Mary held out her arms to Mark. She held him as if she would never let him go and kissed him with fevered lips. She smiled a great deal, although thinly, and they asked one another how they were. She asked him not to forget all those things like brushing his teeth and polishing his shoes, as she had always done.

Andrew read her Peter's latest letter, which was postmarked San Francisco and which contained the news that he was on a destroyer somewhere in the Pacific. As the letter concluded, Mary closed her dark eyes, the way she always did when she prayed. The time came to leave.

"Come home soon," Mark asked her while within her enclosing arms.

"I will," his mother replied, but she never did.

Chapter Four

Andrew sent a telegram to Peter. Then he waited in the parlor until Mark returned from school and Martha from her job at Stern's Department Store. Leaving Mary in the hospital was like being in a dream. He felt as if he was floating on the bosom of a bubbling stream, heading where he did not know. Mary had been in a coma, her eyes minus their blue pupils as if she were gazing upward toward a ghostly presence. She gasped for air once, twice, then again and was gone. He was still holding her thin weak hand when her spirit flew away.

Now, as he waited for Martha and Mark, he knelt by the sofa, stiff, quaking hands clasped in prayer. What could he say? Why did God take her from him? But, he knew, God did not "take" away a devoted soul. What, then? But there was no real answer, not on earth. In heaven? That was his hope, that was his quiet assurance. He rubbed his tears aside.

Later, Martha, who had just turned eighteen, sat beside her father on the sofa. She covered her drained face and turned her head onto his shoulder. She had taken his sad announcement rather stiffly, Andrew thought. Of course Mary's dying had been a long time coming. Martha had been grieving for weeks. She was strong. He wished he had her strength. Now it was Mark he was worried about.

It wasn't long before Mark returned from school. When he saw Martha within his father's comforting embrace, he knew. Dizzy with the certain knowledge that he would no longer feel the sweet comfort of his mother's arms, he tried to absent himself logically from the view of his sobbing sister and stiffly welcoming wave of his father's hand. He used his trick of imagining a chalk brush erasing an unwanted and threatening message from a blackboard. It worked. For a long moment he had no thought at all, even as hot tears burst streaming from his stinging eyes, until the word "never" that his father had used was written on the slate again and again and again, like a punishment exercise. With each written word he heard a sound like an oceanic throbbing roar, and then a voice, whispered at first and then with gathering strength: "Never! Never! Never !"

The days before Mary's funeral and the day after were a vast blur, gotten through with hours of endless activity as Martha and Mark prepared the meals, cleaned the house as it had seldom been cleaned before, followed by hours of talk, and even some bursts of laughter when friends came to call. The parlor was seldom empty, except in the night hours when Mark asked to sleep in his father's room, using his own mattress, which Andrew carried in and set on the floor beside his own bed. In those dark hours Mark would awake screaming at the vision of his mother's waxed face floating in space, her gaunt cheeks rouged, as he had seen them at the funeral home. She looked more like a store mannequin than the dead repository of his hopes.

It was a lonely Christmas. A stubby spruce occupied the usual corner in the parlor, tipped slightly toward the street window, and tied, for safety's sake, to a nail on the wall behind. A life-size bluebird, frail and scratched, its beak broken off, surmounted the tree's central spike. Mark hung the tree with silver icicles, laced it with tinsel and finished the job with globes, several of which were tear-shaped. When he plugged in the electric cord the lights blinked like fireflies.

Andrew insisted on their annual gift-shopping trip to Stern's. Mark carefully prepared himself by plastering back his forelock with Brilianteen. He was setting the part in his hair when he noticed that one of the two flags that embraced Peter's picture on the adjacent wall had dipped, as if lowered to half-staff. Taken in a San Francisco drugstore, the jumbo print showed his brother, legs astride a vessel's stanchion. Hands behind his back, he peered at the camera, eyes blacked by shadows. His tousled blond hair swept back in pompadour style from his smooth broad forehead. His seaman's cap, on the back of his head, was hardly visible. Mark stepped back one pace, clicked his heels and saluted. He straightened the falling flag.

Beside Peter's picture was another, this of Peter's girl, Carol Stevens, standing behind a picket gate in front of her parents' white house on da Silva Street, San Francisco. Her thick long hair, whose color was undeterminable, fell to her shoulders. There were laughter lines under her eyes. Idly, Mark traced a finger over the bold forward leap of her breasts over the gate.

Mark received everything he wanted for Christmas: Super Erector set, an Horatio Hornblower book, a Westclox alarm, and several other gifts he hadn't expected, including three long-sleeved shirts and two clamp-on bow ties. Martha roasted a turkey, for what was Christmas without one? When they sat down to eat, Andrew said the grace: "God bless this food, which now we take, to do us good, for Jesus' sake, amen," the only grace Andrew ever said.

The next day a letter from Peter arrived. He and Carol were married.

Andrew read the letter to Martha and Mark over dinner. Peter's ship had docked at Treasure Island for refitting and supplies. He received twenty-four hours shore leave. Carol's pastor married them in her church. The next day he sailed with his ship. Mark went to his room. He placed one of the two flags over Carol's photo.

On New Year's eve, 1942, a man named Robert Stanford had a date with Martha. When she heard a car horn she kissed her father lightly, wished Mark a happy new year and hurried out. For half an hour Andrew played a game of rummy with Mark, who won every hand. "You're not concentrating, Dad," Mark said. Andrew admitted it and retired to the sofa to scan a magazine.

Mark switched on the Stewart Warner radio shaped like a gothic arch that stood on an end table in a corner by the window. Guy Lombardo was conducting his Royal Canadians. Listening, Mark lay down on the carpeted floor, head on a pillow snatched off the sofa. He felt as if he was floating on a formless empty sea. The wallpaper's horizontal border next to the ceiling sped intersecting triangles around the room. Mark inspected paintings hung on the walls: a moonlit ocean bay, a Rhine castle, a boy riding a chestnut pony, a studio portrait of the family, including Peter in his neat dress uniform. Missing was his mother. Suddenly the music stopped.

Andrew was standing by the radio. "Listen, Mark," he said, hand raised, cautioning silence. The nightly casualty list. " …and four Attumwa men are reported missing by the Navy." Peter's name was not on the list. Andrew sank to the sofa and closed his eyes. The soothing strains of Glenn Miller filled the room.

Mrs. Susan Marshall came to live in Peter's old room shortly after Easter. She wasn't exactly a boarder. Andrew told Martha and Mark that she was to be their housekeeper, which meant she would do all the work that their mother used to do. Mark thought she was a handsome woman. That is, handsome rather than beautiful like his mother. She was in the house when he came home from school. She was wearing one of his mother's aprons as she prepared dinner. After she introduced herself she went about her work while Mark leaned in the kitchen doorway. She was quite tall, almost as tall as his father. When she stooped to open the oven door strands of thinning blond hair fell over her high forehead. She tucked the strands under the plate-size bun at the back of her neck. She was a big woman with big hands and feet, and a broad back and hips. But she was not fat, Mark could see that. She was also very tanned, almost sunburned, from the height of her massive forehead to the base of her long angular neck. Her lips were rather thin, especially when she smiled and displayed her long, very white teeth. Her nose was so narrow that it looked pinched and it too was longer, much longer than his mother's. Her eyes weren't like his mother's either, for they were brilliant blue, a fact of which he was painfully aware since he played the staring game with her. She was better at it. "Had a good look, Mark?" she asked. He shook his head and retired to his room. Over dinner she raised her glass of tomato juice and cried, in a surprisingly soft voice, "Skoal!"

Three months later Andrew began working late, leaving Mark alone many evenings with Mrs. Marshall. Martha came around once in a while. She had moved out shortly after Mrs. Marshall moved in, renting a two-room apartment close to downtown. She had a full-time job at Stern's accounting office and she told her father she might get another promotion soon, since so many men had left to join the military.

It was now Andrew's telegraph job to edit the growing lengthy war casualty lists, which were delivered to press and radio outlets. Most nights, when he came home, Mark was in bed. Andrew tried to escape working Saturday evenings, so that he could play games with Mark at least. On Sundays they went to church together and often spent the afternoon in the parlor, Andrew reading and Mark doing high school homework. Now, however, Andrew was spending most Saturdays and Sundays at work.

Mrs. Marshall was always there. She seldom went out, except to shop. When Andrew was home she sat quietly with them, darning socks or otherwise taking care of their many needs. One night while Mark was in bed but unable to sleep, listening to their voices soaring to his room via the hot air register, he listened, fascinated, to their frank, intimate and highly personal conversation. Minutes later he heard their lowered voices coming up the stairs. He crept to his bedroom door, opened it a crack, and saw them go into his father's room together.

There was some trouble with Martha, the nature of which Mark could not discern. He heard his father and Mrs. Marshall discussing Martha's relationship with Stanford, who worked downtown for Modern Enterprises. Apparently, he learned via the register, Martha had quit Stern's and was now working for the same company. In fact, she was Stanford's secretary. But that wasn't the cause of her father's angry words. Andrew, apparently, had discovered that Martha had moved in with Stanford.

One Saturday afternoon Mark boarded a clanking red street car on the waterfront road, getting off in the heart of downtown Attumwa. He took an elevator in the Transcontinental building to the big telegraph control office where his father worked. Andrew was bent over a pile of yellow carbon copies of telegrams, sorting them into topless wooden boxes labelled "Missing," "Missing, Presumed Dead," "Wounded in Action," and "Killed in Action."

"Want to read a few?" he asked his son.

Mark thumbed through a foot-high pile stacked in the "Killed in Action" box.

"All these?"

"Just so far today."

Andrew swiveled to his typewriter, which sat atop a small table set on casters. He began typing a list of names and addresses under the heading of "Missing." Finished typing, he proof-read the list, making corrections. He inserted the list in a manila envelope on which "Attumwa Star" was printed.

"These," he told Mark, pointing to the pile of telegram copies, "have already been delivered. Mothers, fathers are crying now." He sighed. "Well, that's my job." He stood up. "Let's go eat."

Seated in a Jewel Cafe booth, Mark attempted to talk about Peter, but his father kept changing the subject. "Pretty warm for February," Andrew said. "Can't last though." He resumed eating his burger. Not looking up, he asked "What grade are you in?"

Thinking he hadn't heard properly, Mark asked "What did you say, Dad?"

Andrew eyed his son strangely. "What?" He looked away, apparently examining the overcast sky, perhaps wondering if it would be snowing before nightfall. "Never mind," he said vacantly. "Never mind."

Mark glanced at Andrew suspiciously. Could his father have forgotten that he was in his final year of high school, that he would be graduating in June? Mark felt a sudden chill of fear. His father had changed in many ways in the past year. There was no doubt about that. He had put on a considerable number of extra pounds. He had lost his handsome, sporty look. He was almost completely bald. Despite the hint of jowls and a slight paunch, a certain ruddiness of complexion, tiny capillaries cross-hatched his cheeks, he seemed full of energy that day, for he began to talk about where they might vacation next summer. "Maybe we'll go to the lake again," he said. "Mrs. Marshall could come too."

"Does she have to?" Mark asked.

Instead of answering, Andrew tackled the remaining stack of french fries. "What grade did you say you were in? he asked. "You mean you'll be graduating in June? I can't believe it. Isn't that something? I wish I'd had your chances, Mark. I wish I'd gone to high school." He kept looking out the window, his face contorted, as if fearing there would be a catastrophic storm. "Who knows, Mark, you may even go to college. Now, wouldn't that be something? The first Christopher ever to go to college. What would you like to be? Maybe you would like to get a job in the telegraph office with me. Tradition, you know. I was my dad's apprentice. No reason I couldn't get you in. Start off as a telegram delivery boy." Andrew idly stirred sugar into his coffee. "Hey! There's an idea. Maybe you'd like to deliver telegrams this summer. Ease you into the business."

This was not the first time his father had made the suggestion. Evidently he had forgotten. In any case, Mark had often observed Mr. Sullivan's Boys, as they were called, named after the telegram delivery department's supervisor: the boys in smart, usually too large, blue uniforms and black-peaked floppy caps and black leather puttees, the boys who waited in Sullivan's office on the ground floor, waited for enough telegrams to pile up in their pigeon holes atop Sullivan's desk, enough telegrams to warrant being sent on their bicycling routes.

"I don't think I'd like it," Mark told his father.

"It's not always the way it is now," Andrew said defensibly. "The work is heavy now because of the war. After the war things will get back to normal."

On Sunday morning Mark walked to church alone. Pastor Woods preached about the need for courage in these trying days and of the brave new world to come. Mark couldn't tell whether he was talking about the world after the war or about heaven, or maybe they were the same.

That night Andrew brought home a telegram with his name on it.

Peter was missing in action.

Andrew started taking the street car to work three days a week because his gasoline ration had been cut. Mrs. Marshall increased the number of fish days from every Friday to every third day. The days merged.

Then it was the first Sunday in March. Andrew came home from work at noon. "You're home early," Mrs. Marshall said.

"Not much to do," Andrew told her. "It's such a nice day. I thought I'd just take the afternoon off. Maybe we could go for a drive."

But they did not go for a drive. After lunch Pastor Woods came for a pastoral call. Mark went over to Jack Strong's house to help him run his model railroad in Jack's basement. When he came home, around four o'clock, neither his father nor Mrs. Marshall were there. He was reading about Captain Hornblower when there came a knock on the front door. Mrs. Marshall stood there, a policeman beside her. She was weeping.

Mrs. Marshall gathered Mark into her arms. She guided him into the parlor. The policeman followed and closed the door behind him. Mrs. Marshall told Mark to sit down and he did, on the sofa. She sat beside him and, gathering him up again, pressed his head against her shoulder.

"It's about your father, Mark," she said. "He … he's had an accident." She paused to wipe her eyes, using for the purpose the cuff of her tan suede overcoat. "O God," she exclaimed, "how can I tell you?"

Mark jumped from the sofa. "What? What happened?" He turned toward the policeman and snatched at his blue jacket. "Tell me!"

"He's dead, son." He grasped Mark as he was falling.

Another voice came to him from far, far away: "The bridge, Mark," Mrs. Marshall said. "He fell off the bridge. He was hit by a train."

Chapter Five

Andrew was laid to rest beside Mary in the Methodist Church's graveyard. Among dozens of mourners were a score of his fellow Transcontinental workers. The funeral service was conducted by Pastor Woods, who paid tribute to "one of our most faithful members." Martha and Mark sat side by side in a front pew. Each had been invited to speak. His sister was surprised when Mark volunteered.

Mark was surprised himself. He had enjoyed speaking in high school classroom presentations and had become a member of the Debating Club. But speaking in a church about what his father meant to him was another matter. What was his father doing out there on the bridge? Why? And how could it have been an accident?

Following Martha's brief salutation to Andrew's faith, before Pastor Woods' sermon, Mark closed his eyes and asked for help. Everyone said he did well, but he knew he did not. He refrained from relating stories that meant nothing. Instead he spoke about his father's faith, as he perceived it, not in its expression, but in its action, how it made his father the good man he was. Still, he was not satisfied with himself. There was too much he did not know. The mystery of death's uncertainty, for instance. He tried to put it behind him. He had his own life to live and he was going to live it to its limitations.

Martha took care of financial matters. With the help of her partner, Stanford, she engaged a lawyer to handle Andrew's will, which, surprisingly, left Mark enough to get by for the time being.

Through the darkening months of fall and winter, days of loneliness and fatigue, Mark dedicated himself to his studies. He resisted the constant temptation to engage in after-school activities. He quit the debate club, denied opportunities to play basketball and to attend birthday parties. He could be found following classes in the school library "reading up," as he termed it. He secretly set his goal: scoring first in every subject.

Sarah had been on the telephone several times talking to their Uncle John Goddard in Maine. She explained the circumstances, especially the question of where Mark was going to live after the house was sold.

Uncle John provided the solution. "He's graduating in June, right?" he said. "Mark could stay with my mother and me, at least for the summer. We've plenty of room." And so it was settled. The house sold quickly. The buyers, a young couple who were to be married in June, were willing to wait until then, although they were eager to "fix the place up" as they put it. Mrs. Marshall agreed to stay on until Mark graduated. Martha promised to pay Mark's living expenses.

The brightening days of spring passed. The war ended in Europe. Mark was graduated with honors. Martha and Mrs. Marshall saw him off at the Transcontinental Railway station. They gathered together under the tall statue of Mercury, whose arm raised in salute as if ready for flight. On this very spot they had bid farewell to Peter, his lost brother. There were kisses and hugs and at last Mark turned away, burdened with contrary feelings of leaving sadness and joyous promise of adventure in a new land. With both hands encumbered by heavy leather travel bags, he marched through the arched gate onto the train platform where the Chief waited, belching smoke.

That night, in the closed comfort of a Pullman upper berth, hushed against the clatter of the Chief's wheels, Mark slipped easily to rest. In a dream he witnessed himself parading dark streets again. It was winter, cold and icy. In an alley by a church, where all was gloom, he heard a voice, his own voice, a small boy's plea for help. He stopped before the alley and peered in. Glow from a single street lamp reflected on the ice. There was a depression in the ice, the mouth of an inverted cornucopia, into which water rushed and swirled from the surface all around. On the ice, close to the gaping void, a small boy, clad in white fur, was strapped into a white railed sled, which slid around, helpless, in the torrent. He heard his own name called, a piercing cry, and then Peter came crawling across the ice toward the maelstrom. Peter reached out his hand; their fingers touched; the boy was snatched from the gulf. Mark awoke with sudden fright. It was a dream, a remembered memory, without shape or form, but true. Martha had told him the story long ago. It really happened in Westminster. Peter had saved his life.

The sudden slowing of grinding wheels awakened him. He was packed and ready long before the Chief pulled into Chicago. He spent the time gazing out the window as the whistling train sped by broken brick, sagging narrow back porches, cast-off ice boxes next to upright mops, newsprint blowing in an alley, worn tires jumbled in a mountainous heap, rusted gutted cars, gray painted plank fences tumbling, weeds high along cracked sidewalks, smashed panes in slanting garages, barefoot Negro children wading in mud, faded rags tossing on a cord, rotting rubbish in a pile, unswept trash in backyards, a hopeless stare.

He left his bags in a key locker at the station, ate toast and drank milk in Savarin's, and, because he had three hours until the New York Central train left, he set out to prowl the Loop. A photographer's studio had photos of families fastened to a wall. The Crystal Arcade featured Rifle Range, Tank Trap, Fortune, and next door a wizened man drilled a tattooed mermaid on a sailor's arm. Then, "Exotic! No Movies! All Live! As you like to see them!" In a doorway a tattered drunk rolled over on a piece of cardboard and snored. Past the western side of Michigan Avenue Mark crossed to Grant Park to view the hundred-jet fountain. Through clumps of lilacs in full bloom, filling the air with incense, and then the lakefront and a hundred boats in the marinas. Far out on Lake Michigan a low-slung ore carrier plodded the horizon toward the steel plants of Gary, Indiana. A breeze cast whitecaps on the quarried stone shore. Four lanes of cars roared unendingly north to Randolph Street.

Because the New York Central train was not crowded he got a window seat. He felt an enveloping thrill of adventure. This was desertion of the American West. After Chicago it was Eastern Time, a time to exult over the view of cities and states only dreamed about. He was eastward bound through unknown territory, a land to be envied and before now unreal. Train wheels clicked. A whistle blew. He was on his way to the coveted country, the land of his father and mother, his ancestral home. He uttered the words his mother sang so fondly, "Going home, going home, I am going home!" A train on an adjacent track passed closely by. A girl with impudent eyes stared back at him across the narrow void. He could see both himself and her in the window glass. The girl receded from view.

Gary's smoking stacks darkened the bright blue of the Indiana sky. Then the unending stretch of vast farms, rolling, tilled and turquoise. Mark saw everything: the flat fertile plains of northern Ohio, the swarming avenues of Cleveland and on east the nearby shore of Lake Erie. Darkness crept over the New York border and here was Buffalo, red globes swinging on yardarms, cars waiting impatiently at crossroads. The western sun's rays faded. A porter lowered the upper bunk. An hour later he was drifting away, humming to the beat of steel on steel, "Going home ..."

It was early morning when the train pulled into Old Boston's South Station. Mark took a taxi to North Station, told the driver to wait, stored his bags and returned downtown. He quickly found the Transcontinental Telegraph's four-story building, where both his father and grandfather, Thomas Christopher, had worked. Mark took the elevator to the fourth floor where he exited into a maelstrom of clattering teletypes, clicking repeaters and chattering radio boxes. A sweet-faced woman directed him to the superintendent's office, where his name, Bertrand P. Smith, was engraved in gold letters on the glass door. Mark knocked and entered to the command "Come in."

Mr. Smith sat behind an ancient pocked walnut desk piled with yellow and goldenrod stocks of paper. He looked up from a roll of telegraph paper which looped over Mark's side of the desk and coiled to the tan tiled floor.

"I'm Smith, young man. What can I do for you?"

"My name is Mark Christopher, Mr. Smith. My father ..."

Mr. Smith put down his pipe in an ashtray. "You don't say. Well, come in. Sit down. Well, I'll be damned." He came around the desk to shake Mark's hand. "What brings you to Boston? Want to work here?"

Mark laughed. "No, thank you. I'm just passing through on my way to my grandmother in Maine. Just thought I'd drop in to see where my dad used to work."

"Of course, of course. I'm sorry, about your father. Tragedy. Falling from a bridge. And one of our trains. Fine man, your father. Glad to get out of Boston. Glad to go to Westminster. Attumwa, not a bad town, as they run. Worked there myself once. Glad to be back east."

Mark leaned forward. "Did you know my dad's father, Thomas?"

"Tom? Deed I did. Briefly. Retired, I think, just after I came here. Or did he pass away before he retired? Can't remember."

"Could I see where my grandfather and my dad worked?"

Mr. Smith's brown eyebrows shot up. "Fraid not. New automatic equipment. None of the old stuff left." He stood up. "Nice talking' with you, Mark. Thanks for comin' in. Good man, your dad. Tragedy." He shook Mark's hand and ushered him out the door.

In a taxi on his way back to the Boston station Mark remarked to himself that he had never been told enough about his grandfather. However did that Englishman get to Maine and why? He resolved that he would find out. An unusual sense of being connected more securely to his father's family passed through his mind. And what about his mother's folk? He resolved to discover more about them too.

A few hours later the Boston and Maine train steamed into Portland. He had time to explore the harbor before spending a night in a hotel. At eight o'clock the next morning he boarded a Greyhound bus for the long trip up the coast to Springport. Along the way the bus stopped at several towns. At Camden there was time for lunch and a quick walk down a hill to the small bay where some breed of black birds splashed happily in the dark Atlantic. As he sniffed the salty air Mark was overcome with the universal thrill of a first ocean experience, the true feeling, and perhaps joy, of being an integral, and essential, part of the scene before him. Somehow the feeling was akin to the most solemn, the deepest, he had ever known.

At last: Springport! At last he would witness with his own eyes the town, its people, of which his mother had engaged his fantasies so many times. At last he was home where the Goddards lived and died. Here was the beginning of his real journey, the search for himself, for who he was, and, he hoped, the knowledge of what he was being prepared to become.

His grandmother and Uncle John could wait. He entrusted his luggage to a friendly clerk at Witherhill's store, setting them down between barrels of grain feed. Out again on Main Street he passed between a clutter of two-story white frame buildings: Woolworth's,

Frank's Dry Cleaning, Desmarshais Hardware, a Kresge Five and Dime, Rexall Drugs, Elite Barbershop.

Back of Main Street's east end, slapping against it was the Atlantic water of Springport Bay. Mark made his way to it by a side street named Cotton Lane, which dead-ended in a turnaround occupied by three cars and a pickup truck. The area was bottomed by dun-colored beach sand, darkened by rain and surrounded on three sides by blocks of granite. Mark got to the barrier's top as a wave crashed, showering him with seaspray. Far off, a buoy's bell rang. A kidney-shaped beach ran a hundred yards or so to the right. To his left a clutch of rotting piers pointed bony fingers into the fringe of the sea. It was the same in the other direction, beyond the beach, except the beach was narrow there with pine, balsam and cedar coming down within a few feet of the persistent waves. Flat farm plots interspersed the trees. Here and there piles of rocks jutted into the surf. Far away on the right, a couple of miles distant but clearly visible, a lighthouse, like a stubby white thumb, poked the blue horizon. To the left were two green islands whose dimensions Mark could not tell. In a straight line from the islands to the north the sea fell into the sky until the bay's distant arm embraced it.

The unpaved shore road ran the length of the town, its drifting beach sand held in place by a thin spread of oil, forming a shallow crust. For several hundred yards the bay's constant off-shore breeze was held in check by stilted frame houses, many unpainted, along the shore rocks, but after the houses there was nothing but wild grass to break the breeze. A distance out to sea low dark clouds were forming. Mark found a smooth rock to sit on. For a long while he concentrated his gaze upon the strange formations as the clouding blueness of the sky soon vanished. Behind him the western sun went down, yielding to the impending clouds. Still, the thick salty sea air lost little of its warmth. Mark filled his lungs with it again and again. This was the ocean life he had only been told about. He leaped up and hollered a loud bellow to the new way of life into which he had just been born. He hurried away toward Grandmother Goddard's house.

Chapter Six

Set back thirty yards from the shore road on the south side of a four-acre field facing the bay, the house towered over scrub pines which stretched back another hundred yards to a backdrop of tall pines that poked their chipped mottled trunks thirty feet high. A sea breeze blew in the pines, whose upper, pyramid branches tossed and cracked like snapped whips. The house was thirty feet square, covered by an A-frame roof. Set four feet above the ground on concrete posts, its crawl space concealed by white lattice, the house appeared to Mark to be a fortress built for defense against the elements, with its faded yellow clapboarding, and its narrow framed windows, one on each side of a green front door.

Mark hastened to the rear of the house where a square one-story kitchen was attached. High above its roof a tall brick chimney poured out a constant cloud of gray smoke. Mark mounted three steps to a square stoop, opened the screen door and knocked. There was no answer. He used a nailed-down iron boot scraper to clean the crusted oily sand off his shoes. He pushed open the wooden door.

The kitchen buzzed with the incessant, annoyed protests of a myriad black flies. They pursued one another over a plank table set squarely in the center of the room, over a knotty pine two-level cabinet by the door, over a black iron wood stove with an overhanging warming oven, over the entire kitchen. Many had died on strips of sticky fly paper hanging from the ceiling. Suffocating arid heat rising from the stove drove Mark to the zinc-plated sink. He tried the two-foot red hand pump, forced the handle down and up several times before a stream of cold water splashed out of the spout. He soaked a nearby towel to cool his face, even as flies attempted landings on his hands. He found a metal cup and filled it with water.

The sink occupied the center of a counter under the kitchen's east window. Sideboards stretched from both sides of the sink to the room's corners. Above the counters were shelves of pine cabinets overloaded with stacks of heavy dishes. A row of shining copper pots and pans hung on hooks from one wall to the other. Mark slapped flies away as he crossed the bare planked floor, cup in hand, to the six-foot wooden table that sat precisely in the kitchen's center. Sitting on one of six chairs surrounding the table, Mark again scanned the room. Here was where his mother spent her earliest years. In this kitchen, in all the other rooms he had yet to see, here was where she shared her life with others. Father and mother, brother and school friends. Here was where she matured until she left to work in Boston. He imagined her seated at the yonder spinning wheel, stringing a fine string of wool around it, peddling until a skein was propelled completely onto a spindle.

He heard footsteps, softly padding. The door on the inner southern wall, which led to the parlor and the main rooms, opened.

"I thought I heard someone," Theresa Goddard said.

She was eighty-five but to Mark she seemed older. Her tanned face was fissured by long overlapping creases. As she advanced toward her grandson she leaned on her square-stalked cane, her left hand on her hip. She tapped a kitchen chair.

"Sit down, boy," she said in a rasping voice. "Let me look at you."

Mark sank back into his chair. "How are you, Grandma?"

She laughed, her thin lips askew. "I'm okay. You're a mite thin. What they been feedin' you? Well, never mind. We'll fatten you up." She pushed her cane toward him. "Here, take this darn thing. Help me down." Mark held her by one arm as she wrestled a chair with the other. When she was settled, she eyed Mark suspiciously. "That Mrs. what's-her-name, she treated you right?"

"Mrs. Marshall treated me fine." Mark began to fidget. He brushed a fly off his nose.

"Good." She eyed the empty cup still nestled tightly in Mark's hand. "You going to get me some too, boy?"

Mark sprang to his feet, grappling his chair. At the sink he pumped frantically. The pump had lost its prime.

"Some people don't know nothin'." Theresa exclaimed. Minus her cane, she hobbled to the sink, picked up a dipper next to a pail of water, filled the dipper and poured water into the pump's top opening. "Try it now, boy," she said. Mark sighed, pumped enough to fill the cup and helped her back to the table. Theresa took a few sips. "You got to work around here, boy," she said. "You ever worked on a farm afore?"

He wished she would stop calling him "boy." The kitchen seemed to be getting extraordinarily hot. The flies badgered him as well as her. She didn't seem to mind. Her small eyes were half-closed as if affected by streaming light, but there were only deep shadows in the kitchen now.

"Well, no," he responded slowly. "There aren't any farms in Attumwa."

"Well, that's just too bad, isn't it?" she responded with a slight smirk. "Where's your luggage?" Mark told her. "I'd best call John," she said as she stood up without asking for assistance. She picked up her cane and swished through the door by which she had entered. Mark heard her telephoning. Returning, she passed by quietly over to the stove, lifted a lid, poked the fire and stirred something in an iron pot that smelled like onions. Then she directed him to the cabinet against the eastern wall and asked Mark to prepare the table for supper. He hastily covered the table with a checkered red and black oilcloth and set out cutlery, plates and cups.

Uncle John's entrance was preceded by a car's misfiring raucous coughing, squeal of brakes and an impatient rattling of the door latch. Backing through the doorway, John wrestled Mark's two bags into the kitchen, where he dropped them thumping onto the planks. He saluted Mark with a blackened hand. "What you got in them cases, boy? Rocks?" he asked in a rough baritone. "Good to see you, Mark. Give me a minute. I've got to wash off this gunk." He held up both hands, black palms visible. At the sink he labored at the task, scouring with a five-inch scrub brush. "Thank God for borax," he muttered. "High ya, Mom." He waved toward his mother and winked at Mark. He combed his thick black hair away from his broad forehead, straight back.

Mark thanked his uncle for fetching his luggage. He liked this straight-backed giant of a man, not only because he was his mother's brother but because of his need for John to fill the void in his life. He treasured little hope that Peter would be found alive. More than that: his father was no longer there as his true life support.

John joined Mark at the table. He struck a match and lit the oil lamp standing in the middle. Oddly, Mark had forgotten that his grandmother's house was not wired for electricity. The room immediately brightened. "Any trouble getting here?" John asked.

"No trouble," Mark said, "but on the sleeper, the upper berth, that takes getting used to. The train sways so much, and you got to hang onto the net so you don't get thrown about."

"What they got a net there for?"

"To put your clothes in."

"What'll they think of next?" This from Theresa, who, while stirring the pot, had appeared unconscious of what was being said.

When the three of them were seated around the table Theresa made a signal, an almost imperceptible nod, and John folded his hands, bowed his head, waited for the others to do the same. John quietly intoned: "In the name of the Father and of the Son and of the Holy Ghost." His voice had changed from a clear Yankee drawl to a churchly whisper. He served them all from a bowl of steaming soup.

"How you liking it here, young fella?" he asked Mark.

"I like it fine. And I appreciate you having me here. I want to do all I can to be of help."

John licked his broad lips. "Been thinkin' all day about you. I'm sorry about your dad, Mark. After all, Andrew's was my brother-in-law. I'm sorry we all didn't ever get together once in a while. As a family, I mean."

"That's the way I feel too," Theresa said. "Darn shame." She returned to the stove to prepare the meal's main course.

"What I've been thinkin'," John continued, "not good for a young fella like you havin' nothin' t' do all day. Young fellas oughta have somethin' to do."

"Sure thing, Uncle John. Whatever way I can help."

John turned to face Mark directly. "I been thinkin' bout your helpin' me, here on the farm. Mainly, it's little things need doin', like wood needs choppin'." He pointed toward the four-foot wood box in the corner near the outside door. "Fill the box once a week. It's almost empty, isn't it, Ma?"

"It near is," Theresa replied.

They concluded their meal together with roast chicken, apple pie and tea. John took Mark outside to "show you around." Beyond the outhouse, with which Mark was already familiar, John pointed to a six-foot pile of newly-cut foot-wide firewood. "Found a pine over there," he said, hooking a big-knuckled thumb toward a grove, dimly visible in the darkening night, "that needed cuttin'." He eyed the pile. "Enough for summer, I'd guess." He pried loose a long-handled axe from a splintered rotting stump. He upended a log from the pile and placed it atop the stump. "Stand back," he ordered. Mark backed away. Tall legs spread, black boots firmly rooted, John raised the axe. The log split cleanly with the blow. The severed pieces thumped to the ground. The axe stayed firmly embedded in the stump. John shook his head. "Blade's a bit dull," he said nonchalantly.

From the kitchen, Theresa, lamp in hand, guided Mark through the parlor, where the linoleum cracked beneath his feet, to the central hall and stairway to the second floor. The room to be his for the summer was at the front of the house facing the sea. Within ten minutes Mark sank into the soft bed but he could not sleep. Had his mother once slept in this very bed? Had she, too, tossed sleepless as the sea roared its nightly chant? He edged onto the cold floor, slid into his slippers, wrapped himself with his kimono, crept down the stairs and out the front door into the yard. Stars were shining and a quarter moon peeked over the horizon far out on Springport Bay. The night was cool and still. Across the shore road a seagull cried.

The tide was rising. Mark crossed the road to stand on the brink. The sea spent its strength on the rocks beneath his slippered feet, then melted away whispering into dark pools, leaving its hoary breath upon him. The moon winked once, then plunged like a scimitar into the darkening sea, parting the waves between the islands. A wave roared upon the beach and somersaulted into mist. The wind blew off the islands across the sea and whistled a lonely song in the crevasses of his mind, infinite and unending, a melody whose lyric he could not remember.

Something out of the depths broke the water, perhaps a seal searching for a directing signpost. A tern dipped to snatch a careless minnow. On the islands the eternal sea unwound itself, like a tired cat, and curled upon the shore. A gull flew past where the moon had been. Then there was only silence, and perhaps the crack of ice breaking, or the silent sound of golden money, or perhaps the crackle of fire spitting danger in the air. A tern cried questions, dot-dashing, to the absent moon. Girded Orion shone down fixedly.

CHAPTER SEVEN

That summer was a journey into the past. Mark had to find out who he was.

When Samuel Goddard arrived in Springport in 1870 the village was already old. For a hundred years the sailing men of Maine had gone out to fight the ageless battle with the sea. Year after year, until their beards turned gray and the winters grew longer by the fire, they returned. Then their sons took up the battle. Their mothers sang to them the songs of the sea, and the village's life was tuned not only to the tides but also to the fishing seasons.

In the dry, close warmth of his grandmother's attic, on cracked and ragged ship charts, Mark traced imaginary courses over the sea, noting depths and the cliffs where lighthouses beamed their warnings. In his grandfather's sea-chest, lined by faded pages of The Bangor News, Mark discovered a three-foot telescope with a bright brass ring on each end. One ring was inscribed, in Old English lettering, "Capt. S. Goddard, Springport." He also found drawing instruments, a quadrant, a binocular, a seven-point star magnifying glass, and a 28-second log glass.

At the bottom there was a medicine box. Abbreviations printed on the corks of finger-size vials, each set in a round hole, told what they were: Ant. Tar. Coloc. Cup. Ac. Canth. KaliBi. Spigelia. Below the box there was a log book with a cracked leather binding. Mark took the book to a small table by a low window. He blew off the table's dust, laid down the book and began to read: *Tenth day out of Springport. Weather fine. Saw dolphin playing before us all day. A whale breached. Good catch of herring in the hold. One dory stove in by falling tackle. Will be on outer edge of Banks tomorrow, by reckoning.*

Day by day and year by year the log told the story of his grandfather's voyages. But where was the man himself? Did he have no emotions? Did he feel no joy when the sun rose gloriously from the morning sea? Did his breakfast of biscuits and scalding coffee warm him against the chill of five o'clock? Did the sharp seasoned smell of the sea at dawn stir him to breathe deeply, rapturously? Did the hauling in of the trawling net cause his arms to ache, and did he turn into his bunk with a prayer?

Mark asked himself why the important things about his grandfather's life were absent. Did he miss Theresa and their children, John and Mary? Was the sailor who was sick, the one he treated with medicines from the chest, in pain? Did the cook ever burn the biscuits? When he was on night watch, with blue lights burning fore and aft and on a mast in a dead calm, did he see the morning star, red and glowing like a far ship on the sea? Did he thrill to the wail of the accordion on deck in the slow evening, after a day's fishing was done, and did the words of a sad song make him long for home? Did the storm at night make him curse his fate for following the calling of the sea? Did he dream of far places, of Canton and Hong Kong, of Singapore and the Cape, where the merchant captains of Searsport sailed on giant clipper ships? Had he, himself, standing in the pulpit over the bowsprit, harpooned a swordfish? Did he bargain for a good price for his catch of cod and halibut at Gloucester? Slowly Mark closed the log book and replaced it on the floor of Samuel Goddard's sea-chest.

The brilliant July days passed slowly. Mark determined to learn all he could about Samuel Goddard. One morning he ventured to the north side of town, to the boat graveyard, a weed-strewn field across from the wharves. Castoff, rotting wooden vessels, like whales stranded on a beach, lay every which way, some resting together, others smashed on their sides, and a few sitting tall on their keels, tackled upright to rusted iron pipes driven deep into the ground. The majority of the boats were labeled with women's names, probably of captain's wives: Ruth, Beatrice, Muriel, Miriam and, among the upright boats, one named Theresa.

Mark grabbed a dangling hawser and hoisted himself onto his grandfather's trawler. He pulled up a sliding door to descend to the torrid cabin, where four bunks lined the walls, with a porthole on each side next to the upper bunks. He clambered into the starboard lower bunk labeled "Captain" which had no mattress. As he lay on the slatted hardwood he thought of Capt. S. Goddard lying there for so many nights and for so many years, and dying there too. He pictured in his mind what his mother had told him, how his grandfather had been brushed overboard by a disastrous wave that broke over the trawler during a wild storm. The wave smashed him against an iron railing as the boat tipped. He was washed into the heaving waves and went under more than once before he was able to grasp a lifesaver thrown toward him by the trawler's mate. He was hauled aboard but he had suffered smashed ribs and a concussion. He died in the bunk within an hour. He was sixty-five.

That evening he sat at the kitchen table as Theresa, while darning his woolen socks, told him of the days long ago when his mother was young. "Of course it was a lot diffrent then," she said in her high-pitched voice. "Now we got the bus comin' every day and goin' every day, so we don't feel so boxed in. And we got telephones and electricity. John keeps tellin' me we should have lights, but I don't see the need. Costs too much." She handed Mark the repaired socks. "There you are, boy. Good as new." She picked up another sock, obviously her son's. "Course things gotta change, I realize that. But if we hold onto what we've got, what's the need to change?" She uttered a quiet sigh. "My, I do carry on, don't I? Anyway, things aren't what they used to be, are they? Why, this town used to have decent wharves, but they're gone now. Just a few bustup piers. Why, we used to have our own wharf just across the road, don't forget. Had the Theresa up dry all winter. Took care of it ourselves. 'Course with Sam gone days, or weeks maybe, it was hard, specially for John and Mary. Your mom worked and worked hard, let me tell you. Best darn worker in town, for a girl I mean. Nothin' much she couldn't lend her hand to. Missed her like you couldn't believe when she took off for Boston. Not that we didn't need the money she sent home regular. Happy she got your dad, Mark. Real happy. Good man, Andrew. Good man." She paused at her task, laying down the needles. "There I go again," she said sniffling. Her thin voice trailed off. Mark looked for tears in her pale eyes but saw none. She set her square, hard jaw, deepening the lines of her tanned face. Her forehead, beneath her smooth-backed white hair, remained unwrinkled and calm. She picked up the needles and resumed knitting.

She told of terrible storms at sea, as her husband had told her. The fury of the sea was in her voice. "One time the motor failed and they had to raise the sails, even as they rolled and pitched. Sam was always the one to climb the mast. He'd go up without his oilskin because he said the wind always got under it and would blow him away if the clasps broke and it billowed out. He always got back alright, although many didn't. You can see their names down at the church, on the carved board they have there, the one with the little trawler cut on top."

Theresa paused as she choked sharply and placed a hand over her mouth when she coughed severely. Recovering, she said, "Don't know why my throat's so dry tonight. Talk too much, I spose." Mark brought her a glass of water. She sipped gingerly, suppressing another choking spell. She recovered and continued talking. "Sam came to Springport one day on his boat and he went to my church that Sunday and that's where we met. After that, whenever he docked here again, he always came to call on me. The house I lived in then with my parents isn't there anymore. It used to be near the wharves but an oil company tore it down to make way for the big tanks there. That was after they passed away, and that was about fifteen years after Sam and I built this house. We buried them over there in the woods in a clearing we made. John cut the stones himself. Take a look, Mark."

Mark went out to see those stones the next day. Here lay his ancestors, his mother's grandparents. Carved from hard granite, twin bright white stones rose from a green garden plot, no more than ten feet square. Mark read the names: "Stephen Roger Winters" and "Beulah Severence Winters." Strange that he couldn't remember his parents ever mentioning a family named Winters. Who were they? Where did they come from? He realized that Grandmother Theresa's maiden name was Winters, but since Severence was probably a family name, he would have to search them out too. And another question: birth and death years on the stones showed that Beulah Winters had died only one year after her husband. He decided he would ask his grandmother.

"Forest fire that did it," Theresa told him. They were sitting on camp chairs in the backyard garden, basking in the warm July sun and under a cloudless blue sky. The jarring roar of four-engine airplanes flying high toward Newfoundland caused her to pause a minute. "Can't stand that racket," she said. "It's been that way ever since the war started of course." She shook her head. "Well, anyway, about the fire. It came over the hills there." She pointed north. "Before anything could be done to fight it the flames reached a farm. We all knew it was the Chandler place, it was so close. There were so many men gone to sea that, when the word spread, the women came out too."

Mark held up his hand. "I suppose they all wanted to watch it," he said.

"Watch it? Goodness, no. They came out to fight the fire. I went too. Sam was gone up the bay. My parents were there. We brought blankets and potato sacks with us. The men got a pump working and got a hose up as far as it would go and we soaked everything, sheets, blankets, everything."

Theresa wiped her forehead, which had suddenly beaded with sweat. "We beat at the flames in the bush," she continued. "Like trying to smother the fire in a stove with a dishrag. All we got for our trouble was lungs full of smoke, and the heat, and I went back with my father and mother to their house, where we put them on their bed and placed cold towels on their heads until they stopped gasping for air. My father had a weak heart, from so many years at sea, I suppose, and he died there, on the bed, with my mother beside him. She never got up again and she died, still choking, in January."

She saw the question on Mark's lips. "No, the village didn't burn down," she said. "That night the wind turned and came in from the bay and the fire burned itself out. The next day, although it wasn't Sunday, everyone went to church. No one that I know of had asked us to go. It was the right thing to do. The minister led the service, and we thanked the Lord for saving us. Then, a couple of days later, my father's funeral was held in the church, and it was filled again. Sam said we had plenty of space here to bury our own, so he and John dug the grave. Later Sam and I decided we might as well make the plot large enough for my mother as well, but, when she died the ground was frozen so we kept her in Luke's ice house until spring, and then Sam and John dug the grave and put her in."

The next day Mark ran down the shore road to the Baptist church, whose boarded white face glared in the bright sun. Above the peaked brown shingled roof, set against an azure sky, was a tower belfry open on four sides. A single three-foot bell hung from a beam set diagonally above the opening. Below, inside the heavy front doors open to the sanctuary a rope dangled against a vestibule wall. Mark pushed through a pair of swinging glass-window doors. Sunlight, filtered yellow and purple by rectangular stained glass, blanketed the pews with a soft glow. On the left he saw it: an ornately carved plank topped by a model trawler. Below were inscribed the names of church members who had died at sea: Ephraim Hoskins, Josh Dennis, Ebenezer Walcott, Samuel Goddard. Below, inscribed in an identical script was a Bible verse: *And I saw a new heaven and a new earth: for the first heaven and the first earth were passed away; and there was no more sea.* Pastor Woods had read those very words, and then had thrown the earth three times: *Earth to earth, ashes to ashes, dust to dust.* Then, and only then, was Mark's father lowered into the ground. Mark, racing, heart thudding, the sound of spaded earth scraping in his ears, bolted from the church. Not until he reached his grandmother's house did he stop running.

July's molten days melted into August's. Mark had been exchanging weekly letters with Martha. Now the time had arrived when a decision had to be made about his future. Mark told her that he wanted to go to university. But where? she asked. He replied: Boston. Couldn't be done, she wrote. Putting it simply, there just wasn't enough money. Many expenses had to be paid: attorney and court fees to settle their father's estate, final payments to Mrs. Marshall. The list was quite long. Her conclusion was that Mark's only choice was to stay on with their grandmother until her own financial affairs improved. She suggested that, perhaps, Uncle John could find a job for him at the oil company where he was employed. Mark decided to broach the matter with John.

"No need to panic," John told him. "You can stay with us as long as you want as far as I'm concerned." He grimaced slightly. "Of course we'll have to check it out with Ma."

"Of course."

Theresa agreed with John, saying, with a smile, "I'll adopt him."

"Seriously, Ma," John said. "Mark wants to go to university, but Martha can't afford it."

"Go to college in Springport," Theresa said. "What's the difference?"

"Plenty, I suppose," John replied. "What do you think, Mark?"

"I don't know. Still costs money."

"Don't worry about that. Maybe I could get you something part time."

Theresa tapped Mark's arm. "You go to Community College, Mark. I've still got a bit of influence in Springport. I'll talk to Pastor Gordon."

A week later Mark was asked to report to the college's admission office. Mark brought his high school graduation report with him. He gave it to a secretary who asked him to wait. Eventually he was called into the admission director's office. He was without words when told that he could start classes in September and that the bursary that was offered would cover the total two years of fees.

"I don't know what to say," Mark aid.

"Thank your grandmother."

"I will, but she's far from rich."

"She has influence," the administrator replied.

Chapter Eight

Mark became a student at Springport Community College the day after Labor Day. The war was over. Japan had surrendered. Martha wrote hat she was delighted and wished him well. She assured him that her parents would have been happy too. She had written Grandma Theresa and had thanked her and Uncle John for their kindness and support. She told him nothing about her personal life. He wondered whether her boyfriend, Stanford, was still around. Mrs. Marshall had found another housekeeper job.

Meanwhile Mark had found a kindred spirit, a fellow student named Jim Pettaw, a Wallabot Indian who lived in an old boarding house, Mrs. Mahoney's. It was said at college he cooked for himself over a fire in his room. In a practiced spirit of fun, Mark asked Jim one late September afternoon if the rumor was true. Jim replied "Come up and see for yourself." Jim was about Mark's height, about five-eight or nine. He always stood tensely tall and "looked you straight in the eye," as Mark described him in his next letter to his sister.

Jim Pettaw usually came to college wearing a leather Army Air Force jacket that had several pale spots where a pilot's insignia once adhered. The jacket had big pockets in which Jim liked to stuff his hands. Jim lounged against an elm. Obviously he was not in a hurry to go anywhere. As they talked he kept looking about the wide lawns, now alive with gatherings of students. Soon the reason he was in no hurry to get away became apparent: Helen Desmarchais, the French girl from Quebec City, was approaching.

"What a dish," Jim said as the girl smiled and went on her way, her long jet-black hair touching her shoulders, her shaded brown eyes casting an appreciating glance in their direction, maintaining silence as she passed, reached the highway sidewalk, turned left and slowly faded from view. Mark told himself he would have to get acquainted with this dish.

"Okay, guy," Jim said, taking off at a trot, with Mark right behind him. Just inside the front door of the boarding house, Jim removed his shoes and instructed Mark to do the same. "Rule of the house," Jim said. His room on the second floor faced the street. His furniture consisted of a roll-top oak desk, narrow brass-framed bed and a four-feet wide wood trunk, whose polished nickle hinged lid was covered with carved Indian hieroglyphics.

"No campfire," Jim said, smiling in amusement, brilliant white teeth gleaming. "No firesticks, no firewater."

"Okay. Gotcha," Mark said, winking. "What's in the trunk?"

"What do you expect?" Jim said, affronted, frowning. "So I'm an Indian, so what? You think I should put on feathers and do a war dance, whooping around with a hatchet?" He placed a hand over his mouth, cried "Whoo, whoo, whoo," and danced a jig until Mark yelled at him to stop horsing around.

The brilliant reds and orange of autumn ushered in the deepening snows of winter. Mark passed from the first college semester into the second. On brief late afternoons Jim taught Mark ancient arts using soft leather and bright beads. On Saturdays they trapped rabbits. Once they made a snare of thin copper wire and strung it from a branch overhanging a creek. They placed a shred of lettuce in a hollow scooped in the snow and set the snare. They snowshoed beside the creek hunting an owl's lair, then returned, as the cold sky darkened, to the snare, which held only the bloody stump of a rabbit's leg. Jim removed the leg as Mark turned away with closed eyes. "The rabbit does that," Jim said as he tossed the leg into a bush. "They gnaw off the trapped leg to get free."

On another Saturday they hiked upcountry, where a tributary of the Wallabot River flowed. Jim showed Mark how to cut a hole in the ice and drop in their hooked lines. They sat on their heels watching fish nibbling at the worm bait. Then one fish bit and then another. They pulled in their lines and laughed together as the frigid breeze blew their steaming breath away. On their way out Jim blazed a trail with his hatchet, just in case they ever returned that way some other day. Under tall pines where brown squirrels leaped, showering them with new snow, they scooped a hole in the white forest floor, down to the pine needles. They filled the hole with sticks broken from nearby branches and lit a fire. Jim showed Mark how to spear a fish with a pointed stick and hold it over the flames until the flesh cracked and smoked. He peeled the skin away, trimmed off the bones and pulled off a baked hunk between thumb and finger. Mark said it tasted great.

At college, Jim was always getting into fights with other taunting boys. He licked all of them. The last one to concede defeat was Big Bill Watson, who made the mistake, in Jim's presence, of calling Mark an Indian lover. That did it. Jim was all over Bill in a flash. The rule of the game was: wrestle, but no fists. They rolled around in the snow for fifteen minutes, time enough for a crowd of students to gather, and even some working men from downtown. At length Jim got Big Bill face down and pinioned his right arm. "Say uncle," Jim said as he pushed harder. Finally one man pried Jim off. "Before Jim broke Big Bill's arm," the man said.

One of the students standing around was Helen Desmarchais. While they had been friendly for months, passing one another in college corridors, Mark found he could never meet up with her alone because she always seemed to be accompanied by the same two female friends, and the three of them, since the friends were also from Quebec, continuously chatted in French. However, he maintained a secret yearning, the nature of which he never really saw as a crush, but rather as an unfair snub and a serious injury to his ego.

The day after Jim's victory, when he glimpsed her in a hall leading to a class- room, she hailed him. "Mark, how are you?" Her dark brown eyes surveyed him closely. "I heard why Jim fought that bully. Jim's a real friend, isn't he?"

"Best friend I ever had," Mark said as they entered the classroom together.

Later, Mark waited for her outside. Fortunately, she was alone. "Going my way?" he asked. They talked what he called "school talk," which professors she liked, which he liked, until they reached her house, a plain white frame set back several feet from the sidewalk. "Like to come in?" she asked. The brick steps up to the stoop were icy. Mark offered to help her mount them. She held out her hand. Unsure of himself, he was about to grasp her upper arm when, smiling, she took his hand in hers. He felt a warm sense of attachment, more than mere friendship, but out of desire, out of hope, that she might love him, as he suddenly realized, he loved her.

They were alone in the parlor together, seated side by side in the embracing softness of the sofa. She told him of the great walled city, Quebec, that she came from, of the Citadel there overlooking the broad sweep of the St. Lawrence River, and how she had been raised French Canadian. She was French and she was Catholic. Her parents had lived in Springport for five years, having moved there after her father inherited Desmarchais Hardware from his brother.

A door from the kitchen suddenly opened. Mark rose abruptly to greet her. "Bienvenue." she said in greeting. Helen introduced him. To Helen she asked, "Comment? Este-ill un e`tudiant?"

"Oui, Momma. I'll est en classe avec mois."

"Bon. Bon." She held out a tray of biscuits. She pronounced it "bis-kwee." She was a plump round-faced woman with a pert nose and the same dark eyes as her daughter. She excused herself and returned to the kitchen. There was a fire in the grate. Mark stepped over to warm his hands. Helen stood beside him. She held her palms toward the flames. Suddenly she grasped his hands. "You are cold," she said, looking up at him with dark uncommitted eyes.

"Helen!" he exclaimed.

She backed away. Confused, unknowing, unaware of any reason why Helen behaved the way she did, he blurted out, "Could you help me with my French?"

"Sure," she replied. "Then you can help me with my English." She drifted down to the red soft carpet before the fire. She spread her plaid skirt around her and smoothed it down. Her sweet mouth opened prettily, displaying slim even teeth. She fingered a gold cross suspended from her neck by a silver chain. It tingled just below her white Peter Pan collar. She tugged the broad white band that secured her hair, a movement that thrust forward her enticing small breasts. She looked at him with a saucy, impudent stare. She smiled at him like an innocent Mona Lisa.

"Do you like me, Mark?"

Taken aback, all he could say was, "I sure do."

She smiled, sighed and rose up. Standing by a bridge table she opened a textbook. "Well, I guess we'd better do our homework," she said quietly.

For a half hour he repeated French phrases after her, savoring her voice's sweet inflections, the rhythm of her soft hands, always gesturing with the words, giving them meanings the words of love that were surely implied: "J'aime, tu aime, il aime, nous aime, vous aime, ills aiment."

And then: "Je t'aime," said warmly, with desire, over and over, as he repeated it, holding her dark eyes within his own steady gaze of adoration. "Aime-tu-mois?" with the rising inflection of the question, and his tongue struggling over syllables, and the basic meaning of the words pounding in his brain, and in his heart too, for he believed that surely she was saying those words to him because she meant them for herself, and not because they were merely words without meaning flung out of a text book.

Several days later he borrowed John's skis, with which he had trained, and marched with Helen sideways up the hill above Springport Road. From there they could ski together toward Route One. He discovered that Helen was no more an expert skier than he was. When she fell he picked her up. Always he felt a hammer pulse of joy.

On a Saturday night there was a hayride, along the shore road and up to Route One and back to Springport Road. Cuddled in a blanket under well-dried hay, Helen leaned heavily on Mark's shoulder. He held her hand as the horse-drawn wagon's runners hissed on hard-packed snow. Stars shone brightly as horse bells tolled merrily outside their warm abode.

In April, when the snow had disappeared, they borrowed riding horses and jogged through evergreen forests. Once they lay by a cool stream, side by side on a bank. They sank their faces into the icy water. Then up wild trails to the hill's summit, where the bush was low among blueberry patches, and along the back road, shrieking "Heah! Heah!" The horses galloped, manes trailing in the wind. In the woods where the first robins of spring sang and jonquils and lilies blossomed, where wind whistled in the pines, where the pines dripped their healing honey, where soft needles carpeted the forest floor, where cedars and balsam cast their thick sweet incense, bathing the forest in cathedral air. A hemlock swayed. A whippoorwill called to its mate, yes-I-will, yes-I-will, yes-I-will.

A chipmunk skittered over the carpet. The earth stood still.

CHAPTER NINE

Mark had been attending the Baptist Church since Christmas. Now his turn came to be baptized. Theresa said she would like to attend but her rheumatism was bothering her, would he mind? He told her no, that was alright.

So it was that on the first Sunday in June he walked down the church's side aisle and opened a small door. Three other boys were already in their underwear and were putting on white gowns like choir robes. Mark undressed and covered himself with the smooth white well-ironed baptismal attire.

"You look angelic, Mark," one of the boys said. "May I have the next dance?"

The choir loft door opened and a bald man thrust his head in. "Ready, boys?" They followed him into the sanctuary's front pew. They bowed their heads. Mark looked up as a door on the other side of the choir loft opened noisily. Five quaking girls, with similar garments, came down. They occupied the opposite front pew. At the organ's first notes, Mark wondered if he was ready, even though he was nineteen, far older than the others.

Despite Pastor Gordon's teaching, he had come to the end of the baptismal candidate course undecided. The minister had spoken of confession and forgiveness as if they were realities that everyone could comprehend and practice. The class had reviewed the Ten Commandments, the Great Commandment, the Beatitudes, and the teachings of Jesus, the great familiars, the miracles. The lessons went on to deal with the mission of the church and what it meant to be a faithful disciple "in this day and age." They discussed God as Love,

Guide and Friend, as Father, Son and Holy Spirit. They talked of Him as Creator, Judge and Living Presence. And then the old historic doctrines: Atonement, Forgiveness, Reconciliation, and all the rest. They memorized the Apostle's Creed, and learned of Christ as Suffering Servant, Shepherd, Prince of Peace.

All the while much of the relevance of these teachings escaped him: their relevance to the fire and the storm, the mountains and the valleys, the forest and the sea, the love and the loss. Only when the lessons touched upon the saints, worship, the Church and its sacrificing heroes, did the small dark hope that was within him come alive. And when, at last, Pastor Gordon gave his benign assurance that all came to baptism as sinners, and therefore equal in the sight of God, did he accept the decision that had, really, been made for him long ago when his father held him in his arms and presented his child's infant body for baptism before the Methodist church's altar. The worm of doubt ate at his heart, but that did not matter now, for it was the intention that mattered, the public dedication, to be a faithful Christian follower forever and to give his life to purity of deed, to cleanness of thought, and to steadfastness of service.

Mind at rest, he heard Pastor Gordon intone the invocation and the worship service had begun. Following the opening hymn, *He Leadeth Me*, came the responsive reading of a Psalm, the Scripture and the pastoral prayer. Pastor Gordon, his young smooth face beaming, called the robed candidates to come forward. From the pulpit he asked the formal questions of their dedication and they assented. While four deacons came forward to shake their hands and ask more questions, the minister stepped into a room on the left. In due time he emerged clad in rubber hip boots. The deacons removed floor boards that concealed the baptismal tank. Pastor Gordon descended two steps into the water, shaded blue by an underwater bulb. From the tank he called the first name on his list, Lisa Brown, who grinned as the minister took her hand and safely guided her, shivering, toward her baptism. He recited the proper words, holding her by one of his arms under her neck. The girl held her nose. Pastor Gordon plunged her backward totally under the water, then raised her upright, stayed with her until she opened her eyes fully and grinned.

Watching the proceeding, Mark felt sweat trickle down his back. He clenched his hands and hoped that the tank's water was cool. He heard his name called. Stepping into the tank, he almost tripped on his soaking gown. Pastor Gordon held his arm. The gown floated to the top of the water. He closed his eyes when the minister plunged him under. Raised enough to stand up, he accepted a dry sheet that a deacon wrapped around him. Dripping, he made his way out of the sanctuary to the dressing room.

That afternoon, as they sat on a bench overlooking busy Springport harbor, he recounted his baptismal experience to Helen, who listened gravely. "We don't do it that way in the Catholic Church," she said. "Infant baptism is more appropriate, don't you think?"

"I was an infant when I was baptized in a Methodist church," he told her.

"Then you have just been baptized for the second time!" she exclaimed.

"The first time, I had nothing to do with it," Mark said. "Besides, you have confirmation, and that's the same thing, isn't it?"

"I suppose so," she answered. "But it happened when I was only six. I was all dressed in white, like a child bride. Because that is what it meant, really, becoming a bride of Christ."

Helen spoke of the mysteries of Catholicism, of the candles she lit in the small Catholic Church on the hill behind Springport Road, of her brother who served with Les Fusillieres Royale and was killed in Hong Kong during the war. Mark heard the drawing of a curtain and felt the dark shadow that had come between them.

A month later Helen told Mark she was leaving Springport. Her father's hardware store had failed. The family had no choice but to return to Quebec City, where her father could find a job. Helen was sorry to leave college, to leave Mark, but she had no choice. Their parting was brief. They met for the last time in front of her house, standing together awkwardly as July's golden sun fell slowly and vanished behind a dark gray cloud. She kissed him lightly on a cheek, as old friends do, and was gone.

Jim Pettaw wasn't around to comfort him. He had gone home for the summer. Mark telephoned him. Jim invited him to come to Pettaw Island for a visit.

Even before the bus stopped Mark saw Jim, his face as tanned as ever, his black hair shining, his deep eyes dark in shadow. Mark leaped out and grabbed Jim's hand. For a moment they said nothing. They stood there smiling at one another. "How are you, you son-of-a-gun?" Mark asked.

They walked up New Town's main street between high shabby brick buildings as a slight drizzle began. Past a shoe factory where the raucous sound of turning machines could be heard, they came to a river where they boarded a small barge with a rope railing around its log platform. A puffing little steam tug pulled the barge across the river to Pettaw Island. The rain was falling hard as they hiked along a dirt road by the shore. They stopped before a yellow wood building, standing close to the ground and fronted by a porch under a sagging slanted roof. A sign, hung crookedly, proclaimed Chief Pettaw's--Genuine Handcrafts. Sweetgrass baskets, yellow and red, dark brown and red, hung everywhere: along the porch's rear wall, posts and rails. Inside, on bare pine shelves, were more baskets. A long counter was covered with ash trinkets.

Jim switched on an overhead light. "Hey, dad, mom," he called. His mother, a short, white-haired, rather plump woman dressed in a neat green wool skirt, stepped into the store. "Hello Mark," she said as she reached out her hand. "Jim's told us so much about you, and I'm so happy he found such a good friend."

Chief Pettaw came in from a back room. He crunched Mark's hand. "Welcome, young man," he said. "Welcome." There was a certain melancholy about his face, a depth of experienced sadness.

Over lunch in the kitchen, Jim's father said grace, a long prayer, which he closed by thanking God "for the gift of thy Son, Our Lord and Savior Jesus Christ." Mark was astonished. He knew that Jim attended the small Lord's Mission in Springport, but matters of faith had never been a topic of their discussions.

Later Chief Pettaw asked Mark "How would you like to join the tribe?"

Mark nodded and laughed. "What do I have to do?"

"Sit there," the Chief said. "I'll be right back." He went off to a back room and returned in a few minutes with a small book, which he opened and laid in front of Mark. "Sign here," he said. Mark signed his name below the signatures of other people identified as coming from Maine, Massachusetts, New Hampshire and Canada, among other states and countries. "Raise your hand," the Chief commanded. Mark did as he was told. "Do you solemnly swear, by Gitchimantu, to uphold the law of the great Abnaki Nation, and give obedience to its chiefs? Say I do."

"I do," Mark said.

The Chief shook Mark's hand. "Welcome to the tribe," he said.

Later, Mark and Jim walked up a road toward the other end of Pettaw Island. Black-haired children halted their games to stare. They paused by a cemetery full of wooden crosses. Several bore the name of Pettaw.

"My noble ancestors," Jim said. "If we're so great, how come we're so poor? Come on, I'll show you something really noble."

They went up the road and over a hill to a little church with a slanted roof covered with tarpaper. The church stood on barked timbers, a foot off the ground. It had stained glass windows and a porch that did not lean over, as did the stubby steeple. A wood sign, shaped like a shield, was attached to a post. It read: Rev. N. Rudolph, Pastor. The church door had been scraped bare. "For painting," Jim said. A small table inside bore some Bible tracts. The windows flooded the sanctuary with soothing light. Ten short pews flanked each side of the central aisle. A pulpit was raised a foot higher than the floor in front of a choir stall.

"Very nice," said Mark, who was standing in front of the pulpit.

"Nice!" Jim exclaimed. "It's beautiful." He sat down on a front pew and bowed his head. When he concluded his prayer, Jim found Mark staring at him. "What?"

"Sorry," Mark said. "I'm just surprised that's all."

Jim came over and stood beside him. "Right here," he said, "on this spot, I accepted the Lord Jesus Christ as my Savior."

"You did what?"

"You heard me. I never told you because I didn't think you would understand. I haven't been a very good witness. After all, you being a regular Baptist."

Outside, as they walked slowly together back to the house, Jim said "There's no happiness greater than to know you've been saved."

"Will you please cut it out?"

Jim stopped and looked sternly at Mark. His dark eyes, like soft coals, had changed. "Just being a member of the church," he said, "doesn't mean you're saved. You have to be born again."

Mark cringed. "I've just been baptized," he said. "I'm a full member of Springport Baptist Church."

"Sure you are, but have you been born again?"

"Whatever that means."

"You have to start over," Jim said. "You have to see that your life has been nothing but filthy rags."

"You're nuts."

"Our new pastor, he converted me."

"You're still nuts." Mark turned away and started walking quickly. "Life isn't something to be thrown away, like an old shirt," he said.

Jim pursued him. "You can't be saved until you realize that your life has been all sin until now." He caught Mark's arm and spun him about. "You have to confess your sin and make it right, and realize the Lord is everything, and accept Him as your personal Savior. He is everything!"

Mark pulled Jim's hand away.

"When you're saved," Jim persisted, "you realize the Lord can do everything, and you can't do anything without Him. He's your whole life and you live to serve Him."

"But there is the church---"

"Many churches are agents of Satan."

"Nuts."

"Many church members are hypocrites," Jim went on, his voice rising. "You must be born again!"

But Mark was walking fast ahead, and at last Jim was shut off. The sky darkened. The rain began to fall heavily. At the bus station Mark shook Jim's hand. "I hope we can still be friends," Mark said.

Jim had turned all Indian. His face was inscrutable. "We'll always be friends, Mark," he said. "And brothers." He smiled. "Now that you're a full-fledged Wallabot." Jim turned toward home, his feet slashing in the mud.

Chapter Ten

Mark spent the dark days of August brooding. Even his grandmother's talk about the old days was somehow depressing. As an early evening fog crept in, a stealthy unwanted visitor that made the windows weep, she would begin: "I remember when it was a night like this, and the boats were out, we huddled right here in this kitchen, trying not to think how scared we were for our men." She would stop knitting long enough to say: "The lighthouse be groanin' every couple minutes and we'd keep the torches lit just in case one of those sailin' yachts come cracking up on the beach." To her a beach was the same thing as the shore, whether rocky or sandy.

Sometimes in the night Mark would be wakened by the lighthouse horn blasting across the bay. Or he would wake up from a recurring dream that took him far out to sea where he trod the deck of Theresa, while Captain Sam Goddard would cry "We're lost, we're lost, boy." But that was so unlike his grandfather, that god of the sea incarnate, that he would gaze into the scoured weather-beaten face, whose white beard hung motionless in a dead calm, and he would yell "You're not my grandfather!" and the face would turn away, then turn around again, and Mark saw holes where the eyes had been, and it was the face of death. He would rise and go to the window, open it and look into the formless world swirling in mist.

Missing Helen, and Jim too, he swam alone in the cold bay, dove off rocks that lined the shore road. Sometimes he hiked to Round Pond, a mile back from the bay, beyond the pine grove. He discovered a narrow strip of sandy beach hidden by high bush. During several visits he swam nude in the warm fresh water, often going out too far for safety and then turning back to the beach's welcoming haven.

Some days required time to be spent on farm chores assigned by Theresa. Often, after cutting wood, yoking water or killing potato bugs he would rest in the cool dark comfort of the underground potato storage house, an earthen cave cut into a grassy bank a hundred feet from the house. He would sit on a bench for half an hour or so. He would exit blinking into the sun, which bathed the farm in a warm summer glow. He usually went to bed early and he would toss sleepless. He went to bed late, and he dreamed of Maple Street. He rose early every day because Theresa scheduled breakfast promptly for seven o'clock. By the end of August he was bronzed and lean, and his cheeks had hollowed. "Got to get some meat on those bones," Theresa would say as she piled his plate high with biscuits hot from the oven.

Mark applied himself intensely to his college's second year of study. He looked for Jim for a few days but his friend, he was told by the admissions office, had written that he would not be back. Mark debated with himself what to do. Should he telephone Jim and beg forgiveness for expressing distain for Jim's religious beliefs? Or should he "move on" as other student friends recommended. Since he could not make up his mind, he told himself, in a retreating mood, to "forget about it." He had other concerns, the chief of which was the evident state of his grandmother's health. Meanwhile he applied himself vigorously to his studies, After classes and on Saturdays he worked with his uncle at the oil company, helping him snake writhing black hoses into pipes, struggling with a two-foot wrench to tighten bolts. He welcomed being paid, not a lot, but enough to buy a suit to wear on Sundays and a couple of trousers. On weekdays, after supper, he brought his homework to the kitchen table and often studied until midnight.

One morning, feeling especially guilty and lonely for Jim, he walked to the bus station, speculating that if he took a bus to New Town, Jim might be home and he could patch up their broken friendship. But what if there was no bus that day, then it was pointless to even leave the house. He went anyway.

When he got there he learned that, yes indeed, there would be a bus in an hour. He settled into an uncomfortable metal chair. He still had plenty of time to buy a ticket. He decided to think about the whole thing. A dense fog was rolling in from the bay. The bus would probably be late. And if it wasn't late, then what? Maybe the highway would be closed. What for? Fog? An accident? Anyway, what if Jim wasn't home? Telephone him. Find out. But, seriously, Jim was no doubt still angry with him. There was no assurance that it could be any other way. It was endless lingering, senseless tarrying, a foolish kicking of his boots loudly on the waiting room floor. Mark leaped up, ran for the door, and hurried back to see how his grandmother was doing.

Theresa died the next spring. First she was well, then she was sick. There was no in-between. "Look at me," she would say whenever Mark had a cold and had to stay in bed for a few days. "Look at me," she would say, her rheumy eyes accusing him. "Never seen a sick day in my life, and don't expect to, exceptin' the day I die. And I'll keep workin' till I do." And she did.

She didn't get up one morning. John telephoned Doctor Barnes, a red-faced man with thin strong fingers, who came immediately. Mark followed him and John through the dim downstairs hall, hearing the blue chipped linoleum crack, then up the stairs with the wobbly balustrade, and into the northwest corner bedroom. John approached her bed. "How are you, Ma?" John asked. Her pale lips moved but only a guttural sound came. She looked toward John. "'on, 'on."

It was a stroke. Doctor Barnes gave his diagnosis later as they sat around the kitchen table drinking coffee. "No use you hanging around," the doctor told Mark. "Nothing's going to happen, not today."

By nine o'clock the next morning, seated in a classroom, Mark was uneasy as Mr. Cohn, his history teacher, talked to his students about a paper Mark had written which began *It's a long way from Hiroshima to Springport.*

"I can sympathize with Mark's point of view," Mr. Cohn said as he brushed a hand through his black curling hair, "but I think he jumped too quickly to his conclusions. Anyone agree?" Mark cupped his hands and sank into his chair. Defeated by silence, Mr. Cohn continued, his tired voice droning. "After all," he said, "Japan did surrender and we didn't have to invade the home islands, which would have required the death of thousands of our soldiers. I don't think we have to apologize, as Mark does, for what we did, dropping two atomic bombs." Mr. Cohn scanned his class. "Does anyone think differently? Apart from Mark, that is." Again, silence. Mr. Cohn threw up his hands, a plea for co-operation. None came, so he changed the subject. He pointed to Walt Jones. "Mr. Jones, about your paper concerning the slaughter of millions of Jews---" That night, when Doctor Barnes came in, Theresa was weaker. She had not eaten all day. John turned up the flame on a wall lamp. Mouth open, glazed eyes half shut, Theresa gasped for breath. John grasped her hand. "It's all right now, Ma," he said, hardly more than a whisper. "It's alright." Her eyes shifted toward him. "'on, 'on," she muttered over and over.

"She can't see anything," Doctor Barnes said. "She's saying your name, John."

"I know," John said. There were tears in his eyes. The doctor gave her a shot.

In the long silence that followed Mark examined her room in which his grandmother had slept almost every night of her life. A three-foot walnut bureau, the color of August grass after a drought, stood near the north window. It was covered by a lace-edged scarf that Theresa had embroidered. There were three objects on top of the scarf: a cracked yellow bone-handled hairbrush, its bristles worn short; a thick brown comb with wide-spaced teeth, and a small blue box, the cover of which was inlaid with pearl. A tarnished, cracked silver mirror tilted slightly downward from two scrolled walnut arms.

Across the room, in the south corner by the bed was a solid pine stand with a white washbasin on it. Above, hung on a nail by a thin wire, was a small mirror in a wooden frame. The mirror was dull and browned. Beside the mirror was a picture, about three inches wide. It was a faded brown oval photograph of a woman in a high-necked dress, with balloon sleeves reaching to her wrists; her hair was swept up from the back of her neck and piled high on her head; the woman was not smiling. It was Theresa.

Doctor Barnes sat in a straight-backed chair beside the bed. John sat firmly in a chair that matched the three in the kitchen, except that his one had arms: a chair for a father, doubtless the one that Theresa's husband used for decades. On the other side of the bed was a black end-table that supported a small oil lamp with a cracked oil paper shade. Its light was harsh and yellow. The bedstead was made of rolled sheet brass, with four vertical bars front and back; round balls of wrought brass covered intersections of the tubes at four corners; elsewhere the vertical tubes were inserted into horizontal pipes; iron rails on the bed's sides supported slats, which again supported the mattress on which Theresa Goddard lay propped up by two white pillows.

The room's wallpaper consisted of vertical stripes of dirty white and turgid green; the cornice was a green stripe. The ceiling was gleaming white; John had whitewashed it two weeks before. The floor was covered by a square of linoleum with an oriental filigree pattern painted in rose, lime and lemon The linoleum showed the striped pattern of the pine boards under it. Where the boards failed to join properly the linoleum's color was worn off; the stripes were dull red. Beside the commode was a cross-barred door, leading, presumably, to a clothes closet.

Mark scanned the big bed again, There was a curious hole in the top brass rail of the bedspring's foot. He poked a finger into the hole. John noticed what he was doing. "Grandpa did that when he was cleanin' his gun," he said. Mark felt the underside of the rail. His fingers encountered a slight protruding bump. "Bullet's still in there," John said. "You can hear the bullet if'n you shake the bed."

Theresa's lips pursed and she made a sucking noise. Doctor Barnes tipped a spoonful of water on her tongue. The water dripped down her chin. Then, from deep in her lungs, a low gurgle, like melted snow trickling over rock, sounded, grew closer, burbled, faded. A sigh of air, like a far breeze murmuring in a pine, escaped. Theresa lay still, mouth agape.

Doctor Barnes applied a mirror to her nose and then a stethoscope to her heart. He motioned for silence as Mark softly cried "Oh no!" No one spoke after that. The doctor and John tugged the blanket over Theresa's arms, then pulled the sheet over her head.

In the kitchen, after Doctor Barnes had left, Mark and John made a pot of tea. As they sat at the table, Mark told John that he would be returning to Attumwa as soon as he was graduated from Springport Community College in June. John urged him to stay through the summer, there being so much work to do, but Mark was adamant.

"I'm applying to Attumwa University," he said. They talked until dawn painted Springport Bay rose and red. Morning birds chirped in the trees.

After the undertaker, Frank Griffith, took Theresa away, Mark helped John strip her bed. They dragged the mattress to the ground floor, then to the back yard where they burned it. Dark smoke spiraled toward the rising sun.

The funeral service was conducted by Pastor Gordon in the Baptist Church. Mark sat stiffly, silently, wiping an occasional tear. The sanctuary was filled almost entirely by elderly men and women, the fishing and farming folk who had known Theresa all their long lives. They sang sad hymns in advance praise for the afterlife, sniffed and shuffled through the sermon praising Theresa's imagined saintly life in elongated phrases capturing the lonely years of a fisherman's widow. She was laid to rest in the neighboring cemetery. Mark and John cast earth onto the descending casket.

CHAPTER ELEVEN

Martha was waiting for him the night Mark's train arrived at Attumwa's Union Station. Scanning dozens in the waiting crowd he caught sight of her almost immediately. He recognized her red hat shaped like a strawberry box, a hat not unlike the one she had worn when they had seen Peter off to war so many years ago. In seconds she rested in his enfolding embrace.

She kissed him profusely on his tanned cheeks. "Oh Mark," she cried in a plaintiff voice, "you've grown so tall!" And he had. He was surprised himself that he was looking down at her, because when he had left her two years ago she was the one who looked down at him. She also appeared to him to be younger than he had pictured her. "Martha! Martha! I have missed you. Honest. I have so much to tell you." He stepped back a foot or two. "Let me look at you." Smiling, she removed her hat, loosening her long tan hair so that it draped a shoulder as she posed for him, turning slightly left and right. She was beautiful. His sister was gorgeous.

Her eyes were dark, almost as dark as Helen's, and although they were frank, they still withheld a secret. In a taxi she squeezed his hand. "I can't believe it," she said. "You're home again." But whose home was it to be? Hers? Or Stanford's? Either way, it could never be his. And yet, as the taxi took them down King Street to Main, and then through downtown's throng of shoppers, he had the feeling he had never been away, that his two years in Springport were a dream, and that he had awakened. He was older but nothing else had changed, or had it? Perhaps he had changed, but how could anyone discern such a thing about themselves?

He was certain that Martha had changed. The teenager he had known had vanished. In her place an exciting person had taken her place. Of course she wore a lot of makeup, including black false eyelashes, but there was no denying she had a marvelous face, perfectly pinched nose, the tip of which projected to a point that almost begged to be twitched, and red lips that were both full and enticing, but still had a tendency to appear aggrieved. Not that she displayed an unsavory pout, for she smiled constantly, displaying marvelously bright teeth, but there was a certain obstinate quality about the way her lips protruded, as if she were keeping them deliberately that way in search of the right words to express whatever she was thinking.

At last the taxi unloaded them and Mark's heavy travel bags at the door to Martha's apartment building. The rattling old elevator slowly rose to Floor Five. Martha unlocked the door and flicked a switch. Three standing lamps with identical tan shades lit up. The room contained a sofa bed slip-covered in gold, two matching stuffed chairs, a coffee table with a glazed glass top and spindle legs. Against the rear wall was a combination television and stereo console, including ornate twin oak speakers. The walls were painted a flat eggshell light brown, offset by a deep slab of maroon carpet.

Guiding Mark on what she termed "the grand tour," Martha showed him "your room" first. It had a double bed covered with a spread with interlocking blue circles, nightstands on either side of the bed surmounted by gooseneck lamps; a red leather lounging chair, with a bridge lamp standing behind it; a walnut office desk with chair; all set upon an azure-blue carpet. Mark whistled in acclamation.

"Like it?" she asked.

"It's wonderful," he said. Hugging her in true gratitude, he felt relieved of the fear that he was intruding upon his sister's life. A tremor suddenly shook him. This had been Stanford's room! He turned aside. "Where's the kitchen?" he asked. "I'm hungry."

On the way to the kitchen they passed into the dining room. While the parlor and his bedroom displayed his sister's taste for the finest, the dining room was truly opulent. There was the table, polished to mirror reflectivity; a matching buffet, and a china cabinet with lacy wood cutouts on its glass doors, framing three shelves of gleaming silver and etched glassware. Martha's modern up-to-date kitchen featured a built-in stove with electric burners, the newest flat-topped white refrigerator, and birch cabinets with antique copper hinges running both sides of a gleaming steel sink with two taps, hot and cold. "If only grandmother could have seen this," Mark exclaimed.

Martha smiled. "Oh, I don't know," she said. "I'm sure she had friends with kitchens like this."

After they snacked on leftover salad and fruit from the "fridge," as Martha called it, she asked Mark if he would like to see her bedroom. "Sure," he said, rather reluctantly, because he had been raised to demur to the common knowledge that children and brothers should realize that the bedrooms of parents and sisters were "off limits."

Martha's bedroom was as finely furnished as he expected. While a massive double bed dominated the room with its satin coverings and high, glossy frames, it was the gathering of cosmetics on her bureau that attracted his astonished stare. While he knew little of mature female requirements, he knew, at least from the movies, that a person had to be "in the money" to own such a generous conglomeration of expensive refinements.

On the rear wall, above the bed, hung an ornate framed painting that consisted entirely of broad slashes, some straight, some scrambled, of black to verdant heavy colors. "I see you like modern art," he said.

"Do I like modern art?" she repeated. She made an upward chopping motion, using both hands. "I adore it."

"Well, I don't understand it," he replied.

Martha shook her head. "You don't understand modern art?" she exclaimed again as they returned to the kitchen. "You don't have to understand it. You feel it. The artist tries to convey a feeling. He expresses his thoughts about the world and life itself in lines and form and color. I just love it, really."

Over tea and cake, as they sat at the shining dining room table, Martha said, looking at him earnestly, "I can't get over it, you're so grown up. When you went away you were just a boy, and now you're back and you're a man!"

"You've changed yourself, you know."

"Well, I suppose I have," she said, looking away as if she was in doubt.

"How's your job going?"

She looked askance at him. He wondered if she noticed the inquisitive glance he had given her. "It's going fine," she said quietly. "I'm still at Modern Enterprises. I've been promoted. I'm more than a secretary." She paused slightly, obviously concerned as to what her brother's reaction would be. "I'm assistant to the manager now," she said. What could he say? Two years ago she had been living with Stanford, sleeping with him in the very bed he had just seen. He shrugged as he told himself to mind his own business. It was time to do something about getting into Attumwa University. The admissions officer had encouraged him, after receiving the report of his graduation from Springport College, to arrange an interview as soon as he could. He decided he would do that in the morning. It was mid-August. Classes would start right after Labor Day. There was no time to lose. He had completed two years of college and he wasn't getting any younger.

The interview went well. He was rather taken with the interviewer, not only because she charmed him with her good looks but also because she was a post-graduate student studying for a master's in social psychology. To him that would be an ultimate goal. She asked him what major he was interested in.

"Well, I'm not sure," he said.

"What did your father do?" she asked kindly. She had her eyes upon his resume. "Oh, I'm sorry. I see he is deceased. And your mother too."

"That's okay. He was a telegrapher, with the Transcontinental."

"Sounds interesting. And your mother?"

"Housewife."

"Well that's important." She shuffled his application pages. "I see you plan to apply for a scholarship. That's fine. Most of our students need outside help. Do you have other means of support?"

"My sister helped pay for my two years at Springport, but I'm not counting on her continuing to do that. Hope I can get a part-time job."

She told him he would hear from her within a few days. He gave her Martha's phone number and asked her to leave a message if he wasn't in.

On Saturday morning Martha asked him if he would like to go shopping with her. "You bet," he said. It was years since he had been in a real department store. "Let's go to Stern's."

Martha looked at him critically. "You need a new suit," she said, a finger to her chin. "That suit doesn't fit you. You can't go around looking like that." She came close to him and began to straighten his tie. "This tie has to go too."

Over lunch on the second floor restaurant of Stauffer's, she said "Wonder you don't get indigestion the way you eat," but he let it pass. At Stern's men's department he had to pirouette five times in front of a mirror before she approved a tan cotton suit he had selected. Fortunately a tailor was available to stitch up trouser cuffs, permitting him to wear the suit as they left the store. Sarah scolded him for taking his old suit with him.

She spent an hour fixing dinner of roast stuffed boneless chicken with giblet gravy and cranberry sauce, When he complimented her for it she said "Someone has to take care of you." He was mostly silent for the rest of the meal. As they were doing the dishes she said "I'm glad you've had some kitchen practice."

That did it. He thwacked his rolled dishtowel on the sideboard . "Just cut it out, Martha!" The cup that Martha was holding slipped from her hand and smashed into pieces on the tile floor.

"Now look what you've done," she cried out. She stooped to gather up the broken pieces. Mark stomped to his room and slammed the door. He was inside only a moment before Martha came in after him. "Just like dad," she shouted at him. "He had a temper too."

"If he did, he never used it on me." Mark stepped away from her.

Martha pursued him. "That's because Mom kept him under control," she said. She switched on the light. "Because if she ever let him out of her sight—"

"That's not true!" Mark backed into the bed. He sat down on its edge, gripping the blanket.

Martha let go of the doorknob. "You didn't have any way of knowing, one way or the other," she said. She shook her head. "Sons never know their fathers the way daughters know them. Besides," she went on with a toss of her head, "Mom confided in me."

"Who the hell cares?" Retreating from her, Mark leaned back on his hands. "It's looks to me you don't care very much about him."

"I knew him better than you did," said Martha stiffly. "He wasn't a saint, you know." She sat on the bed beside him. "Don't be mad at me. I'm sorry. I apologize."

Mark didn't feel like it, but he said it to gratify her. "That's okay."

Hanging her head, Martha continued. "I didn't mean to act like Mrs. Marshall."

Mark studied her. Was she serious? "Mrs. Marshall didn't act that way. I remember."

Raising her head, attempting a forgiving smile, Martha insisted on continuing the debate. "What can you remember? You were too young. In Sunday school with some old woman prattling about gentle Jesus meek and mild. When I was a child I spoke like a child, but when I became a woman I put away childish things."

"Not quite what Paul wrote," Mark said. "Paul wrote *man*."

She stood up and looked down at him. Her hands went to her hips. "I know that. I'm not a religious illiterate. I went to that church too. I know the Bible as well as you." She turned her back on him and flashed out of the room, closing the door behind her with a thud that shook the walls.

Legs dangling, Mark lay back on the bed. The ceiling appeared ready to settle on him and he would be found there covered with lath and plaster. It was a senseless ceiling, flat, plain and very white. It had no character. The ceiling was merely there. No one talks to a ceiling. It absorbed sound like a sponge. No communication.

The door opened a crack. Martha put her head in. Her dark eyes peered at him. She held out a few sheets of typewriter paper. "Here," she said, waving the sheets. "Read them. You'll learn something."

"Can't you bring it here?"

"Come and get them."

"Oh, alright."

He treaded slowly to the door and took the sheets from her hand. Martha closed the door quietly. Mark sat on the bed near a pillow and slanted the gooseneck lamp so that its rays shone on the pages. It was a letter to Martha, dated the month before his father died. It was signed simply "Dad."

Mark adjusted the first page and began to read his father's will:

Dearest Martha:

I have your letter asking for a loan and I can understand your wanting to write rather than asking me in person, but you need not have been embarrassed. I will be glad to do it. I enclose a check for $300 which I hope will be enough for you to put with what you want to pay Mr. Stanford for the furniture. I am sorry he has left you, for your sake, because I know how well you loved him and I understand, now, how he loved you. This may sound strange to you, coming as it does from your stern old father, but it is something I had to learn. It is something your mother taught me, almost too late. When she was dying in the hospital she wrote me a note, here is just a part of it. "Andy, now please don't think so badly about me. I've had a good life, thanks to you (as if I had given her anything). After I'm gone, I want you to find a good woman and settle down with her. You must not ever think that the memory of me stands in your way. You have your life to live." She told me how you had used the $200 I gave you, that you had used it for an abortion. Yes, I have known all this time. To be honest, at the time your mother told me I was ready to put up an awful scrap, but I can see now the situation you were in. Mr. Stanford did his best by you, and I'm sorry his wife would not give him a divorce. I think he did a good thing in leaving you and so did you in parting as you did. It meant his job I think, maybe his career. But with his qualities I am sure he will do well in Chicago. It was best for you--without the possibility of marrying him there was no future in it for you. I am concerned about Mark. I know you will take care of him. If anything should ever happen to me, everything I have will go to you and him. Of course until he is of age you must hold his half in trust. It won't be much--the furniture, the car, some insurance, but it might be enough for Mark to go to college. I hope he does. He has a bright mind, but he has a lot of maturing to do. Please help him all you can. I know you will. Please don't consider what I am enclosing as a loan. It is a gift. I have given you precious little. I can afford it. There is money in the bank, now that the bills for your mother, the funeral and all that, have been paid. I don't want to leave you any debts. When the war is over--well, you will see, something good will come your way. Love, Dad

Mark went out to the parlor, where all the lights were on. Martha was sitting rigidly on the sofa. He handed her the letter. "Now you know everything," she said. She wiped her tears. She reached out to him and drew him to her. She hugged him closely. "I love you, Mark," she said. "You're a good brother."

After a time, when their tears ceased flowing, and when Mark, eyes closed, felt he was drifting slowly on a shadowed river flowing swiftly to an unknown sea, Martha aroused him. "Let's have a cup of coffee," she said.

Seated with her by the dining table Mark asked "Did Dad leave some money?"

Martha took a deep breath. "About a thousand dollars," she said. "And I was able to sell the car and some furniture for another thousand. The insurance came to five thousand. Half that's in your trust account. But you can have my half now, if you want."

"Let's talk about that later. What about Dad?" From far away the roar of the open sea pounded his aching brain. Why did he have to ask? Why now? What was the point? The words from his father's letter to Martha rattled his reason: *It's been a good life* his father had written.

He took Martha's hand tightly into his own. It was time. The question had to be asked. "Did Dad kill himself?"

Martha's eyes darkened. She was struggling to avoid the answer. "What makes you ask that?" she asked quietly. "Did Mrs. Marshall say something to you?"

"Of course she did. She said it was an accident. She said Dad fell off the bridge accidentally." Like surf on rocks, pulsing blood pounded inside his skull. "But I've always wondered—"

"Wondered about what?" Martha asked coyly.

"Why was he on the bridge, sitting on the railing, over the railroad?"

Martha sighed. "I don't know. All I know is what Pastor Woods told me."

"What did he tell you?"

"Well, as he put it, he accused Dad of living in sin."

Mark threw up his hands. "Living in *sin*?"

"That's what Pastor Woods told me. After the funeral he came to the house to comfort me." Martha laughed scornfully. "Comfort me, hah! You were at school, so I was the one to benefit from the full treatment. He told me that he had been warning Dad--warning him, mind you-- about Mrs. Marshall. He had warned him that he was living in sin with Mrs. Marshall, that for the good of the church he had to let her go."

"Stupid!" Mark exclaimed. "What did you say?"

"I said thank you very much, Pastor Woods. Thanks a lot."

"Idiot!" Mark shouted the word.

"You can say that again." Martha raised an upward palm. "Can you blame me for never going back to that church?"

Mark grinned. "You stopped going to church long before then," he said.

"Alright. And you know why. Well, my past is an open book with you now."

"It's safe with me, Martha." He massaged the back of his neck.

"What's wrong?"

"Headache, all of a sudden."

"You better get to bed," she said. She pointed at him with an admonishing finger. "Can we continue this tomorrow?"

"No we can't," he said. "I couldn't sleep, not knowing what really happened. Did he kill himself, Martha? Was it really suicide?"

Reluctantly she settled back on the sofa. "As for that we can't be sure. He was feverish, a little crazy I think. He had been working day and night. He didn't tell me much, but I'm sure just the fact that he had to sort through umpteen dozens of casualty lists every single minute of the day, and the fact he put in so many hours of overtime, must have got him, breaking him down, so to speak. Imagine the strain, and, on top of everything, thinking about Peter, not knowing if he was dead or alive. Could have gotten anyone down. How much can anyone take?"

Mark was feeling the strain. He asked himself what was the point? His father was dead. All their talk could not bring him back. "What about Pastor Woods?" he asked Martha. "Living in sin, hah!"

"I agree with you, Mark. It was a terrible thing to say. Anyway, poor Dad, with Mom gone, Mrs. Marshall may have been good for him, considering his state of mind. Who's to know?" She reached over and gently touched Mark's hand. "He had eight months with her. I can't say why but I think she depended on him as much as he depended on her. In a way they were the most peaceful days he had since Mom passed away. In any case," she continued with a shrug, "what does it matter whether he fell accidentally from the bridge or if he jumped? He was sitting on the railing, that's the point, waiting for the train. Why? He went crazy, lost his mind, at least for as long it took him to get his legs over to the other side of the railing."

Martha stood up. "Now, off to bed with you."

Startled, Mark suddenly became aware that Martha's soft voice, the words she had just spoken, and the quiet, self-controlled way she spoke, even the phrases, mirrored their mother. More and more, as he had studied her brisk way of talking, he became aware of her radiant composure. Her way of smiling sweetly echoed the image he had retained of his mother throughout his Springport days. Of course Martha, in mothering him through his high school years, honestly reflected the love and care both his mother and his father gifted him.

When he awakened the next morning Martha was already in the kitchen. He hurriedly downed his breakfast and was soon on his way by bus to visit Mrs. Marshall. The address that Martha had written for him was that of a five-story brownstone, one of a solid row of houses on Attumwa's prosperous north side. A slight push on a brass knocker summoned a liveried butler to the door. He looked up suspiciously at Mark's taller figure, examining him closely. Apparently satisfied, he at length ushered him through a capacious foyer into a snug waiting room. "I will inform Mrs. Marshall of your presence," the butler said smugly.

Mrs. Marshall greeted him warmly with a tight hug. She stepped a pace away. "Mark, my goodness, how tall you've grown." She herself had not changed much. Her long blond hair, tightly braided, was as he remembered. She was, perhaps, somewhat heavier, but the way she spoke, with a measured tonal tendency, was still an engaging characteristic. She insisted that they pursue their conversation in her suite on the top floor. She assured Mark that it was perfectly appropriate, that friends frequently visited her there. A small rattling elevator took them up. Her parlor overflowed with mementos, each celebrating her Norwegian background: Carved ivory figures, perhaps impressions of patriarchal gods, crowded a mantle. A score of framed photographs covered half a wall. Glass door bookcases displayed shelves of Norwegian books: Vesaas' Vindarne, a complete Ibsen, Evans's Englandsfarere. Mrs. Marshall insisted on making tea and she went off to the kitchen. Mark examined the photographs. They were obviously of her friends and family. Then he saw it: a faded photograph of his father standing on a wharf, his fishing pole held proudly aloft to display his catch. His father grinned in triumph.

Later, returning with hot teapot, cups and saucers on a tray, Mrs. Marshall asked "How is dear Martha?"

"Very well," he replied lamely. He was eager to press on with his mission. "Martha has a new job."

"I'm glad to hear it, Mark." She began pouring tea. "She never liked me, you know," she said, but her words lacked condemnation. "Except for once on the street, when she said only a few words, I've not seen her since--since your father died."

"You mean since he killed himself, don't you, Mrs. Marshall?" He was standing opposite her on the other side of the tea table, and had been waiting for her to sit down. A look of surprised hurt came into her pale blue eyes. Perhaps he had been precipitous. Now she would never tell him anything.

Mrs. Marshall stood up, teacup in hand, and strode toward a sofa covered with a knitted red and white afghan. She sat down carefully. She took her time before responding. "I suppose Martha told you that. In a way, she's right. But when you lose the will to live, well, anything can happen. The coroner said it was an accident. Why shouldn't I believe that? Anyway, what does it matter?"

"It matters a lot to me," Mark said. He suppressed an inclination to accuse her of being unfeeling.

"I assumed it would," she said. "Did Martha tell you about?" Obviously aware of Mark's growing sense of alarm, she paused. "About your father and me?"

He could see the door closing, long ago, behind them as they entered his father's bedroom together. "Yes, Sarah told me," he said.

"Your father needed me and I needed him," Mrs. Marshall told him. "It was as simple as that. It wasn't a normal situation for either of us, what with your mother having passed away, and not knowing what had happened to Peter. We were thrown together by, well, by circumstances. If I was of some comfort to him in those unhappy months I'm glad, I have no regrets." She laughed, a high hopeful laugh without a tinge of self-conscience anxiety. "Mark, do you remember New Year's eve? All those pots and pans! You wanted to stay up until midnight so you could make a joyful noise, banging away."

He remembered. "But you wouldn't let me," he said. He heard the door of his father's room close without a sound.

"You were a good young man, Mark." Coolly, she raised her cup in salute. She had a faraway look in her eyes. "You always had a certain---certain quality of heart and mind I admired. For one thing, you cared what happened to people. I suppose you can't remember, maybe you do, helping me with the dishes, telling me about your day in school, asking me homework questions. What I'm getting at is: I was like a mother to you, wasn't I, Mark?" She looked at him through the gulf of years. Her thick blond eyebrows peaked. "Wasn't I, Mark?"

"Yes, you were, Mrs. Marshall."

"Not that I wanted to take care of the place," she said, "You needed to be cared for and, well, I was there. Why do you think I stayed after Andy, your father that is, died? To take care of you, Mark, until you finished high school, until you could go to Springport. I stayed on to take care of you."

For Mark, that wasn't enough. There must be something she wasn't telling him, but what was it? "Well, Martha paid you, didn't she?" It was wrong to say that. "I'm sorry Mrs. Marshall."

"That's okay," she said. "Heavens above! Did she tell you that?"

"No, she didn't," he replied, rather sheepishly. "I presumed"

"Incorrectly," Mrs. Marshall interrupted him. "In a way she did pay me. She didn't charge me rent. But I didn't get any pay from her. I worked for Mrs. Creighton, your neighbor, two days a week. I managed." She drank tea in silence for a moment. "You remember the day we saw you off at Union Station, me and Martha?"

He remembered. Mrs. Marshall had packed his cases, being careful to put in everything he wanted, even including a pack of gem-size pebbles from Echo Lake. They were still in the cases, together with the photos of Peter and Carol.

"Why didn't you write me?" he burst out, regretting it. He had failed to write her himself.

"And if I had written, what could I have said?" she asked. "Could I have written that I missed you, as I did. Could I have told you that you meant everything, because you were Andy's son?" Lips quivering, she took a deep breath. "How many times I started to write, and then tore it up. I knew you had to begin again, to make a new life for yourself, and it was better for you to forget the past." She reached across the table and took his hand, a tingling touch. "Forget the past, Mark. You're young. You've got the whole world ahead of you."

Mark stood up. A flash of regret cut a trench through his tensely confused thoughts. "Please, Mrs. Marshall, don't go on. I shouldn't be bothering you."

"Bothering me? Why, heavens, Mark, you don't bother me. What a thing to say. If you knew what it means to me to see you again." She brushed her tear-filled eyes. "I'm sorry, Mark. You bring it all back." Her shoulders heaved. "I loved your father so much, so much."

He felt torn, divided as if he were two selves. He wanted to retreat, he wanted to stay. He blurted out: "But did my father love you?"

Mrs. Marshall pushed herself upright and stood away from him. Her blue eyes gazed at him with icy intensity. "Must I prove it to you?" she asked him bitterly. "What are you made of, Mark?" She moved quickly to the back of the parlor and opened a buffet drawer. She withdrew an envelope and handed it to Mark's trembling hand. "Read it," she commanded. "It's a letter your father wrote to me." He hesitated, but she insisted and retreated to her bedroom. Mark resumed sitting on the sofa, adjusted a nearby floor lamp, and began to read:

My dearest Sue:

It's late at the office and my work is not done yet. Will it ever be? I don't know why, I got this sudden urge to write to you. It just seemed right that I should do it. So many times I wanted to say something to you that would tell you how I felt. It isn't easy. I have never written a letter like this before. I suppose Peter could have done better, at his age, or even Mark, he has such a skill at words. I suppose you might call this a love letter. I hope you will receive it as such, for I want to speak from my heart. And please don't think that I write merely out of gratitude. I am so thankful for you--you have done so much for me and Mark. If anything ever happens to me I hope you will take care of him. He's all I've got now, besides you, and do I really have you? These past few months have been like a dream. Some days I think I will wake up and find they never happened. But, Sue, believe me, they have been the happiest days of my life. I have no wish to bind you to me, and yet I want you forever. I don't wish in any way to hurt you, and yet I have. I can make no claim upon you, you are not mine to be claimed. I can't in any way speak for the future, there is no future I can see. When I first saw you, it was as if I had always known you, so we have the past as well. If this is all we have, then so be it. I would not have it any other way. Shall I say it? That I love you? It sounds so trite, and, besides, you know I do. Rather, my life depends on you. If you should ever be taken from me … But that is something I dare not think about. I do love you, truly. Almost, I never knew such love before. Sometimes I think I must be very weak, to feel this way, knowing it is wrong, but I can't help myself. You came into my life unknowing. Was there a fate in this? One woman who came to my door, in answer to the ad, might have been a tottering old woman, but it was not. It was you--you! When the war is over (isn't everyone saying that?) we may have a chance at life together. We may not. So what counts is now. This can never be taken from us. Andy

With tender fingers mark refolded the letter and returned it to the envelope, where his father's dark secret would remain secret forever. The mist was lifted. Now he knew his father.

Mrs. Marshall told him what she had done that final day. She had searched The Flats. At length, not finding his father, she went to the police. She was at the station when the word came that his body had been found. But that was long ago and far away. Now Mark had places to go and people to see. And not much time. He had discovered his father. Now he had to find himself.

Chapter Twelve

Mark was admitted to Attumwa University as a third-year student. He was content to drift through the first semester, which required make-up math and science courses in addition to a scattering of liberal arts. Apart from classes, he devoted hours in the university library to devouring the novels of Thomas Wolfe and others of their type. Saturdays were devoted to sleeping until noon and seeing a movie downtown.

On Sundays he sampled services at the university chapel, Trinity Episcopal Church near the Capitol, and even went to St. Mary's Catholic. Most often he attended Madison Avenue Baptist, which was within walking distance from the apartment.

He went with Martha only once to the Methodist Church, his family's church. Although Pastor Woods had been transferred and was succeeded by a likeable young minister just out of seminary, Mark found it a painful experience. Sitting quietly in the pew with Martha, he felt the ghostly presence of Peter, his mother and his father.

He was not getting enough sleep and he knew it. He would get up in the middle of the night, creep into the parlor, careful not to waken Martha, pick up whatever novel he was reading, read a few pages, drift off, give up and sleep.

He had a few dates with university girls who also lived at home, where they were easy to reach. One of them, whose name was, incredibly, Cherry Hill, invited him to her house on Upper Maple Street that was a bust because Cherry's mother made them leave the porch at ten o'clock just when things were "looking up," as Chase Drummond would have said.

Chase Drummond, whose father was board chairman of Drummond Pulp and Paper Company, was not Mark's friend. That role was filled by rolly-polly, happy-go-lucky Ted Swain, who didn't live in a mansion as Chase did. In fact, Ted lived on The Flats, and that was why, Mark presumed, they got along. In any case, they chased girls together a few times, attended the Gayety Burlesque a few times, and generally "bummed around," as Ted called it. Ted was a great beer drinker and would haul Mark into the Swain kitchen to "down a few," but Mark always refused.

"Holy, holy, holy," Ted would say, his beady eyes committed to laughter.

"Go to hell," Mark would reply.

Still, there was some truth in Ted's taunt. For some reason, tradition perhaps, on many weekday mornings, before taking a bus to the university, he sat down on the sofa, picked up his Bible, opened it at the page where he had laid a marker, read a chapter, then closed his eyes. He would sing quietly to himself "Holy, holy, holy, Lord God almighty," or simply hum any tune that came to mind, and he would pray. That was his "Quiet Time."

He eased through the second semester and suddenly it was June. He passed the dull, boring courses with minimum grades. He was sick of being tested and tested again and again. What was the point? Being a university student was not living. It was, mainly, wasting time. Most of the stuff he had to learn was irrelevant to his dream. But what was the dream? There had been a dream, on the beach at Springport, perhaps, watching the tide roll in, the gleaming sunswept waves smothering the sand, the rocks, his very life, with a bright vision of a future that would take him to the promised land. But where was that wonderful country, that dream of fulfillment?

In early July he was drifting around the crowded downtown streets and just because he did not have anything else to do, on an impulse, he entered the Transcontinental Telegraph building, where his father used to work. He did not need to knock. He merely opened a door that he recognized as the one he had been through a few times. There was the long table, still overloaded with noisy equipment, just as he remembered it when his father demonstrated how he earned the pay that meant his family's survival.

A tall, white-haired man approached. "Why if it isn't Andy's son," he cried out loudly enough for a few others in the noisy room to hear him. "Hello Mark," he said. "I'm Lance White." He shook Mark's hand warmly. "My gosh, you were in high school last time I saw you. What are you doing now?"

"I just finished my third year at Attuma U," Mark replied. "Just another year to go, thank goodness."

"And your sister, what's her name?"

"Martha. We share an apartment. She's fine. Has a good job."

Mr. White, fingering his chin, observing Mark closely. "Say, you working this summer?"

"No. Just taking it easy."

"Tell you what. I need some help here," Mr. White said, glancing around the room. "You type?"

"Well enough."

"We're drowning here with telegrams." Mr. White glanced shyly at Mark. "You know, just the way things were when your dad worked here. Not that busy, of course. Not like during the war but a couple of our guys will be going on vacation soon. I'd appreciate it if you could help us out, okay?"

In a sense, Mark was thinking, he would be walking in his father's shoes. The irony of it caused a chuckle. "Sure, okay," he said. "When do I start?"

"Right now," Mr. White said. He paused. "That is, if you're free."

"I'm free," Mark responded instantly.

"Day shift only. We haven't had night shift for a long time. Stay with us until you have to go back to school, okay?"

Work hours, pay and other minimum details were agreed upon. Mark took a place at the end of a table, uncovered a typewriter, was given a stack of printed forms and a box full of telegrams. Within a half hour he was typing his first lists.

In late July, Mark received a letter from Jim Pettaw. It was the first time he had heard anything from Jim. When, long ago, they parted company at the Maine bus station, he believed that their friendship was over. The bond that kept them together at Springport Community College had been severed by Jim's religious passion. At least that was the factor upon which Mark placed the blame for the ending of their friendship. Not that the Indian had not figured hugely in his thoughts, because for weeks he castigated himself for being a fool not to accept Jim for what he was. That had nothing to do with his being an Indian, but had everything to do with his being deeply engaged in Christian fundamentalism.

Jim told Mark that he had returned to Springport Community College after a year's absence due to need of money. It took a year for his father, the Chief, to afford sending him back. The Chief had done well at his job with the New Town shoe factory and his gift shop was prospering due to an increasing influx of moneyed tourists. Now his father wanted his son to go to university and that was why Jim was writing to Mark. He wanted to know if Attumwa was a "good" school. Which, Mark knew, meant: Would Attumwa accept an Indian?

Bypassing the admissions office, Mark went immediately to Chaplain Mordecai Davis, who assured him that prejudice was a dirty word at Attumwa U. On Jim's behalf, Mark picked up the required application papers and airmailed them to Jim.

Within two weeks he filed the appplication himself, adding his own written recommendation to those of three Springport College professors, the college dean of students and Jim's Pastor Rudolph. An admissions office secretary assured Mark that the application would be "expedited." Jim was admitted.

Mark met him at Union Station. Jim was standing beneath the statue of winged Mercury, as they had arranged. They shook hands respectfully. Jim hadn't changed his comedian style. "How!" he said, saluting, smiling broadly. It was Jim as he had known him, darkened thoroughly by the summer sun, somewhat aloof but grinning nevertheless. Mark stepped forward, closing the gap between them.

"You nut," Mark said. "How ya doin' fella?"

"Big Chief lonesome. Miss reservation."

"You stupid nut." Mark embraced Jim for a moment. He knew they would always be friends.

They took a taxi to the apartment. In the evening Martha prepared supper and went to bed early. Mark and Jim were up until one o'clock reviewing their time together in Springport. Not once did either make a religious comment. Mark gave his room to Jim; he slept soundly on the parlor's sofa bed.

They arrived on the campus at ten o'clock, just in time for Jim's appointment with an admissions officer. Jim was assigned to Wayne House, a university residence. Mark helped him carry his luggage to the second floor.

Afterward, as they crossed the quadrangle, Jim shaded his eyes and looked toward the roof of McMaster Hall. He pointed upward.

"What's that ugly thing?" he asked.

"That thing on top? It's just a cupola. Why?"

"Sure looks like gold, doesn't it?"

The sun struck a halo around the shining tower. "Symbol of the university," Mark said. "All that glitters, etcetera."

"Enough to blind you."

They met as often as they could after that, in the cafeteria, in the library stacks. in Jim's room, which was meant for two men. It had two beds and two small desks. Although the university was crowded with returning war veterans, Jim was alone. Mark made no comment and neither did Jim.

In October, Mark was accepted as a pledge by Phi Zeta Rho, which had a house off campus. Like any neophyte, he went about with one pant leg rolled up. He was assigned janitorial duties. In February, when the snow lay deep, he was initiated. But first he had to accomplish thirty-four tasks. There was little time. Between nine o'clock in the evening and three in the morning he had to prove himself worthy of being a Phi Zete.

"It can't be done," Mark protested to Chase Drummond, with whom he was paired. "Nobody can do it. It's a joke. No one has ever done all thirty-four!"

Chase threw up his widespread hands in despair. He was a big, broad-limbed man with a constant sneer. He fingered his gross mustache and flipped his fingers through his thick black hair. "There's nothing to it," he proclaimed loudly. He talked as if he had done it all before. He had sung a temperance song in a bar. He had borrowed a G-string. He had found a page of Freud's Dreams, a brick, a green glass, a wedding ring, a condom. He had sung a serenade to the girls in the windows of Kappa Rho Delta, He had begged for a dollar at Union and Bank streets.

Mark was ready to give up at midnight. But Chase, acne scars flaming, said "The hard part is over." Chase knew his way to Eastview, knew the house to go to. The women there gave him two G-strings just by asking a stripteaser. They sang *By the Light of the Silvery Moon* under Kappa Rho windows. The girls waved their panties. The night grew long and the moon went down. They begged for dollars and sang a duet, *Daddy, Poor Daddy* in Donavan's bar. Pennies were thrown toward them. Chase, bending the rules, gave Mark a condom. They had carried two bricks with them, but still no black cat. Chase was the genius who did it. He cornered a gray one in an alley, netted it into a potato sack, took it to his room and there applied to the cat a coat of shining black shoe polish. All done by three o'clock and only the gold to get.

They were blindfolded and led unseen by Phi Zetes, by means of a fire escape, to the roof of McMaster Hall. A brisk wind wrapped around the tower. Coatless, Mark shivered. He felt himself being raised on shoulders. He reached up, as instructed, but his hands fumbled in a void. Another boost and he was up, the sharp tower's edge under his fingers. He angled forward, blindly, until he felt the hard curving surface of the cupola. A metal burr scratched his stomach. He uttered a small cry. He reached out. His fingers touched the gold. He pried a flake loose and it fell into his sweating palm.

"Phi Zete!" he screamed. The sound echoed down the campus. He was lowered to the roof.

Later, standing with his fellow initiates in the dimly lit basement of Phi Zeta House, right hand upheld, he swore allegiance to the fraternity, promising to be faithful forever, never to reveal its secrets, to share tribulation together, brothers bonded by the mysterious golden pledge by which they were joined to eternity.

Now that he was a Phi Zete he had a lot to do, which meant he saw a lot less of Jim Pettaw, but the fraternity nights were important. There was an open question to be argued: Should the atomic bomb be unleashed?

Chaplain Davis was invited to lead a discussion about the war. Fraternity brothers filled every seat in Phi Zete's wide parlor. They stood along the walls and in the archway to the vestibule. Mark found a place to stand in front of the arch.

When his audience quieted down the chaplain, hard jaw thrusting forward, glanced severely around his audience. "Korea is one war that we need never to have been fighting," he said gravely. A sheltered hoot echoed around the room. "Some of you disagree with me about that," he went on patiently. He was a well-groomed man about forty. As he talked a handful of graying hair dangled over his forehead. "Those who disagree may not be aware of the facts. War is an admission of failure, the failure of good sense and wisdom to prevail over saber-rattling. I'm not saying our men in Korea are fighting in vain. Don't get me wrong. What I am saying is that Korea is a stupid, senseless war that could have been prevented by foresighted statesmanship and a willingness to face the fact that we are fighting a war in the wrong place, at the wrong time, and against the wrong enemy." Again, howls of derision around the room. Chaplain Davis glanced coldly at his detractors. He was a former Navy chaplain, had served on an aircraft carrier in the Pacific. He was obviously used to loudly expressed contrary opinion. "I realize that some of you aren't in favor of this cease-fire proposal we are trying to negotiate. May I ask, what is the alternative? An endless war?"

Chase Drummond, tall, erect, his pocked face flaming, shouted: "We can win. We should order MacArthur to drop the bomb." Ted Swain, squiggling on the floor at Chaplain Davis' feet, asked "Yes, Chaplain, why don't we use the bomb?"

Before Chaplain Davis could answer, Mark burst out: "I suppose there are those," he hollered above the hubbub, "who wouldn't mind a world-wide atomic war, as long as they weren't under the bomb."

Chase Drummond pointed at him. "That talk of a general war is just a smokescreen for cowards." It was a typical Chase Drummond remark, cutting and personal. Chase knew very well that Mark's sympathies lay with Chaplain Davis, a man of reason and sanity.

"War as an instrument of national policy is obsolete," Mark shouted.

He heard Ted Swain's snicker. "The cliché," Ted muttered, "is the last refuge of the fence-sitter." There was a lot of laughter.

Chaplain Davis held up his hand, commanding silence. "We're getting off the subject," he said. "Both sides should sit down together to achieve an honorable agreement."

"Or to save face." This from Chase Drummond.

"Alright," the chaplain said. "To save face." He looked defeated. "And what is wrong with that? Would you rather have this civil war go on forever?" He glanced around the room, his eyes nervously twitching. "Would you rather that we settle down to a war of attrition?"

There were cries of "No, no" and others of "Drop the bomb!"

Mark raised his hand. "It's not a matter of saving face," he said. "It's a matter of saving lives. That's a Christian concern."

Some applause. Some hoots by others.

Chaplain Davis again commanded silence. "Well, what does Christianity have to say? What kind of a world do we want? One in which a war, once started, must result in the annihilation of mankind, or one in which means are available to stop little wars from flaming into big wars? It appears to me that we have the chance in Korea to prove we are for peace."

"At all costs?" shouted Ted Swain.

Mark slipped out silently to the hall. He felt very tired. The discussion would go on for another hour. Chaplain Davis, having lost control, would excuse himself and talk would turn into a free-for-all in which no resolution was possible.

He walked slowly across the dark empty quadrangle to Wayne Hall. Jim hardly ever locked his door. "What's the point?" he would ask. "I don't own anything worth stealing." Mark entered and quietly closed the door behind him. He switched on a ceiling light. Jim's room had the severe look of military neatness: beds covered by green and yellow bedspreads, Jim's few books upended in a neat row between gunmetal bookends atop his desk, the bureau top covered by a white linen scarf, a loudly clicking silver Westclox with a bell on top, a brush, a comb, and a blue ceramic box with a lid, upon which two hand-holding cherubs formed a handle. Mark was examining a photograph of Jim's mother when Jim came in.

"Well, hello there," he said pleasantly. "Good looking, isn't she?" he asked, pointing to the photograph.

"Pretty," Mark replied. How much Jim looked like her. Jim had the same dark tired eyes, heavy-lidded and deeply recessed, with cross-hatched lines beneath. And there was the same heavy look, the forehead massive and lined, slanting back from heavy brows, the nose quite narrow, the cheeks bony and cavernous, but the same mouth, generously wide, not in repose, as if always on the verge of saying something profound.

Standing before the mirror above the bureau, Jim combed back his thick mass of black hair. He ran a finger over the crack that split the mirror. "Look at me, Mark, here in the mirror."

Mark came over to stand beside him. "Good grief!" he exclaimed. The mirror divided Jim's image along a jagged crack from top center straight down to the bottom of the mirror. "Is that you or twins?" Mark asked.

Laughing, Jim replied "Split personality. Typical injun."

"Let's go over to Kappa Rho," Mark said, "and scare up some girls, one for me and two for you."

"No, its one for you and none for me."

"You and your Indian fatalism," Mark said. "Does there have to be a double meaning in everything you say and do? Does nothing ever happen to you by sheer accident?"

"God has a plan for everyone."

"I was baptized as well as you."

"That should guarantee you a place in heaven," Jim said sardonically.

"It was only symbolic. It didn't mean anything."

Jim shook his head. "No, it was more than a symbol. It was a sign of your ingrafting into Christ."

"Baloney! I don't go for that mumbo-jumbo any more. It's what a man believes that counts."

Jim gave Mark his raised-eyebrow look of reproach. "Do you believe, Mark? Luke eighteen, seventeen."

"Just like my mother," Mark said. "She seldom quoted the Bible, just chapter and verse. When she wanted to scold me about not doing my homework she'd say 'Second Timothy two, fifteen'." He paused and sat down on Mark's bed. "Tell you the truth, Jim, sometimes I was curious about that chapter-verse thing. I'd look it up in my Bible. Come to think of it, I learned a lot of verses that way." He laughed mildly. "Funny thing, she'd open her Bible anywhere, close her eyes and point a finger on a verse. That would be her message for the day."

Jim was listening quietly. "I wish I'd known her. It's late, what else is on your mind?"

That was another thing he liked about Jim Pettaw. He was intuitive.

"Chase Drummond accused me of being a coward," Mark said. He was taking a chance. He never could predict Jim's reactions, because Jim was not only intuitive, he was inscrutable.

Jim looked at him inquisitively. "There is evil in the world to test the good."

"Darn it, Jim. Come down out of your pulpit."

"Alright then, Chase Drummond is evil. So what?"

"He would like to have us drop the bomb in Korea, not because he really believes that would win the war but because that's the farthest-out attitude. Whatever's the wildest, that's what Chase Drummond is for. Why? Because that's the way Phi Zetes are supposed to be. They have always been that way. Chase Drummond was cast in the true heroic Phi Zete mold. He will be remembered as the Phi Zete who was the prime stickler for tradition."

Jim was listening quietly. He heaved a sigh. "Mark, ease up. I'd never be a Phi Zete. I don't want to and they would never have me. So what?"

"So what! If I were president of this esteemed university I'd run 'em out of town. That's what."

"This too shall pass," Jim said. "Why in the world did you ever join?"

"I wish I hadn't," Mark said, eyes lowered. "Prestige, I suppose. Ego."

Jim raised himself on one arm. "Bless you, my son. You are forgiven." He looked at his watch. "It's late, Mark."

Mark apologized. "Sorry, I got carried away."

The next day Mark investigated the Phi Zete bookcases that lined one wall of the parlor. Ted Swain had told him that Phi Zete had a long history and that he had read about it in a manual-sized publication detailing its founding and prestigious standing among university fraternities. Mark found the manual after a brief search. He took it to a nearby chair. He wanted to know about Phi Zete's hazing practices. He skipped over pages until he found a history of McMaster Hall.

There was a wet-plate photograph of the hall taken before the Civil War. There was no cupola. Another picture dated "About 1880" showed the cupola, in black and white. On the next page was a color photo. A caption explained that "real gold" had been applied at the time of the tower's construction.

Mark could find no record of a date when Phi Zeta added chipping gold from the cupola became a required action for initiation. However, a later account called attention to the fact that the cupola was commonly referred to as the "Chipped Chalice." There was a time when chipping was frowned upon. Editorials in the campus Eagle called it "Dross Loss," a catch phrase popularized by those who doubted the gold was real. But it was real. For years flakes of the stuff were legal tender. It was suspected that only upperclassmen were responsible for cupola banditry, because who could suspect a freshman or sophomore of the proper motive? Only juniors and seniors, it was argued, had a right for the gold. In the early years anyone caught with a bit of gold in his laundry was either paddled or forced to swallow a guppy. When the country went off the gold standard the university's trustees replaced cupola gold with a synthetic. At first brass filings mixed with linseed oil did the job. But since the end of World War One anodized aluminum paint had been substituted.

What Mark had climbed so high to get was a fake!

Chapter Thirteen

The next Friday, the day after Thanksgiving, was also a holiday. There were no classes. The campus was nearly empty. Mark spent the day studying at the university library. Martha had to work, however, and thus he arrived at the apartment under a cloud of dark fatigue and loneliness.

The same old question festered: "What shall I do?" Tonight and tomorrow and Sunday were future long depths of emptiness, to be got through somehow. He would rather be in class, or at a Phi Zete rally, or with Jim or Ted Swain than here, alone. He wished that Martha would hurry up and come through the door, happily greeting him with a warm hug. It wouldn't be unusual if she did not come tonight. She usually spent her weekends somewhere else, at a girlfriend's house, she would tell him. He could not help feeling suspicious that she had a regular boyfriend. Mark would never enquire and she never identified exactly where and how she spent her time away from the apartment. That was her business. Still, he wondered. He thought so much about it that he slowly realized that he missed her, that he needed her. Jim had tagged him a "lone wolf." Mark had protested, but he knew now it was true. He only pretended, to himself, that he liked being alone. This evening, however, the truth assaulted him: he did not like being alone.

Reluctantly, he decided to prepare a meal for himself. He filled the kettle and placed it on the stove to boil, then took a potato from a bin and began to peel it For some reason, perhaps it was the fact that he had a knife in his hands, he thought about his boyhood friend, Jack Strong, how they knifed their way through brush to create a trail. He had lost track of him after his father died and he went away to Maine. Where was Jack now? Mark swore when he cut his left thumb.

He was in the bathroom attaching a bandaid when he heard the front door open and Martha's bright, cheering call. "Mark! I'm here." He dashed out to greet her. "You're late," he said.

"Well, I'm here." She hugged him. The fit of depression vanished. She was his sister. She was his family. Martha deposited a quart of New York icecream and a bottle of gingerale on the table.

"What's the occasion?" he asked nervously.

"Why must it be an occasion?" Martha replied, as she removed a pin from her purple flowered hat and hung the hat and her raincoat on the clothes tree.

"I peeled the potato," he said brightly. She nodded. His stomach tightened. Martha, he was beginning to suspect, was preparing him for bad news.

She wrapped an apron around her waist and turned around so that he could tie the strings. "You look tired," she said. "What's wrong?"

He laughed lightly. "I'm depressed," he said, "about the state of the world."

"Who isn't?" Martha bustled about as if the greatest joy she had in the world was to prepare him a meal. Her dark eyes flashed. As she moved about the kitchen her long black hair swished on her shoulders. The way she acted, so joyful, not a care in the world, he knew she was going to desert him. She noticed the bandaid. Mark clenched his fingers together. "Let me see it," she demanded.

"It's nothing," Mark said. "Just a scratch." She hustled off to the bathroom and returned with a small bottle of iodine. "That'll hurt," he protested. She zipped off the bandaid, anointed the cut with a few drops of iodine. He cried out dutifully.

Over their meal, Martha appeared to Mark to delay her intention by telling him, at needless length, about her day at the office, how a salesman from New York pestered her for a date, how the office girls were forever squabbling. "You have no idea," she said, "what I have to put up with, not that I mind so much, because I am helping you with your education, that's the important thing, isn't it?"

Mark stood up, arms akimbo. He looked directly into here upraised eyes. "You're going to leave me, aren't you? " he asked brusquely

She swept him with a sidelong glance. "Don't be angry with me, Mark."

Mark collapsed into his chair. "Don't be silly," he said, above the hurt that stung his heart. "It's what you wanted, isn't it? " He didn't really know quite what to say. He had long suppressed the feeling of uncertainty he had whenever he questioned her concerning her future, what she anticipated, what she really wanted. Deep down, as he lay sleepless, here in the apartment that Sarah had shared with another man, he lived with the gnawing conclusion that one day she would be gone. He was her brother but nevertheless he had a rival for her affection, and that was Stanford, who had moved to Chicago, leaving Martha behind. His sister left hints around the apartment, especially in her room, that Stanford was still a presence in her life. His prized painting over her bed, a photo of her lover on her cosmetic table, and probably other mementoes of their intimate relationship here; yes, here where he himself lived with the dim but warning discomfort that one day he would lose her.

Martha told him that she had been offered a promotion to an executive position at the national headquarters of Modern Enterprises in Chicago. She eyed him carefully, obviously waiting anxiously for his reaction. She covered her chin with clasped hands. "We will see one another often," she promised. "I will miss you."

"Stanford will be happy," he said in a vain attempt to disguise his dismay.

"I'm not going because of him."

"Don't try to kid me, Martha. You've been wanting to go back to him for a long time. Forget about me. I'll be okay."

"I'll send you money whenever you need it."

"Admit it. You're going to Chicago to be with Stanford."

Martha's face flamed. She stood up and threw down her napkin. "Stop it, Mark. Just stop it. I'm not going to put up with your pettiness. I didn't ask for the job. It was offered to me."

"Divine guidance, I suppose." Mark was on his feet. They squared off in the center of the parlor. "The hell with Stanford," Mark said rather quietly.

She eyed him coolly. "So that's it. At last you've come out with it. You don't want me to go because you hate Mr. Stanford." She folded her arms. "Well, I've got news for you. His wife is going to divorce him and then we're going to get married. You'll have me off your hands for good. You won't have to worry about me anymore." Slowly she bowed her head into her cupped hands. She sobbed as her tears descended. "Maybe then you'll appreciate what I've done for you."

Despite her tears, Mark was unconvinced. She was using her weakness against him. He paced the carpet and looked down into the street lights. "Do you think I care if you go to Chicago?" He gazed blankly at his dark image in the glass. "What does it matter to me? I can get along without you. It's not as if I can't take care of myself. Go to Stanford if you have to. See if I care."

A door opened and closed. He turned around. Martha was gone. He tried the door to her room. It was locked. "Martha," he called softy. She did not answer.

He stamped around the parlor wondering what to do. He turned on all the lights. He placed a record on the player, the first record that came to hand. *Peer Gynt*. Martha's favorite. He replaced it with *Eroica*. He sat down on the sofa and picked up one of his textbooks, *English Prose and Poetry*. Coleridge! The passion and the life, whose fountains are within. Who said these poets were romantic? He flipped the pages. Byron: *And men forget their passions in the dread of this their desolation.* Mark hurled the book to the floor. Musings of long-dead poets. Cheap thoughts to amuse inbred minds. A romantic attachment to the past had no place in the middle of the Twentieth Century. All that nonsense about a passionate attachment to life didn't belong in a world that demanded scientific detachment. The best brains were calling for a new commitment to the search for solid fact. The mystery of the universe was to be found inside the atom, and out there among the stars. Think small was to think big. As for heaven, who could find it? He turned on the television set. Robert Ryan, the star, comes into a room. He has a so-sorry look. He holds a revolver. There is another man in the room, a Japanese room. The man is taking a bath in a barrel. Robert Ryan points the revolver and shoots several bullets into the barrel. Water spurts from the holes. The man in the barrel leaps and screams, leaps and screams. The tall man walks over to the barrel. He grasps the corpse by the hair and says to the staring eyes "You know I had to do it." Cut to a commercial. A beautiful woman takes a bath in a gleaming white tub. Bubbles cover her to the armpits. Slowly she raises a slim leg and lathers it. Mark switched off the television.

A dull buzzer sounded announcing that somebody was in the building lobby. That somebody was walking up the stairs. The front door opened. "Hello Mark," he said, "I'm Joe Stanford."

Mark couldn't remember him. Stanford eyed Mark up and down. "You don't look at all like your father," he said. "But I do see a resemblance to Martha. Yes, especially around the eyes. It's quite remarkable, really."

As he spoke he shook Mark's hand firmly. Mark shrank as far away as he could. All he could say was: "Mr. Stanford. What a surprise." He wanted to sit down. Why did he feel that his legs were a little wobbly?

Stanford was taller than Mark, at least six feet with a quarterback's lithe body. He wore a crew cut like a fedora, stiffly upright. His face was all rugged planes: flat rough cheeks, high scored forehead, long and slightly crooked nose.

Suddenly Martha came up behind Mark, so quietly that he was moved aside involuntarily. "We both look like Mother," she said. She was heavily made up, cheeks rouged, lipstick thick and red. "At least not as far as his looks are concerned," she added. Mark noted the ambiguity.

Mark wished there was some place he could hide. "What difference does it makes who I look like?" he asked sourly.

Martha took Stanford's arm. "Mr. Stanford," she said, "came from Chicago for the weekend. We're going out. I won't be late."

"That's alright," Mark said firmly, almost as if she had asked his permission. "Do you have your key?"

Martha patted her purse. "I'll be quiet."

Stanford helped her into her raincoat. He shook Mark's hand. "Great to see you again, Mark."

"Nice to have met you, Mr. Stanford."

"What's this mister business? Joe to you. When you come to Chicago be sure to look me, rather us, up. Modern Enterprise Ink."

In his dream that night Mark was in the house in Westminster. He had just returned from the hospital in Attumwa. That was when it was thought he had polio. Martha floated in. She laid her cool hand on his forehead and whispered angel words. He did not want her to take her hand away, but she did take it away. He could not protest because he could not speak. He was sure he had moved his eyes and he was sure she had seen them move. But she only looked at him. Then his mother came in and smiled as she fondly mussed his hair. He was unable to smile back.

He was awakened by the squeaking of a car halting outside. Mark went to the parlor window as Stanford held Martha in his arms for a long time, right there under the street lamp, then slowly walked her to the entrance. Mark retreated beneath a dark window curtain. He heard the key turning in the lock. Martha quietly entered, tiptoed to the bathroom, then to her bedroom. And all was still. Mark crossed the parlor to her door and poised his hand to knock. What could he say? She was going away, and that was that. He returned to his room, where he slept fitfully.

Chapter Fourteen

The Phi Zeta parlor was crowded for Professor Hugh Johnson's talk about sexual relations. The teacher of English literature emphasized the weight of his argument by furrowing his brow half-way up his bald scalp.

"Let's face it," he proclaimed, "you may be educated, but what are you good for?" He flagged his arm as if waving down a train. "For nothing, that's what." And then the point of his dry joke: "Goodness knows no blessing."

(And something Mark's mother used to say: "Be good, and if you can't be good, be careful." Not obviously a joke to a ten-year-old, but now he knew what it meant.)

"It's not a question of sex per se," Johnson went on, gazing at his attentive audience through a hovering haze of smoke. "It's your attitude toward sex. Say you have this girl in your car. She wants to and you want to. The question is, should you take her to a motel, which you can't afford, or do it there in the car and risk the chance of being caught by a cop, thereby causing her to be exposed?"

The room exploded. Chase Drummond, standing next to Mark, leaned over and said "That guy kills me. What a hell of a guy." Chase levered his cigar to the other side of his mouth and hissed his approval through gritted teeth. Ted Swain groaned and bent his head into his hands. While Mark chuckled as loudly as anyone, he somehow felt guilty.

Johnson saluted his audience, and when they had quieted down, he continued in his high condescending tone. "I can see you fellows understand me completely. Isn't that your way of escaping confrontation with a changing morality? You talk sex. You talk it all the time. Not dirty. I don't accuse your generation of that. Not in the traditional sense of dirt. But you treat sex like it was something to be hidden under a bush."

Again he received the welcome accolade of polite guffaws.

Chase Drummond, cigar revolving, hand high, his voice suspiciously deep in his throat, called out: "Is it true, sir, that it is possible to contract a social disease in a public toilet?"

The professor's furrows erased themselves. He smiled, puckered his small mouth as if in serious thought. "Young man," he drawled, "your question has real merit. I advise you to stay away from public toilets. It would be an embarrassing place to be caught with a girl."

A respectful holler of appreciation was honored by a Johnson salutation. "Let's get on with it," Johnson said. "I must remind you that you invited me into your distinguished company tonight to assist in your deliberations on a most pressing subject." Again, guffaws trickled through his audience. "Well, enough of that. Seriously, man to man, you fellows are going out into the world ill-equipped to take your place in a society that is changing, evolving, into a demoralized, I use the word deliberately, demoralized and fractured mess. Now I know many of you fellows hell around. Some of you go to Eastview on Saturday nights, and you fellows have to be hard up to go there. Hard up, I say. Alright, no more of that.."

As the hiss died around the room, Mark felt a dryness clutch his stomach. Was he less mature, less sophisticated, than Chase Drummond, who gleefully hugged himself with joy? Was he less experienced than Ted Swain, who doubled up as in pain from groaning.? Or was he feeling sick because the verbalization of sex dragged into mind images long fondled both for their fulfillment and their lack of fulfillment? These questions had to be faced or else he was merely a prude.

Johnson looked around the well-upholstered parlor as if to make sure he still had their attention. Seemingly assured that he had, he dropped his voice to a bass register and spoke as if in deepest confidence. "You fellows are lucky," he said. "You are living in an age of enlightenment, when youth has access to knowledge denied my generation. Let me be explicit. You know all about sex, all about it, before puberty. Some of you were disillusioned. You refused to believe the stork story was a myth. You got over that. You were helped over the stile by biological education which successfully tore the veil of mystery and wonder from sex. Yes, you would stand today in awe of sex but for the blunders of the sexologists. You would stand not in fear and trembling of the unknown but in anticipation of delight. You know that sex is but a mixing of the genes and you can't quite believe all that hokum about the blending of spirits. Now, can you? Sure, all that about the union of male and female being the bliss of heaven is a joke, isn't it?"

Johnson flung the question into the hazy air. The question hung there while Johnson poised his next shaft. "Ah, I can see you don't believe me. You think I am mocking those who, like Havelock Ellis, proclaim for sex the role of faun-like fun and delight? Well, I'm not. Trouble is, not one of you will discover what real sex is until you practice it on the only basis that present-day society condones and that nature assures us is correct. Sex is the sublime gift for the maturing of a man and a woman who desire one another in a candid and non-compromising way. What do I mean by compromising? I mean honesty. Ask yourself, are you honest in desiring good for the good and good only? If you desire sex on any other basis, be honest about it and admit it. Deflate yourself, but do not deflate sex. For sex can be noble and good when those who perform it are noble and good, but when you must engage in it furtively, under cover--I'm sorry--you are admitting you are transgressing the common law of society. Perhaps not the law of nature, for God knows there are lovers who have little recourse but to flaunt society's laws. But I do say this, that if you truly have the interest of your partner at heart, you will consider all the angles. Will this sex hurt her? Will it hurt you? If your answer is yes, let sex wait. And if it can't wait, then--"

The professor's words trailed off. Chase Drummond waited a moment in silence before calling out "What then, professor?"

Mark could stomach no more. He stumbled across spread-out legs and arms to the hall just as the Phi Zetes broke ranks and enfolded Johnson in a mass ringed embrace, each wave pressed to the next, as tide ripples encircle a rock on Springport Bay. Mark had no questions, desired no private counsel. He went upstairs to Chase Drummond's room, entered and waited for him, intent on baiting him for wallowing in Johnson's oppressive filth. Because, he felt, it was filth wrapped in tinsel of let's-be-modernized, tied with the golden cord of man-to-manism, it was still filth. Johnson's words dripped like effluvium on open sores. Something within him churned his spirit, not Johnson's words, but over what he believed Johnson was. In sidelong glances he had observed the professor's cosyness with certain Phi Zetes, whose names he did not know but whose faces merged now in one vast framework of flame and darkness, like the night-marching redcoats of the university band. Thus his first words to Chase Drummond, as he pounced in, were: "He's queer, isn't he?"

Chase raised a can of beer and drank hugely. "I'm not sure," he said. "At least he attempts the appearance of being homosexual." Chase worked the beer as if it was mouthwash. "If that's too profound for you, Mr. Christopher, let's say he pretends to be an angel when he's really a fairy. You heard, Mark." Chase mocked the words that Johnson had spoken: "You fellows are going out into the big bad world, so let me tell you something, guys, about the big bad world." Chase sat down roughly on his bed. "Only he didn't get to that part, did he? Only as far as Eastview. Want to bet he's never been to Eastview. Not that I hold that against him--I am sorry--" Chase shook his head. His black hair danced over his eyes. "Come to think of it, Mark. That guy has a dirty mind, doesn't he?"

"A fake!" Mark cried. "A phony!"

"I wonder," Chase said, as if to himself, "if he's sleeping with a student? And I don't mean a coed."

Something was going on in a room next door. They heard the soft sound of music. "We've reached the age of true enlightenment," Mark declared, "when love means only one thing. However, I used to be a true believer. I love thee … mark! … I love thee. Mrs. Browning."

"There's a lot more sex in that than you think," Chase said. He screwed his tight lips, flung out a long arm. "Translate this into modern English: *If thou must love me, let it be for naught except for love's sake only.* Shall I translate it for you? If you must make love to me, make love for the sake of sex only. Makes more sense, doesn't it? Trouble with the romantics was they were in love with the idea of love. In other words, they lacked experience. But Mister Browning! He had the right idea. Mistresses with great smooth marble limbs. And this isn't for anyone under eighteen: *I plant a heartfull now; some seed at least is sure to strike.* Artful soul, wasn't he? There's more sex in those romantics than might at first appear."

Sure enough, Mark could hear Frank Sinatra singing some soulful ballad. "I prefer," he said, "the candor of the Elizabethan age. The plays. Marlowe. Shakespeare, Samuel Johnson."

"Ah, yes!" Chase said in agreement. "Our friend the professor has so much in common with them. The submerged pun, the unwitting jest, all slickly planted, such as I am sorry. I'm thinking I agree with you, Mark. Johnson is a fake."

Mark heard the shuffling of feet from overhead, "What's going on in the attic?" he asked.

Chase lifted his can of beer. "Just a dance."

"Women in Phi Zete house? Who are you kidding, Chase?"

"I was kidding."

The shuffling noise above them turned to stomping. Mark straightened up. "Must be women up there" he said.

"Be quiet, Mark. You want to be heard all the way to Alpha Beta House?"

"You know women aren't allowed here."

"So what? You want the house to be closed down?"

"None of my business," Mark said. "I suppose this isn't the first time."

Chase whacked Mark on the shoulder. "You are amazing!" he exclaimed. "Truly amazing. They don't make guys like you anymore. Are you putting me on?" Chase pushed closer, solemnly examining Mark's face. Mark retreated a foot, avoiding the sight of Chase's pockmarked jowls. "Tell the truth, Mark," he said harshly. "You haven't heard about our parties?"

"I don't believe you," Mark declared.

"Go up and see for yourself."

Mark crept down the corridor outside Chase's room. He opened a door that led to a stairway leading up to the attic. He could hear Mario Lanza singing a passionate love song. If it turned out to be only a dance, the joke would be on himself. Because he did not swear, drink or go to whores, Mark told himself, it was probable that Chase classed him with

Jim Pettaw. No doubt Chase was playing a game with him, but he had to see for himself. He started to climb the stairs.

He blinked in the glare as he opened the attic door. In a square surrounded by several beds five or six couples danced to a Tommy Dorsey piece. Ted Swain held a girl whose buttocks nearly burst her black leotards. Doug Porter drifted by, his arms full of a blonde whose yellow skirt swished up when she turned, revealing long smooth thighs.

Somehow he scurried down the stairs without falling. He was about to burst into Chases' room to call down the wrath of all the gods upon him, but he had second thoughts. It could be only a dance. Presuming the worst, there could be no clear proof that the girls were there for the night.

Chase, sitting in an easy chair, flicked ash from his cigar onto the tiled floor. "Are you convinced?" he asked.

Mark shrugged. "It's only a dance."

"Then why," he asked triumphantly, "do you look as if you had just discovered sex? Haven't you ever been to Eastview?"

"Everybody's been to Eastview."

"There's a house has a broad build like Marilyn."

"I haven't had the pleasure."

"Well, you'd remember if you had." Chase winked at him. "I'd like you to have one on me, as your reward for keeping quiet about our--our parties."

"Chase, you're a true friend," Mark said acidly. "A bosom pal. Oh, I am sorry. But I'd have to be hard up, oops, to accept a bribe like that."

Chase threw up his hands in mock dismay. "Why, Mark Christopher, you dirty old man! I do believe you have been corrupted by our beloved frat. I shall have to recommend that you be expelled. Immediately!"

Mark pulled the other chair closer to Chase. "Tell you what, Chase. I'll go to Eastview with you if you invite me to the next party."

Chase rubbed a cheek and bellowed. "Who's kidding who? You won't go to Eastview and I'll never invite you to a party." He looked at his watch. "Really, old boy, I do hate to throw you out, I have a pressing engagement. I am sorry."

Mark stood up. He was ready to leave but he felt he had to challenge Chase once more. "How do I get an invitation to a party?" he asked, adding "Or are the parties reserved for residents of this house?"

"I'm respecting your morals, old boy. Now get the dickens out of here."

Mark got out. There was no need to rush a showdown with Chase Drummond. He would bide his time, wait for the opportune moment, then make his lightning strike. Besides, he had to concentrate on his studies and, for another thing, he was convinced that it was student politics that permitted the parties to continue: collusion in high places protected the participants, who were safe and untouchable.

And so he remained aloof, above it all.

He continued to attend the Phi Zete discussion hours. In February, President Coffman asked the fraternity to consider a gift to the new auditorium, then under construction, and which, it was rumored, was to be named Coffman Hall. In March, Dean Wright spoke about the ideal citizen as a person who sought justice for all, because everyone was equal in the sight of God and the Constitution.

When the first signs of spring touched the campus, crocus sprouting, flocked starlings, a fresh warm breeze, it was Professor Hugh Johnson's turn again. This time he raised the Phi Zetes fever by hinting that premarital sex was alright, as long as the participants knew the possible consequences, which he enumerated for an hour. Afterward, several Phi Zetes gathered in Chase's room for the usual post-mortem.

Mark was standing by the window looking into the quiet street. He gripped the sash, for he had quite enough of Chase's bragging about his sexual prowess. He heard: "And that one I had, she couldn't get enough. 'Do it again, do it again.' 'I'm tired,' I said. I really was. But she insisted. So I did it again. Man, I nearly flunked out."

He gathered from the talk which drifted from Chase to Doug Porter, to Chase and back again that, with the lights out, the couples exchanged partners during the night. Doug, on this last occasion, was partnered with at least three girls. Only Chase appeared not to be promiscuous. "That babe of mine!" he cried, saliva drooling. "God, I won't be any good for a week. Who says blondes are frigid?"

Gentlemen that they were, they named no names. Their descriptions of the party girls were veiled in vague adjectives, such as stacked, hot, easy and slick. They talked easily in Mark's presence, almost as if he was not there. Or were they punishing him for being an anachronism, a throwback in the world where all-night parties in a frat house attic were no more than routine, to be equated with basement ping-pong and parlor rummy?

He wondered how much longer he could be loyal to his fraternity brothers. Their parties were stupid and foolhardy. He kept thinking that he ought to do something, anything, to put an end to their behavior. But his oath precluded outright condemnation and complaint. Still, despite being captured by a disturbed conscience, he slavishly continued his fellowship with those he looked upon as friends, as indifferent as they were to their fanatical obsession with what they universally termed "having a good time." Mark assumed he was powerless to change their ways and impotent to charge them with evil-doing, even though, as Jim Pettaw assured him, when Mark told him about the parties, they were all "going to hell on a greased skid."

Doug Porter, his fat legs flung widely, lay on the floor. Mark outflanked him on his way out. "Where you goin'?" Doug asked. Mark leaped down the stairs, almost bowling over a descending girl.

That night, kneeling by his bed in the darkness, he thanked God he had escaped living in Phi Zete House. Then, even as he knelt, he could see the marbled thighs of girls clanging up a fire escape to their attic rendezvous. He bent his head into his gripped hands, pounded the mattress, wrung the blanket, as if by doing so he could squeeze dry the image in his brain of attic beds and sweating bodies coupled in lust. He rose from his prayers. He cooled his hot face at the bathroom sink, then returned to bed to twist the night away as in his dream images came again and yet again and refused to leave him, until at last he damned the empty apartment as a prison and a gate forever hinged, barred and shackled against his day of pardon and release. He awoke before dawn. He turned in torture for an hour, and then sprang up to sting away his dreams under a lashing shower. His body was fevered: he had risen tormented and ashamed.

In the parlor he raised a window high. Starlings squabbled in the elm. He breathed deeply the sharp cold spring air, filled his lungs with the promise of life's renewal, but felt all the while that this was nature's well-played trick, for the concrete sidewalk below looked hard and cold and inviting. When, gripping the sash, he realized what he had been thinking, that he had imagined his sore body crushed and scarlet on the concrete, he dashed down the window, splintering the glass into a dozen pieces.

He sat down at the writing desk that Martha always used and picked up a sheet of blue note paper. He wrote his name: Mark Christopher. He held the paper so that it faced the window light. He examined his name. He had sometimes thought of his name as a curse. He wondered if Saint Mark had ever experienced discouragement, but of course he had, for he gave up, quit, when Saint Paul needed him for that first perilous mission. Saint Mark was a quitter, a deserter. He ran away in the face of danger. Still, he made up for his cowardice. He acquitted himself well in the service of Barnabas, and had been commended by Saint Peter himself.

As he continued to gaze at his name, he told himself that he had never been a quitter. Some might have believed that, with his name, he had two strikes against him. No doubt his parents expected him to "live up to your name." Among those guilty of saying that to him was Uncle John, who compared him to Grandfather Goddard, who never came back from the Georges Bank without cod in the hold.

"Didn't matter if it were November," Uncle John had said. "Paw would stay out until the cod ran into the net, and he wouldn't ever come home till he had a fair catch for winter. He made a name for himself in Gloucester, let me tell you, because many a year he sailed in there with ice on the sheets so thick you could chop it with an axe,"

Uncle John would roar, as he dumped kindling into the black kitchen stove, "That old man of mine, he'd rather die than give in." He would spit into the fire and the flame would fly up. He was stubborn, he was. Oh, he was a stubborn man. It's bein' stubborn that killed him." Uncle John would turn his dark eyes upon Mark. "Let that be a lesson to you, boy," he would say.

Mark had never been sure what the lesson was. Perhaps to be stubborn was a virtue, like a fearless ambition. On the other hand, it could be a vice, like pride. Stubbornness fed Grandfather Goddard's family through the brittle Maine winters, but stubbornness was his undoing. On his last voyage he stayed out too long, and the swollen November sea claimed him. Mark wondered whether his grandfather was killed as much by pride as by stubbornness. Perhaps he was murdered by pride, for he was ashamed to come home from the sea without a decent catch.

Of all the Goddard virtues, or vices, which was of value now? What virtue would there be in clinging to the naïve notion that he could, single-handedly, change the character of Phi Zeta Epsilon? And who would thank him even if there might be, by some queer quirk of fate, given to him the axe to fell the rotten tree? Might as well try to trim a star, or harness the moon, as to expect that by some individual act he could change the status quo, the way things are. Still, his middle name being Goddard, if there was a way he would find it. If there was a price to pay, he would pay it.

No sooner had he come to that conclusion he recognized his conceit. He had been told that few, by character and talent, have the power to reverse the course of events. Professor Johnson himself had said that. "The day of rugged individualism is dead," Johnson had propounded before the gathered Phi Zetes. "The day of cooperation is at hand. Why? For the simple reason that the individual is an anachronism. The individual, as such, can be replaced." Of course Johnson made such atrocious statements to stir up discussion. This was the academic method. Johnson played the devil's advocate. Soon Johnson revealed his hypocrisy: Anyone who believed a word he said, he had told the fraternity, was either a dunce or a throwback, a Neanderthal.

Mark's first target was therefore the obvious one: Hugh Gifford Johnson. He baited the high-domed professor in his office one floor beneath McMaster Hall's golden cupola. Johnson, although deep in a clutch of poetic themes, rose and put out a friendly hand. "Christopher, isn't it? Yes, I remember you. A Phi Zete, I believe. Admirable fraternity." Johnson spread himself on his chair like an old coat. "Stairs too much for you? After three years climbing to this den you get used to it. You begin to accept the fact you're a physical wreck."

Mark grinned despite the pain in his chest, which he hadn't noticed while climbing the three flights of steps, but which now stitched his side like an open wound. He cursed himself for a fool. What plan did he have other than to discover what knowledge, if any, Johnson had of the attic parties? And what possible use could he make of a Johnson admission that he was aware of them? In any case, it was unlikely that Johnson knew anything about the parties, for would not a professor have done something to stop them? Mark's tongue felt like a stone and his lips as if stapled shut. Johnson, lolling in his chair, fiddled with a black pipe, turning it over and over, inspecting its roughness as if seeking for a flaw. Despite Johnson's let's-be-pals attitude, there was something about the man that forbade confidence. Perhaps, Mark thought, it was Johnson's imperious self-control, the way he wrinkled his forehead as another person might raise an eyebrow.

Between heavy breaths, Mark said: "It's about the fraternity, Professor Johnson. Maybe you already know. I mean, everybody knows it." Johnson continued to inspect a typewritten sheet of examination paper. "But, you're busy," Mark said nervously.

Johnson, seeming to sense a problem, dropped the paper on his desk and leaned forward, all attention. "Not busy at all, Christopher. Why don't you come out with it? I won't eat you."

Tales of Johnson's marathon counseling sessions with students now came to Mark's mind. Ted Swain rolled in sweat after a bout with Johnson that lasted all afternoon. Chase had termed Ted's experience a draw and suggested to Ted that he ask for a rematch, but Ted would have none of it. Thereafter Ted tossed into a wastebasket each Johnson summons to a conference. "He can flunk me if he wants," Ted declared defiantly, "but I refuse to attend another Johnson séance."

Ted refused to reveal the nature of his encounter with Johnson. Now, Mark became increasingly certain he was about to be enlightened. Johnson held his pipe between his thumbs, bit the stem, stretched his lips, a grimace that made him look like a grinning skeleton, and sucked air through the pipe's empty bowl. "I've been watching you, Christopher," he said slowly through gritted teeth. "I've had my eye on you. You're a rather serious chap, aren't you?"

Mark noticed the Oxonian terminology and inflection creeping into Johnson's speech. "I suppose I am," Mark replied simply. He felt completely outmaneuvered by this buck-toothed, nervous-lipped man, who reminded him of his favorite chimpanzee, Eugene, in the Attumwa Zoo. Offered marshmallows, Eugene puckered his lips, clapped his teeth and chattered for service.

Johnson leaned back contentedly and clicked the pipe stem on his lower teeth, like a campus cop clicking his stick on iron pickets. "Yes. I dare say you are a thoughtful fellow, Christopher. You don't talk much, do you?" Mark nodded, then shook his head. "I thought as much, but I know you are a gentleman of ideas. One paper of yours, on Coleridge, wasn't it? Yes, Coleridge. You ranked him as a Romantic. Now that was clever of you, very clever. But we have to distinguish between the early Coleridge and the late Coleridge. And we don't find one the same as the other, do we?" Johnson peered down closely at the bowl of his pipe, so that his eyes crossed. "We must be more precise in our evaluations. Or don't you think so?"

Mark listened as well as he could, but his mind began to fill with thoughts designed to resist Johnson's attempt to crush him. For, he realized, Johnson had turned tables on him. Cornered in his lair, Johnson fought back by purring. Still, Mark knew that Johnson's back was up, and Mark could fairly see the hackles rising.

"You have a good head on your shoulders, Christopher," Johnson went on, resigning his pipe to his palm. "I know you have a high I.Q. You wouldn't believe me if I told you what it is. Suffice it to say that many so-called geniuses wouldn't score as high. Now don't let that go to your head. Genius, as who said it? Edison said, is ten per cent inspiration and ninety percent perspiration. It's the ninety percent that counts. Now you, Christopher, don't sweat enough. You try to get by on language alone, your literary talent, let us say." Johnson humped over his desk, his brow lowered as his eyes glinted. "Why do you do it, Christopher?"

"Do what, sir?"

"Try to con me." Johnson leaned back, as if to relieve pressure on an aching back. "You're much too smart to try those cheap tricks on me." He sucked in his breath. "Oh, you can get away with it with some of your instructors, and I won't name names. You know who I mean. They have their readers." Johnson raised his fist and pounded the stacked papers. "I do my own reading. Not one word gets by me!" His voice rising to the screech of a snared rabbit, Johnson cried, "Personal attacks will get you nowhere!"

"Sir?"

"You are disposed to make me believe you do not understand?" Johnson asked oily. "You prefer the pose of the innocent?"

"I'm not quite sure--"

"Oh, you follow me alright," Johnson rebutted. "Shall we talk about Keats, or Shelley or Byron? To say nothing of Oscar Wilde. By what right, may I ask, do you attack their personal lives, the flavor of their living, one might say, when your assignment is to criticize what they wrote? Answer me that, Christopher."

Feeling as if his thoughts had been turned inside out, as if Johnson's stabbing eyes pierced his brain, Mark turned away, blinking in the glare of the wide window that gave a blazing view of the quadrangle. The shadow of the golden cupola stretched across the campus. Johnson knew him, he thought. Johnson had not missed the meaning of the simple allusions in Mark's papers, which sought to expose the hypocrisy of those poets who clamored for love, all the while being incapable of real love.

"Objectively," Mark began, not turning around, "we may sympathize with the poets for their peronsal problems and still admit their genius. After all, they were men who---"

"The likes of whom we will never know again!"

"Perhaps," Mark said, "but men like ourselves."

"When you get out into the world, Christopher," said Johnson, resuming his purring voice, "you will find everything isn't black and white. There are many shades of gray that you would have to accept if you want to get along."

Stung by Johnson's sarcasm, Mark swung swiftly about. His chair rose with him on its front legs as he leaned on the desk. "What makes you think I am not in the world now? And why don't I have the right to say what I think? I've seen more hell than you will ever see, Johnson--"

Johnson interrupted him. "What hell?"

He could not help himself. He'd never felt this way, as far as he could remember. A student was expected to respect his teachers, even as much as he had been raised to respect his parents and all elders. Then why did he not respect Johnson? It was obvious that Johnson had no problem with the fractured, spoiled, intemperate and often indecent lives of the poets he himself admired, even adored. Johnson had a right to his academic views, however distasteful. But there was something else, something densely disturbing that Mark could suspect but failed to decipher.

"My father committed suicide," Mark said in lowered voice. Immediately he was overcome with disdain for saying that, for revealing a secret, betraying Martha. Why in the world would he reveal such a secret?

"What's that got to do with what we're discussing?" Johnson asked coldly. He looked at Mark with a glassy stare, almost as if Mark had told him that it was going to rain. "What I expect of you, Christopher, is to shape up and ignore your opinionated moralistic views that distort your appreciation of literary masterpieces."

Mark stood up abruptly. Johnson was surveying another paper.

"Thank you, sir," he said. "Thanks a lot." He strode stiffly from the room.

For weeks Mark succeeded in avoiding direct confrontation with Johnson, although they had frequent nodding encounters in corridors. Only once had Johnson acknowledged his existence, and that by merely granting him a hissing smirk. Attending Johnson's class, he always sat in a back row, beset by a strange lonely emptiness. He seldom left the apartment in the evening, forsaking Phi Zete discussions, ignoring Jim Pettaw's invitations to visit him, telling Jim that he was behind in his studies and simply did not have the time.

He slept fitfully, waking often during the night to assuage his thirst by fetching a glass of water, and also by analyzing himself. He not only stayed away from Jim, but he excused himself from the company of Doug Porter and Chase Drummond. He was jealous of them, for their cool sophistication, their callous behavior. They appeared to suffer no twinge of conscience. They did what every red-blooded young American man was expected to do, given the opportunity and the physical stamina. Indeed, his friends gloried in the attic's challenge. The attic was there, it had to be conquered. Such brute amorality was calculated. His friends knew the risk, to themselves and their beloved fraternity. And yet they continued to enjoy the parties, perhaps partially because of the thrill of "risking it."

As he continued his dark nightly exploration of motives relative to his own activities and behavior and his own moral attitudes, he wondered if the attic party participants believed they were guarded from indictment by some devil's angel. Obviously they believed, or at least sincerely hoped, that they could get away with it. Or perhaps this was the key to knowing what the difference was between himself and his friends. He could only conclude that he was jealous of them.

There was no one who needed to know. He was jealous because he envied his Phi Zete brothers their impudence in the face of traditional views of what was moral and what wasn't. They rejoiced in their newfound freedom from rules of behavior they had adhered to for most of their lives, including through high school. Now they were totally immersed in the outlook and attitudes fostered by higher education. They had been freed from accepted adherence to traditional values and social structures in which they had been raised. Intellectual rebellion was expected and breaking cultural and religious principles was encouraged.

While some Phi Zetes were open in their dismay concerning the attic frivolity and, nevertheless, the flagrant nonchalance of most of their brother frats, many, like Mark, were deeply and sincerely appalled, not necessarily nor entirely on moral grounds, but simply because the activity was going on within the walls of Phi Zeta Rho House.

Mark thought about resigning from the fraternity but that would be going too far. That would be an act of cowardice and he wasn't a coward. Neither was he a quitter. He pondered whether he should send a letter to Attumwa University President Coffman. But he discarded that idea when he remembered that his month-long silence compromised his right to protest. But there was no need to panic, he thought. Apart from the real possibility that Johnson would fail him, or at most give him a D, he could search for some person in authority who would listen to his story of incredible corruption. Thinking about that, he laughed at himself, dryly and joyfully. He might hold the power to command Johnson's future. He could create a scandal that would rock the entire university. He assumed he had the power and thus he could wait for the right opportunity to play his hand.

Time, however, played a trick on him. He received a letter from Martha telling him that she and Stanford had married and that meant she had to quit her job at Modern Enterprises. Stanford was now a vice-president and judged it imprudent for his wife to hold an important position under his supervision. Her husband, Martha wrote, desired her to be a full-time housewife, and that was that. She had lost a paycheck and that meant she could no longer send him a monthly allowance. In addition, the money their father had left him was running low. He telephoned Jim Pettaw.

He couldn't wait to see his Indian friend. They had visited one another infrequently through these winter months. They kept each other informed of their activities. Jim was always angry when Mark told him about Phi Zete discussion nights, the attic dances and his encounter with Johnson. Jim was hard at work typing out a class paper when Mark came in. "Jim boy," he exclaimed. He gave his friend an enthusiastic hug. "How've you been?"

"Fair to midlin'. Would you believe Johnson kept me two hours this afternoon finding fault with my latest paper."

Mark told him about his similar encounter with Johnson. "I'll be lucky if he passes me," he said. They discussed the implications of Johnson's discussion nights, especially Chase Drummond's advocacy of dropping an atomic bomb in Korea.

"Some day," Jim said, "Chase will see the light."

"Sure, sure," Mark replied. "The flash of the bomb."

Jim sounded tired, old. "No, it's not God's will that man should be destroyed."

"Thank God for people like you, Jim. Everyone else believes the world is going to be blown to hell."

"No," Jim said with finality. "We will endure as long as God endures." From his easy sitting position on the bed, his steady gaze fixed upon Mark. He was silent for a moment.

"What?" Mark asked. "Did you say something?"

"Sorry, I was just thinking."

"Okay, what were you thinking?"

Jim sat up straight, his dark eyes fixed on Mark. "You've been saved, right?"

"Darn right," Mark responded automatically. You didn't argue with Jim Pettaw.

"Have you been called, Mark?"

He knew what Jim was referring to: Had God called him to His service. He paused to think about it. He had long believed that God had a plan for his life. Most Baptists did, and Methodists too, for that matter. He had to be careful not to offend his friend. At length he said "No, I'm sorry Jim, I can't say I have."

"That's alright, Mark." Jim smiled graciously. "God calls in His time, not ours. It's our job to be ready when He does call. Are you ready, Mark?

"Ready for what?"

"The call, of course. That's what we're talking about, isn't it?"

Mark laughed with a friendly frown. "It's a serious matter, I realize that. But why are you asking me about it, I mean right now."

"Because you would make a great minister, Mark." Jim held his piercing gaze on Mark, who was feeling quite uncomfortable.

"You've got to be joking."

"Think about it, Mark. Why do you think you're at this university?"

"I almost didn't get in. The registrar questioned my credits from Springport."

"But you were accepted."

"I had pull. My sister's boyfriend put in a good word."

"Didn't make any difference, Mark. You were accepted because it was God's will."

"I can understand that. I won't say God can't do it." He shook his head. "Anyway, most of what happens to us is the result of our stupidity, our ignorance, our greed. Have you been called, Jim?"

"Of course I have." Jim laughed lightly. "Don't tell me you're surprised."

"Well, not exactly surprised. I'll tell you one thing. I'm grateful you told me."

Jim accompanied Mark to the bus stop. "Let's get together at my place, Jim."

"You bet," Jim said. "Give me a call."

A few days later Mark received a note from Chaplain Davis, asking to see him about a scholarship. For what? The next day Mark entered the university chapel, a rather medium-sized church with a slim steeple just off campus. He found the chaplain's office in the basement.

Doctor Davis unlimbered his tall angular frame from behind his desk, reached over it and shook Mark's hand with a tight grip. "We've met before, haven't we?" he asked. Mark nodded in assent. "Now I remember. Jim Pettaw mentioned you. He asked me to recruit you for the chapel committee, but you turned us down. Still, you're here and I want to talk to you about another matter." He eyed a paper on his desk. "I see you're up for graduation this year."

"I hope so."

"Good. Jim tells me you are quite serious about your faith," Doctor Davis said. He paused, his eyes focused on Mark's. "Of course there's no reason to rush a decision about a career in the ministry."

"The ministry! I've never thought about the ministry."

"Jim told me you were considering it."

"I'm not surprised. Just like Jim."

Doctor Davis grunted. "You wouldn't mind some financial aid, would you?"

"What for? I'll be gone in June."

"I mean it's for a master's degree." The chaplain took a card from his desk. He studied it carefully. "You're a Methodist. No, a Baptist." He looked up at Mark. "Which is it?"

"As an infant I was baptized in a Methodist church, but when I was a teenager I was baptized in a Baptist tank. I like Methodist."

"Well, it doesn't matter," Davis said. "This scholarship doesn't have a denominational tag. It pays full tuition for three years at Attumwa University's Divinity School." He looked up to observe Mark's reaction.

Mark looked and felt stunned. "I don't understand," he muttered .

The chaplain ignored his remark. "What did you say?"

"What do I have to do?"

"All you have to do, Mark, is sign here." He placed a paper in front of him.

Mark examined it. Above the line for his signature were these words:

It is my intent, as much as in me lies, to declare, that I will prepare myself for God's Holy Ministry within

> *a Christian Church subject to the approval of the*
> *Scholarship Committee.*

Mark signed his name. Chaplain Davis folded the paper and returned it to a drawer. "I must say you don't waste any time signing your life away."

"It's a formality, isn't it?" Mark asked. "I mean, it's just an application."

Doctor Davis frowned. "You will need letters of reference from three ministers," he said coldly. "I will be glad to write one of them, if you wish." He stood up and put out his hand. "The scholarship Committee meets here at two o'clock next Monday. Be there."

"I will, sir."

"By the way, Mark. Aren't you interested in who provides the scholarship?"

"Of course, sir."

"Drummond Pulp and Paper Company."

"That's fine, sir. Thank you again."

Chapter Fifteen

Mark had to act quickly. He needed to find two ministers to recommend him as being worthy of getting the scholarship. Three whole years! A master's degree!

He had to hurry. He was on his way to visit Pastor Woods at the Methodist Church in The Flats. He had the uneasy feeling that he was trespassing on holy ground. There was Mr. Samuelson's grocery, but it wasn't a grocery anymore. It was Speedy Dry Cleaners, with a neon window sign flashing on the waterfront road side. *Same-Day Service.* When he was a kid Mark used to buy penny candy from Mr. Samuelson, black licorice whips and yummy brown moons. Sometimes Mr. Samuelson let him help himself. Mark would go behind the glass cabinet, slide open the door, reach in and pop the candy into a small paper sack. Always he put in a sucker, placing it upside down so that he could wrap the top of the sack around the sucker's stick. That way he kept the candy from falling out as he raced toward home. When he handed him a nickel Mr. Samuelson would bow his gray head in mock gratitude.

The Elite Tonsorial Parlor on the opposite corner had disappeared. Where the single story tarpapered house once stood was a four-story brick apartment building with aluminum framed windows. He could not remember the barber's name, but he did remember what he looked like: a very tall thin man with long graying hair, slicked back, and a mustache that sprang straight out in sharp hard points. It was like the mustache of the Kaiser, whose picture he had studied in his father's *Popular Encyclopedia of Modern Facts.* The barber always gave him a sucker, and he always petted Mark's hair and said, "Be a good boy." Mark would smile and pay him the cost of the cut with a dime.

Mark glanced down Maple Street toward the house in which he used to live. He could not make out, searching the long block of look-alike houses, which one was his. Once-green lawns were now dusty patches of bare earth. Tiny gray porches sagged. Only the Creighton's house across the street, under whose stoop he used to hide never to be found, appeared as well kept as always. He wondered whether Mrs. Creighton and her huge Persian cat were still there. He used to see the cat each afternoon on the way home from James W. Barker School. Once he dared to pet the cat's shaggy soft fur. That was when Mrs. Creighton, who wore her hair in a bun, was sitting on the porch reading her Bible, and the cat (what was his name?) was tied to the post by a leather strap. He asked Mrs. Creighton about that. She told him, seriously, that the strap was needed to keep Noah (that was his name) from chasing dogs. Mrs. Creighton was one of those Bible-reading women of Maple Street. She and his mother were members of the Sunday morning women's Bible class at the Methodist Church. That was during the Great Depression, which his father claimed was the fault of big businessmen like Chase Drummond Senior, whose mill had laid off hundreds. Mark sauntered down the street toward his old home. The mill's acrid, sulphuric odor burned his nostrils. His father had termed the mill "the surface emanation of a volcanic underworld." A dog barked and chased a cat up a tree. A garbage man hoisted a can and tossed the contents high into his truck. Then, there it was: 35 Maple Street. The lawn, which his mother had tended so carefully, was overgrown with sodden weeds, The house's brick walls were cracked and flaking, as were the three steps to the stoop. Mark rang the doorbell.

The door opened a few inches. A woman in a pink chenille dressing gown, her hair in tight pin curls, thrust her head out. "Whatcha want?" she asked.

Mark had no answer to her question. He would like to see his old room, to assure himself that this woman and others who lived in the house had taken care of his home out of respect for its former tenants. He wanted to reconstruct faulty memories of the exact positioning within the walls of his parents, his brother and sister, in relation to himself, and to discover the shape, size and power of the forces of brick and plaster that had enclosed the image of his life. He could see into the vestibule where the black walnut coat rack still stood, with its mirror, taller than himself, reflected his image. And there was the dark hall and the stairs leading up to the second-floor landing and the room in which he had slept and dreamed.

"Whatcha selling?" the woman, irritated by his silence, asked. She folded her arms, on which her ample bosom overflowed, barring his view, as if she suspected a forced entry.

"I once lived in this house," he said weakly. "My name is Mark Christopher."

"Well, nobody with that name lives here." She slammed the door.

Mark told himself it really did not matter. What would he have seen? Grimy dishes in the kitchen sink? The triangulated wallpaper in the parlor faded and torn? Nothing would be the same as it once was long ago. He sighed and returned to the waterfront road.

He walked north a few blocks past rows of gray unused sheds, and started up the bridge over the Transcontinental Railroad tracks. He stood on the spot where his father had stood. He grasped the flat railing upon which his father had sat before falling to his death. He gazed on the area far below where the body, smashed and bleeding, had been tossed aside by the train's cowcatcher. Mark held tightly to the cold iron. His body trembled as he continued over the bridge toward his destination, the Methodist Church and Pastor Woods.

The church's stone walls were darker than he remembered. The long years under the mill's belching smoke had blackened them. He passed by the wide steps that led up to the sanctuary door until he came to the attached Sunday School building. He stepped up to its double-door entrance and went inside. He was struck by the sense that he was going back in time, because here was the same familiar stuffy warm odor of air shut up too long without the refreshment of open windows. Just down the corridor was the small, glass-fronted classroom where Mrs. Browning had taught him, each Sunday afternoon at three o'clock, the fascinating stories of Samuel and David, of Andrew and Paul, and chiefly of Jesus and the wisdom that He taught, lessons of love and faith.

He pushed open a swinging door that led to the front of the sanctuary. The oval theater was dim, almost dark. The rising rows of pews were deep in shadow. For a moment he hesitated, overcome by the ancient shy feeling that he ought not to intrude upon God's holy place. He stepped inside. The road traffic was hushed, almost silenced. He walked slowly up the carpeted side aisle, under stained glass windows of Mary, Jesus and Joseph, and sat down in the highest pew. The dark mahogany pulpit, centered on a stage, seemed small and insignificant although when he was a boy it had appeared huge. He shifted uncomfortably on the hard wooden pew, counted the number of pews in front, stood up, crossed to the center aisle and strode down to the fifth row from the front. He sat down in the left pew. This was the very pew in which he had sat with his family for ten years. Usually he sat between his father and mother, his father always beside the aisle. Martha sat to his mother's left, and then Peter. They all entered the sanctuary together. Their pew positions never altered.

Mark could hear Pastor Woods' booming voice. He could see the minister's gestures, especially when he pounded the pulpit. That happened at least once during a sermon and usually at the climax. One Sunday the pastor stopped preaching as he waited for Harry, the sexton, to hand him a note. All was quiet as he told his people about Pearl Harbor.

"Mark, is that you?"

The voice sounded from far away, perhaps behind a closed door. It was Pastor Woods' voice, not as strong as he remembered it, but still commanding. The minister drifted slowly toward him out of a shadow. "Mark Christopher? Why, for a moment I thought it was---why, you look so much like your brother Peter. That was his name, wasn't it? How long has it been, Mark? I do lose all track. But I did hear from you last year, didn't I?"

"I spoke to you on the phone. That was two years ago."

Pastor Woods sat down beside him, bracing himself by grasping the back of the next pew. His hair was very white and quite thin on top. His face, once ruddy and an indication of good health, was a flaccid white. "I do remember, of course. We talked about your poor father. Let's go to my study, shall we? I'm sorry to confess it, but the pews here are too hard on the anatomy. I've been telling the board that we need pew cushions, but there's no money."

Sitting together comfortably on a parlor-type sofa in the study, Mark told him that he was surprised to be meeting with him in The Flats church. "I was told you had transferred to another church long ago," he said.

"I was," the pastor said, "but a few years later the bishop asked me to return here as interim pastor. You see, Mark, this church can't afford a full-timer any more. Come on Sunday and you will see why. Two thirds of the pews are empty. Mrs. Woods died three years ago---"

"Oh, I'm sorry. I didn't know."

"Yes, well, she's safe, she's with the Lord." He touched Mark's hand kindly. "So here I am, taking care of things. I've never liked preaching to empty pews. Discouraging, you know. But what can you do? People move away. More industries building in The Flats now. Tearing down houses every day. But, tell me, what's on your mind?"

Mark told him about the possibility of getting a graduate degree scholarship that would allow him to attend Attumwa University's Divinity School and asked him if he would write a letter of commendation. Pastor Woods clapped his hands. "Wonderful, Mark, wonderful. Of course. My oh my. So, you want to be minister? Wonderful."

"Well, I'm not sure. Lots of people go to divinity schools without necessarily wanting to join the ranks of the clergy."

Pastor Woods looked at him curiously. "So what's the commendation for?"

Mark felt trapped. "The application, Pastor Woods. It states that my goal is ordination to ministry."

"And you signed?"

"Yes I did."

"You have reservations?"

"I don't know what kind of minister. Some are pastors. Some are chaplains. Some are professors. All depends upon what I'm called to do."

"By the Lord?"

"Of course."

"Then I don't see any obstacle. The Lord is faithful. He will guide you to choose what kind of ministry is best for you--and Him. Let me write the letter now so you can take it with you." He retired to his desk. In five minutes, letter in hand, he handed it to Mark and settled back on the sofa. "Now, I heard about Peter. Tell me about Martha. How's she doing?"

"She's fine. She's married. Living in Chicago."

"Good, I'm glad to hear that." Pastor Woods leaned toward Mark, hands clasped under his chin. "Now, how about you, Mark? I can't help remembering about what happened to your poor father." A sudden gasp escaped Mark's tightening throat. The minister noticed it. "I'm sorry," he said. "If you don't want to talk---"

How could he forgive Pastor Woods for the memory of that conflicting afternoon that Martha told him about? "It's alright, Pastor Woods," Mark said. "It was a long time ago. I've talked about it a lot with Martha."

"Your father was a good man," Pastor Woods began. "Why, there wasn't a better man in this church." He held up his hands as if in prayer. "Mark, tell me truly. I know you were troubled, as young as you were, over your father's death. Losing your mother, too, and she was so young. I know what it was like. My wife and I were married sixty years. We married young, you see. That was during the First World War. I'd thought about joining up, maybe becoming a chaplain. But we had our first child on the way, our son, John, our only son, who went into the Army and died in Italy."

Mark struggled with Martha's accusation that Pastor Woods had told his father, the afternoon of his father's death, that his relationship with Mrs. Marshall was sinful. How could this old minister have had anything on his mind than his father's well-being? Perhaps they had spoken together about the meaning of salvation. Perhaps his father had a troubled conscience. Probably despair and grief over his wife's death and not knowing whether Peter would ever come back alive. How could anyone, pastor or not, alleviate his father's deepening grief? Pastor Woods had ministered to the entire family for many years. He spoke of Peter, Martha and Mark as if they were his own children. Now all the bitterness that Mark had harbored against Pastor Woods all these years was drowned in pity for this disappointed, sincere and grieving old man. "Thank you, Pastor Woods," he said. "I admit I've been confused about

Dad for a long time, but I have come to the conclusion that Dad's death wasn't an accident. He sought death because there was no other way to escape the torment of his grief, and I will let it go at that." He heaved a sigh of relief. May I ask you another question, about the scholarship?"

"Sure. Fire away."

"One of my friends is Chase Drummond Junior, he's in my fraternity."

"The son and heir of the owner of Drummond Paper? There's a conflict?"

Mark laughed. "No. I don't think the younger Chase would ever want to be a minister. It's about his father's company, which is donating the scholarship."

"I'm sure Mr. Drummond earned his money honestly."

"I don't question that," Mark said. "It's not as if Mr. Drummond was in the liquor business, or even tobacco."

Pastor Woods laughed. "Basic Methodist prejudice. What I meant was, money is a-moral. Render unto Caesar, Jesus said. You do believe in God's guidance, don't you? I would think seriously before rejecting the scholarship, if it is offered to you. How I could have used that kind of help when I was in seminary. You are fortunate, Mark. Take the money."

Mark shook his head. "And if, later, I decide that I don't want to enter the ministry, what then?"

"The money won't be wasted. You will have received a good education."

"I don't understand, Pastor Woods. I always thought you had to be called. And then there is the matter of being worthy."

Pastor Woods tapped Mark's shoulder. "You're much too serious. This is the modern age, Mark. God guides in many ways. You may be struck by lightning, so to speak. More likely, you will be guided by such opportunities as this. Don't take that the wrong way. The very fact that you have asked questions shows you are not opportunistic. That is a fine trait. But, you see, I know you. I knew your family. Why, I practically raised you, in the spiritual sense. Take the scholarship, Mark. Later, when you have doubts, and you are sure to have them, don't hesitate to come see me again."

Later, as he waited for the bus on the waterfront road, Mark fingered Pastor Woods' letter. It had been too easy. Pastor Woods was almost too eager to help. The minister asked no questions concerning his beliefs. He failed to probe his past. He had expected an inquisition designed to prove his Christian beliefs. Surely Pastor Woods was too lenient. He should have been tested on Bible knowledge and theology. Instead, the minister accepted him because he knew him. Knew him? How could that be? This was the first time he had seen Pastor Woods since he was thirteen. And yet the minister appeared convinced of his character. Mark had misgivings, but he was grateful.

As soon as he returned to the apartment he telephoned Baptist Pastor Gordon in Springport. Mark asked him to telegraph a recommendation to Chaplain Davis right away.

Chapter Sixteen

Johnson had begun his usual boring English 105 lecture when Jim Pettaw handed Mark a clipping from that morning's *Eagle*. He pointed to the Letters and then to the one signed Hugh Gifford Johnson. What Johnson had written was more interesting than what he was saying at the moment:

> Recent discussions of sex in various campus groups led me to the conclusion that Attumwa students are suffering under the delusion that they are answerable to their elders concerning their private sexual practices. For myself, I have never required that any student either apologize or plead a defense for the method nor the partners he or she selects for sexual satisfaction. This is a private, personal concern, and has much to do with the preservation of individual liberty. God knows we are living in an era when the rights of the individual are being slowly eroded by mistaken authoritarian and bureaucratic intrusion into an area which is the individual's own business.

Signaling his disgust, Mark returned the clipping to Jim. "Johnson's a fool," he whispered. Meanwhile, Johnson continued to ramble on about the manners and morals of the nineteenth century. He derided that era's hypocrisy, apparently unaware he lad lost his audience's attention. Johnson talked to the ceiling, to the walls, and to the windows. All the same, the students remained silent and stiffly alert. Mark felt a physical wrenching in his gut. The close air stank of nine months of Johnson's derision and cynicism. He wanted out; he itched; he felt a cold clammy sense of isolation.. At last the dreary hour ended. Mark hurried into the cool free air of the corridor. He was no sooner there, walking toward his next class, when Ted Swain touched his arm.

"Pass the word," Ted said. "Johnson has been fired."

Mark's whoop rang down the corridor. He leaped, he laughed, he was overcome with joy. Soon Chase Drummond and Doug Porter joined in, slapping his back, until he doubled over with laughter and every breath was painful.

They hurried to Phi Zete House. The parlor was already crammed with a noisy mob. Amidst the excitement, Mark noted, only a few sat silently.

Chase mounted a chair. "Hey, guys," he called out loudly. It was a tribute to Chase's evident position of leadership that there was an immediate hush. "Okay, we all know what's happened. The powers that be have finally showed their hand. They fired Professor Johnson. The question is: are we going to let them get away with it?"

Mark was taken so completely by surprise that he nudged Ted's arm, interrupting Ted's rejoicing shout of support for whatever it was that Chase was getting at. "What's going on?" he asked.

"Rebellion," Ted said simply.

From his raised position Chase shouted "Destroy free speech and you destroy everything." He eyed his audience with an insidious grin.

A few hours later the Phi Zetes marched across the quadrangle toward McMaster Hall. Placards, magically produced, proclaimed: *Support Johnson*. The Zetes howled the Phi Zete song:

"We'll march all the way together,

"We'll always and ever loyal be.

"We'll be friends to every brother

"Of Phi Zeta Rho from sea to sea."

Mark, still feeling confused, followed the enthusiastic rebels. The Zetes paraded back and forth, attracting the attention of other students, many of whom came over to find out what was going on. Ted waved a placard asking *Is This Russia or America*? Doug Porter's proclaimed *Johnson Railroaded*.

They had been parading for half an hour when Dean Wright lunged down the Hall's steps. He held up his hand. "Thank you, fellows, thank you very much." He had a loud voice, which helped. Mark drew closer to hear him.

"You are mistaken," the dean said. "Doctor Johnson has not been fired. He's only been suspended. His case is being considered by an administrative committee. I'm sure you wouldn't want to prejudice his case."

Reluctantly, the Phi Zetes lowered their placards. For a time, after Dean Wright left, Ted Swain pleaded "Don't give up." It was too late. The picketing was over.

That evening, before the assembled Phi Zetes, Chase Drummond defended his position. "Phi Zeta Rho," he said, "has a reputation to maintain. That reputation is that we always cooperate with university authorities on important causes and issues. That is why I consented to Dean Wright's request. We have not given up the fight. Far from it. We are here to plan the next step. The meeting is open for suggestions."

From the back of the parlor someone shouted, "Burn President Coffman in effigy!"

Another called: "Boycott classes!"

And still another: "Meet with Johnson."

Chase pointed to the one who made the suggestion. "Details, please."

Crash McCone, a football hero, stood up. He squared his boxy shoulders. "I suggest we invite Professor Johnson to a meeting to explain why he wrote that letter."

"Invite everybody," someone yelled.

Acknowledging the wild applause, Chase said "I take it that we are agreed on an open meeting at which Professor Johnson will be the principal speaker. We will invite him to enlarge upon the views he expressed in his letter. Now, where will this meeting be held?"

By the speed of the suggestion and its quick acceptance, Mark knew the meeting had already been planned.

Several meeting sites were suggested, including the university auditorium and gymnasium. All agreed that a very large hall was necessary.

Chase smiled. "May I suggest," he said, "it would be much better for the meeting to be held outside the campus. As a matter of fact, I doubt we would be allowed to have the meeting on campus, considering the circumstances." A roar of concurrence. "I suggest the meeting be held in a place with which most of you are acquainted. I refer, of course, to the Gayety Theater. Arrangements will be made by your officers."

Shouts of "Yea! Yea!"

"Good," Chase said. "Now, a rebuttal has been suggested in the form of a letter signed by those Phi Zetes desiring to do so, to be given to the *Eagle* tonight. What is your pleasure, gentlemen?" Again a round of applause. "In that case the draft of the letter may be presented. Ted?"

Ted Swain, his voice tinged with due solemnity, read from a sheet of paper. The letter was filled with passionate support of Johnson's right to speak freely as a private citizen. It criticized the university administration for cavalier treatment of the Phi Zete hero. After several whereases, the letter concluded: *We, the undersigned members of Phi Zeta Rho, do hereby respectfully request Professor Johnson's immediate reinstatement and a declaration by the university administration that all faculty shall hereafter be accorded their due privilege of speaking their minds on issues of the day.*

Another volley of rebel yells. A rush toward Ted, who happily held forth the letter for signing. In the turmoil no one appeared to hear the knocking on the fraternity's main entrance, a solid oak door that Phi Zetes seldom used. The door slowly opened. A deep voice announced: "They're all here, Modecai."

Dean Wright's tall shadowed figure loomed through the doorway, followed by Chaplain Davis. They marched directly into the parlor. Chase Drummond leaped to his feet. "Welcome to Phi Zeta Rho," he said as he shook Dean Wright's limp hand. "Our fraternity is honored."

Clearing his throat, Dean Wright said "I'm here to make an announcement."

"Well, come up here by me," Mark said. He smiled meekly.

"No, I will say what I have to say from here." He moved back a step toward the open door. "Gentlemen you all know Chaplain Davis. He has accompanied me," he went on as the chaplain bowed slightly, "to answer your questions." He glanced coolly over the expectant faces. "I am here to inform you that this fraternity is no longer recognized by Attumwa University."

It was a long time before the meaning of Dean Wright's words penetrated his audience. The color drained from Chase Drummond's face. His mouth popped open. The parlor was utterly silent.

Dean Wright's face became stern, immobile. "What this withdrawal means to you will be explained by Chaplain Davis," he said. "You will want to know the reasons, of course. These will be outlined. Meanwhile, I assure you that this action has been reviewed by the university trustees and has nothing to do with your protest over Professor Johnson's suspension. In tomorrow morning's mail some of you will receive notices of dismissal from the university." Dean Wright remained to soak in the scene of forty Phi Zetes too stunned to breathe.

Chaplain Davis was striving to answer questions raised by a few Phi Zetes when Mark escaped by way of the kitchen. He quickly crossed the road that led to the campus, then slowed down as he marched toward the quad. His reason seemed to have been throttled. No more Phi Zeta Rho? How could that be? Why? He hastened to see Jim Pettaw.

Right away Mark could discern that Jim was in a state of shock. "What's wrong?" Mark asked. Jim kept pacing around his room like a caged bear. Head low, eyes fixed on an invisible point in space, shoulders slumped, legs buckling as if he bore a great burden, he went to the window, leaned against the frame, arms upraised. He fingered a crack in the glass.

Suddenly Jim turned to face Mark. "You're not going to be expelled," he said bluntly. "You're a lucky guy."

"I was on the picket line too," Mark protested. He felt a quivering chill.

"That's not why the fraternity was suspended," Jim said. His voice quivered. His body trembled.

Mark stared at Jim incredulously. "How do you know that?"

"Because I know, that's all. It's all about the attic parties."

Now Mark was on his feet. "How come you, of all people, know why?" A cold sense of foreboding froze him. He could not move. All he could do was try to suppress the rising fear that Jim might have gone to the attic. But he knew that was impossible. He knew Jim. He knew that Jim could no more have participated in an attic party than he could have himself. Besides, Jim wasn't a Phi Zete. He could never have been initiated. He was an Indian.

"The picketing led to the suspension," Mark insisted. "I saw Chaplain Davis watching me."

Jim was only partially successful in harnessing his obvious agitation. He sat down on his bed and observed Mark quietly, as if he was not sure of what he should say next.

"They've got the names, Mark," he said sadly as he awaited Mark's reaction. "They've got all the names."

"Whose names?" Mark asked. "How do you know whose names?"

Sweat beaded Jim's forehead. He wrung his hands. "The names of those who went to last night's attic party."

Mark burst into wild laughter. "You're pulling my leg. Tell me you're pulling my leg." Surely something darkly morbid had captured Jim's mind, something insane was torturing him. This was not the Jim he had known all the way from Springport to Attumwa. "Please don't kid me, Jim," he pleaded.

Jim's whole body tightened. He spoke through a muffled sob. "It's true," he said. "I squealed."

"Oh Jim. Oh Jim! Was it Johnson who told you?"

Jim frowned and lowered his head. He moved on the bed until he could rest his back against the wall. "How could it happen, Mark? My first year here was wonderful, but this year I got all messed up." He was silent for a moment. He seemed to have drifted away on a foggy sea of doubt. "What did I do?" he asked at length. "Nothing. And everything. I started something I couldn't stop. Now it appears to have been inevitable. Somehow I knew that this was going to happen, and yet I couldn't do anything about it. It was like being in a car you know is going to crash, and you can't get out, you can't get away. What's worse, all this could have been prevented if I hadn't been such a fool. It's all my fault, you see. I'm to blame." He laughed bitterly.

Mark reached across a widening gulf to touch his friend. "Jim, you've got to get hold of yourself. Tell me what happened. I can help you."

"Do you believe in the devil, Mark? I do. I believe the devil appears in many forms, in many disguises. One of those disguises is Chase Drummond."

"For God's sake, Jim, tell me what happened."

"All right." Jim left the bed and sat down in the second chair. He pulled it closer to Mark. "If what I have to tell you sounds mixed up it's because I am mixed up. I've been over it a dozen times, trying to separate the truth from the lies, the temptation I've had for months to go to the attic myself, as if they would let in an Indian, and the temptation to squeal on them in revenge. And it's mixed up with the fact that I wanted a Drummond scholarship."

"I applied myself," Mark said. "If I had known--"

"It doesn't make any difference, not now. I never would have gotten it anyhow, even if what's happened hadn't happened. The fact was I needed that scholarship. There was no hope that my father could pay the cost of three more years here. But let me tell you from the beginning."

This is Jim's story as Mark remembered it:

One winter Friday night Chase Drummond had sauntered into Jim's room. During a long conversation, Chase described the attic parties. Jim was shocked at first but at length found himself enjoying Chase's way of making the parties sound like no more than innocent fun. However, when Chase deliberately and crudely described what the "boys and girls" were really doing, Jim objected so strenuously that they got into a wrestling match. Chase ended up being pinned to the floor.

Their conflict did not deter Chase from baiting Jim with descriptions of how much fun the parties were. One night Chase learned from Chaplain Davis that Jim wanted to apply for a scholarship, the same one that Mark was seeking. Jim pleaded with Chase to put in a good word for him with Chase's father. Chase told Jim that he would do it on one condition: that Jim would come to the attic parties as a bouncer. It would be an easy job. He would stand guard in the corridor below and admit only certified "guests." Jim refused. But Chase didn't give up. He told Jim that Johnson had blatantly "demanded" an invitation to a party.

"For a week," Jim told Mark, "I couldn't stop thinking about it. Maybe I could get even with Johnson, because Johnson continued to give me failing grades and calling me to his office to cajole me about my ignorance of what he called the American way of life. I had it. The notion that I could get even with him by catching him attending one of those blasted parties---well, Mark, it was stupid, but I told Chase that I would take the job on the condition that I'd do it for that one night only and that Chase would pressure his father to get me that scholarship. I didn't know what Chase was up to. I suspect that he wanted to get Johnson fired. Chase had his reasons. Maybe Johnson threatened to fail Chase if he didn't get that invitation."

Jim was silent as he paced about his room.

"Did you go, Jim?" Mark asked.

"Yes I did. I took the job. The next morning I went to Chaplain Davis and gave him the names. You see, as they came toward the stairway to the attic I asked each one to give me their name, then I secretly wrote down the name."

The two men were silent. They retired to separate sides of the room. Jim could not look up and neither could Mark.

At last Mark was up, pursuing his friend. "You!" he screamed at Jim. "You did it! You squealed!"

"The guilty must be punished," Jim said.

"You knew that Chaplain Davis would have to tell the dean. That's it, isn't it?"

Jim shrugged. "Don't try to make excuses for me, Mark. I knew what I was doing. You can't compromise with evil. I did that for too long."

"But why did you report the names? You didn't have to tell the names!"

"Because they were there!" Jim faced Mark, his eyes blazing. "Get off my back, Mark. I was there because I wanted to be there. My purpose was to expose them all. Chase and the others, they had it coming. And so did Johnson."

"Johnson was there too?"

"Oh yes. He even congratulated me for doing a good job."

Mark tried to grab Jim's arm but Jim eluded him. "You got the fraternity suspended," he cried out. "And who knows how many of them will be dismissed from the university? The girls too." He caught up to Jim and forced him to turn around. He thrashed a hand across Jim's face. "You're a squealer, Jim Pettaw."

CHAPTER SEVENTEEN

The next day, a Sunday, Mark paced the empty streets. He turned from Union Avenue into Orchard, where the elms were tall against the blue sky. Planted spring daffodils puffed their fragrant odor into the cool air. A car was passing by. A woman, sitting beside the driver, looked at him boldly. I will never see her again, Mark thought. And yet he would remember her. Smooth black hair, dark eyes and fair skin, a high smooth forehead. But, why her? She was like a thousand others whom he had passed on the street, seen on a train, jostled on a bus, and what did these others mean to him? Surely he could not go through the rest of his life feeling that these strangers, whom he would never see again, meant more to him than those few whom he called friends. Was there something in him that led him to smash a friendship? One after another his friendships had turned sour. Why, there was not a professor that he really cared for.

He stopped in front of a row house. He looked upward toward the summit. The brick façade, the color of autumn sumac, brightened under the rising sun. Suddenly he recognized the place. It was the house in which Mrs. Marshall served as housekeeper. He debated with himself whether he should press the welcoming bell button. How was it that he should have been passing by her house? He had no intention of going to see her. He had only been meandering around, attempting to banish from his mind the vision of Jim Pettaw holding himself in check after receiving Mark's devastating blow. Mark stepped forward and rang the bell.

Mrs. Marshall, standing tall and smiling, opened the door. It was Sunday, the butler's day off. "Well, I declare," she said. "What in the world you doing up so early?" They rode up the cranky elevator to her apartment. "What brings you prowling about at this unearthly hour?" she asked. "Don't tell me it's a girl."

Mark felt a healing warmth as he looked around the parlor. It was a homecoming and his welcome was embracing him. Not a stick of her furniture had been moved. There was the tall oak buffet still covered by an embroidered scarf. There was the generously padded sofa inviting peaceful rest. Not much had changed about Mrs. Marshall either. She looked slightly broader, that was all. Her eyes glittered a merry steel blue. Beneath the enormous curlers in her hair, which she was now removing, was the pleasant rotund face he now associated with his need for loving attention to his brittle, injured spirit. Mrs. Marshall hummed a Grieg tune as she departed to the kitchen to make the tea.

She returned bearing a painted tray loaded with what she termed the necessities for a light breakfast. She asked "How is dear Martha?" Mark told her that his sister was "doing great" and that she enjoyed being a housewife. "I plan to visit her this summer," Mark said, "if I can afford it." Mrs. Marshall told him she would be glad to help him pay for a train ticket.

She was looking at him keenly. "My goodness," she said. "You're looking more and more like your father."

"Martha says I look like our mother."

"Of course I've only seen photos of her, and those were black and white."

Mark had a mental image of her looking at the few faded photos he had of his mother, those sacred pictures he kept safely in his father's strong cashbox. He was aware that what he was thinking was irrational but he could not help himself. How could his father have permitted Mrs. Marshall to see them? They were his own coveted sacred property. Just the same, he admired Mrs. Marshall. She had been loved by his father, and for that she more than deserved his respect.

Over tea and biscuits she continued to shower him with praise. "You know, Mark," she said, "you have so many fine qualities. I don't mean to embarrass you."

"Everyone likes flattery," he said.

"But I don't intend to flatter you, Mark." She smiled slyly. "First, you are direct and sincere in your beliefs. Oh, I know you won't admit it, but you are. That's what people are like today, I can tell you. They think they can pick up this year's model of beliefs and values as easy as shopping for a new car. But I've never known you to do that. Your beliefs may be old-fashioned, in the sense that you retain what you grew up believing. That's something. And that's the way I am. I'll say again, you're like your father. People would have called him old-fashioned, the way he hung onto his beliefs. Believe me, your father was a wonderful man. You talk like him, you know. You have your father's, how shall I say it? Attitude toward others. Call it kindness, tolerance, I don't know. I know you have been kind to me, by your attitude, I mean." She laughed nervously. "I'm not used to talking like this. Mark, I wish I could have talked with Martha like I can talk to you." She wiped her eyes with a tissue. "People who despise others actually despise themselves."

Mark listened carefully. He wanted to tell her about himself, how the agonizing tumor of regret gnawed at what he wanted to be, at what he actually was. Somehow, their roles had switched. He had always felt that Mrs. Marshall needed his words of comfort. Now she was speaking words of comfort to him just when he needed those words to ease his rising distress. How did she fathom his need? How could she subvert her needs to counsel his? Long ago he had resented her because she had taken his mother's place. Then, for a time, he was glad she did, because she had provided his father with the love he needed.

"I must tell you something," he said.

"Good!" she exclaimed. "I was wondering what was eating you." She settled back on the sofa. Mark told her how he had been on the verge of telling Johnson about the attic parties, about the firing of Johnson, the suspension of Phi Zeta Rho, about seeking a scholarship, and concluded by telling her what happened in Jim's room the night before.

Far from displaying shock, Mrs. Marshall was highly amused. She suppressed a chuckle, but once it burst out, rising to a laugh of tremulous heights.

"Jim Pettaw did the right thing," she said as soon as she recovered. "Nobody should be an ostrich, unless they want to lose their head. And it seems to me you did the right thing in applying for the scholarship. You just can't turn down an offer like that. If you get it, that is."

"I'm not sure I want to be a minister," he protested.

"Well, maybe this is a sign, a sign you should be a minister."

"I wasn't struck blind or anything, like Saint Paul."

"That only happens in the movies, and you know it," she said. "Anyway," she went on, "you will make a handsome minister. I'd love to see you in a clerical collar."

"When I was growing up Pastor Woods wore the thing all week long. Nowadays you hardly ever see a collar like that, except on Sundays."

"Cool it, man," she said with a laugh. "No one gets anywhere unless they have a plan. Most people I've known drift through life That's what their problem is. They don't know where they're going."

Mrs. Marshall suggested he go back to his apartment and take a nap. She asked him to keep her posted. He kissed her goodbye.

Back in his room he tried but he could not sleep. He kept feeling the sting of his hand where it had struck Jim. What could he ever do to make amends? Jim would never want to speak to him again. Perhaps he would be dismissed by the university, sent away with little hope of receiving a scholarship anywhere. He might plead for Dean Wright not to kill the fraternity. One thing he could, that he must do, was to find Jim and to apologize to him, on his knees.

His trip was slow agony. An automobile collision at Main and Union backed up traffic for blocks. The bus hit all the red lights. When he arrived at the campus stop, he raced to find Jim. His room was empty. Back outside, near McMaster Hall, a crowd was gathered. As he approached he became aware of a strange quietness. Ordinarily the quad was alive with jocular voices. This afternoon the crowd, mainly made up of students, but with many faculty people too, emitted only low whispers.

A freckled student with long hair and a burgeoning beard broke away from the crowd and walked hesitatingly toward him. "What's going on?" Mark asked him. The guy seemed not to hear. He had his head down and his hands thrust into his pants pockets. Mark touched his arm. "What's going on?" he repeated.

A wild-eyed stare. The student drew back as if he had been touched by a reptile. Slowly, as if his questioner had asked the impossible, as if the answer was inexpressible, the student pointed up toward the golden cupola gleaming in the brilliant light of the western sun. His mouth opened, his lips moved, and then a slow guttural "Ah!" stuck in his throat.

"For heaven's sake, man," Mark said, acknowledging his annoyance. The young man said nothing as he walked away. Mark continued toward the hall until he reached a group gathered in a tight knot. They seemed to be leaning on one another. They were speechless. No one paid attention to him as he pushed his way closer. Then he saw Ted Swain coming toward him in the company of a red-haired girl he was sure he had never seen before.

Ted raised a hand in salute. "Mark, Mark, I'm so sorry." Mark wondered what he was sorry about, then figured that it was because he had failed to properly introduce him to the girl. Ted expertly corrected himself. "Mark, I'd like you to meet Laura Duquesne. Laura, Mark Christopher." He quickly shook her cool hand.

"How do you do?" she said somewhat differentially. She was tall, not as tall as he was. She had a radiant, comfortable smile. In other circumstances Mark would have paid more attention to her. She regarded him with a long frank glance. "Isn't it strange," she said. "Ted and I were just talking about you." Then: "You were a friend of Jim Pettaw's weren't you?"

Suddenly he observed a mist separating himself from her. She seemed to zoom in and out of focus. A strange tingling sensation gripped his eyes. Ted reached out to stop him from falling.

"My God," he heard Ted exclaim. "He doesn't know!"

As Ted and Laura held him and began to walk him away, he was possessed by an image of Springport in the summer when he worked on Uncle John's farm and rejoiced as the field sprang alive with sweet odorant hay. Perhaps he would return there. He would plant potatoes in the field and go boating on the bay, ignoring the spray's sharp sting as he gunned the outboard toward the island, *their* island rising golden from the sea and green higher up where cedar and balsam hid lovers from a storm. He would sit on the shore where he had with Helen and watch the long slow march of the unraveling waves---

He heard Laura say, "I know how you must feel." It was Ted who told her: "Yes, Jim was Mark's best friend."

Mark thought: I will have to earn a lot of money. I will work at the oil company. Of course I don't know as much as Uncle John but I will learn. Anyway, there isn't much to learn. You hook the snaking black pipe to the pump, open a valve, and *blurp blurp* the oil sucks into the high round silver tank. And all the while the tanker in the bay, relieved of its burden, rises higher until the hull gleams orange in the sun—

"What a horrible thing," Laura was saying. "Let's go now. Nothing we can do."

What he could do, Mark thought, as he tasted the tang of the sea, is repair Grandmother Goddard's house. Leave a house long enough and it just falls down. That could happen. The shutters would droop, putty would crack, shingles warp, and plaster cascade—how crabbed the campus looked with its old dull brick and tramped-down grass. Why, at Springport, back of the farm, was enough land to hold ten universities right side up.

The sun struck a halo around the golden cupola. Mark tried to raise his hand to shield his eyes but the hand, dumb thing, would not rise. And then he felt the soft moist grass under his cheek, cool and utterly comforting.

The next day the whole story was printed in the *Eagle*. It was after midnight that Jim Pettaw was captured by four or five Phi Zetes. He was taken from his room, beaten and dragged across the campus to McMaster Hall. There he was carried up a fire escape to the roof, where he was bound to the golden cupola. During the night he fell to the ground and there he died. His half-naked body, arms flung out to either side, was found at dawn.

Chapter Eighteen

The afternoon was fair, as fair a day as he could remember. As he was sitting on the bus he looked out the window, but he could see nothing except Jim's agony as he slapped his friend's face.

The chapel sanctuary was cold. He passed down a side aisle until he reached the door to a brilliantly lit parlor. He entered quietly. Chaplain Davis and three other ministers were gathered around a long dark table. Mark was surprised when they all rose in a respectful greeting. Chaplain Davis came over and held out his hand. "Mark, I was sorry to hear about Jim Pettaw."

"Thank you, he was my best friend."

Doctor Davis introduced him to the other clergymen, Mr. Fleming, Mr. Elkin and Mr. Munro. Mark was invited to sit down. He took the chair next to Doctor Davis. He placed his hands on the long gleaming table, thought better of it and placed them in his lap. Mr. Fleming, whose bushy hair stood up as if electrically charged, was seated at the other end of the table, upon which his fingers drummed a tattoo. Each minister was deep in the contents of a file of papers. Mark presumed the files contained secret information concerning his life. But that was alright. What he had to tell them was not in his file.

At last Mr. Fleming looked up at him, disclosing by his stern frown that he was presiding. "Now, young man," he began, "you have applied for the Drummond Scholarship?"

"Yes, sir."

"And you have declared your intent to enter the ministry?"

"Yes, sir."

Mr. Fleming leaned back and folded his hands over his heavy paunch. "Will you please tell the committee what led you to this decision?"

"Well, sir, it's because I'm a sinner."

Mr. Elkin, an emaciated man with a thin mustache, who had until that moment been engaged in twisting and turning a gold signet ring, jerked his head. "What did you say?"

"I said I believe in original sin."

Mr. Fleming tapped the table. "Answer my question, young man."

Mark clasped his hands over the table. He glanced from one minister to the other. "We're all sinners," Mark said. "But I confess my sin. You see, I have been carefully taught. It's not good for me to go about bearing a burden of guilt. No, I wish to share my guilt with you."

Mr. Monro, a young man who wore his clerical collar as if it were a yoke, turned to Mr. Fleming. "I think Mr. Christopher is out of order," he said.

Mark laughed, a giggle. His head felt as if it were full of bubbles. "Yes," he said. "I am out of order. I am in need of repair."

Mr. Fleming whacked the table. Mark could see that Mr. Fleming was skilled in wielding a gavel. "Young man, this is no laughing matter."

"Ah, but, you see, it is," Mark replied coldly. "A friend of mine died yesterday, all because of sin. Not yours, not mine. You must understand that." He leaned back. "Well, come to think of it, I suppose we all had something to do with it."

"With what?" Mr. Elkin asked. The minister seemed rather dense.

"With the death of Jim Pettaw."

"What does that have to do with your application, Mr. Christopher?"

"Mr. Welkin—"

"Elkin."

Mark gasped, an open-mouthed gasp. "Oh, I'm so sorry. You must pardon me. I'm having a rather trying day, as the saying goes. After all, you don't have your best friend die on you every day. Well, that's neither here nor there." He leaned toward Doctor Davis. "May I have a drink, please?" he asked.

The chaplain left the room. All was quiet. The reverend gentlemen appeared to be in prayer. The chaplain returned with a glass of water. He tripped on the carpet but managed not to splash away any water.

Mark drank it in a gulp. He looked around at the severe faces of his questioners. The walls of the room appeared to be receding.

"Where was I?" he asked. They appeared to him to be rising from their chairs, like a fellow he once saw raised by a levitator on the stage of the old Majestic. "Ah, yes, about the ministry," he said desperately. "It seems to me, gentlemen, that we have more sick souls than we have sick bodies. Why? Good question. Because we don't have enough doctors, physicians that is, for the soul. Now Saint Luke was a physician, a doctor. He cured the body. But he knew that wasn't enough. So he went along with Saint Paul, and---well, where was I? Where are you gentlemen going?" He sipped some water. "Ah, that does taste good. Thank you, Doctor Davis. Thank you very much. I was thirsty and you gave me to drink."

There were whispered comments around the table. "Can't you see the boy's sick?"--"He needs a doctor."--"My car's outside, I'll take him to the hospital."---"Call an ambulance."

Mark rose up. "No need, no need," he told them. "Didn't I tell you? Jim Pettaw has passed away. Yes, my friend Jim is safe in the eternal arms. Safe! Ah, Jim!" He sat down again. The ministers remained standing, their heads together, circling him. "Won't you gentlemen come down?" he asked. "I said you can come down now."

To his satisfaction, they all came down.

Doctor Davis drove him to his apartment. The chaplain insisted that Mark needed someone to care for him. Mark telephoned Mrs. Marshall.

"Help me!" he cried as she arrived. "I killed him! I killed Jim Pettaw." He told her what happened as best he could. "I killed him," he repeated over and over again. He could not suppress his tears.

"No, no, don't think that," Mrs. Marshall said as she held him closely. "You weren't to know." He bent his head onto her breast, as he had against his mother the night the monastery burned and he thought the priestly brothers had been killed, and maybe God too.

A few days later a letter arrived. Written on Drummond Company stationery, it curtly informed him that he had been awarded the full scholarship he applied for. The next day he filed a long form requesting qualification to enroll in Divinity School, beginning in September.

Follow-up stories in the *Eagle* reported that Phi Zeta Rho was banished from Attumwa University's roster of approved fraternities and that several students had been dismissed. Chase Drummond simply resigned. It was rumored that he had applied for transfer to a private college in Connecticut. As for professor Johnson, no one seemed to know. He simply disappeared.

Chapter Nineteen

Mark was graduated in June, receiving honors in English literature. An honorary degree was granted Jim Pettaw, whose father received it proudly. But the Chief had not stayed long enough for Mark to talk to him at length. However, he did provide Mark with some details about the funeral service in Jim's Baptist Church. Tearfully, he gave Mark a handsome feather that he recovered from Jim's room. Everything else had been shipped to Pettaw Island.

Early in July he arrived at Chicago's Midway Airport deep within the city's south end. The two-propeller airplane made a rough landing. It was Mark's first flight. He felt somewhat groggy as he stepped carefully down a moveable stairway onto the bare concrete tarmac.

Martha greeted him warmly as he exited directly into the airport's bright arrivals building. She hugged him fondly, stood back to size him up and down with her still stunning eyes. Her beauty, surprisingly retained and even enhanced beyond the year he had seen her last. She told him that he was looking "just fine," that he was more "mature." He kidded her by responding "So are you, Martha."

It was an hour's drive in her Chevrolet to the west side of Evanston where she and her husband, Joe Stanford, were living. Her house did not appear to Mark to be as large and stunning as Martha had described it in her letters. The ranch house stretched widely parallel to the elm-rich street. They stepped out of the car onto the paved driveway. Martha walked over to the single garage, which stood on one side of the house, and tugged strenuously on a handle to raise the car-wide door. Then, having driven the car into the garage and dropped the door, which banged soundly into place, she locked the door with a key.

"Look over there, Mark," she said, pointing to the house next door. "They don't need to kill themselves raising the door. It's motorized. I've asked Joe a dozen times to get us one. I'm still waiting."

Joe got home about six-thirty. Mark was in the parlor, which Martha called "living room." He could hear them very well. Martha was scolding her husband for being late. Joe protested loudly that the traffic was "horrific." He also complained that it was his turn to park his Cadillac in the garage. "What's the point?" she asked him. "The garage is too narrow. You scratch your car every time."

Still agitated, they entered the parlor to bestow upon him fond salutations. Joe was particularly enthusiastic. "Great to see you Mark," Joe said warmly. "Hear you're on your way to California to see your brother's wife."

Martha put her arm around Mark. "Take me with you, brother mine," she said seriously.

Mark was about to ask "Why not?" but Joe immediately interfered. "Not a chance. We've got this banquet next Saturday night in honor of Mr. Duquesne."

That was that. Martha retired to the kitchen to prepare "dinner," as she called the evening meal.

Mark wanted to know. The name sounded familiar. "Who's Duquesne, Joe?"

"He owns my company. Billionaire."

Later, still hungry because Martha served only hunks of dry flat fish and heavy baked potato, Mark related events that led to acquiring a scholarship. "Means I can go to the Divinity School for three years and graduate with a master's degree."

Martha gave him an accusing stare. "Whatever for? Don't tell me you want to be a minister!"

"Not necessarily," he said. "All depends upon my major."

"Like what?" Mark began to resent her attitude. Martha always had been inquisitive. She admired accuracy. Always dot the I and cross the T, she would say. "Want to teach?"

"Could be anything. Social work, prison chaplain."

"That sounds like fun."

"There are military chaplains, hospital chaplains. Why, I heard not long ago of a company that hired a minister to be the chaplain for workers in a big factory that makes automobile parts."

Joe was listening carefully. "Makes sense to me," he said. "Sometimes I wish we had a chaplain at Modern Enterprises."

Martha scoffed. "Good heavens, why? Seems to me there are more than enough ministers wherever you go."

Joe threw up his hands. "Have it your own way, Martha. You usually do." Joe winked at Mark. "If we had a chaplain at my plant I can think of dozens of ways he would be helpful."

"You can't be serious!" Martha exclaimed. She kept her eyes on Mark as she scratched her forehead, twirling two fingers. She mouthed: "He's crazy."

Mark briefly summarized recent events at Attumwa University, condensing details as best he could. He kept hurtful memories to himself. Perhaps some day he could bring himself to divulge the whole story. But not yet, not now.

Later, when Joe had left them to make some telephone calls, he confronted his sister about her obvious discontentment,

They sat apart on the sofa. "I'm worried about you, Martha," he said flatly.

"Good heavens, this from my kid brother."

"I'm serious. You seem to get upset so easily. What's wrong?"

She turned away from him, as if it pained her to be challenged.

"I don't know," she said. "But you're right. Sometimes I just can't stand myself. I haven't been like that in the past, have I?"

"Actually no. At least not since you stopped trying to mother me."

"I never did!" She looked at Mark inquisitively. "You're kidding me."

"Of course I was, Martha. Seriously, are you happy here?"

"Doesn't make sense, does it? Great husband. Nice house. Good friends."

"Then what is it, Martha?" Mark persisted.

"My first guess is that I'm bored. I wasn't cut out to be a housewife."

"And?" He looked at her sternly. "I'm your brother, Martha."

She extracted a tissue from its nearby box. She dabbed her eyes. "Alright, Mark. You win. We don't have enough money. Joe got stuck with having to pay a terrific amount of alimony every month and he's stubborn about not wanting me to get a job. Not the thing, in our class, to do, he says. There's nothing I can do about it."

And there's nothing I can do about it either, Mark thought. They continued talking for an hour before Joe returned. He yawned widely. "God, I'm tired. I've go to get some extra sleep tonight." He reached out to Martha. "Sorry, Mark. See you at breakfast. Coming, Martha? Show Mark to his room, will you? I've already put his bag in there."

Martha shrugged and shook her head sideways. She pursed her lips. "Follow me, Mark." The small guest room contained a single bed, a pine bureau, a chair and little else. He picked up his bag from the floor and placed it on the bed. "Looks very comfortable, Martha. Thank you."

"How long can you stay?" She gazed at him sadly.

"My plane leaves tomorrow morning, Martha."

"I suspected it, Mark. Just as well. I'm not much fun to be around anymore."

He held her to him as she laid her head upon his shoulder. She sobbed uncontrollably, even as she attempted to suppress the sound of her sorrow.

Martha was still on his mind as the plane flew over the deep blue of Lake Tahoe. What she would have given to be free, to be with him on this adventurous flight! Far below, California's verdant forests, spiked with pines, glimmered in the afternoon sun as the great four-engine Constellation glided toward the Pacific. Then the long slow descent over San Francisco Bay's silent enlarging waves. Mark stiffened his legs and held tightly to the arms of his seat. A gentle thump as the monster plane settled down to its turbulent ride along the gleaming runway.

He took a taxi to the Stevens house, a five-mile run up staggered hills, then down toward the Pacific coast, San Francisco on his right.

Long ago Carol had sent him a photo of her parents' house, the one she lived in after Peter sailed away never to return. There was the picket fence, and the gate on which she had leaned. But the house and grounds looked different now. The grass was parched and brown. There were no flowers.

Mark opened the gate, which creaked in protest. The house was set low on the ground with a red verandah running its full width. Four fluted white columns supported the convoluted Spanish tile roof.

He pushed the button beside the front door. Somewhere deep inside the house a bell rang loudly. There was the sound of running feet. The door flashed open. Six-year-old Peter Junior flung himself into Mark's welcoming arms. Young Peter hollered "It's Uncle Mark! It's Uncle Mark!" The boy leaped high and clung to his uncle's neck. Mark hoisted him up and staggered into the hall.

"Okay, Peter, you can get off now." Mark ruffled the boy's full crop of crinkly brown hair. He went down on one knee and held Peter's small hands. He looked solemnly into the dark eyes. They were the eyes of his brother. "You look just like your daddy," he said. Peter nodded vigorously. "Where's Grandma?" Mark asked.

The boy led him by the hand to the kitchen, where Mrs. Stevens was trimming roses over the sink. She kissed Mark lightly on his cheek. She was rather plump, with squared shoulders and hips. Her white hair, which she wore in a page-boy, framed delicate brown eyes, a thin sharp nose, and a narrow mouth with a pendulant lower lip. She smiled constantly. Mark liked her.

"Oh," she said, "it's so wonderful! I've been looking forward to seeing you for so many years. And now you're here I can't believe it." She stepped back a pace and looked up at him. "I didn't know you were so tall. And, I can't get over it, you look so much like your brother." She looked away. "Oh, he was a handsome man, and so loving. When I met him for the first time, I knew he must have wonderful parents. And Carol! She fell for him. Did she! Like a ton of bricks, as they say."

Peter was tugging on Mark's hand. "You wanna see Grandpa now?"

"Don't be too shocked," Mrs. Stevens said. "Roger's been laid up more than a year now. The fall at the plant, you know. But I suppose Carol told you about him." Mark assured her that, in her letters, Carol had mentioned her father's fall, but he couldn't recall that he had been "laid up," as her mother put it, for so long.

Peter led the way upstairs to the room in which his grandfather lay, propped up by pillows, on a wide double bed.

"The way you yell," Mr. Stevens said to Peter, "everybody in San Francisco heard you." Mrs. Stevens, who had just come in, advised her husband that he shouldn't shout either. An unlit cigarette dangled from his mouth. She tugged it away. "Good grief, Roger, you're the limit," she said. He threw her a kiss. His face was all flat planes, square forehead, equine nose, jutting chin. His cheeks and nose bore tell-tale fine red lines, cross-hatched. His protruding stomach and meager chest were covered by a blue sheet up to his shoulders.

Mrs. Stevens was fingering the retrieved cigarette. She waved it before her husband's nose, then smashed it into an ash tray that lay on an end table next to the bed. "What did Doctor Tanner tell you?" she asked. "Where did you find those terrible things anyway?"

"Don't baby me, woman," Mr. Stevens grumbled loudly.

"You don't have to yell. I'm not deaf."

"I never yell."

"You do too." This from Peter.

"Who's asking you?" Mr. Stevens asked Peter, lowering his voice. He made a face at Peter and asked him to sit down. "You and I, Mark, we're going to have some fine talks," he said. "Yes sir, some real long talks."

"I'm looking forward to it," Mark said politely.

"How about a story?" Mr. Stevens asked young Peter. "You might not believe this," he said to Mark, "but Peter reads to me." The boy was advanced for his age. He picked up a paperback western and, seated on the bed near his grandfather, read a page with clarity and emphasis. They all congratulated the boy, who beamed enthusiastically.

"You must excuse Roger," Mrs. Stevens told Mark as she prepared dinner in the kitchen. "He's always been a tease, and since he's been laid up he's been worse. Once I got so mad when he teased me about my diets. But it's not easy to just lie there doing nothing. Once we get television it will be a blessing." She shrugged. "What can you do? That's the government for you. So, Roger spends his time writing letters to Sacramento, claiming he isn't getting enough workman's compensation. That may be, but you'd think he'd find something better to do with his time. When you have time on your hands you get to thinking all sorts of mean thoughts. Having you here, Mark, that's cheering me up. I hope you won't mind talking with him." She kept on chopping carrots, her brown eyes darkening. "Talk to Carol too, Mark. She's another brooder. She will listen to you."

The front door opened. Carol Christopher entered Mark's life.

She was beautiful. She kissed him full on the mouth, soft and promising, causing his blood to rise. She said "Ummm-huh!" She paraded around him, inspecting him, noting his height. Mark pivoted and inspected her.

There was no doubt about it. Carol was beautiful. Like Maureen O'Hara in Miracle on 42nd Street, but that was black-and-white. More like Technicolored Greer Garson in The Forsythe Saga, which he had seen in Springport because Errol Flynn was in it, but it was Greer Garson's picture, shining red hair to her shoulders, wonderful blue eyes. And it was Carol's bright red hair that compelled him toward open-mouthed adoration. Carol was wearing a black suit with wide lapels and a V-cut revealing high swelling breasts, emphasized by a belt with a three-inch brass buckle that pinched her slim waist. Her spiked heels clicked on the kitchen's tile floor.

"You do have your brother's looks," Carol told him.

"As I remember him he looked like our father," he said.

"Carol," her mother said, "don't you think you'd better give Mark a bit more time to get used to us?"

"Nonsense." Carol held Mark's hand. She smiled up at him. "He knows this is his home as long as he wants to stay. Mark's one of the family."

Peter rushed in. "Grandpa says he's hungry enough to eat his pillow," he announced.

Next morning, after Carol left for the aircraft plant where she worked, Mark took Peter for a walk down da Silva Avenue, where trees bordered wide lawns and sprinklers swirled, arching embryonic rainbows from hedge to hedge.

When they returned, Peter went to the yard to play. Mrs. Stevens had gone to her hairdresser's. Mark went upstairs to have "that talk" with Mr. Stevens, who was reading a book and smoking. Sun slanted through double dormer windows onto an oval Spanish-red scatter rug.

"Mr. Stevens, how are you this beautiful morning?"

"For God's sake, stop calling me mister," the older man said sourly. "I do have another name. Call me Roger, damnit." He squashed the cigarette into the ash tray that teetered on his stomach. He practically demanded that Mark fetch him a fresh pack of cigarettes from the top of the bureau.. Opening the pack, he offered one to Mark. "Gives you a lift," he said. He looked whiffed when Mark refused.

Mark drew up a chair with a rattan covering. "Mr. Stevens, 'er Roger, what was my brother like?"

Roger looked inquisitively at Mark but did not hesitate to reply. "Finest boy I ever met," he said. His eyes shuttered against the impacting sun. "Most generous too. Always bringing presents for everybody, never waiting for birthdays. Said there wasn't time. As if he knew he wasn't coming back from the war. Not that he was morbid. Not at all. He was always cheerful. Carol would protest sometimes about his going away, but he'd say, 'The war won't last forever.' He asked me to be sure to take care of Carol and Peter Junior. I knew what he meant. Her mother used to have this atrocious fear that Carol would be kidnapped---"

"Kidnapped?"

"Sure. As a child. My wife got that phobia right after the Lindbergh kidnapping. She would tell Carol never to talk to strangers and never, never accept a ride in a car. Well, one day Carol came screaming home and it was a long while before we got it out of her that a car had stopped at the curb while she was walking home from school. A man had opened the door and motioned her to come to the car. But Carol, good girl, screamed and ran all the way home. My wife, she said 'You see. It can happen,' and she told Carol, 'You did the right thing, the man wanted to take you away and do bad things to you.'" Mr. Stevens smashed his cigarette into the tray. "The guy may have just wanted to ask directions. Anyway, I told my wife it wasn't right, her scaring the kid like that. During the war there were a lot of bad sorts in the Navy roaming the streets in gangs, looking for a skirt, but, you know, Carol would wave to them from the porch and they'd stand by the fence talking to her." He massaged his waist. "Damn brace," he muttered.

"Anything I can do for you?" Mark asked.

Mr. Stevens shook his head. "That's where she met your brother." He pointed toward the window. "Right out there. They sure married soon enough, didn't they?" Mark nodded in agreement. "After Peter was reported missing, there was none of that why-does-it-have-to-be-me? Once when Carol was small she was playing with her dolls and her favorite fell off the window sill and smashed. Any other kid might have cried her eyes out, but not Carol. Another time, when she was in high school, there was this boy she had a crush on. But he took up with another girl. Carol just shrugged. There was always another boy hanging around. But that boy who jilted her came back and said he wanted to date her again, and she said okay. If you ever saw a rabbit hop! Boy, if she told him to come at eight, he was there at quarter to. If she didn't like the color of his socks, he changed them. Things like that. When she had him hooked, she jilted him. I told her off good."

That evening, after little Peter had gone to bed and her mother was sitting with her father, Carol showed Mark her photos of Mark's brother. Like Mrs. Marshall's collection, they were mounted on a wall in her bedroom. There was the venerated sailor in his tight Navy whites leaning against the picket fence, another holding Carol's hand in a restaurant, Peter grinning in the garden with Mr. Stevens, Peter on the parlor sofa between Carol's parents, Peter in his swim trunks on a beach shielding his eyes against the sun, Peter in uniform with a buddy, their arms around each other's shoulders, Peter incumbent on the verandah hammock, his hands under his head, a wide smile on his tanned face.

And these also: A studio portrait of uniformed Peter signed "With love and affection," Peter in working tans on a palm-fringed beach, Peter in sparkling dress whites with shipmates lining a destroyer's rails, Peter with Martha and himself taken long ago in Westminster when they were children, Peter as a bridegroom sailor with Carol in shining white and a veil, Peter and Carol holding hands before a log cabin with stark rock mountains mirrored on a lake.

"That's where we spent our honeymoon," Carol said. She was standing close behind him, to his left. When he turned he bumped solidly against her. He reached out to steady her, gripping her arms, and Carol laughed. "We never had enough time together," she said. "Peter was always so conscientious. Why, he'd even take somebody else's duty, jut as a favor. He was a real flag-waver, let me tell you." She sat down on a plush, silvery chaise-longue. "He thought it was just glorious to be in the Navy. Mr. Spick-and-Span himself. He used to say that everyone who got promotions was neat about those things. He's the only Navy man I ever knew, and I've known plenty of them, who could defend discipline and officers. Of course," she said, as she leaned back and unbuckled her belt, a white leather strap binding to her slim waist the folds of a pleated jersey dress, "he was a volunteer in the regular Navy and most everyone else was an escapee from the Army. He loved the Portland, that was the name of the destroyer he was on, like he had built it with his own two hands. He was so proud of that ship that, before Pearl Harbor, he took me on a tour and we even had to go down to the engine room!"

"I would have liked to have seen it myself," Mark said.

"That's what Peter was like," Carol went on as the sun went down and darkness settled in the room. "Once he brought a buddy of his home, a big ugly fellow, an oiler, I think. God, was he ugly! Grabbed my hand and almost broke it. Six five, three hundred pounds. Bald, a fat broken nose and teeth that looked like they'd been smashed by a bat. Well, this jerk was Mr. Cheerio himself. He picks me up like I'm a basket and swings me around. He says to Peter 'So this is your girl.' That's the kind that Peter brought into this house. He always seemed to associate with the crudest types." She paused and looked across the room at Mark, who was sitting on the edge of her bed, which was covered by a quilted pink spread with a lacy orange fringe around it. "I suppose Peter had some sort of need," she continued. "Anyway, I told him never to bring that jerk, or anyone else like him, into this house."

"He only wanted to show off his friends," Mark protested.

"I despised his so-called friends. They only wanted to take him away from me for a night on the town, for poker and heaven knows what else."

Mark felt a strangely growing unease and sense of embarrassment, being somewhat overcome by Carol's frankness, indeed eagerness, to tell him such details about her life with his brother. Had he traveled so far from a distant world, a different way of life, that he felt so out of place? And why was his beautiful sister-in-law presuming that her private life would interest him? Not that he wasn't interested. He was intrigued by her account of what his brother was like during all those years when they were separated by half a continent. He decided to change the subject.

"Are you going to get married again?" he asked abruptly.

Carol looked at him inquisitively. She laughed heartily. "What a thing to ask!" Her room was dark as the evening light departed. "Oh well. It could happen if the right man came along, I suppose. They don't make men like Peter anymore." She let out a light, charming giggle. "Present company excepted of course."

"Of course."

"I'm not entirely the merry widow, but I do date. Once in a while I have a male friend over to dinner. They take one look at Peter Junior and vanish."

"Peter's a smart kid," Mark said.

"Isn't he though? Father really enjoys him."

"What's wrong with your father?"

Carol appeared alarmed. "What do you mean?"

Mark leaned forward. He was only a few feet away. "I mean there's nothing wrong with his back, is there? Sure, he was hurt, but his back isn't broken. And it's been a year."

"How did you know?" Carol swung her feet to the floor. "You're pretty smart yourself."

"I knew, that's all. I don't know why I knew. But I did."

"Well, you're perceptive, Mark, I must say." Carol swept her feet back onto the chaise-longue. "You're right. Dad uses that accident as an excuse. He had this boss at the plant he hated. When he accidentally fell he accused his boss of all sorts of things, as if his boss was responsible. So the boss fired him. Dad sued the company for building a faulty scaffold. The suit will be settled out of court. How long it takes depends upon Dad's ability to keep up his charade, and then he'll have to go back to work. He'll have to. I'll be damned if I'm going to support him much longer. And Mother can't go to work, because she takes care of Peter. She won't admit that Dad's faking. She coddles him. If I were her I'd roll him right off the mattress. That would fix him. Of course, Dad had a lot of tough breaks in his time. He was laid off and we were on relief in the Depression. That's when I went to work, as soon as I finished high school. Then the war came and Dad got a job at the aircraft plant. Then I met your brother right out there in the front yard."

"I heard about it. What happened next? I don't mean to pry."

"That's all right," she assured him. She leaned back again. The light of a street lamp lay on her face like a yellow mask. "It was at a USO dance. He just swept me off my feet. While we were dancing he gave me a line a mile long, how beautiful I was, and that he was going to marry me. Yes! That's what he said. I only laughed, but he insisted on taking me home, to meet his future in-laws, he said. He was crazy, I tell you. He came over from Treasure Island almost every night after that. We were married a few months later by a justice of the peace."

"Peter was like that at home, too," Mark said. "He wanted to join the Navy and he just went down and signed up. My mother didn't like that, but Dad was real proud."

"I'll bet he was," Carol said. "Dad thinks of Peter as his own son." She paused.

"I'm sorry if I appear callous, but I haven't talked about Peter to anyone else for a long time." She tried to muffle a quiet sob to no avail. "Sorry," she said. "Shouldn't be so long-winded. After all, it was your loss too. I can imagine what you and your parents went though."

"Mainly it hurt so much because we didn't know for certain what happened to Peter. All we were told was that he was missing in action."

"I know, I know," Carol said. "What we know is that his ship blew up."

Startled, Mark said "What did you say?"

"Just that we only know that his ship blew up."

"No. It was sunk, by the Japs."

"There was an explosion, Mark. An officer at Treasure Island told me. The ship's magazine blew up. It was an accident. Japanese ships were reported in the area but none were sighted. The Portland was escorting a convoy. At first they thought it was a submarine, but the other destroyers couldn't find a trace of one."

"It could have gotten away."

"I'm sorry, Mark. There were some survivors. They knew what happened."

"Why were we not told?"

"We were told, Mark. After the war, remember?" Carol paused. "O my God! You never got the message! The Navy officer came to the house and gave me a folded flag. Of course, your parents had passed away, Martha had moved, and you were in Springport. Oh, Mark! All these years, not knowing." She took him into her arms, sobbing out of her dismay. "I could have written to Martha and you. I could have."

From somewhere long ago and far away Mark heard Peter say *So long, Mark, take care of yourself. See you soon.* And Mercury looked down with a cold eyeless stare. Mark told his friends that his brother had died a hero in his country's service, for his country's honor, and there was pride in that, for had not the Japanese ship that sunk *Portand* dipped its rising-sun flag in salute as the dauntless destroyer went down in glory? The darkness was deep in the room and curled like a hissing cat in the corners of his mind.

The next day, a Friday, Carol and Mark had dinner on Fisherman's Wharf. They clung to a clanging open trolley over Nob Hill to Market Street, where Carol had parked her red convertible. They drove over Golden Gate Bridge to Sausalito where, under a million stars, Carol had a glass of wine while he sipped a Coke. Then back across the bridge, through Golden Gate Park, and down the rugged coast between high cliffs and pounding surf. They stopped at a motel in Santa Cruz. Next morning they were off to Monterey and, by way of the 17-mile route through the city, followed the coast road to Carmel, where they watched seals through binoculars. They bought a bucket of fried chicken and ate on the beach, their backs against a smooth sea-sculptured log as Pacific waves boomed high and long. Southward toward Big Sur and beyond, Carol wheeled the car around pin-turns where the cliffs dropped steeply into eternity and the sun slanted across the calm Pacific. The highway dipped and rose, carried far out to windy points, slid around an inlet, across a concrete bridge and back to the shining sea. It was dark when they reached San Simeon, but they caught a glimpse of Hearst Castle sparkling high like a medieval fortress on the hill, pale and ghostly under a rising moon. The next morning they sped inland through Santa Maria and Alamos until they reached the sea again at Santa Ymez and passed through Goleta to Santa Barbara. They turned toward the water, along a palm-lined boulevard and stopped at a motel fronting the beach. Carol asked at the desk for adjoining rooms and signed the register Carol and Mark Christopher.

They had dinner at a restaurant on a pier overlooking the flat oiled water of Santa Barbara Channel where they could watch tankers sailing up the coast in front of the islands. Later they swam in the motel's heated pool, and then sat together on the terrace as the moon strode through the stars. They talked until a cloud covered the moon. Across the channel the island lights blinked. On the beach a ripple chased a sandpiper. To the northwest, high up, the wing lights of an airplane blinked red and white. Far away against the hills a train shrieked through the lingering night.

As waves sloughed on the beach, Mark was drifting into sleep, when, vaguely, he was aware that the door between their rooms was opening. A slice of light stabbed him awake. Carol stood in the light, her hand on the doorknob, her slim legs silhouetted. She came in silently and sat down on the edge of his bed. She was wearing a negligee which folded to her thighs. She began to stroke his hair.

"Love me, Mark," Carol said softly.

He could not tell her that the abyss yawned. One step (the fire will warm, the shadows hide) and he was over, slipping, eager, to her warm embrace.

"You had better go back to your room," Mark said.

"What kind of a man are you anyway?"

"I am Peter's brother."

"I suppose you think you would hate yourself in the morning."

"No, it's not that."

Carol stood up, hands on her hips. Her hair shone light flame. "Well, I'll be," she said mildly. Shoulders high, she walked slowly toward the open door to her room. She turned and smiled. "Jilted again," she said. She threw him a kiss.

All the way back to San Francisco she never mentioned the incident. She talked about his brother and her father, but there was a distance between them.

Mark spent another week with the Stevens. He used the time mainly for sightseeing, then he said goodbye, knowing it would be a long time before he saw them all again. At the airport Carol permitted him to kiss her cheek.

Chapter Twenty

"Haven't we met before?" Mark asked the girl. He knew, of course, that he had met her but he could not for the moment remember where. He had just sat down opposite her at a two-chair table in the cafeteria of the university Student Center.

"Yes, I think we have," she replied. She smiled and beckoned toward the empty chair. "Won't you join me?" As he sat down he observed her closely. A red-head whose hair reached to her shoulders, she was wearing a pretty starched pink dress with cherry prints and a Peter Pan collar. She regarded him intensely. "Aren't you—" She had forgotten his name, so he promptly provided it.

"The friend of the Indian?" Apparently she noticed his disapproval of the racial identification. "No offense, Mark. I've never gotten over what happened to Jim."

"Now I remember," Mark said. "You were with Ted Swain. You were crying. I appreciated that. You are the only student I know of who cried for Jim Pettaw."

"Well, I've always been a cry-baby."

She was delightful. She smiled at him, never failing to look directly into his eyes, and not flinching either as he held her gaze for moments longer than was appropriate under the circumstances. Her deep-set eyes, which were as blue as Springport Bay on a mid-summer morning, and not dark like Helen's, examined him with candor, but not unkindly. He thought she was interested.

They ate in silence for a while. She had a peculiar way of handling a fork: a quick stab, a twist, the fork balanced between thumb and two fingers, in a pattern that never varied. Her hands were slim and delicate, impeccably manicured but without polish. Her dress had long sleeves with one-inch fluted cuffs, which struck Mark as somewhat old-fashioned. She smiled a quick easy smile, displaying flawless teeth, and he knew she had caught him at his observation game.

"To tell you the truth, Mark, you've passed me by a lot of times. I wondered when you were going to speak to me." Her voice, clear and lilting, had a nervous tremor. "You don't remember my name, do you?"

Mark flushed. "I ought to remember," he said. "I really don't have an excuse."

"There's no need to be embarrassed," she said with a smile. "It happens to me all the time. I'm a dope when it comes to remembering names." She looked at her watch. "Wow! I've got a one o'clock class. See you." She rose, collected her books, and started off.

"Hey," he called after her. "What *is* your name?"

"Laura Duquesne." She laughed and hurried away.

Of course! How could he have forgotten? If there was one name that was famous in Attumwa that name was Duquesne. It was one name that people knew how to pronounce—dew-kane—even if they could not spell it. Laura was the daughter, the only child, of William E. Duquesne, the chairman of Duquesne Corporation, which was a holding company. One of its holdings was Drummond Pulp and Paper Company. Another was Modern Enterprises! That meant: Laura's father was the same Mr. Duquesne who Martha's husband was meeting in Chicago!

In the days that followed he looked for her in the cafeteria but she was never there. As he crossed the quadrangle on the way from the library to Divinity Hall or to the Student Center he watched for her. She never appeared. Once he ran into Ted Swain and he managed to bring their brief conversation around to the subject of Laura.

"She wouldn't be attending Attumwa University," Ted told him, "if her old man hadn't built the science building."

"What's she studying?" Mark asked.

Ted squinted suspiciously. "What's it to you?" he asked. "If you're trying to date her, forget it. Poor boys don't have a chance."

"Is she doing graduate work?"

"Social studies," Ted replied. "Just for kicks. She's not the social order type. Anyway, can you imagine her dad allowing her to wallow in the slums? Take my advice. Forget Laura Duquesne."

But he could not forget her. He looked for her everywhere. He thought of telephoning her and twice inserted a dime in the box but could not work up the courage to dial.

He was in the library stacks looking for Toynbee's latest book when he collided with her, knocking to the floor several books she was holding. She appeared dizzy for a moment. Mark insisted she sit down on a nearby bench while he picked up her books.

"How about coffee?" he asked her. He added, with a sure smile, "Laura."

They found a booth in a corner of The Knight's Gambit, a student-oriented coffee shop in the basement of a brownstone across Main Street. Posters of movie stars—Robert Taylor, Clark Gable, George Brent, Errol Flynn, Cary Grant—draped the walls, one over each booth. A girl in leotards, short black skirt and black sweater, took their order. Except for one other couple near the front window, they were alone.

"I was hoping I would see you again, Laura," Mark said.

"Have you?" Laura asked without commitment.

"I kept looking for you in the cafeteria."

"I guess our schedules must be different. I always eat at noon."

"That's the trouble, I guess. My classes run to twelve-thirty, Tuesday through Fridays. I don't have classes Mondays."

"That's a coincidence. I don't have classes on Mondays either."

"Laura, I've been wanting to see you an awful lot. May I ask you something, something personal?" She nodded. "You aren't going steady or anything, are you?"

Laura shook her head. "Not steady. Or anything."

"Do you know the park behind the Capitol?" Mark asked. "If you're not busy on Monday would you like to go there with me?"

"What's wrong with Saturday?"

Mark brightened, then looked gloomy. "I don't have a car," he said.

"If it's alright with you, I'll drive. I'll pick you up a your place."

And so it was arranged. Mark dreamed about her each night.

Promptly at eleven Saturday morning she parked her car outside the apartment building and honked the horn. He waved to her from the parlor window where he had been watching for half an hour. On the street he whistled approvingly at her gold Desoto convertible with huge tailfins. Laura was sitting on the passenger side. She motioned to him, pointing to the driver's seat.

"I wish I could," Mark said., "but I can't drive." Laura laughed and moved under the steering wheel. She drove with intense concentration, eyes severely focused on the traffic ahead. She raced along the Rayoodoo River Road past the quiet university campus and then over a narrow iron bridge onto the canal road. High elms, leaves turning autumn red, clasped hands overhead. Scarlet maples tossed their heavy branches on either side. She flung the car into the one-way drive leading to the promontory behind the great stone Capitol and pulled to a skidding halt next to a high stone wall which, at that point, edged the cliff high above the river. Several couples had already staked their claims on the lawn which curved behind the State Senate Chamber and slanted down toward the cliff. Mark spread a blanket a dozen feet from a couple engaged in a strong embrace. "How's this?" he asked Laura as she was already taking the makings of their lunch from a picnic basket. He studied her with admiration. She was clad in a white angora sweater with short sleeves, which emphasized the perfect shape of her appealing figure. A white band secured her fine red hair, which draped to her back. Lipstick appeared to be her only cosmetic. Mark knew he was falling hard.

Later, they lay side by side in the warm late-October sun observing the patterns created by slow-moving clouds. On the river a tug, trailing a clutch of logs, spewed a froth of spray and tucked its bottom deep in the trough. Beyond the river the Attumwa Hills flowed softly to a dim horizon. Mark stretched out his hand, reaching for Laura's. She enfolded his fingers in a sure undemanding grasp.

On the return journey through the city their conversation turned on difficulties each was having in particular university courses. Just the same, at least for Mark, time flew. Two miles past the city limits, along the Rayoodoo River, Laura pointed to a three-foot stone wall which edged the highway as far as he could see.

"On your right," Laura announced in the fashion of a sight-seeing guide, "the Duquesne Estate!" A half mile further she cut a sharp right turn between high stone pillars capped by shingled cones. Black iron gates stood open on either side. The winding drive through molting sycamores and ancient shagbark hickories opened all at once upon a greensward sloping up to the mansion. Laura drove past the pillared porch, around the corner of the house, and parked in a blacktopped courtyard between a four-car stone garage and a stable which, except for the absence of wide doors, was identical to the garage.

Laura led the way into the stable. Only two of five stalls were occupied. "This one is mine," Laura said, indicating a sleek-coated gray roan. "Hello there old Betsy," she said in a deep imitation of Katherine Hepburn. "The wild one," she added, pointing to the other horse in the next stall, "is Daddy's."

"He doesn't look wild to me," Mark said. Indeed, it was the mildest-looking horse he had ever seen. A chestnut, the horse was as old as Laura's and only slightly taller.

"Don't let appearances fool you," she said with a warm laugh.

A complete riding habit had been laid out for Mark in the vacant groom's quarters. "One of Daddy's old things," Laura explained. "You can change here while I go up to the house."

He had trouble getting into the boots, and the breeches were too short and had more than enough width. Laura returned outfitted in immaculate breeches and white sweater. She pressed her riding crop to a hip as she examined him. "You are a sight," she said.

They were riding together not too far into the woods along a cinder bridle path when Laura lashed her mare and was soon five lengths ahead. Mark caught up to her in an enclosure of gothic birches as quiet as a church sanctuary. He dismounted and helped Laura down, then tethered the horses.

They sat together on a grassy knoll with their backs against a moss-green log. Slender shadows of pine needles flitted against them. The damp air was sweet with the scent of pines. Mark put his arm around Laura as she shut her eyes and moved close to his side.

Later, after he changed back into his street clothes, Mark met Laura on the mansion's wide verandah. They were sitting in a hammock watching the crimson descent of the sun across the narrow Rayoodoo when Laura's father came out of the house. He was dressed in a tuxedo and was making an adjustment to his black tie when he saw them. "Oh Laura," he said, " I didn't know you were home."

Mark bolted off the hammock. Mr. Duquesne marched toward him, hand outstretched. Laura introduced Mark. "He's a graduate student," she said.

"What are you studying, m'boy?" he asked. "Physics? Business?"

"I'm at Divinity Hall," Mark replied rather sheepishly.

"Heading for the ministry are you?" Mr. Duquesne asked sharply.

Mark shook his head. "I don't know yet."

Mr. Duquesne looked up at Mark. He was at least six inches below Mark's height, but he certainly was much broader. He studied Mark for a moment. "Haven't we met before? Your name's Christopher? It seems to me I've heard that name somewhere. Not long ago either. Oh well. It's pleasure to meet you, sir." Mr. Duquesne was on his way down several stairs leading from the verandah to the driveway when he paused. "Don't keep my daughter up too late, m'boy." He laughed hollowly. "Got to get her beauty sleep, you know."

A long black Imperial crept up the drive, coming from the courtyard. "Well, here's Bromley," he said. "Good. He's polished the car. Will you tell your mother, Laura? That's a good girl."

Laura took Mark by the hand. "Let's go in and see my mom," she said. "I want to show you off."

"Not much to show," Mark said. "Maybe she's busy."

"C'mon. Don't be such a ninny."

As it happened, Laura's mother appeared that minute. She was dressed warmly. She wore a dark brown fox stole over her shoulders, partly covering a sparkling white ankle-length gown. Her marcelled hair was bluish gray. Laura introduced him. She flashed a dazzling smile and blinked heavily darkened eyes. "How do you do?" she said cordially. Her husband hastened up the incline, mounted the steps and helped his wife descend to the waiting car. "Good night, dear," she said. "Nice to have met you, young man." From inside the car she opened the window and waved a white-gloved hand.

In the mansion's vestibule, which was larger than his apartment's parlor, Mark watched as Laura inspected herself in a gilt-framed mirror of ceiling height. She ran her fingers through her wind-tousled hair. "What a mess!" she exclaimed. She took his hand, a soft touch, and led him into the formal dining room where the table was set for two with glittering silver. The centerpiece was a bed of pink and white carnations surmounted by three white glowing candles. Above the table hung a chandelier whose every globe was surrounded by fragments of cut crystal that spun off diamond rainbows. Except for the table area the room was otherwise shadowed. An entire wall was blanketed by a dark maroon drape with helter-skelter white lines running through it. Purple avenues flowed to curving cornices and the sculptured ceiling.

Laura insisted that he sit at the head of the table in a sway-backed captain's chair while she took the chair to his right. "Now where can Nancy be?" Laura asked the ceiling. She picked up a small golden bell and was about to ring it when she changed her mind. "I hate ringing this thing," she said. She set the bell down. She excused herself and ran to the other end of the room, opened a door and disappeared. Mark felt a distant chill. The dining room was really a banquet hall, a baron's eating place. Even the carpet, a plush silver, soft and deep, was uncomfortable. He went over to the drape and was behind it searching for the cord when Laura called him. He emerged sheepishly.

"What are you doing?" she asked, laughing loudly. "Playing hide-and-seek?"

She pointed to a button behind him. "Push it," she said, still amused. He did. The drape slid across the carpet, revealing an enormous oval window. The sun, like a huge balloon, dusted gold on recumbent clouds across the river.

Laura returned with Nancy, a handsome dark-skinned woman with a brilliant smile. Laura introduced Mark. "How do you do, sir," she said pleasantly with a slight bow. It was not long before they were served braised tips of beef and egg noodles. He picked up the first knife that came to hand and began sawing beef without result. Laura handed him another knife, thin-bladed and slim-toothed for the purpose. Nancy delivered sliced carrot cake. Mark was about to use a spoon but, just in time, Laura waved a small fork in his direction.

Laura suggested they go for a walk along the river. He wasted no time discussing her suggestion. He was on the porch waiting for her while she retrieved a sweater from somewhere in the mansion's depths.

As they descended to the river the sun dipped beneath the jagged faraway horizon and the sky blazed pink and ochre. They rested on a bench close to the quiet river. Idly, Laura tossed a stone into the water. Circles rippled on the calm surface. The plop echoed in the poplars whose branches leaned over them like sheltering arms. Mark, clasping his knees nervously, looked at this woman beside him, as if with a sudden clearer vision. Something alerted him to the awareness that he had found what had been his secret yearning, like a revealing dream. He knew her! She was the one! The last rays of the sun filtered through dancing poplar leaves, mottling Laura's wonderful features with flecks of gold. She was leaning back, her palms flat on her knees. Her white sweater, buttoned only at the neck, hung loosely on her shoulders. Her eyes were shadowed, but she was smiling, an angel smile. He loved her!

"So, what did you think of our house?" she asked him. The spell was broken.

"It's a great house," he mumbled. "I like it. I really do."

"You don't have to fib. It's a museum. To me it's a prison. I can't wait to get away from it. You don't know what it's like living here, being alone in the evening."

"You? Lonely?"

"A big house only makes it worse."

"I never would have imagined---"

"Poor little rich girl?" Laura leaned forward and imitated his position. "That's me." She laughed and shook her head. "But I'm a fine one to complain. You live alone, Mark. You know what it's like, don't you?" She touched his clasped hands. He shivered, but it was with delight.

"You learn to live with it," he said. But he never learned to live with it, had he?

Laura looked at him intently, but now the sunlight was gone. She seemed to retreat into the shadows. Night was coming on quickly. Mark peered through the trees but there were no stars.

"I often come here alone," Laura said. "I sit here a long time watching the water, listening to the birds. There's a mockingbird. There! Do you hear him? No, it's a thrush. But the mocking bird often sings here at night."

"There aren't any mockingbirds in Maine."

"Is that a fact? How can you be sure?"

"At least I never heard any."

"It must be nice there--in Maine, I mean. I've never been there. In fact, I've never seen the ocean. Were you born in Springport?"

"No, I just went to a two-year community college there. I was born in Westminster."

"Where's that?"

"North of here, about a hundred miles. It's a small railroad town. My father was a telegraph operator. He used to work in Boston. My brother and sister were born there."

And so it went. For an hour he told the story of his life. From time to time he asked her if she had heard enough. She insisted she was not tired. She appeared to be enthralled by the dramatics, by the touching, yet calm way he had of narrating his story, so that when he came to the way in which his father died, she was in tears. He was alarmed and grateful, both at once. She reached for him and drew him, as her eyes watered, to her side. "Mark, Mark. What you have endured! You're so strong." She released him. She dried her tears. She laughed a little, telling him that it was wonderful the way he had coped with tragedy.

"You deserve a medal," she said.

Somewhere high above them, probably on the mansion's driveway, bright lights chased away the darkness. "Must be your folks coming home," Mark said.

"I've got to go back," Laura said sadly.

He helped her up from the bench. He was surprised by the intensity of her response. She held him closely. Neither said anything for a while. Mark ventured a kiss and he was rewarded. Their lips joined intensely.

"I love you, Laura."

"I love you, Mark."

Chapter Twenty-One

Laura told her father she was in love with Mark Christopher. Her father went into one of his ridiculous fits. "No daughter of mine is going to marry a minister," he said, "and that's an end to it." He slammed the dining table. The candelabrums danced. "I told you not to go to that university."

"You don't have to shout, Daddy," Laura said calmly. She quickly left him in the dim dining room and flew upstairs. She flung herself on her bed and burst into tears.

Laura had grown up in this room. Her childhood companions were scattered here and there between the gaily papered walls, still bearing a few nursery images of angels and puppies. Laura leaned over to hug her favorite panda bear, the one with only one black-ringed eye. Her menagerie also contained a kangaroo, a monkey and a sloe-eyed deer, all remnants of happy birthdays and Christmases.

Laura's mother, Doris, had selected the room's wallpaper before Laura was born. She could never replace the original window curtains. She always swelled with motherly love and pride when she affectionately felt the soft organdy and vast blue ruffles.

It was a bright room, situated in the southeast corner of the house so that Laura had a free view of the lawn and the river. During a clear morning the room was flooded with golden light the instant the eastern sun dawned. Even at sunset it was beautiful when the south-facing windows caught the glance of the setting sun. There were four doors: one to the upper hall, two opening to her vast clothes closet, and the fourth into Laura's bathroom.

Except for her infant years, when Laura's cot occupied the space between her parents' twin beds, her room, her personal home, was the center of her mansion world. It was here, at her wide spruce desk that occupied half the wall beyond the foot of her bed., she did her homework, from elementary school to university graduation, and where, still, she placed her sociology books and studied for post-graduate tests. Six-tier bookcases stood tall on either side of her desk. The southern wall had no windows and was covered almost entirely by framed photographs, mainly views of each and every birthday party, from when she was four years old until the present year, a comprehensive record of her development from a small girl to a mature woman. Even so, there was a tameness about the pictures which stemmed not so much from their identical theme as from the intensity of Laura's smile. As each of the photos was taken, Laura responded with vigor to her father's command to "Say cheese!" Another similarity was that in each picture she was wearing a new dress, a birthday present from her mother.

It had been her parents' habit to mark each birthday with a party at which the three of them were the only ones present. An elaborate cake with the appropriate number of candles graced the formal dining table and it was always brought in by a shining-eyed Nancy and placed in front of Laura, whereupon her mother told her to "make a wish," and her father commanded her to blow out the candles before they dripped wax on the icing. With the candles out, it was then Laura's duty to cut three slices, and the remainder of the cake was sent back to the kitchen to be shared among the servants. Not until their meal was finished was Laura permitted to open her presents, each of which was expensively wrapped by the stores at which they had been purchased. A kiss of thanks to each of her parents and the ritual was over for another year. Laura would retire to her room wishing that this year her wish would come true.

She wished for nothing else than that her captivity might be ended. The birthday parties of her friends in the Rayoodoo section were always crowded affairs replete with parlor and lawn games, depending upon the season. Laura, of course, pressed her parents for similar parties but her father couldn't stand the presence of noisy children. When Laura was grown he couldn't see the point. There were so many parties at the Rayoodoo Country Club that a party at home would be redundant.

Besides, they said throughout her undergraduate years, she didn't have the time. A birthday in May was inconvenient since in that month she was studying for final exams. But Laura suspected that her parents were punishing her for enrolling at Attumwa University when they wanted her to go to Radcliffe. They had relented enough to make tentative plans for her Coming Out, which would be held in February of her senior year. In January she applied for acceptance to seek a post-graduate degree in sociology. Laura's mother immediately cancelled the Country Club reservation and thereafter meditated in the mansion library for three hours each afternoon. She was convinced that her daughter was destined to live in spinsterhood for the rest of her life. She expressed her outrage to her husband .

As for William Duquesne, he washed his hands of the affair. Laura had always been a clear-headed, sensible type who gave him little trouble. When he thought about her he pictured a little girl with golden curls, a Shirley Temple doll, who climbed onto his lap each evening to kiss him goodnight. That she was a grown woman simply never occurred to him. Certainly there were boys, so many that he lost track of them. They all looked alike to him, and Laura never confided more interest in one than another. When Mark Christopher came to the house that evening he was simply one more boy in a series of boys and meant no more than any of the others. If Laura's boyfriends had one thing in common it was their complete lack of ambition. One boy, he couldn't recall his name, was introduced as a potential YMCA worker. Another intended to study international relations and become a State Department servant. Still another, this one he did recall as thin enough to be ascetic, was going to be a professional poet. William Duquesne would have preferred an up-and-coming young man like Chase Drummond, particularly since a marriage alliance with the Drummonds would make sense in Attumwa. But Laura, when he attempted to discuss Chase with her one evening, expressed nothing but contempt for the boy. Laura was indeed difficult.

When Laura felt that time enough had passed for her father to compose himself she descended to the library room where she knew her father would be. Her knock echoed dully beyond the thick oak door and her father called pleasantly, "Come in, Laura." He was sitting in his recliner with his legs up. He removed his glasses, laid them carefully on the reading table and closed his book. "I'm glad you came down, dear," he said carefully. "I think we ought to have a little talk."

"Yes, Daddy." Laura sat down in a dark green leather chair opposite him. The library was her second favorite room, the first being her bedroom. It was a man's room, her father's private sanctuary, but he permitted her to use it when he was away. She had little interest in his books, which lined three walls to the ceiling, as they consisted primarily of complete works of the classics. Most of them had never been opened. They were mainly for show and her father readily admitted it. He had contracted with a bookseller to furnish the room with books at the same time as he had the entire house furnished, and did it with little thought. This was not to say that he did not like to read, for what he read was not on the shelves but in a case with solid doors next to the liquor cabinet. His books came and went, for if he did not like a book he simply threw it away. One shelf contained nothing but mysteries, another science fiction, and another current events. He could read one of each concurrently. He had no use for television or radio. He read The Wall Street Journal assiduously. He had a magnificent collection of classical music records which he stacked indiscriminately on the changer in a four-foot console. He was little concerned that he never listened to a symphony right through. Let a record fall from a Beethoven first movement to a Schumann third, who cares? He stacked the records in piles atop the console, for he had no time to replace them in their paper sleeves; neither would he permit anyone else to do so. When he was away and Laura came into the library for an hour or an entire evening she chose the records carefully and played them one at a time in proper order. The trouble was that many records from album sets were missing, since her father discarded records as soon as they became scratched, which happened with alarming frequency.

The flip side of Mozart's twentieth symphony was playing as Laura awaited her father's "logical argument." He entered quietly and immediately removed the record from the player. He cleared his throat and folded his hands together. Although it was well into the evening, he wore everything he had worn when he left the house that morning: tie, collar, vest, jacket. Even his well-fleshed bald features bore their morning freshness, for he had shaved again before dinner. Although his hair had receded an inch or two, it was, except for a narrow fringe, as black a it had ever been. The only thing about her father's face that Laura did not like was his mouth, which was narrow and thin, too narrow and too thin for his prominent, sensitively chiseled nose and sleek oval cheeks. His eyes, which usually glinted a commanding gray, were shaded to the warmth of pearl for Laura's benefit. He smiled often as he spoke.

"Your mother and I have discussed this matter thoroughly," he began, "and we have come to the conclusion that you are not to see this Mark what's-his-name again. Of course," he said with a dismissing wave of a pudgy immaculate hand, "we are in no position to enforce this decision, but you are a sensible girl and I am sure you will see the logic of our argument."

"Speak for yourself, Daddy," Laura responded impatiently.

William Duquesne laughed nervously. "There is no disagreement between your mother and I on this point, Laura. I know you like to set your mother and I against one another, but that tactic won't work in this case. We are only thinking," he added with a smile, "of your welfare, of what's best for you."

Since she had often been in this situation with her father, Laura knew that he was merely stating his premise. Her father had a logical mind, and could never understand why others could possibly disagree with him. That is why, she supposed, he was a successful business man.

"It's no use, Daddy," she said. "Mark Christopher is the man for me. I've decided."

"That is an interesting statement," he said coolly. "What makes you so sure? Has he asked you to marry him?"

Laura hesitated. "Well, no. But he will." She had to brace herself as strictly as her father because his stonewall attitudes were natural to him. He knew he could argue anyone out of an opinion that disputed his own. She could never admit, or even hint, that she had only tentatively made up her mind to marry Mark. But since her father would be the chief obstacle and not Mark himself, she would have to deal with the chief obstacle first.

"The principal reason I admire you so much, Laura," he said, attempting another tactic, "is that you are honest. I don't think you ever deceived me in your life and I don't think you are deceiving me now. So, I believe you. Now, let's get down to the basic argument. Mark Christopher is studying for the ministry. You know my attitude about ministry."

"You never told me. What is your attitude about ministry?"

Her father crossed his legs. It was evident he did not want to get into this aspect of the argument. The less said about holiness and self-sacrifice and dedication the better, because these were abstractions, and abstractions had no place in a logical argument.

"You take Pastor Fleming," he said. "He's a good man and has a fine mind. He could have been a good salesman. But he's warped. He thinks he knows everything. What is it about ministers that makes them think they know everything? He thinks he's a psychologist, a psychiatrist, gets himself in hot water with the elders all the time by spouting off in the pulpit about politics and race relations and other subjects he has no business talking about.. He thinks he's an expert in everything. That's what sets the layman against ministers. You can't reason with them, or be logical with them, because they simply aren't reasonable and logical. It's the seminaries that are at fault. They don't train men to run churches and preach a simple sermon anymore. They train them to spout off on subjects in which they have no more competence than the janitor. I don't know what the church is coming to these days with men like Fleming being allowed to upset everybody Sunday after Sunday. And look who he lets into the church, all those long-haired students who don't believe in anything and are even proud of being atheists. And besides," he said with an easy smile, because he judged by Laura's expression of interest that his logic was getting though to her, "the ministry is a waste for a man with ambition."

"The trouble with you, Daddy," Laura replied tartly, "is you think any job outside business is a waste."

"Don't be impertinent, young lady." It was evident he was feeling the heat rise to his face. He attempted to "maintain his cool," as everyone was saying these days. "There are many professions I admire. Law. Medicine."

"As businesses."

"Well, they do contribute a lot more to the economy than ministry. He paused and, to Laura's dismay, lit a cigarette. "That's probably too broad a statement," he continued. But it's the psychology of the man who wants to be a minister that troubles me. This has nothing to do with your young man, who, I am sure, is a very fine young man. I'm speaking generally. Ministry is like teaching. They say that those who can't, teach. Same with ministry. He couldn't make a go of it in business, at least not after he's gone though any seminary you can name. That's where they ruin a good man. And I'm not speaking without facts. Mr. Drummond, who provides those theological scholarships, knows what's going on, and he's opposed to it. He's thinking about putting a halt to it."

Laura caught her breath. "He wouldn't!" she exclaimed.

Her father noted her alarm. "Oh, I see. Your man is receiving a Drummond scholarship, is that it?"

"Yes, he is."

"And how's he to get along if he doesn't have it? His family has money?"

"He doesn't have a family. Only a sister."

"All the more reason for you to consider the financial reasons for not marrying a minister. They don't get paid much, not even the best of them. Personally, I'm opposed to that, and I argue with the other trustees all the time for a higher salary for Pastor Fleming, despite the way he's splitting the church. Laura, I'm only concerned for your welfare. You know I've always wanted you to marry someone of your own class." He knew he had lost the argument. To raise the argument of class was Victorian. No matter that he was perfectly convinced that class was a logical argument, it was lost on idealistic girls like Laura. "You know I'm not a snob," he said, attempting to repair the damage. "I suppose we have to have ministers. In their place. But I'm thinking of the life of sacrifice you would live. Look around you. How could you give up all this, a life like this?" But he knew immediately he had again said the wrong thing. He had wanted to use good psychology, but he had botched the argument. He awaited the logical rebuke.

"Well! At last you've come right out with it, Daddy," Laura said firmly. "All that nonsense about ministers in general. You don't want me to marry Mark because he's poor. Don't try to deny it! Every argument you raised convinces me that I would be doing the right thing marrying him."

Her father wearily reached for another cigarette. "All I want to know is, do you love him?"

"Yes, Daddy, I love him," she replied.

"How do you know?" her father asked.

Since the night she had sat by Mark's side on he riverbank she had asked herself the same question many times. All her life had been a planned sequence of events. She had never seen anything ahead of her except marriage to a man of her class, a man who would be astoundingly successful in business. She would live nearby in a smaller home and when her husband became a company president they would move into a mansion and she would give birth to four children, two boys and two girls. It was all pre-planned. But when, in her junior year of high school, her mother made the mistake of burdening her with the catalogs of Radcliffe, Bryn Mawr, Smith, Wellesley and the rest, she was dating an Attumwa student named Jack Schroeder whom she had met at a youth social hour at First Presbyterian Church, of which she was a member and where his father was a staunch ruling elder. Ordinarily she would not have given him a second glance, but Jack was a war veteran and had killed men in France and Germany. He was twenty-five at the time and wanted to be a doctor. But then the Korean War came along and Jack joined up and was killed. For weeks she wrote in her diary remembered descriptions of him: tall, angular body, eyes brooding with idealism, an earnestness and goodness beyond anything in any man she had ever known. She chose Attumwa University with the faint notion she might study to be a doctor, but since she was never much good in biology she knew she was cut out for something else. She had resisted her mother's defeated tears and her father's logical arguments. She became a student at Attumwa University, a triumph over her parents. Even so, they still told her she had made a grievous error.

It was true that Mark's poverty was an attraction for Laura. Many times she had asked herself whether she suffered from a kind of reverse snobbery. Perhaps she pitied him. In a way, she did, and that was because Mark did not pity himself. He was more fearful than envious of her station in society. Her world was not his world, but neither was her world her own. She had been born into it, and yet it was not, in a way, hers. In spirit she was more a part of Mark's world than her own. She did not have the slightest idea what kind of a life a minister's wife lived, but what did that matter? She was perfectly confident she could manage. What was important was her own feelings toward Mark and those feelings were difficult to define. She was physically attracted to him, and she was certain he was toward her. But there was something more: he was committed. This was what she wanted because she had never really been committed to anything in her life. She wanted to be committed but she had not found anything to commit herself to. If she committed herself to Mark she would be committing herself to ministry as much as him. Here was the difference. She could marry a businessman and be indifferent to his business. She could marry a doctor, a lawyer, or even a mechanic, and she would remain indifferent to her husband's choice of career. But when she married Mark she would marry his ministry as well. She had to admit to herself that she needed Mark more than he needed her.

Perhaps to avoid an unforgivable break in her inevitably lifelong relationship with her father, Laura felt she must reply to his question of how she knew that she loved Mark. "I think I can grow to love him," she said quietly. She said that despite her firm knowledge that she did love Mark. But that was not all there was to it. She loved her parents too.

"That's more honest," William Duquesne said. He felt he was making progress. Laura was indeed sensible. She had a good head on her shoulders. If he stopped pushing her she would soon outgrow her infatuation. She would be wasting her life if she married a minister. "My best advice to you, Laura, is to take your time with this young man. Examine your motives, girl. Examine your motives."

Laura returned to her room and dutifully attempted to examine her motives. She came to the conclusion that she did not have any. It was a dreadful conclusion to come to. All her life she seldom had doubts concerning her motivation. As a matter of fact she was contemptuous of those who vacillated and lacked purpose and will. She thought she knew exactly what she wanted. That is what her mother always told her.

"Some day you're going to discover, young lady," her mother used to say, "that the world isn't run to your particular desires and wishes. The trouble with young people today is they think they know it all. Well, let me tell you something. Don't be so sure of yourself. What you're going to get out of life isn't necessarily what you want. And don't ever forget it."

Doris Duquesne was not usually a scold, but sometimes her daughter got her goat. She could never remember the circumstances that caused her to give Laura a particular piece of advice but she could always remember the exact words she had spoken. She was quite skilled in reminding Laura of "As I once told you …" Laura remembered the occasion well, however, since it was the time of her first date with Jack Schoeder. He had escorted her to the Rayoodoo Country Club, where he was a member with his parents (Mrs. Schroeder was a second cousin of Mr. Drummond. Mr. Schroeder was at partner in the law firm Schroeder, Watkins and Raymond.} Jack had behaved badly by getting tipsy and staggering around the dance floor with Laura in his arms. The news reached Laura's mother before Jack unloaded Laura at the mansion. While it was after midnight it was not too late. Even so, Laura's mother was waiting on the porch.

"I forbid you to see that boy again," her mother had proclaimed. "I won't have a daughter of mine going with a man who's so much older."

"But he wants to be a lawyer, " she said.

"I forbid it."

"What's wrong about him?" Laura protested. It was then that her mother had scolded Laura as a know-it-all. Laura denied it vehemently.

But now, because she felt that she had won the debate with her father, Laura was certain she could survive her mother's scolding too.

Doris Duquesne entered Laura's room, offering her daughter's her nightly glass of milk. "Your father told me what you said about wanting to marry that boy," she said abruptly. "I forbid it!"

"Mom, I'm not a child."

"Well, we'll see about that."

In the days that followed Doris Duquesne kept her peace, although her mind was busy plotting the many ways in which she could force Laura to give up her ridiculous notion. In the case of Jack Schroeder, it had been easy. She merely phoned Jack's mother. But this Christopher fellow had no parents. She was at her wit's end what to do until one night her husband happened to mention that he had bought Modern Enterprises, a Chicago corporation which was managed by a man named Joseph Stanford, who was married to, of all people, the sister of Mark Christopher. A full-blown plot leaped into her mind. She told her husband what to do. He phoned Stanford, who reported a few days later that Mark's sister, whose name was Martha, would try to reason with Mark the next time she visited him. William Duquesne reported this to his wife, who made the mistake of telling Laura.

"Of course I think this puts an entirely different complexion on things," Laura's mother told her. "Since your young man's brother-in-law is head of one of your father's companies." She paused to regard Laura's evident consternation. "That still doesn't alter our basic opposition."

They were on the verandah waiting for Bromley to bring the Desoto around. A cold December wind blew strongly across the snow-covered lawn.

"Mom, do you mean to stand there and tell me …" But this was simply unbelievable. That her mother would go to such lengths! Laura resolved to leave home. A few days later she found a one-room apartment in town and that night she packed several suitcases and ordered Bromley to bring the car around. There was no need to explain to Bromley, but she did. "I'm moving into town," she told him, "and if you tell my parents I'll beat you."

"Yes, Miss," Bromley said, attempting to suppress a smile.

Since her allowance would no doubt be cut off, the next step was to stop attending classes and find a job. She became a research clerk in the State Senate Office Building and after a bit of shifting around was permanently located in the Senate library. When she had time she would go to a window and glance down at the promontory lawn where she and Mark had talked together that afternoon. But now it was the depth of winter and the snow lay hard on the ground. On the river a ferry butted furiously against the ice flow.

The following Friday she received her first paycheck. She opened a bank account. She went to the Westminster Fellowship at First Presbyterian Church for the first time in weeks.

Chapter Twenty-Two

"So you see," said Laura, "I think you'd better ask me to marry you."

She was quite out of breath. She had raced through her story, forcing him not to interrupt her until she had finished. If she had any doubt before that she loved him she had none now, because she had told him everything.

It was in Laura's nature, Mark presumed, for her to make such a lengthy bold accounting for her three-week absence. He had searched for her daily in the Student Center cafeteria. She had phoned him once, telling him only that she was unusually busy, that she had to study hard for upcoming January examinations, which climaxed her first semester.

Now, as they sat facing one another on the parlor sofa in his apartment, he felt as if he had known her always, that perhaps it was ordained that the awesome wonder of her was like a dream come true, a blessing no longer disguised, a revelation long waiting to materialize. He knew he could tell her everything and she would receive what he said with understanding and sympathy.

He held her gaze for quite some time and she did not shrink from it. Her eyes were blue with a hint of silver in them and they had the beauty of drifting summer clouds. Laura was calm with inner strength and her whole face shone with exciting promise. He recognized her as the one for whom he had been searching, although he had not known he was searching. And he knew she recognized him in the same way. They reached out and touched one another, softly at first and then more strongly until they were holding one another for what they knew, for what they were absolutely assured, was a life together, bonded for eternity.

Their kisses signaled their bonding, not only bodily, but also in spirit. They sealed their spirits, their trust, their faith that would enable them to surmount all difficulties, all defiance, all obstacles to their mutual and everlasting trust in one another.

Mark was caught up in joyful surprise. He felt an exultant happiness rising within him that was physical but which also involved him wholly and without holding anything back. He gave himself utterly to Laura and even his body felt strong in its resignation.

Laura entered his embrace with the full force of her body, as if she could give him all that she was. Although she was close to him, shoulder, breast and thigh, she could not get close enough. Her body felt surprisingly light, as if it was melting, and her head was going around and around and around.

"I love, I love you, I love you," Mark said softly.

"I love you too," Laura responded. "Oh, I do love you." She was surprised that she could love him this much, with a freedom and a total giving of herself that was utterly unbounded and without guile or cunning whatsoever.

They gave themselves to one another in ecstasy of contentment and fevered joy, as if their hunger for love could never be satisfied. And when at last they lay back and looked into one another's eyes, they knew that they would never again suffer famishment for love.

Mark could have laughed, danced, shouted for joy. There was no need for speech because everything that needed to be said had been said in the closeness of their lips, their hands, and their arms. Laura nestled contently in his embrace, knowing that this was shelter enough for a lifetime.

"Will you marry me?" Mark asked at last.

"Of course, silly."

"You will never regret it, Laura. I will make you happy."

"I am happy," She replied. "I always thought of happiness being related to something exterior to what I am. Right now I've never been happier in my life."

Laura tilted her head to look at him. "Do you believe I'll make a good minister's wife?"

"Of course you will. I want to marry you, but I'm scared it won't happen. Laura, I love you. So much. So much!"

"Then there's no reason to be scared." She sprang off the sofa, took him by the hand. She helped him stand up. "How long does it take to get married?" she asked.

"Three days, I think. We'd have to get a license. We could get one tomorrow." He paused, thinking. "We'd need our birth certificates, wouldn't we? To prove we're of age. I could phone to find out. Why not? That's right, why not? We have the apartment." He waved his arm, sweeping the parlor. "You can move right in." He looked at her doubtfully. "You can, can't you?"

"Why do you think I left home, silly? Why do you think I got a job?"

"Why, you plotter you! You had it planned!"

"To tell you the truth, I did. You don't mind, do you?"

"I suppose I should be," he said with a laugh. "A man's prerogative and all that. But I don't mind at all. I wanted to call you, to see you, but I thought it would be hopeless, useless." He held her close. "You being so darned rich.," he added with a joking laugh.

"Well, I'm not rich right now. I'm a working girl and I intend to support you."

"Like fun."

"Like it or not, you've got to finish Divinity School."

"What about your own career? I won't hear of you giving that up."

"There'll be plenty of time for that, silly. Your career is more important than mine. To tell you the truth, I really don't want to be a social worker. Two more years and you'll be finished and I can stop working and be a plain old minister's wife. I heard it's a career in itself."

"Divinity Hall has special courses for ministers' wives."

"I'll take them, when I can. And some theological courses as well. Evening classes. I want to be of help to you. But first I want to learn to be your wife. Let's get married right away."

"Aren't we forgetting something?" Mark asked.

"I hope not."

"Your father and mother. I have an idea they won't be exactly enthusiastic."

"To tell you the truth, Mark, I don't give a hang. They'll be as mad at me as all getout, but they'll get over it. Who do we ask to marry us? A justice of the peace?"

"I'd like it to be in a church, don't you?" Mark laughed. "I presume First Presbyterian isn't eligible."

"Hardly. Daddy would throw a fit. Come to think of it, he'll have one wherever we get hitched."

"I've got it! Anything against being married in a Methodist church?"

"Not as long as it's legal."

"I'll ask Pastor Woods."

Laura clapped her hands. "Wonderful. From what you told me about him, I'd rather have him than anyone else, even Pastor Fleming." She was silent for a moment "Oh, Mark, I must tell you something." She looked at him seriously.

"Oh, oh. Bad news?"

"Mark, I have to tell you. My father's firm bought the company that your sister's husband works for."

"I thought it was owned by the Drummond company."

"Well, Daddy owns that too."

Mark sat down slowly on the sofa. "I don't get it," he said. He was silent. Soon the portent of Laura's message struck him. He laughed heartedly. "Well, I'll be. I'll marry the daughter of my brother-in-law's boss!"

"More yet." Laura said. "Daddy practically ordered Mr. Stanford to see to it that your sister Martha try to persuade you not to marry me when she comes to see you at Christmas time."

"Oh, good and gracious Lord!" Mark paced the floor. "I think I'll ask Joe Stanford to be my best man! Do you think that will get me into good standing with your father?"

Laura stood by him, watching him fearfully. She began to cry. "Oh, Mark, I'm so sorry. My mother told me she was the one who thought up this stupid plan. I'm so ashamed!."

Mark held her closely. He was almost tearful himself. "Martha!" He practically shouted. "They don't know Martha. She has a mind of her own. She's not the kind that can be influenced by blackmail. And that's what it is! Using my own sister against me. Or, at the least, trying. But it won't work, Laura. Don't worry a single bit about it. She's a good sport. She likes to mother me. After all, she was the one my mother depended on to keep me in the straight and narrow. Martha! Good grief! You will like her, Laura." He laughingly patted Laura on the back and kissed her hugely. "Cheer up. If anyone can help keep us on good terms with your parents, Martha can, believe me. I can hardly wait until she gets here. We'll have a jolly good Christmas and you can ask Martha to be bridesmaid. Let's set wedding day, Laura. Day after Christmas, Boxing Day. If we have to fight the world, Laura, we'll fight." He hugged her again. "God, do I love you!"

Martha arrived at Attumwa Railroad Station three days before Christmas. She kissed Mark agreeably on his cheek and then held him at arm's length. "You look fine, Mark, just fine." She was wearing a coat of silvery fur with wide sleeves and a white box hat with a flimsy veil. He was startled to note that her black hair was turning gray at her temples. "And how is Laura?" Martha asked

He suspected that her question was her first thrust, but she looked at him with such genuine interest that he began to doubt her intent. "She's looking forward to meeting you," he told her.

"And I want to meet her!" She picked up the smaller bag while Mark handled the other two. They found their way to a taxi.

During the brief ride to the apartment Martha did not mention Laura again but confined her exclamations to the beauty of the snowy night and his progress at Divinity School. As soon as they entered the apartment Martha said "You've rearranged the furniture!" As he helped her out of her coat she added: "Where did you get that horrible painting?"

"Knock it off," he muttered . He was glad she appeared not to have heard him. The last thing he wanted was an argument. So far, Martha was acting true to form.

"I thought you'd at least have a tree," Martha said as she looked at herself in the wall mirror while removing a hatpin. "You still have the decorations, don't you?"

Mark felt another touch of annoyance. "Of course I still have them," he snapped. "They're under your bed."

"First thing tomorrow, Mark, you go out and buy a tree." Martha looked around the room. "Let's see, you'll have to move the TV to put a tree in the corner, where I always had it. And the sofa will have to go back against the wall. "You'll have to get rid of that painting. Where in the world did you get it? It's awful."

"I found it in your bedroom, over the bed," Mark said smugly.

Martha covered her face with her hands. "Oh my gosh! Oh, Mark, I'm sorry. What a ninny I am. I never recognized the thing."

"I hung it here just for you, Martha."

"Don't rub it in." She hastened to his side and hugged him tightly. "I feel so stupid." She laughed heartily. "That's a good one on me, isn't it? Please, Mark, don't tell anyone, especially Laura."

"No problem," Mark said as he removed the painting from the wall. "What shall I do with it?"

"Sell it. It's worth a lot of money. Keep the money."

"You've already given me enough, Martha."

"No, I haven't." She looked at him through teary eyes. Dark streaks of mascara tainted her beauty. She was wearing a black sheath which looked like silk. She had put on a little weight since Mark had seen her in Chicago but otherwise she was quite svelte and appeared as much a woman-of-the-world as ever.

After a modest meal of pork chops and baked potato, which Mark had prepared, they adjourned to the sofa. Martha held his hand. "Tell me frankly, Mark, are you seriously intending to marry Laura?"

"Yes, I am. You've come here to tell me I shouldn't do it, haven't you?"

"I came here because I've always wanted to spend Christmas with you."

"I heard that your husband was contacted by Laura's father."

"So I understand. Joe told me what her father wanted." Martha began to laugh. "Mark, you should see the look on your face. "You think I'm against it, don't you? Well, I was at first. I'm sure that Laura is a perfectly wonderful girl, and I am dying to meet her. But I was thinking of the years ahead before you get your divinity degree. I was worried about how you could possibly manage. But then I thought what a dope I was."

"We'll manage alright. I guess you didn't know. Laura is giving up her studies. She has as a job and her own place to live. It's temporary of course. Whether we can live together here, in your apartment, is up to you."

"As far as the apartment is concerned, Mark, I plan to turn the lease over to you. I will continue to give you whatever you need."

"That's too much, Martha. I don't want to be dependent on you forever."

"Hear me out," Martha said impatiently. "Joe wants to keep Laura's father happy, and so I. Joe's job depends upon it. There wouldn't be much point in trying to talk you out of getting married, even if Joe and I wanted to, which we don't. And Joe pointed out to me, quite frankly, that he could do worse than having a brother-in-law who was married to Mr. Duquesne's daughter!"

"Then you're not opposed to me marrying Laura?"

"Certainly not. She's a real catch."

"I wasn't fishing," Mark said grimly.

"Don't take offense," Martha said with a pout. "I only meant if you had to marry someone why not someone as rich and well-connected as Mr. Duquesne's daughter? In this case, what could be better for Joe--- and me?"

"I'm not getting married for your benefit."

"Of course not, don't be ridiculous. You ought to be grateful for what my husband is doing for you."

"What's he doing for me?"

"Well, he hasn't done it yet. But he will. I'm to telephone Joe tonight. Joe will report to Laura's father that you have thought it all out carefully but that you are a very stubborn lad and you refuse to give Laura up. I entreated you, I implored you, but you stood your ground. Love conquers all!"

"You devil you!" Mark leaned over and gave her a hug. "Thank you, Martha."

"I know we are taking a chance," she said. "But in our family, blood is thicker."

Chapter Twenty-Two

A latent snow hung heavily in the air as Mark entered the Methodist Church on the waterfront road. He held open the door for Martha. In the sanctuary Harry, the sexton, was standing by the lectern making last-minute adjustments to the linen Bible markers so that they draped exactly six inches from the Bible on the congregation side. The markers were yellowed with age and some strands were missing from the gold fringes. Harry failed to look up. He had not heard them come in. He left by a door in the chancel's rear wall.

Mark and Martha were walking down the central aisle when the overhead suspended chandeliers suddenly brightened. The sanctuary took on a soft still glow, yellowish and demanding quiet conversation. The chancel door opened, revealing Pastor Woods. He was clad in a clerical collar and a black gown.

"Ah, there you are," he said with obvious delight. "I thought I heard someone. Ah, Mark. Are you nervous? Don't be. And who's this?" He came close to Martha. "Why, my goodness, it's Martha. Wonderful." He gave her a gentle one-arm hug even as he clasped Mark's hand.. "Where's the bride?" he asked.

"She'll be along," Mark said. "A friend of mine, Ted Swain, is bringing her."

"And who else?" Pastor Woods asked.

"No one else, I'm afraid."

"Oh well, you told me this had to be secret, at least for the time being. I said I'd do it, and I will, but I favor a wedding with a big congregation present." He stepped back a pace. "Martha, you look lovely." He laughed. "I presume you are going to give the bride away? Of course not. You are the Matron of Honor, right? Okay, and Mark, your friend will be your best-man?" Mark nodded. "Shall we begin? Rehearse?"

Under the circumstances, Mark thought, the affair was being somewhat overdone, but Pastor Woods was adamant. "We don't want to be tripping over one another, do we?" He looked at his watch. In ten minutes the rehearsal was over. There was a scuffling noise outside the sanctuary's roadside entrance. The sexton opened the door. He turned to see whether those up front were ready. He stepped aside. Ted Swain removed his winter coat. He waved a greeting, turned and opened the door again. Laura entered with measured step. She removed her heavy overcoat. The sexton took it away.

Mark gazed from afar upon the vision of loveliness and love. She appeared to him to be floating down the aisle toward him, her hand lightly upon Ted's upraised arm, smiling, nodding as if the pews were filled by an appreciative audience and an organ was playing *Here Comes the Bride*. She took her place by Mark's side. She was holding a bouquet of white carnations. Martha stepped beside her. Ted, looking quite handsome, winked at Mark.

Pastor Woods stood before them, wedding service book in hand, ready. Ted felt inside a vest pocket, obviously assuring himself that the ring was still there. Laura was wearing a two-piece gray suit with wide cloth-covered buttons. She handed the carnations to Martha, looked up at Mark and smiled, a winsome gift of adoration.

Because he had envisioned himself a dozen times standing thus before Pastor Woods and listening to the magic immortal words which would make Laura his wife, Mark felt as an actor must upon speaking stage lines ad infinitum. Until noon that day his mind had been upon the arrangements for their marriage, including, most of all, their honeymoon. He felt equal to everything and somehow was able to draw upon some secret well from which he gained strength to endure the longing of the night to end, for the dawn to break, and his wedding day to begin. He did survive the night. He arose clear-minded, strong and eager for the morning to pass. Now that the day had come all doubt faded. He wondered what there was to be afraid of. He had lived to the day and thus triumphant over whatever fates had haunted his life---those same fates which had taken, one after another, those whom he had loved best in the world.

He stood clear-eyed before the old minister, meeting his gaze whenever Pastor Woods patiently awaited a response to a question. He felt his breath coming and going in its regular order; he was surprised at how regular it was. He felt strong, in his legs especially, which bore him well as he flexed and raised himself lightly onto his toes. He could feel his arm muscles tense and vigorous, and there was a curious tension in his neck which sent a shiver up the back of his scalp. His shoulders quivered involuntarily; he had never been more aware of his body. He glanced at Laura She was intent upon the words Pastor Woods was saying, as if she was deaf and she was lip-reading. In profile she was even more beautiful. She wore an eager alert calm like a bright mantle. He returned his attention to the minister, who was saying something as he smiled, and then Ted was touching his arm and passing him the magic ring. He slipped it on Laura's upraised finger and repeated words after Pastor Woods. Laura did the same. The minister pronounced them husband and wife. Mark said to himself, *I'm married! I'm married!* He bent his head and kissed her, a light touch, and then Ted, and then Pastor Woods. It was quiet in the church. The quartet retired to the pastor's study to sign the required papers, then passed quietly out of the sanctuary's yellow glow to the outside world of cold snow.

Mark and Laura said their farewells to Martha and Ted, and thanked them profusely. Martha would be returning to Chicago. Ted was going back to the university grad school after New Year's. Laura's car was nearby. Mark kissed her as she was about to unlock a door. "Hello, Mrs. Christopher," he said.

Laura drove down the waterfront road and crossed the river bridge. Mark felt a qualm as they passed over the place where his father had died. He gave it only a momentary glance. For some vague reason he felt he had been released from that dark image that often possessed his memory. With Laura by his side, his mind was free to possess the future and forego the past. His body felt very much alive in every muscle and every fiber, a strange sensation of strength which was like the feeling he once had when his mother took him to Stern's a long time ago to buy him his first Sunday jacket. He remembered going to the store's basement, where the Boys Department was located. He tried out many jackets until he came to the one with the Clark Gable back, like the one the actor wore in *It Happened One Night,* with pleats from the shoulders to the cloth band across the back. That jacket made him stand up straight and bold. He would flex his arms and shoulders like snapped cords. He became quite conscious of new muscular strength. His mother bought him his choice. He carried the jacket home in a box. He dressed himself in that jacket. He stood tall while his father and mother and Peter and Martha examined him and told him how grownup he looked.

Now the bridge was passed, behind him and nearly forgotten, as the Attumwa Hills stretched halfway across the bright horizon and the falling snow was brushed, swish-swish, off the windshield. He pulled down the visor and relaxed, admiring his new wife's skill behind the steering wheel. He told himself it was about time he learned to drive. Laura could teach him. The car moved on as if with a life and motion of its own toward the first upward slant of the road.

It was nearly five o'clock when they reached their destination, Monarch Inn. As they left the car in the parking lot the sun was setting far away beyond the Rayoodoo. The river was dark beneath the dying rays of light. They satisfied their hunger in the hotel's dining room among a joyous group of Attumwa students who invaded the hills to ski. Having eaten hungrily, Mark and Laura took a stroll on the motel's wide terrace. They prolonged their walk under a dark sky that promised more snow. They looked at one another with knowing secret glances and returned to their room.

Laura prepared herself. Mark was already in the broad queen bed when she came to him in a pink dressing gown, and, beneath it, a matching flimsy negligee.

The day before, when Mark had left Martha behind in the apartment in order to visit Laura in her rented room, they had hardly been able to keep their hands off one another. They had admitted their virginity. "Let's not spoil our first-night honeymoon," Laura said. Now, in the hotel, there did not appear to be an exactly appropriate time to begin. They both pretended that they were not tired. They were not sleepy at all. So what was the rush? There was no need for haste. Thus they lay on the bed, in each other's arms, for a while. Even so, when they were ready, it was impossible. Laura cried until Mark made a joke of it. Then they laughed and so stayed awake half the night laughing about their failure. The next day they rented boots and skis and spent the day on the slopes. In between runs they talked at length about her hopes for him, and his hopes for her. That night they were successful, at least as far as they knew. Now Mark truly came to know his body and the strength that it was capable of. While he had always felt strength on the surface of his body, now he felt an inward strength. It flowed through him, even as blood flowed in his veins. Since the depth of his newfound strength became known to him, he was not afraid. And this too: the strength of love renewed itself, and renewed again, and there was no end to it and never would be.

All of this had a center and a heart: Laura herself. While they exchanged the usual words and the usual physical tokens expressing their love, there was something stronger and deeper and wider that communicated itself in terms which made no use whatever of their other means. When he bought her wedding ring he had the jeweler inscribe inside its narrow band the words *Mark-Laura-Forever.* Nothing had happened in his life which he trusted utterly to go on forever, nothing except this one thing. He had come a long way and he had found her, they had found each other, and this was the meaning of forever. Whether ordained, predestined, meant-to-be, fated, or whatever, this was the meaning of this marriage. There was no need to ask questions about it, to reason why, or to suggest that he might have married someone else had that someone happened along. Well, there had been Helen, but that was long ago in Springport, on a day dark with parting, an impossible island which had never known the meaning of forever or even was meant to have the chance to discover it. Parents were forever with one another, and a brother was forever until he died, and a sister was forever. But how small was the golden circle which *forever* enclosed! Life promised a little or a lot depending upon its impingement upon that circle. And only that! Ever since his father died there had been only one other person, Martha, in that circle of his life, and now there was Laura. The polarity of his life had been dissolved, and as that happened everything outside the circle took on a new meaning and became related to the circle, but always everything outside was of temporal importance. Only within the circle was anything forever.

New snow had fallen during the second night while they slept. He stretched the lazy languor from his limbs. He opened the window. The cold air, which flushed the room immediately, aroused Laura. She sat up, making no attempt to cover herself.

"For heaven's sake, Mark," was all she said.

Chapter Twenty-Three

William Duquesne was, to say the least, not in a good mood when he summoned Pastor Woods to the mansion. Bromley rushed the old minister into the library. After polite chitchat about the latest violent snowstorm and such, Mr. Duquesne could stall no longer. "With all due respect, Pastor Woods, why?" He shook his head, indicating furious bewilderment, when actually he was embarrassed. His wife had insisted, to put it mildly, that he place Pastor Woods on the carpet. He paused and looked away.

"Why what, Bill?" Pastor Woods had been acquainted with Mr. Duquesne long enough to address him by his nickname. They had served together on a few civic groups, most recently The Flats Restoration Committee.

Mr. Duquesne grimaced. "Why did you marry my daughter to that divinity student?"

"Because Mark and Laura asked ."

"They didn't tell you that my wife and I were against it?"

"They told me."

"You didn't call me. Why?"

"It was none of my business. They are of age." Pastor Woods paused. "Laura told me that you didn't approve because Mark wants to be a minister."

"That's true. Laura and I had quite a debate about it."

"Bill, you're wrong," Pastor Woods leaned forward. "I know you don't think much of ministers in general. But you do have clergy friends in particular. Why is that?"

Mr. Duquesne laughed. "You got me. To tell you the truth---"

"Please do."

"I have nothing against the young man. He strikes me as quite a smart fellow. It's about Laura, what's ahead for her, money wise."

Pastor Woods beamed. "I have three kids myself and they're doing alright."

"Of course. I didn't mean that …"

"What did you mean?"

"Laura is our only child. She will inherit millions."

Pastor Woods smiled. "I'm happy to learn you won't disinherit her. Look at it this way, Bill. They're crazy about one another. She's not a runaway bride. Be sensible. Ask yourself, do I love my daughter? Do I want to lose her?"

Mr. Duquesne shook his head. "I love her very much and I don't want to lose her," he said quietly.

"Then go to them. Don't wait for them to come to you. They are afraid of you. Bill, listen to me. I've known Mark and his family for years. Mark is one of the finest young men I've ever known. Your daughter is very fortunate."

Pastor Woods could hardly believe it when Mr. Duquesne wiped a tear from his eye. "You're a good man, Bill," he said. "Do the right thing."

"But Doris …"

"Do you want me to talk to her?"

"No. Better leave it to me."

"Alright then, Bill. But do not put it off. You need Laura and Laura needs you, almost as much as she needs Mark Christopher."

Within a week Bill Duquesne telephoned Mark and Laura and asked if he could visit them at their apartment, where they were now living together.

"Hello," he said softly when their phone rang and Laura answered. "May I speak to Mrs. Christopher please?"

"Oh, Daddy!" She exclaimed.

They arranged for her father to visit them that evening. Doris Duquesne would have nothing to do with it. Laura said she would tell Mark, who wasn't in, and she would have a hot meal waiting.

There was no way she could get in touch with Mark to warn him. When he came home just before six, he could not think of proper words to say when Laura's father stood up to shake his hand. Laura helped him out. "Daddy's brought us a present," she said as she kissed him. She pointed to the table. A huge box lay there. Emblazoned on one side was the word *Microwave*.

"What is it?" Mark asked .

"An oven, Mark, latest thing."

"Thank you, Mr. Duquesne."

"Come here, you two." Bill stretched his arms widely. They sidled up to him and he hugged them both. "Listen. Would you both please call me Dad."

Laura laughed. "Yes, Daddy."

Her father grimaced. "I mean, Dad."

They rejoiced to have her father with them. Not one of them displayed a single iota of tension. As the three held hands in a circle Mark said a prayer of thanksgiving. They all said an amen.

Later, they talked together in the parlor. Laura's father told a few of his favorite jokes, most of which had to do with business faux pas. He said nothing about money matters. He wished Mark the best in his studies. He told them he would tell Laura's mother about his visit and assured them it would not be long before she "got over her current disposition" and they would all get together at the mansion.

Mark and Laura breathed huge sighs of relief when he was gone.

For the next several weeks Laura continued at her job while Mark attempted to assimilate the newest methods of learning theology and at the same time battle assaults upon his faith. He joined Laura in her renewed attendance at First Presbyterian Church, enjoyed Sunday services led by Pastor Fleming. They also went to the Friday night meetings of Westminster Fellowship.

The Fellowship was also attended by several undergrad students, who, having discovered that Mark attended Divinity School, turned to him to answer difficult questions raised during regular Bible study discussions. One question was: "When Jesus descended into hell after he died on the cross, where did he go?" Although he was annoyed by the question, he was able to provide the group with a satisfactory, even if ambiguous, answer. He was gratified that he was accepted as a Bible expert. Laura told him that he was good at "learning by doing," and she encouraged him to continue doing exactly that. He discovered, because of his amateur leadership, that the students were more interested in issues such as war and peace, race relations, sex outside marriage, and urban renewal, than they were in hair-splitting over the Apostles Creed.

Learning by doing was the theme song of one of his Divinity School teachers, Professor Campbell. His principal teaching assignment was preaching, or "homiletics," the formal name. Mr. Campbell concluded all his lectures with the same words: "Your preaching themes should always grow out of your pastoral experience."

Professor Campbell abominated "social indifference" in the pulpit. He once interrupted one of Mark's practice sermons to lecture him for muttering as his argument weakened. "When in doubt, shout like hell!" the professor proclaimed.

Whenever a student preached, there followed a fifteen-minute opportunity for fellow students to comment on the sermon. All were given a chance to comment because a comment was required. A majority of the class responded negatively. Mark considered some comments asinine, especially when he was asked "What did Paul mean by *thorn in the flesh*?"

It was a week later when he had a telephone call from Pastor Fleming, the one who had bugged him so much when he was being interviewed by the Drummond Scholarship Committee. The committee would like him to attend its meeting the following Tuesday. "Do I have to?" he asked tremulously. The answer was strictly affirmative. Mark said he would attend. But why? "Review of your first semester, Pastor Fleming said firmly. "Committee will be in session, so just knock and I will let you in. Come at four o'clock, will you? Same place as last time. Campus chapel." There was a moment's pause. "By the way, I hear you got married."

"Yes I did."

"Well, don't be late."

Laura was immediately fearful, although she attempted not to show it. "I'm sure it's nothing," she said. One of their first tasks after moving her things into the apartment had been to review their finances and fashion a budget. There was just enough between them to pay the rent, and buy food and clothing. "If we have to," Laura said, "we can always sell the car." She paused thoughtfully. "Thank goodness I have a job."

Laura had no intention of selling her car. She would sell her fur coat first. She really did not believe that anything serious would happen. "After all," she asked Mark, "what can they have against marriage?"

Mark agreed. "It isn't as if we had done anything wrong," he said uneasily. "What can they possibly do?" They were seated at the small table in the kitchen, where they felt strong and secure. Now, however, he was overcome by a strange sense of guilt. There was only a hint of fear in Laura's eyes, just a mote. He did not like to see her being afraid. He wanted to protect her from the world and its cruelties--she who had lived a secure and protected life. They could hurt him and he did not care, but do not let them hurt her! Then why this guilt, growing like a lengthening shadow? He should have told Pastor Fleming, but he had been afraid. He had always known that the agreement he signed with the Scholarship Committee required that he would need the committee's approval to get married if he wanted to retain the Drummond scholarship. Of course he could not fault Pastor Fleming. The minister was following the rules.

"I don't care what they say," he told Laura. "What you mean to me is more important than any scholarship." His voice had a hollow ring to it. He was begging the question. There was no way he could continue his studies without the scholarship. That was important enough. Even more important was his acceptance by the committee that he was a bonafide candidate for ministry.

For Laura's sake he turned their conversation to other subjects. The next few days were filled with a growing sense of doubt. And thus, when he entered the parlor of the campus chapel with foreboding, he still had a splinter of hope that the committee would accept him as a married man and let it go at that.

Mr. Elkin and Mr. Munro were at Pastor Fleming's left and right. Mark was asked to sit at the end of the table opposite Pastor Fleming, who was presiding in Chaplain Davis' absence. As if searching for the proper words, Mr. Elkin pressed his hands together, palm to palm, fingertip to fingertip. He tapped his forefingers against his thin pursed lips. He stared at a point on the gleaming table. Without looking at Mark, he began.

"I understand you were recently married, Mr. Christopher." His voice was tipped with irony.

"Yes, sir," Mark replied as calmly as he could. He found it difficult to speak above a whisper. He also kept his eyes upon the table.

"You were aware, weren't you, that permission of the committee was required."

"Yes, sir."

"Speak louder, Mr. Christopher."

"Yes, sir," Mark repeated loudly.

"Under the circumstances do you expect the committee to renew your scholarship, Mr. Christopher?"

Mark was silent. He felt the floor slipping from under his feet.

Pastor Fleming raised his hand. "Mr. Elkin, I think we may assume that Mr. Christopher would like to continue to receive the scholarship. We already have the facts in hand. What's the point of baiting the boy?"

"You would think," said Mr. Elkin, "that he'd at least do us the courtesy of explaining his actions, since they are so clearly a violation of the committee's rules. I consider his actions a violation of trust that displays a character fault."

"Now, wait a minute!" Pastor Fleming said loudly. "Such a conclusion is the prerogative of the committee as a whole." He drummed the table. "Mr. Munro, do you have a question?"

Mr. Munro adjusted his tight clerical collar. "I concur with Mr. Elkin," he said.

"Any questions, Mark?" asked Pastor Fleming kindly.

Mark shook his head.

"Then I must ask you, Mark, to step out for a little while. I'm sorry."

Instead of remaining in the hallway Mark mounted a stairway and entered the sanctuary. He sat down in a pew near the front. Like many churches on wintry weekdays, the sanctuary was very cold. He reflected for a moment that this meant wise economy but made a mockery of a sign on the chapel's front door that said the sanctuary was open daily for prayer and meditation. He felt even colder among the empty pews. He folded his hands and rocked back and forth, all the while gazing at the communion table on a dais. It was beautiful. It was made entirely of stone, the base of granite and the top of gleaming white marble. On the front of the base were the carved initials *IHS*, which to him meant *In His Service*. The front edge of the table top was inscribed *This Do In*

Remembrance Of Me. Some day he would stand behind such a table and lift the bread and cup. You had to be holy to do that. Only a holy man could dispense the elements of bread and wine. He prayed that he would be holy by the time he was graduated from Divinity School and ordained. But that was a long way off. There was plenty of time to become holy. He had thought that dedication would do it, that and steadfast purpose, an unswerving loyalty to the cause. But that was not enough. You had to know the rules and obey them. He had broken the rules and now he was somewhat flawed. It would never be possible for him to be holy, not unless he obtained forgiveness. But forgiveness for what? You sought forgiveness when you committed a sin. Had he committed a sin when he married Laura? Or did his sin consist of not having the committee's permission? But he never thought of that action in terms of sin, at least not until now. An unforgiven sin would certainly disqualify him from continuing toward the ministry. But a worst sin would be to give up and deny his calling. Without it, how could he possibly manage? Well, it was out of his hands. He would have to be guided by the committee, by his superiors, by those holy men who were already ordained. He went back to the hallway below and paced the floor until Pastor Fleming opened the door and called him in.

Pastor Fleming was alone. "They had other appointments," he told Mark as he sat down and opened the file folder. Mark resumed sitting at the opposite end of the table, far away. Pastor Fleming examined papers in the file. He drummed the table, then cleared his throat.

At last he spoke. "I have to tell you, Mark, that the committee's vote was unfavorable."

"Yes, sir."

"The vote was two to one," Pastor Fleming said, "to reject any consideration of a renewal of your scholarship." He closed the file. "That means," he said as he looked up, "that you will continue on your present scholarship through the end of your first year. That's the best I could manage."

"I appreciate that."

Mark rubbed tears from his eyes. He covered his face with his hands and dug his fingernails into his cheeks. He had to struggle to find his handkerchief. "I suppose I did wrong," he said.

"Nonsense!" Pastor Fleming struck the table. "Laura is a fine girl. She is absolutely one of the finest girls I've ever known. Her father is a stubborn man, and I'm glad to know he keeps in touch. As for her mother, well, what can I say?" He held out his hand. "Please come to see me, Mark. I have an idea. I think I can help you."

Mark shook the offered friendly hand. "I'm scared," he said.

"I know. That's natural. I understand. But don't allow this, what two men on a committee did. You will make a fine minister, Mark. Believe that. Come and see me. Give me a call."

That evening he told Laura what had happened. "I can't believe it!" she gasped. "It sounds to me that somebody doesn't like me."

"Why you? Why would you have anything to do with it?"

"My mother." Laura threw up her hands. "Well, doesn't that beat everything? This is the last straw." She strode quickly toward the wall telephone. "I've got one word to say to her."

Mark grasped her arm as she was passing by him. "No, Laura," he said. "That's not the way." He told her that Pastor Fleming had offered to help them. Laura agreed to do nothing until Mark found out what her minister had in mind.

Three days later Mark entered Pastor Fleming's study inside the long brick Christian Education building behind the massive First Presbyterian Church. Situated near the state Capitol in downtown Attumwa, the church had dominated its prime location for eighty years. Built of polished gray granite, surmounted by a forty-foot square tower, it stood at the heart of the Presbytery of Attumwa's extensive boundaries.

Pastor Woods rose promptly from a chair behind his desk to greet him warmly. He was almost Mark's height. He had a precise way of standing that revealed his military experience, for he had served as an Army chaplain in Europe during the war. He remained active as a chaplain in a reserve unit, which took him away each June for two-week drill camp. He had been voted year-long presbytery moderator two years before. He was currently chairman of the Presbytery's Ministerial Relations Committee.

There were two padded leather chairs in front of the desk. Pastor Woods invited Mark to sit down in one of them while he took the other. "Comfortable?" Pastor Woods asked. He observed Mark closely. He appeared to Mark to be "sizing him up," as the current slang would put it. Pastor Wood's bushy blond eyebrows raised and lowered. He was clad in an open-collar white shirt, minus a jacket, even though the study was on the cool side.

"You're probably wondering why you're here, Mark." he began. "I won't keep you long. I need your help."

"I appreciate it," Mark said as calmly as he could. He felt slightly chilled, despite the fact that he was warmly dressed.

"You don't have to give me an answer right away. But I would like you to give my suggestion serious consideration. Our denomination has been assisting a few nearby small-town churches who are struggling to stay alive. Starting during the war they have lost a lot of members, so many that they can't afford full-time pastors. They depend upon our Presbytery to assign part-time *Student Pastors,* as they are called. Some of those part-timers are retired ministers, others are Divinity School students like you."

Mark leaned forward. "Yes, of course. I know a couple of them."

"Mark, if I could help you obtain one of those part-time pastorates, would you be interested?"

Heart throbbing, Mark said firmly "Of course I would."

Pastor Woods leaned back in his chair and clasped his hands together. "You were planning to become a Baptist minister, right?

"Well, I suppose so. It seemed natural. Why?"

"Simple fact, Mark. We call our part-time pastors 'stated supplies.' So far as I know, they are all Presbyterians."

"Of course. That's logical."

"Laura tells me you're a Baptist." Pastor Fleming laughed. "And you were raised in a Methodist Church! Well, son, you do get around. I'm just kidding. But, tell me, do you have a strong connection with either?"

"I was immersed. I believe in it."

"Of course, but you were also baptized as an infant in a Methodist church."

"Sorry, Pastor Woods. I don't see the point."

The minister frowned. "Well, let it go. Here is my suggestion. Would you be willing to become a Presbyterian? No need to answer now. I must talk to Laura about it. After all she is a member of my church. And her parents too, of course."

Mark smiled. "Good family relations, I presume."

"It's a serious question, Mark. Take your time."

"Certainly would be helpful financially, I suppose," Mark mused.

"At least three thousand dollars a year. Quite possibly a provided manse too. Please, Mark, give it serious thought. As far as joining my church and obtaining Presbytery's approval, you have my vote. I truly believe you would be welcomed as one of Presbytery's ministerial candidates."

As they shook hands Mark felt that an unexpected door was opening. He always had the kind of deep faith that if God closed one door He would open another. He recognized the hand of God was welcoming him into another room, perhaps another way of life. After all, it had happened several times in his past. It is the way he was always guided in his search for fulfillment of his destiny.

A cold wind was blowing. It whistled through the high bare elms and strummed on power lines. Head down, bending into the wind's cruel bitterness, Mark plunged through the gathering darkness. Slowly at first and then with determined fury, it began to snow. He stood waiting for ten minutes for a bus. One came by, but it was full and did not stop. Mark pulled up the collar of his thick winter coat and plunged forward, tramping through the snow.

He told Laura about Pastor Fleming's offer. She promised she would visit the minister as soon as possible. Laura took his temperature. She insisted that he go to bed in Laura's room, which had remained unused since Martha was there at Christmas time. She telephoned the Duquesne family doctor, who called in a prescription to a local drugstore and ordered it delivered. Mark was soon downing a spoonful of the nasty syrup. He was sweating profusely.

Mark was confined to bed for three days. Laura took his temperature regularly, He did indeed have a fluctuating fever. Mark took his medicine every four hours. He had little faith that it would do him much good, and it did not. At the end of the week the doctor came in and tested him. He was a hatchet-faced man with flat back hair. Mark took an instant dislike to him. His name was Conrad and as soon as he was gone Mark called him Ramrod. He came again the next day, gave Mark a shot of penicillin and told him he had reserved a room for him at Civic Hospital. He was assigned to a semi-private room on the fifth floor and given the bed farthest from the window. His roommate was a corpulent man in his early thirties. His name was Tom Benedict. He immediately asked Mark if he had a cigarette.

"Sorry," Mark said. "I don't smoke." Mark was standing by his bed attempting to tie his gown via a cord behind his back. He gave it up and resumed occupation of his bed.

"You don't smoke, eh? That's a helluva note." He picked up a copy of Time. There was a photo of President Truman on the cover. Tom's face was as round as a platter with not a crease on it. His cheeks were so round that when he smiled, which was often, his eyes were almost hidden. He was completely bald. "What are you in for?" Tom asked.

"Nobody seems to know," Mark told him. "I'm here for tests. I had the flu, some brand of virus infection. Maybe I still have it." Mark turned on his side to face the window. "My bowels aren't right."

"With me it's my heart," Tom said. Tom pressed his chest. "I have a bum ticker."

"Oh, I thought it was—" Mark stopped himself from saying the obvious.

"Cancer," Tom said. "That too. Bum ticket."

"What are they doing about it?"

"The usual. Chemo. Doc says I have only one more shot. Just routine, he says. Routine, like hell! I've been here two weeks already. Doctors these days don't know what's flyin'. If they knew what was flyin' they'd tell me, wouldn't they? I'll be lucky if I get out of here alive. He says I can go home next week."

"My mother died here," Mark said, for no apparent reason. He knew right away that it was not proper, considering Tom's condition.

Tom gave him a look of dismay. "That's a helluva note," he said. "When did she pass away?"

Mark noted the religious connotation. "When I was eleven," he said. "Your mother still alive, Tom?"

"Yeah, sure. But my dad died." Tom pointed to his chest again. "Same thing. Runs in the family. I wish to hell you had a cigarette."

"Guess they don't let you smoke," Mark said obliquely.

"With my heart? 'Course not. Well, that's life. Were you in the war? I was in the Navy. Pacific."

"I had a brother in the Navy. He was also in the Pacific. Lost at sea."

"Too bad," Tom said. "You wouldn't have known me during the war. I was skinny, believe it or not. They keep me on that damn diet I'll be skinny again."

"Maybe that's your problem," Mark said. "Being overweight, I mean."

"Naw. It's congenital. My dad had it. Runs in the family. I'll live until I'm fifty. Then I'll go." He snapped his fingers. "Like that!" He looked at Mark acutely. "You married?"

"Yes. I just got married."

"Too much for you, eh?" Tom's whole body shook as he laughed. "I'm married too. Got two kids. Where do you work?

"I'm a student at Attumwa University." Mark hesitated. He wondered if he ought to tell a stranger. "I'm studying to be a minister."

Tom laughed, a deep-throated guffaw. "Good God! A godamned minister!" He looked steadily at Mark with grave interest. "Why in hell anyone would want to be a minister beats me. I'm an agnostic myself. So take everything from me whence it comes. I just don't believe in all that heaven and hell crap. In the war lots of guys I know got religion when they thought all that mumbo-jumbo would steer a bullet in the opposite direction. Knew a guy once kept a New Testament over his heart. It had steel covers on it. Said he'd heard of another guy once did the same and the Scripture saved his life. That's just so much crap." Tom turned toward the window. "If you're going to kick off, you'll kick off. Doesn't matter much when or how." He lapsed into silence. His big body heaved with a weak prolonged breath.

Chapter Twenty-Four

Laura completed her mission to support Mark by visiting Pastor Fleming. The only thing she was concerned about, she told him, was Mark's health. "How much can anyone take?" she asked.

Pastor Fleming was sympathetic. "I know, from my own experience." He was silent for a moment. "I know studying for the ministry isn't as demanding today. We're beginning to learn, from surveys and practical experience, that preaching is not the be-all and end-all of ministry. People are. Pastors are the shepherd. They must tend the flock. That is exactly where a minister's wife can be of most help."

"I agree with that," Laura said. "Some day women will be pastors."

"Well, we will see." He sighed. "It's still a man's world, isn't it?"

Laura settled back in her chair. "You know, Pastor. I once dreamed about being up there in the pulpit preaching away! No offense, I can't see any reason why it shouldn't happen. Not, I assume, soon, but one day!"

"Takes a lot of learning, Laura."

"You mean for a minister's wife?"

"That too. Lots of clergy wives teach." He paused. "In Sunday School, Women's Association."

"I have an idea, Pastor," Laura said. "I just this moment thought of it. I want to get some theological education. You know, Mark always talks to me about what he's learning, especially in theology, but it's all Greek to me." She laughed heartily. "Funny I should say that. It's only a common expression."

"Did you know, Laura, that in my time Greek and Hebrew were required both for seminary graduation and ordination?"

"That's one reason why Mark likes the university's Divinity School. Greek and Hebrew are optional."

"To get back to why I asked you here," Pastor Fleming said.

"Of course. About Mark becoming a Presbyterian. I'm all for it."

"I've been told he seems to enjoy answering theological questions. I mean, at Westminster Fellowship."

"He's got a fine mind, Pastor. He's really more interested in social studies, same as me. He knows his Bible, but for him that's not enough."

"Laura, I'm going to leave it up to you. I think he will fit in with us just fine. Tell him there's a church in Plato that's in desperate need of a pastor. I think I can pull a few strings. Plato's only thirty miles away. The Ministerial Relations Committee meets in early March. That's when pastoral appointments are made. And when Presbvtery meets next month he must be approved as a ministerial candidate, being taken under Presbytery's care. Under its wing, so to speak."

"Leave it to me, Pastor," Laura said. She laughed. "I can wrap that fella around my little finger."

And she did. Mark had recovered. Laura presented him with a thin book entitled Presbyterianism Made Simple. He got through it in an hour. Laura told him about the church in Plato.

"I always said I wanted to be a Presbyterian," he said with a satirical grin.

"Like all getout you did!" Laura said. " Who are you trying to kid?"

Actually his enthusiasm knew no bounds. What difference did the insistence on protocol make? There was a church, no, people who needed him. Not just anyone. Him!

The first step was to become a member of the national Presbyterian Church. That step, Laura explained, was taken via a local congregation. Pastor Fleming excused him from the usual process of required attendance at a six-week series of weekly classes for would-be members.

"I'm going to railroad you through it," Past Fleming told Mark when they met in his study. Fortunately there was a meeting of the Session, the body of elders, mostly older men, who were elected to rule the congregation in spiritual matters. The Board of Trustees took care of church property, budget, and such. It was complicated but necessary. The Presbyterian Church was ruled by elections, much like the democratic government of the country. It had books of laws and courts of justice too. Mark would have a lot to learn.

The Session elders, with whom he met at an evening meeting in the Board Room adjacent to Pastor Fleming's study, were more interested in him as the husband of Laura Duquesne and son-in-law of her parents, than they were in his former church memberships. . They were not interested enough in Pastor Gordon's letter to read it. One elder did ask, "Where in the world is Springport?" They endorsed him for presentation to the congregation. During the next Sunday morning worship service he was called to the front of the church where the congregation received him into "the fellowship of the church." He was now a Presbyterian.

Mark spent all day the following Saturday writing, and rewriting, a five-page Statement of Faith for presentation to a Presbytery committee. Much of it was autobiography. The remainder was his faith-based aspirations and understanding of what it means to be a Christian. Fortunately he was not required to reveal his confusion about Presbyterian law and order. That would come later.

Meanwhile, Laura's father had launched an investigation. He was prompted to do so after church two weeks later. As usual, he and his wife exited by way of the narthex. Pastor Fleming was shaking hands with departing worshippers. "Mr. Duquesne, good morning," he said as they shook hands. He leaned closer. "Bill, meet me in the study, will you? Yes, right away." He never called him Bill in earshot of other church members.

Bill left Doris behind to wait for him in the Desoto. She protested. "Well, you can always talk to Bromley," he said. He hurried back through the sanctuary and exited into the hall. He inspected photos of former pastors that decorated the walls. A photo of his bearded father was hung in the midst of several distinguished elders of the past. Although he was familiar with the words of tribute on a brass plate below the photo of his father, he read them aloud: "In honor of Bartholmew Duquesne, beneficent supporter and servant." He bowed his head. "Thank you, father," he said.

He heard a voice behind him. "He was a great man, your father," Pastor Fleming said as he unlocked the study door and followed Bill inside. "Sorry to keep you waiting, Bill. I wanted to have a word with you about Laura and Mark."

"They appear to be fitting right in," Bill said.

"Best thing is they're sitting with you and Doris. I presume Doris has eased up on her negative views of Mark."

"Well, she stopped making a fuss about it. So have I."

Pastor Fleming eyed Bill for any sign of reluctance. Apparently seeing none, he said "I'm glad about that, Bill." He picked up a paper from his desk. "Bill, I want you to do me a favor."

Bill blinked knowingly. "Who needs money now?" he asked with a jovial smile.

"Laura and Mark." Pastor Fleming waited for Bill's usual cautious response.

"Laura said they didn't need any help from me."

"But they do. Did they tell you that Mark's scholarship will not be renewed for his final two years, beginning in September?"

"That's ridiculous. This is the first I've heard about it. What happened?"

"I was voted down, two to one by the committee."

"But why?"

"There's a rule. Mark needed the committee's approval to get married. He didn't, even though he admitted he knew the rule. He simply forgot about it, I suppose."

"Stupid rule," Bill said. "I didn't know about it myself." He was thoughtful for a moment. "I'll fix it. Mr. Chase Drummond Senior is going to hear from me. It may be a company gift but I own the company! Let me get back to you."

And he did. Bill reported that Mr. Drummond had listened to his son, Chase Junior, who accused Mark of some fraternity mischief. In essence, he ordered Mr. Drummond to rescind the committee rule about marriage. Pastor Fleming telephoned Mark the good news. He would continue to receive the scholarship until he was graduated.

Time went by. Laura went to work every day. Mark passed from his second semester into hot summer months. He spent two weeks in July helping out at his church's Vacation Bible School, another three weeks employed by a Presbyterian camp for boys and girls high in the

Attumwa hills. Martha had promised to visit but she did not have the time. She and her husband were away for a month on a European tour. Mark heard from Carol in San Francisco that she had married again, a Marine who, she wrote, was away on sea duty more than he was at home. Her parents were doing fine. Her father was back to work. Young Peter was growing up fast.

In July Mark was able to buy a used 1948 Buick Roadmaster, still in good condition. Laura taught him to drive. He passed his driving test and received his license. His second year at Divinity Hall began. The Presbytery appointed him, at the request of Plato Presbyterian Church, to be their student pastor for one year. He was to be paid two thousand dollars for the year. He negotiated an automobile allowance sufficient to pay the cost of gas used for the benefit of his church. He met with the church's elders in the first week of September. He preached his first sermon the following Sunday.

The congregation was small, about twenty, the majority women. There were four children, all of whom departed the service as he adjusted his sermon notes. They were ousted in the charge of one of their mothers, who had told him "so they won't annoy you as you preach." He had been made aware of this traditional ousting, to which he had uselessly objected. More than half the pews were empty. Plato was a small town, no more than a village centered in agricultural areas of the county. The church itself, although located on Main Street in the middle of town, retained its rustic appearance. It could have been mistaken, at first glance, as a one-room schoolhouse were it not for a ten-foot belfry in which an iron bell could be clearly seen.

The sexton, Max Smith, a tottering man about eighty years old, struggled to pull the rope that descended from the belfry into the church's small vestibule, which worshippers entered through painted white double doors after climbing six worn wooden steps. Just before the service was about to begin, Max came down the aisle with a stars-and-stripes flag mounted on a six-foot pole. He planted the pole in a heavy holder in a corner a few feet from the pulpit. He saluted and hurried back up the aisle to sit beside his wife, Mary.

Mark felt at home. Memories of Springport Baptist came to mind: the clear simplicity of the authentic American, challenging the autocratic, unafraid to live close to nature's challenge and nature's glory. There was an authenticity, an awareness that influenced him to speak plainly, never in a derogatory fashion, but directly to their humanity, their needs, their defeats, their victories,

He cited Bible verses as signals, guideposts and not as laws or rules. They were all equal, undivided, innocent of guile and deceit. Certainly there was sin, anger, obsessions with both what was wrong and what was right, what was good and what was bad, what was freedom and what was oppression, what was conceit and what was innocence, what was work and what was slavery, and, above all, what was abuse and what was love.

They called for their favorite songs and hymns to sing. They sang clearly, from memory, *My country 'tis of Thee*, *The old rugged cross*, and *Until we meet again*. They sang as if they were love songs, which they were. They sang well. There was an old foot-peddled organ in a corner, but no organist to play it. Still, they sang and, standing now, cried for more. Mark led from the pulpit as well as he could. During the moments when the familiar words escaped his mind, he conducted like a choir leader, until Laura came up from the congregation and took over for him. She knew more of the words than he did. She sang along with her people, because they had suddenly become her people as well as his.

When the service came near its close, he prayed like he never prayed before. Magically the words found their way to his people and they said "Amen, amen," looked up to him as he rocked with pleasure and relief that the Spirit had invaded his spirit. He felt at home, as one with this fraction, his fraction, of humanity. They were his people and he was one of them.

He stood by the open doors as they lined up to greet them. The men shook his hand as if in gratitude. Some of the women hugged him. No one sought to praise him with "I enjoyed your sermon," and he was thankful for that. Preaching was not intended to be enjoyed. It was a celebration, a gift of joy, a measured sadness, an expression of love that can heal pain, suffering, guilt, loneliness and fear. Laura hugged him. "I love you, Mark," she whispered in his ear.

Throughout the coming months he endured Divinity School courses that appeared predicated on his ability to memorize incisively the placement of Bible chapters and verses, to describe the characteristics

of varied Judaic tribes, to trace the sources upon which the new
Revised Standard Bible books were based, and why the Apocrypha was
included in some older Bibles and not in this one. Might as well ask
him how deep was the Dead Sea. He did not care. He studied the great
theologians and the sermons of famous preachers. He was enthralled by
the witness of Methodists like Wesley who braved the wilds of Georgia
to bring the Gospel to the outlands and establish churches in their
midst. He cherished the old fashioned hymns when he sang in the
Divinity Hall choir. He admired those who had gone to Korea and
established Presbyterian churches. He studied church history in the
Americas. He bewailed the forces that brought disunity and praised
ecumenical efforts toward building brotherhood among varied self-
centered denominations. He was trained by a voice teacher to project
his voice to the rear pews and to enunciate clearly.

On Saturdays he drove to his far-flung parish to visit his flock.
He concentrated on those who lived farthest from town. He learned a
considerable amount about farming, especially about farmers who had
cows. He often wondered why Earl Brown, whose farm was three miles
away on a flat between two modest hills, was often late for church. He
found out why. Earl was always up by five to milk his large herd but on
Sundays it had to be four o'clock if he was to have time to bathe and
dress for church. "That's why country services always start at eleven,"
Earl told him. During the winter he plowed the Buick though deep snow
to watch a horse give birth. In March he entered a Sugaring Shack to
observe boiled maple syrup being ladled into jars. In May he mounted
a tractor to turn over the thick damp soil of a cornfield.

In July he received a telephone call from Pastor Gordon in Springport.
Uncle John Goddard had been killed in a fall off the top of an oil tank.
Could he come right away and participate in the funeral service in his
Baptist Church? Laura insisted that they ask her father to pay for the
airplane tickets. "I wouldn't think of not going with you," she said. Her
father agreed.

It took them all the next day to get there. After a flight to Boston
they took a bus to Springport. They went immediately to John's house,
which, they quickly discovered, had been electrified. Gone were the

kerosene lamps with their fluttering flames. Mark flicked a switch near the kitchen's outside door. The bleak room blossomed into light.

Laura gasped. "It's not as big as I imagined," she said.

"Appears to me it's shrunk."

They toured the house together. The upstairs rooms, except for John's, appeared as if they had not been touched since Mark left them. Was it only three years? Laura was interested in the bed Mark had occupied for two years. She laid upon the puffed-up blankets. "Not very comfortable is it?"

"Comfortable enough," Mark replied.

They examined his grandmother's room, the one in which she died. Except for the bureau and washstand, still bearing the heavy weight of the white basin, a lonesome chair, the bare spring bed without a mattress, the room bore witness to the emptiness he felt. She was family. Was she the last of the Goddard women? He did not know. Immediately he felt somewhat guilty. Did she have brothers, sisters? He tried to remember her maiden name, but he could not. Perhaps it was the shock. He could not even remember her first name, her Christian name. But, of course, it was Theresa. His sister was named after her: Martha Theresa. And so was he! His middle name was Goddard. He determined that, as soon as he returned to Attumwa he would do something about it. He would start a family tree. He would seek out some cousins. Maybe tomorrow he could search around Springport. He could ask Pastor Gordon. Perhaps some unknown cousin would show up for the funeral.

Springport had not changed much. Down by the bay they noted several men and women painting, their artist easels supported by tripods raised gingerly at varied distances on the rocky shore. One of them, a man who apparently was their instructor, told them that Springport was growing as a favorite place to practice their talent. "I see a growing art community here," the man told them as he waved a brush toward the calm blue water. "Could rival Rockport one day! Maybe Gloucester!"

They passed by the Community College but did not go in. They passed by the house that Helen lived in. She was only a sad memory now. He felt strangely that he could envision her features, but they were blurred, as if by a dim fog. He wondered if, now that he had found his true love, Laura, if one day he would no longer be able to envision anything but fog. They continued their journey through the Main Street shopping district. He recalled events that happened here---not here, over there, maybe somewhere near here. The hardware store that Helen's father owned was gone. Looking south beyond the bay were the soaring wide oil and gasoline tanks. A single oil tanker was tied up at the pier waiting to be filled, or possibly unfilled, who knew? Where was Uncle John when he fell? That one? Or that one? What difference did it make? He was gone now. He would be buried beside his mother in the family plot outside the Baptist Church.

Viewing time was scheduled for seven o'clock at the Travis Funeral Home. Mark and Laura had dinner at a small restaurant nearby. Laura remarked that Mark was unusually quiet. "Thinking about what I can say tomorrow," he told her. He looked at her fondly. "Holy smoke," he said.

"Holy what?"

"My brother Peter had a high school girlfriend that he brought to our house once or twice. That's what Peter said all the time. When he looked at her. That's what he said, in front of everybody. She was good looking, as far as I can remember. But she had nothing on you. Holy smoke, you are really beautiful."

Several of Uncle John's friends had gathered in the funeral home's parlor. One of them, a veteran fisherman by the looks of him, said he missed Mark's uncle because, for years, they played "craps" every Monday night in the back room of a nearby bar. "Lots of other guys we played with coming to the service tomorrow." Also, there were a few of his uncle's fellow workers at the oil plant. And, he noted gravely, a gray-haired woman dressed in black. She was also wearing a black hat with a wide brim pulled so far forward that Mark could not see her eyes. Laura was surrounded by a ring of admiring gamblers. Mark approached the mystery woman and introduced himself.

"Did you know my uncle very well?" he asked shyly. He felt a sudden misgiving that he had asked. He had lived in the same house with Uncle John for two years. They attended the Baptist church together, although there were many Sundays when his uncle excused himself. He said Saturday night was "My night on the town." Mark was often awakened in the middle of the night by a closing kitchen door and creaking steps on the stairs.

"Well enough," the woman said. She told him her name was Leslie Morgan. "We went to school together," she said. She would not look up. Her voice was slighted slurred. "You the minister?" she asked. There was a ripple of laughter across the dimly-lit room. The group around Laura was enjoying her company.

"Not yet," Mark said. "I'm studying so I can become a minister."

"Pastor Gordon told me about you," she said. "You're preaching tomorrow."

"No, just talking about Uncle John. There'll be others wanting to speak too, I suspect. How about you, Miss--- is it Mrs.?"

"Call me Leslie. Everybody does."

"Have we met before, Leslie? I don't recall."

She laughed meekly. "I was your Sunday School teacher, soon as you came here to Springport."

"That Mrs. Morgan! Oh, I'm sorry. I should have recognized you."

"Don't worry about it, Mark. My hair wasn't gray then."

"Are you still teaching?"

"Heavens no. I gave that up a few years ago. I'm getting tired. Let's sit down. There's something I want you to tell me, if you can."

They relaxed on a nearby sofa. The parlor was getting noisier as visitors came and went. Laura was still engaged by her enthralled audience.

"Is something troubling you, Mrs. Morgan?"

"Of course not," she said in a slightly irritated tone. "Sorry. Gets to my legs, standing too long." She rubbed her knees vigorously. "Ah, that feels better. Where was I? Oh, yes, your uncle. This is confidential, Mark. Did his mother ever say anything against me?"

"Against you? Whatever for?"

"Because of my, ah, relationship with your uncle."

"I don't know. I lived with them for only two years."

She gave him a highly surprised look. "Don't tell me you didn't know?"

He tried not to look irritated. "Know what, Mrs. Morgan?"

"That his mother wouldn't even listen to him talk about marrying me!"

He was bewildered. Grandmother Goddard had been, as Uncle John remarked more than once, "A tough old bird," but why would she have opposed her son, to say nothing of the fact that he was a grown man and free to do as he pleased? Mark shook his head. "I'm puzzled," he said. "What reason would she have?"

"Because Theresa Goddard was a dang stubborn woman, that's why. She was indifferent to the fact that John always came to my place every Saturday night after he had a couple of shots at gambling," She drew a deep breath, as if she was thinking she had told Mark too much.

"Is that all?" Mark asked. He was getting into something beyond his depth and he knew it. "Please tell me, Mrs. Morgan. I'm sworn to confidence." He knew that was going too far but he would chance it.

"Alright, then." She leaned a little closer to him. She spoke slowly. "John told me what his mother told him. She told him she needed him to work that little bit of land they grew things on. He suggested that I could live with them after we were married. She would have none of it. She said she wouldn't be wanting another woman in the house because she wanted to run the house the way she wanted. She was right there. She was stubborn and bossy to boot."

"And Uncle John said he couldn't move out?"

"He told me he couldn't because she threatened to cut him out of her will and, since she had all those acres back to the pond, he'd need to sell some land so he could have enough money to live on after she passed away. He knew Springport was growing fast, that more vacationers were coming in and building summer homes. His mother's land would go up in value in no time. That's what he told me and that's why we couldn't ever get married." She stifled an impending tear with a finger. "Now John's gone and I'm all alone. And I still have my own lonely house. Mark, why?"

"Why didn't you marry him after his mother died?"

"I don't know. He said he was used to life the way it was."

"He didn't want you to move in with him?"

"We talked about it. Pastor Gordon wouldn't like it. Besides, I liked my own house. At least it had electricity."

Mark did not know what to say. He really wanted to know why she was telling him all this. Was it because she thought he was a minister? It certainly was not because he was Uncle John's nephew. What difference did that make? Something in his mind, his awareness of where he was, a sacred place, and what he was, a man dedicated to a goal of future ministry. Mrs. Morgan opened her broken heart to him with secrets she could tell no one else. She had been compelled to live a lonely life by a selfish woman. She needed healing, not only because of the loss of her lover, her intimate friend, one whom she loved and could not have to herself, one whom she was compelled to share with another woman who had no right to enslave them both.

He held her hand. "Mrs. Morgan, truly, I was unaware. My uncle honored his mother, as he had been taught. I am only making an assumption. I really don't know the answer to why some people behave as they do, but they do, despite the suffering they cause." They stood together. He hugged her gently. He introduced her to Laura.

"One of my best pupils," Mrs. Morgan said. She turned her attention to Mark. " How's your Indian friend doing? I forget his name."

"Jim Pettaw, he died, an accident."

"I'm sorry. A nice man. He came to my class once."

"Only once?"

"Oh yes. At our church. Indians are not allowed. Nice to meet you, Laura. See you tomorrow." Mark and Laura left the parlor and entered the next room where Uncle John lay on white satin, eyes peacefully closed.

The next morning Pastor Gordon advanced to the lectern and welcomed the congregation to the funeral service. Despite prediction, the sanctuary was only half filled. Old tired faces were lifted to sing *Blessed Be the Tie that Binds*. Mark and Laura occupied the first pew on the right. They were Uncle John's only relatives to attend. Behind them were the few remaining fishermen, members of the church, who once sailed with John Goddard's father. Across the aisle John's gambling friends and a few oil company employees were grouped together. A dozen aged women, including a few who were too weak to stand, occupied rear pews. One of them was Mrs. Morgan. Mark presumed they were faithful members of the church, with whom he had undoubtedly worshipped at Sunday services for two years long ago. No doubt they had been mourners at Grandmother Goddard's funeral too.

In due time Pastor Gordon invited Mark to the pulpit. He introduced him as a former member. Mark cringed slightly when the minister mentioned that Mark had been baptized "right there," pointing to the space between the first pews and the raised pulpit where the baptismal tank lay concealed under the floor.

"John Goddard was not only my uncle but my friend," Mark began. "Friendship can mean many things to different people. They may be called pals, acquaintances, dear friends, dearest friends, old friends and new friends. But would you ever tell anyone you didn't like your friend?" He paused to look keenly, as if he was inspecting the congregation, singling them out. One of the older women in a rear pew was holding a hand to her ear. He spoke louder. "Of course not. Did you ever tell someone 'I would like you to be my friend,' or 'I would like to be your friend,' when you didn't like them? Of course not. I liked Uncle John, not only because he was a likeable man, but because he liked me. He may have told me so. I can't remember. But I knew he liked me. There was no doubt about it. I lived in his mother's house. He asked me to help him cut wood, dig potatoes, got me summer work at the oil plant." That received a polite murmur of appreciation from John's co-workers. "The thing is John didn't need to tell me he liked me. He didn't need to tell me that he was my friend. He told me by the way he helped me. He talked with me. He worked beside me. He was truly interested in how I was doing in college. He was interested in meeting my friend, Jim Pettaw, and talked to Jim as a friend. Yes, John Goddard was more than a helpful uncle. He was my friend. He gave me love, he gave me confidence. He cheered me up when I was down. He understood my loves and sorrows. Especially when his mother, my grandmother, died. We comforted one another. Even as Jesus comforted his brothers, his followers, like Jesus, John Goddard comforted me. Not only me, but many of you I'm sure. May John Goddard live in our memory and our lives forever."

Pastor Gordon preached. He talked about the afterlife. John Goddard was now happy in heaven with his mother and father. The service was adjourned to the church cemetery. Mark and Laura joined others in tossing bits of sand onto the descending coffin.

Chapter Twenty-Five

Luckily the old Buick started without a gasp. Mark drove slowly up South Street past the dark blotch of the fire station, the block-wide brick Neeby Foods plant, the Victorian red clapboard mansion of Claibourne Browne, the undertaker, with its painted turrets outlined darkly against the sky, and then into the gravel of South Hill. He shifted into low gear. The Buick spurted smoothly up the center of a dusty road toward the summit where the rising sun smote his eyes. The eastern sky faded from dark blue and took on a tinge of orange. Mark pulled over at the top of the hill and stepped out of the car onto the road's shoulder. The summit edged a plateau stretching for miles in a semi-circle. The immense valley below sheltered Castle Rock. At the very center of the town, which appeared to Mark to be quite small, rose a square tower and white spire that surmounted Mark's new church, barely visible through a rising mist. On all sides of Castle Rock, stretching to dim horizons, lay vast farms framed by a maze of strait dirt roads running both east to west and north to south. Here and there racing pickup trucks trailed clouds of dust. Far back from the roads, amid groves of trees, tops of lonely farmhouses and barns sparkled brightly.

It was mid-summer. Sheltering elms and poplars hid the manse, his new home, but Mark could make out the church's stained-glass window which lit the stairway leading to his study. Below the tower two white Corinthian columns supported the porch roof that covered the main entrance to the sanctuary. This was his new church. This Sunday morning he would preach again before his new flock. He knelt on the soft damp grass. He prayed that God would find him worthy of the gift. Although he was still a student he had been given this charge.

The Castle Rock Presbyterian congregation had triple the number of Plato's members. It was a town church but many of his people lived on the surrounding hills of Chesterton county. He thanked God for Laura, his partner in ministry. He thanked God for the manse, their first real home. He asked God to bless his people, his new flock, and make him worthy to bring the gospel message of trust and truth. His people would be waiting for him, to bring them a message of hope and love, a message that would truly help them through days of trouble and tribulation. "Thank you, Lord," he said as he rose up.

A month before, Pastor Fleming himself had met with the elders. He promised them that Mark Christopher would be "a right fit" for their ministerial need. He was mature, he was experienced. Laura was a great "helpmate" as the Bible promised. He asked them to request that Mark be appointed their student pastor. They said they would seriously consider it, but first they wanted to meet this man and his wife. Most of all they wanted to hear him preach. They termed this "preaching for a call," the same as when the church had enough members to afford a full-time ordained clergyman. Some would have liked an older man, such as an experienced retired minister. They were the last to vote in favor of, at least, hearing Mark before they would vote in favor of the appointment.

Mark had preached about the meaning of the Church as a means of grace. "See those flowers," he said, pointing to a vase of mountain columbine atop the Communion table, "No creature hand can raise a flower from the dark soil. No man-made promise of life again can cause a seed to flower in its season." As he had been taught, he made his "significant pause." He surveyed the pews. "No!" he thundered. "Only God can raise from this circling planet, a mere speck poised in His creation, those whom He has made in His image."

Tightening his grip on the pulpit, he felt secure. He began to feel a familiar sequence of sensations which always came when he lost himself in his preaching. It was like being on a train, going on a long journey, and watching signals flash by. The signals told him when to make the significant pause, the exclamation of warning, the probing illustration to illuminate a point, the exhortation of caution, the hiss of scorn, the twin-pronged thrust of paradox and dilemma, which he had learned from Professor Masters. He drove his sermon forward on high ringing bridges of affirmation, twisted it through haunted valleys of doubt, affirming ties that bind, stopped at stations of the Cross, all the while rolling along on the worn webbed rails of allusion, allegory and parable.

"This is the promise," he had continued with a glance over the heads of his people intended to sweep away every doubt, "The promise is made this day, the promise that God holds forth to you and to me the greatest gift—life eternal!" Suddenly he had stopped preaching. The next sublime words he wanted to say, the words he thought his people waited to hear, escaped him. During his silence there was a ruffle of annoyance throughout his audience. They waited patiently, silently, anxiously, to hear what could only be his concluding appeal for righteousness, because that is what they were accustomed to hear. All Mark could think of saying was: "Let us pray." Mark knew that his people had come to hear the Word of God, but he had given them stones instead of bread. However, the elders liked the sermon. They voted to ask Presbytery to appoint him as their student pastor. They were aware that only an ordained minister could conduct the sacraments of Communion and Baptism. Pastor Fleming had instructed the elders to obtain the service of an ordained minister for that function.

The next week Laura came with him to open the manse, a white frame house across the street from the church. It was simply furnished. From their Attumwa apartment they brought bedding and clothing sufficient for weekend use. Mark's Divinity Hall classes, beginning in September, would be limited to Tuesday through Thursday. He would serve his new church on Friday through Monday. Laura would quit her job as soon as she could. Her father increased her allowance. She understood Mark's insistence that he needed her but that he also needed the field experience in order to pass examinations for his last two semesters.

Mark visited his people where they lived and worked. Before the end of July he knew them. When they came to church he knew them. When he looked upon them in the pews he almost knew what they were thinking: Orson Coffey was thinking about the cow that had the colic; Ruth Neeby was wishing it wouldn't rain, as forecast, because rain would ruin her afternoon trade at her tavern; Mrs. Garson was thinking about the spasm of pain that was constantly in her side; Mary and Fred Lewis were both thinking about Mary's chronic tiredness; Steve Roberts was wondering how to avoid becoming an alcoholic; Larry and Joann Bryson were thinking about Joann's mental condition, for she had recently been very depressed; Howie Mason, sitting beside his wife, Lucille, was blaming himself that his wife was childless; Mrs. Lincoln felt as if her dead husband, who sat beside her in the same pew for forty years, was still beside her; and Blinko Crowley was wondering if he ought to marry Claudia, with whom he was living.

He saw and heard Duane Roberts cough; Cincy Zenkorski looked evilly at her brother, Joe, who was cuddled to their mother's lap, while her father, Abner, who hadn't been to church since Easter, looked as if he was asleep; Lucius Levoning sneezed and was thinking about the possibility of promotion from his position as teller at the Chesterton National Bank; Cray Brown, whose real first name was Creighton, his mother's maiden name, stole a glance at Cincy, and Cincy smiled back; Lemuel Orduff was thinking about the strike at the Chesterton Steel Company and wondering if it would ever end and he could return to work; Russ Neeby, president of Neeby Foods and Ruth's father, was hoping that Mark would end his sermon on time because he had to catch a plane to Chicago; Harry Ironwood was really sleeping, despite the jabbing that his wife was giving him; and Sarah Shamley, the librarian, was counting the members of the church whose books were overdue.

The choir was singing an anthem while Mark took notice of sunshine piercing the stained glass windows on the east side of the sanctuary. Images of a burning bush, a dove and a laurel wreath dwelt timidly upon his people. Leaded shadows crossed themselves on uplifted faces. Suddenly he observed for the first time that all the faces were white. This fact of their single color had never concerned him before. He immediately knew the reason. That afternoon he would be preaching for the first time to a new flock at Doug Bryson's migrant camp.

The day before, as he was polishing the Buick in the driveway behind the manse, a pickup truck had paused at the curb. The driver, a husky Negro who identified himself as Buck Washington, introduced himself. He was the migrant crew chief at the big Bryson farm, the Xenophon. He had asked if Mark could come to the camp the next afternoon to preach. Mark consented without asking details. Laura thought it was a good thing to do.

The final hymn was sung. Mark closed the service with prayer. He raised his arms and said the benediction, and as his people sat down to pray silently, he walked up the center aisle to the narthex, where he shook every hand. Lillian Ironwood handed him his weekly pay check. Some remarked "Good sermon, Mark," and some said "I enjoyed your sermon very much." When all had left, Mark climbed the stairway from the narthex to his study, which was located under the belfry and outside a sanctuary balcony for which there was no need but which had no doubt been used many years before. The congregation was founded a century ago and the present church was built sixty years before. Mark had read a history of the church. In the early nineteen hundreds the church had two hundred and fifty members. He removed his gown, which he had borrowed from the choir, removed his tie, put on his "loafing around" sweater and crossed Main street to have lunch with Laura in the manse.

That afternoon, driving on the road toward Chesterton, two miles from Castle Rock, Mark turned his Buick onto a gravel road. He passed by the two-story green-gabled Bryson house. He turned west on a dirt road that kicked up a cloud of dust. There was the migrant camp: a wooden bunkhouse stretching two hundred feet or more opposite a huge red barn.

He parked the Buick back of the barn. Laura came with him as he walked into the yard between the two buildings. Buck Washington came out of the bunkhouse. Mark introduced Laura. Buck was at least five inches taller than six feet. He moved with easy grace. He had the breadth of shoulder and the thickness of chest and arms to go with his height. Shifting from one foot to the other, Buck seemed shy and self-conscious, a sharp contrast to his appearance the day before when he spoke boldly and had even seemed slightly condescending. Now, however, Buck refused to lift his eyes from the ground. He kept his hands in the back pockets of his blue jeans. Buck was a very dark Negro. Mark's father would have said "Black as the ace of spades." The day before, Buck had not hesitated to shake Mark's hand. Now, when Mark said simply, "Hi, Buck," slipping into an easy familiarity, Buck appeared fearful.

"I would like you to meet my wife," Mark said.

Still, Buck would not look up. He kept looking at the ground until Laura put out her hand. Even so, Buck gave her hand only a quick touch. By this time they were surrounded by a full circle of the migrant workers. There were about forty, men, women and children. They came quietly across the yard from the bunkhouse and almost, it seemed to Mark, from out of the nearby thicket of trees. The migrants stared at their visitors with passive curious eyes. Mark held Laura's hand. Several laughing, smiling children circled around them. Laura bend down and reached out to one of them, a shy, hesitant girl who, one finger between her lips, touched Laura's hand and gazed up at her with wondrous eyes. Laura picked her up and kissed the little one's cheek. The child hugged her.

Mark had the feeling that he was being examined like a strange specimen. He was in a strange land with strange people. Buck was silent. Mark knew he was waiting for him to say something to them all.

"Hello, everybody," he said at last, loudly enough to be heard by all of the expectant eager people surrounding him. He made a friendly gesture with his right hand, not quite a wave, but a greeting. Not knowing what else to do with his hand, which hung for an awkward moment suspended in the crisp summer air, he clasped his hands behind his back. "I'm very glad to meet all of you," he said awkwardly. "I want to know all of you, personally." Not a dull, perplexed expression changed. Mark wished he could get behind something solid, like a pulpit. "I'd like you to meet my wife. Laura, would you like to say something?"

Laura smiled distantly. All she could think of saying was what Mark had said. "Hello everybody," she cried out dryly. She was wearing the simple three-button tan coat she had bought at Sears Roebuck the week before. She felt she was overdressed. Compared to her, the migrants were wearing rags. On clearer inspection, however, she saw that their clothing was clean and well-mended. The women's dresses were of every hue, faded but neatly pressed. The children especially looked scrubbed and polished and the girls had neat red ribbons all over their heads. "I would like to meet everyone," she told the crowd. She turned to the person closest to her, a tall woman with snow-white hair.

"Hi," Laura said, offering a friendly hand. "My name is Laura."

The woman backed away. Laura looked to Buck for help. "Her name is Beulah," Buck said. "My wife's mother." He turned toward the older woman. "Come on, Maw, she won't bite you." Beulah bowed slightly and slowly shook Laura's proffered hand. Buck introduced Laura to his wife, Naomi, who smiled broadly. Naomi was pregnant. A couple of months to go, Laura figured.

Mark and Laura went around the circle shaking every hand, including those of the children, who were not nearly as shy as their elders. One little girl who told them her name was Thistle clung to Laura's leg and refused to let go until her mother pulled her away. She immediately began to cry but stopped when Laura picked her up and patted the ribbons on her hair. The girl hugged her hugely.

Everyone sat down where they could, on upended crates, rocks and lengthy logs. They began to sing *Steal Away to Jesus*. Laura sat down on a wooden box that Buck placed for her. Thistle joined her. Seated on the sandy ground, Thistle looked up at Laura with quiet curiosity. Laura lowered her hand to Thistle's shoulder. Buck sat on a log between Naomi and Beulah.

Mark stood in the focus of their semi-circle. He took a small Bible from his jacket pocket and opened it tremulously. He said a silent prayer to stem a rising sense that he was inadequate to the task before him. The Bible was a morocco-bound King James version that Laura had given him. It was both a Christmas and a wedding present. He read the resurrection story from Luke's gospel. His sermon was a straight exposition of the text, as it had been in church that morning, but now he felt new freedom. There was nothing between him and this new congregation, neither pulpit nor pew.

"Jesus was raised from the dead," he said, "to show us there is life after death."

"Amen!" someone shouted.

Startled, Mark felt a shiver down the nape of his neck. He preached as he had never preached before. His new flock seemed to drink in every word, as if every word he uttered was the most important word they had ever heard. Soon each of his sentences was punctuated with a cry of "Amen!" or "Praise Jesus!" He felt as though he could preach forever. The responses mounted. Beulah stood up and performed a little dance. She kicked up dust from the sandy yard. Everyone began to clap in rhythm. His sermon, whether he liked it or not, was finished. Mark joined Laura in the innocent joy of praising God by clapping.

His newfound people were still clapping and dancing as Buck came over and invited Mark and Laura to see the camp. He led them into the clapboard bunkhouse. The long interior was divided into seven cubicles along one side of the interior, leaving a narrow corridor on the other side for access to the cubicles, which were divided from each other by one-inch-thick board walls. Buck opened the door to the first cubicle. Made of three widely-spaced planks, the door opened on creaking hinges to reveal, along the walls, two tiers of bunks, three bunks to a tier. A ladder was nailed to each tier. The walls that separated the cubicles did not reach the building's flat roof. Each bunk was outfitted with a straw ticking, a thin pillow and a single faded blanket, all laid on rough boards. Along the wall, left of the door, was a row of crates of various sizes which contained shirts, jeans and other clothing. By the other wall was a small table, about three-feet square, covered by cracked oilcloth. The table was piled high with an assortment of dishes and an oil lamp. There were three chairs with spindle backs, the residue of different kitchens. The room smelled of sweat and urine. The walls were the reverse sides of the building's outer walls. Daylight streamed between the wall planks throughout the building. There were no windows. The floor, made of unpainted pine boards, was worn smooth, except for areas close to the bunks that were full of splinters. Buck explained that families were kept together as much as possible. Children slept two to a bunk.

The clapping and dancing had stopped. Except for Beulah and Naomi, who were tending a fire under a steaming kettle, the yard was deserted. Laura joined the women in the barn attending to their duties of sorting potatoes into various bins. Some children were with them. Others who were older went into the fields or woods to play. Mark went with Buck to examine the outhouses behind the shack. There were three two-seat lean-tos set against the bunker's rear wall.

"It seems to me," Mark said, seeking to control his rising sense of outrage, "you should have something better than this."

"Mr. Bryson had them built last year," Buck told him. "You should have seen what we had before."

"Do you depend upon Mr. Bryson for everything?"

"Except for what we get from the churches. Once in a while the county nurse, Miss Herkimer, comes out."

"What happens if someone gets really sick?"

"We manage best we can. Oh, you're thinking about the hospital. None of us allowed there, at least to stay. An accident, that's different."

"I was thinking of a baby being born."

Buck grinned. "You know Doctor Roach? He's the county doctor. He comes out. Him and Miss Herkimer. They arrange everything."

"So I've seen," Mark said. "Is there anything I can do, in addition to the Sunday services?"

"A couple of years ago we had movies on Tuesday nights."

"Would you like me to show movies?"

"We'd be much obliged."

"Well, I'll have to see Mr. Bryson and ask his permission. Will you go with me, Buck?"

Buck laughed. "You don't know Mr. Bryson very well. That man, he'll give you a hard time. You want to, tell him we need a generator for electricity. You'll need one to run the movies. But don't expect nothin' from Mr. Bryson."

Before going to see Sam Bryson, Mark led the regular Sunday evening meeting of the Young People's Society at the church. Eight members showed up. Mark showed a filmstrip and led a brief discussion. It was only eight o'clock, a half hour before the usual time, when he adjourned the meeting. Lester Ironwood, Harry's son, led the march to the soda fountain across Main Street. Mark stopped Jenny Glen at the door and asked if she would sing a solo at church next Sunday. Jenny, a remarkably pretty brunette, agreed. "Then don't forget rehearsal Friday night," he called after her. Ted Gore, whose mother, Margaret, operated a laundry in town, tried to hold Jenny's hand but she shrugged him off. Cray Browne had better luck with Cincy Zenkorski, however, which made Mark worry about them. They were inseparable. Mark hoped they would get through high school before, as Laura once said, "getting into trouble." Mark hurried through the church turning off the lights. He paused a moment in the darkness of the sanctuary to absorb its quietness and peace, then quickly went out, locking the front door behind him.

He returned to the manse and telephoned Sam Bryson to ask him if he could drop by. Sam grumped a little, then said "Okay, come on over." Laura objected but he told her he would not be long. "You'll wear yourself out," she said.

Mark halted the Buick below the white-columned porch of Sam's house. He strode up the path with head high and shoulders square. All the way from Castle Rock he thought about what he would say to Sam, but now the moment had arrived and he knew that nothing he had planned would work out. He had talked too often with Sam and had seen him in action too much at Session meetings to anticipate an easy acceptance of a proposal regarding the migrants. Not that Sam was not generous. After all, he had offered to make up the church's annual deficit. The point was, as everyone knew, Sam could not tolerate interference in the affairs of Xenophon Farm.

On the porch, Sam offered Mark a wicker rocking chair next to his, then a cigar. Mark put the cigar in a pocket. He was relieved that Sam was in an affable mood.

"I had a great time at the migrant camp this afternoon," Mark said. "I led a service. I wish you'd been there to see how well those people responded."

Cigar smoke curled around his head, Sam leaned back. He peered off toward the eastern horizon where a star was rising. His tanned knobby features reflected the porch light, now under siege by several moths. "You going to do that every Sunday?" he asked.

"With your permission."

"No need to ask that."

"I really came to ask you to improve conditions over there."

Sam's face clouded as the sky darkened. His rusty hair, cropped to his scalp, looked black. "You preachers are all the same, seems to me," he said. "You're all so fired up with the love of Jesus that you want to change the world overnight."

"As an elder you ought---"

Sam pounded the arm of his chair. "Don't tell me what I ought to do."

"Well, I wasn't---"

"Seems to me you preachers got it all against us laymen. Same with Alf Brent, your distinguished predecessor. Don't you know he came here crying how shameful we treat our niggers?"

"I wish you wouldn't call them that."

Sam's growl was deep in his throat. "Aarh! Last year I put in the new shithouse. They don't even pour the lime in."

Mark's arms grew tense. "Sam, in the name of decency!"

Looking coolly at Mark, his eyes in dark shadow, Sam said "You want that church deficit paid?"

Mark jumped to his feet. He felt as if his head would burst. Temples pounding, he crossed the porch to the steps. Despite an attempt to control himself, his hand came up, accusing finger pointing. "If one of those poor people dies this year," he said, his voice edged with fear, "I'm holding you responsible."

Sam rocked easily. The porch boards squeaked. He puffed his cigar. "Hell, Mark, don't be so damn melodramatic. Those niggers of mine have been coming here for years. Anyone gets sick I take care of 'em. Anyway, it isn't my responsibility. The county's got the right to come in here anytime it wants. Every time they come they give me a clean bill of health. My conscience is clear."

"I suppose you know I'll have to fight you on this."

"You go ahead," Doug said jauntily. "Be my guest. You got the right, same as anybody else. Just remember, this is private property."

"That doesn't give you the right to mistreat---"

"Who says I'm mistreating them? They get paid, twenty-five cents an hour, the going rate. More than they deserve, some of them, specially the kids." Doug crossed his legs. "Besides, what's the point of giving them anything decent? They only wreck it. Don't think I haven't tried. Seems to me if they want something better, well I admit what they have isn't much, they'd be willing to help build it. Trouble is, they're too damn lazy. Anyway, you didn't hear any complaints from the niggers, I'll bet."

Doug had a point there. Not even Buck said a word of complaint about the camp. Nevertheless, that did not excuse Sam. "I'm showing movies at the camp Friday night, " he said.

"You go right ahead." Doug spoke clearly, without avarice. "You go right ahead. You do all you want for them." Sam came across the porch. He put out his hand. "You're new here, Mark. As I said, you aren't any different than those other preachers in Castle Rock. They've been tryin' too. But they gave up. They came to realize those niggers don't appreciate." Sam sighed as he shook Mark's hand lethargically. "But I suppose, being new, you've got to find that out for yourself."

Back home at the manse, Mark told Laura what Sam Bryson had said.

"I'm not surprised," she said. "Castle Rock has its bigots and Sam Bryson is the worst."

Mark eyed her sharply. "At the camp this afternoon, Laura, you didn't feel uneasy?"

"I suppose I was, in a way. Why shouldn't I have felt uneasy? I must say, Mark, you did very well."

"Sam Bryson scared me," he said. "Who am I to judge Sam Bryson? Maybe I'm bigoted myself."

"It's a sickness," Laura said, quoting Kierkegaard, "that's what bigotry is, a sickness unto death."

On Tuesday he returned to what Laura termed his "other life," that of being a theological student. It was a life devoted to Dodd and Strong and C.S. Lewis, and on to Bultmann, Brumer and Karl Barth. At night, in bed with Laura, he read them, seeking the true light until Laura would object, telling him that the only true light is in life. Mark would respond: "But if one rejects objective Biblical revelation, how can one make your view compatible with a belief that God is in control of history?"

Laura would say: "Oh, for heaven's sake, Mark, go to sleep."

Chapter Twenty-Six

The next evening, Monday night, Mark entered Steve Roberts' apartment. Steve stretched his thin body on the sofa. He raised himself up sufficiently to grab a half empty glass of whiskey from a side table. Mark quickly snatched it away. Aren't you ever going to learn?" Mark asked him roughly. Ruth tells me you haven't been to AA for three weeks.

Steve slid off the sofa. He raised the glass. "Here's to Alcoholics Anonymous."

He took a long slow drink. "And how come, since I'm supposed to be so anonymous, that you know so much."

"I'm a snoop," said Mark. He skipped over a pile of old music records on the floor to get to the kitchen. "Don't go anywhere," Mark commanded. "I'm going to get you some coffee."

When he returned, hot coffee in hand, Steve was fast asleep on the floor. Mark dragged him up to the sofa, arranged him in sit-up position and held him there with one hand while his other hand raised the hot cup to Steve's lips. Mark helped Steve to his feet, guided him to the bathroom and held his head above the sink with one hand while he turned on a deluge of cold water.

"Okay, don't drown me," Steve fairly screamed.

When Mark presumed that Steve was sober and dry enough, he led him back to the sofa. Steve opened his eyes. "You still here?" he asked.

"Fine deacon you are," Mark said,

"Don't tell me you've never laid one on."

"No excuses, Steve. You keep this up and it's going to kill you."

"Hurrah!"

"Don't be facetious. Think of your mother, think of Ruth."

"Okay, okay. I'll even think of Dad. What brings you here? Must I confess?"

"On Friday night you're going to help me show movies at the migrant camp."

"In the first place I don't know how to show movies. In the second place, are you crazy?"

"That's beside the point," Mark said. "Will you go with me?"

"Why should I?"

"Because I need your help."

"Oh, that's different. What do you want me to do?"

"Just be here at six o'clock Friday. I'll get the equipment. I'll pick you up."

Friday night came. Steve was sober but he was quite nervous going to the camp, especially since it was getting dark. Mark drove the Buick up to the barn door. Soon the car was surrounded by excited children and curious adults. Buck came over to help. Steve shrank back a step when he saw this giant of a man approaching. "I'm done for," he muttered. Buck and Steve hauled the generator into the barn. Steve assured Buck that he knew all about generators because he was an electrician at Neeby Foods Plant. Buck returned to the car and helped take in a projector and a stand to put it on. Mark carried empty reels and a couple of films. Buck came back to unload a six-foot screen. He took it into he barn. The migrants clapped and cheered as he opened it up and set its tripod legs firmly on the sawdust floor.

Steve strung an electric wire from the generator across the floor to the projector. He flicked a switch and the screen sprang into brightness. There was a roar of expectant delight from the potato bins that rose from floor to ceiling where the children sat on timber, bare legs dangling. From titles to the end of the Abbott and Costello comedy the barn echoed with laughter. The people laughed and cheered and clapped their hands. They hissed the villains and hollered encouragement to Lou and Bud.

Afterward, while Steve and Lonny, one of the Negro men, packed the gear in the car, Mark sat down with Buck on one of the birches. Darkness had descended like a mantle. Buck was almost invisible. Mark wondered how to begin. He had been thinking about it all day. He felt uncomfortable in the presence of this black man. There had been a few Negroes at university, but those few had remained aloof and apart, grouping themselves in class and in the cafeteria. The Negroes remained as dark and mysterious to him as if he had just encountered them in a dark forest. Was it merely sentiment, the singing in his childhood of Negro spirituals around the piano in the house on Maple Street as Martha played the piano as she read the music of the Seth Parker hymnal, or was he actually afraid of Buck Washington? The man had such power: those calm passive eyes, that humorous mouth, that touch of the lion in his body. Mark shrugged. Books on race relations were not much help as he sat, side by side, with a Negro on a bench. Books did not tell him that the two feet between himself and Buck might as well be two miles.

Buck started chuckling to himself.

"What's so funny?" Mark asked.

"That Lou fellow." Buck roared aloud.

Were they indeed, as Mark had heard, like children? Childish in their innocence, happy in their innocent souls? That was nonsense, and he knew it, or thought he knew it, better than anyone. Buck was the wise one. He was at perfect ease, secure in his knowledge of his superiority. Yes, superior, because Buck brought to this bench, here in this gathering darkness, the centuries of his aloneness, which gave him strength, while Mark felt like a curious boy standing outside looking in.

"Buck," said Mark, "I want all of you to come to my church on Sunday."

At first, from Buck's end of the bench, there was utter silence. Then the bench shook as Buck rocked with laughter.

"Church! Did you say church?"

Without the cooperation of the migrants themselves, Mark knew, what chance was there of doing anything for them? He could not see anything to laugh at. "Of course, if you prefer some other church," Mark said.

Buck's voice was quiet, subdued. "Pastor Christopher," he said, "you haven't been around much, have you? Where did you come from?"

"Attumwa."

"They got Negroes up there?"

"Of course."

"Those Negroes, they go to the white folk's church?"

"Well, no. They have their own churches."

"You ever been to a Negro church?

"No, I haven't." He remembered one evening service in the Methodist Church on the waterfront road at which a Negro minister gave the sermon. That was long ago when he was in high school. The Negro minister was the only Negro attending the service. The reason he remembered the Negro minister was because it was Race Relations Sunday, a day in June, and Pastor Woods had pointedly, in his introduction, said it was important for the races to understand one another. He could not remember anything the Negro minister said, but he did remember being disappointed because his sermon contained not a word about race. He had merely preached the Gospel.

Buck touched his arm and said "Mark—" For a moment Buck was silent. Mark was startled . It was the first time Buck had spoken his first name. "Mark," Buck continued, "don't you mind my telling you, but you've got a lot to learn." Buck dug the tips of his boots into the earth. "It isn't that we don't appreciate—. Well, they're nice folks in Castle Rock. They give us clothing and other stuff, and we appreciate that. We like you folks coming here. And we like talking to white folks. We like the movies. But going to your church, that's different, that's a whole lot different."

"Everyone is welcome at my church, regardless," Mark told him firmly. "I want the young people to come to our youth society Sunday nights too,"

"That's kind of y'all, but I don't see how."

"We will send cars. Mark wondered who he could get to drive, but he would worry about that later.

"We could get there aw'right," Buck said. "We have the truck. No question we could get there."

"What happened to your voice?"

"What do you mean?"

"I mean the way you're talking."

"That's nigger talk."

"You don't need to talk that way to me."

"White folk expect it."

"Well, knock it off."

"Okay. I just wondered whether you were serious," Buck said with a laugh.

"I am serious."

"We don't have white folks clothes."

"Is that nigger talk?"

"Yes. If I thought I could get past the front door."

"I'll meet you at the door. You and everybody."

Buck knocked Mark on the shoulder. "Damned if you ain't the most."

"Will you come?"

"No, not a chance. I'm not about to get spat on."

"I doubt if that would happen, not in Castle Rock."

"You got a lot of livin' to do," Buck said.

"Maybe I have. Castle Rock is as good a place as any to start."

"Alright then," Buck said vaguely.

"Alright what?"

"I'll come. Just me. Nobody else. I been spat on plenty."

"Everybody can come."

Buck slapped Mark on the back. "I don't think you're a fool, Mark, but you sure act like one."

"It takes two, Buck."

Buck stood up. He towered over Mark. "Ain't it the truth though?" He sauntered away to find Naomi. "See ya," he hollered over his shoulder.

Steve was waiting impatiently. He was sitting behind the wheel of the Buick. "I'll drive," he said. "Where you bin?"

"Sorry. I was having a long talk with Buck." He was glad Steve did not ask him what about. Steve backed the car to the road. Beulah was stirring clothes in a big steel drum. As she stirred she sang:

I am happy in the Lord
For the love He shows to me
He sweetens all my days with pleasure.
Not a naught can harm my soul
His great salvation no one can measure.

The stars poked their bright lights through the sky's black canopy.

"What's the beef?" Mark asked Steve, who had remained darkly silent.

"Didn't you notice the smell?" Steve sniffed as if the strong pervading odor of the camp was still in his nostrils.

"I smelled it," Mark said.

"How could you stand it?"

"It was pretty bad, wasn't it?"

Steve jerked the Buick out of the ruts. He turned into the gravel road leading to the highway. "It's not that I'm squeamish," he said. "In the war I had a belly-full of those niggers." He half-smiled. "Excuse me. Negroes."

"Well, thanks for your help."

"It was nothing," Steve said. "There was this one black bastard I knew. He was a corporal, can you imagine? But damned if he didn't have guts. One night we were on this hill, on the forward slope, and this nigger was in the hole next to me. It was dark as hell. I kept seein' the Japs comin' up the hill, at least I thought they were Japs; probably rats, I dunno. Anyway there I was, fagged, stoned, you know. All of a sudden I feel myself being dragged up out of the hole. It was so damned dark I couldn't see what was goin' on. But I knew. A Jap was grabbing me. I yelled, which was the worst thing to do, because it could have meant a knife in my gut. Then I wasn't being dragged anymore, and this nigger corporal, just a cook, we called him Chick, was standing over me, and when I got up on one elbow I saw what he'd done. The Jap was dead at his feet with Chick's knife stuck in him. Now that's the kind of nigger I admire."

Exactly at seven-thirty the next night, Saturday, Sam Bryson entered Mark's study. Steve's father, Duane Roberts, and Russ Neeby were already there. Duane stood up, coughed, and shook Mark's hand. Russ, from the chair, waved. Orson Coffey was due any minute. Unfortunately, Fred Lewis, the grocer, whom Mark expected would be sympathetic, was unable to attend because his wife, Mary, was not feeling well. Harry Ironwood had a Grange meeting.

Because Orson was habitually late—his single cow seemed to need as much care as a herd—Mark was sitting in his swivel chair ready to preside. It was not the official monthly meeting of the session, as the church's ruling elders were called, but a special meeting requested by Doug. It was the custom that special meetings could be called to discuss only one topic. Mark said a prayer asking for God's blessing, expressed thanks and mentioned Mary Lewis' failing health. He had no sooner said "Amen" than Duane, who had worked at Chesterton Steel all his life, began coughing, apologized, and coughed again.

Mark had no doubt that the elders knew what the meeting's topic would be. It was a sure bet that Sam had told them. Mark attributed the good turnout to the topic's nature. Getting a quorum at a regular meeting was difficult. This meeting had a quorum, an ominous sign.

"Thank you all for coming," Mark began. He looked carefully around the circle of faces. Each was a tragedian's somber mask. "I presume you know that I was asked to lead a service for the migrants on the Xenophon?"

"Not by me," Sam Bryson said. He looked solemnly about, crossed his legs and sat back, smiling. "I just want the record to be clear. Got that, Duane?" Duane nodded. He was the Session's Stated Clerk. It was his job to take the minutes.

"Mr. Bryson," Mark asked, "are you saying I needed the Session's permission?"

"Not at all, Mark. I'm just saying you didn't need my permission to enter my property, that's all. I asked for the meeting because I think the matter needs discussion."

"The meeting is open for discussion," Mark said.

"As far as I'm concerned," Sam continued. "I'm all for giving the niggers what they want. Doesn't do any harm to preach hellfire and damnation to them. Matter of fact, it helps."

Duane coughed an interruption. "Seems t' me that seeing it's Sam's farm it ought t' be up to him to decide if he wants services up there, that's his business. But that doesn't mean we oughta let Mark here to do it. Just because we okay the services doesn't mean we okay what Mark does. There's the difference."

Although Mark had told himself not to hope, he felt a surge of optimism. These were decent men. They were fine Christian elders, faithful to their church. Perhaps he had lacked faith in them.

"Folks hereabouts," said Orson, "need more visitin' as it is. I hear lots of folks haven't been visited yet."

Mark deduced that his ministry had been examined and found wanting. It was true. He had not visited every single one of his people. He ought to visit many others more often.

"Any more comments?" Mark asked.

Russ Neeby adjusted his heavy black-rimmed glasses. The president of Neeby Foods, where Steve Roberts worked, was a man of few words, but what he said usually made sense. If Mark had to name his favorite elder, he would have named Russ Neeby. Mark knew that the elders were in for one of Russ's scoldings. "As I understand the function of a pastor," Russ began, "he has the duty, and I use the word advisedly, to perform the ministry as he sees fit. He is responsible to the Presbytery, not to the Session. I have reminded the Session many times of this, and I don't hesitate to remind you again. As elders we have the responsibility to share in the ministry." Russ removed his glasses and twirled them. "That means we have a responsibility to assist Mark in his ministry. Let Mark tell us what he would like to do for the migrants and tell us the way we can help."

Mark refrained from smiling. Yes, he had lacked faith in his elders. They had been raised in the Presbyterian system, and that was the value of the system. They shared in the ministry. Mark waited for further comments.

Russ nodded toward him. "Mark, you have the floor."

But, for Mark. having the floor was an unexpected turn of events. He said a silent prayer and plunged in. "I invited the migrants to come to the service tomorrow." This was not what he had intended to say. He realized he had gone too far. Every one of the elders looked horrified. "I'm sorry," he said. "I misspoke. What I meant to say is: I invited the migrants' foreman, Buck Washington, to come." He expected a smile, not a retort.

"You let one in you let 'em all in," said Duane Roberts.

"Our people will never stand for it," said Doug Bryson. He looked around for support. All nodded. They said "Sure thing," and "Being segregated is best for everybody, " and "Now's not the time."

"Anyway," Sam Bryson continued, "what's the point? Stirring up trouble? It's pretty obvious Mark here wants to make a case out of what he thinks of as a racial issue. But that isn't the way it is at all. I'm all for better race relations, same as the next man, but they're migrants. They don't live in the county. They come here only for the summer and fall, and there isn't any opportunity for us to integrate. I mean, it isn't the same as if we had a lot of Negroes living in Castle Rock and hereabouts, which doesn't mean I'm against them, mind you, I'm just as glad—" There was a round of light applause and an approving "here, here."

Sam nodded in gratitude for their support. "What we have to keep in mind," he continued, "is we're talking about migrant labor, transient. They come and they go. Many of them are shifty. I know a lot of people don't like me hiring these people, but they're mighty glad to have the economic benefits. Some mistakenly blame the Xenophon, me, for bringing them in here. You know that migrants work on most of the big farms hereabouts, but this isn't always known and the Xenophon gets the blame when one of them niggers gets caught breaking in and stealing, or getting drunk and making a noise. Well, I do my best to control that, with Sheriff Delaney's help, and I think, by and large, we do a pretty good job." He looked around to affirm that he still had their approval. "Now the point is: do any of you want those niggers coming into town nights? Would you, Russ? Well, I know I don't. Because they'd all the time be wanting to get into Ruth's tavern. And if Fred Lewis was here he'd back me up on what I'm sayin'. Fred wouldn't want them coming into his grocery store anymore than any of you wants them coming to the church."

Mark raised his hand as if he were a pupil. "Well, now—"

"Them's my sentiments entirely," said Duane Roberts.

"Thank God someone's looking out for our women folk, 'specially the kids," said Orson Coffey, who was childless.

They looked toward Russ Neeby, who, as chairman of the church's Board of Trustees, was primarily responsible for seeing to it that the annual budget was raised. Russ took his time. He extracted a handkerchief and polished his glasses. His hazel eyes looked as if they were about to shed tears. "We all know," he began, "that we have a responsibility toward the migrants. After all, they're here, in our midst, and we can't very well ignore they are. The fact they live at the Xenophon doesn't make them any less our responsibility." He looked around to make sure they were listening. "As you know, I'm mighty interested in keeping Castle Rock a decent place to live in. We have very little crime here---"

"That's a laugh," Orson put in.

"Well, except for the Negro district," Russ admitted. "Now I'm not saying all crime is caused by Negroes, and that's a fact, but if you study the statistics, as I have, you'll see that the number of crimes by Negroes is far out of proportion to their numbers. We all know they're disadvantaged, and we've got to help them, but that doesn't change the facts. After all," he said, smiling, affable, "we've got to be realistic. Christian compassion is one thing, but going against the facts is another." Russ replaced his glasses over his brilliant blue eyes. He looked studious.

"As I understand it," said Mark, "you have no objection to my preaching to the migrants on Sunday."

"That's your prerogative," said Doug Bryson.

Mark smiled. "And this church is open to anyone who wants to worship in it."

"Of course," said Russ Neeby. He held up a warning hand. "But under the circumstances—"

"I only wanted the Session's advice," Mark said. He looked around to make sure he had their attention. "Buck Washington is coming to church tomorrow."

Sam Bryson looked at him in consternation. "He's the migrant foreman," he said for the benefit of those who were ignorant of that fact.

Orson waved his hands. "He won't get past the door," he cried.

"We won't let him in," said Duane.

"Try anything like that and you'll be sorry," cried Sam.

"I advise you, Mark," said Russ, "not to do it. We've tried to be fair to you. You should be fair to us."

"Buck Washington will be here," Mark replied firmly.

"You're a stubborn fool," Sam said.

One by one they left the study and clomped down the stairs toward the narthex. The front door clanged as they left. Orson told Mark that he would "live to regret this." Russ said he was sorry.

Mark followed them to the sidewalk where the elders gathered in an arguing group. Mark slowly crossed the street to the manse.

He told Laura what had happened. "I knew this was bound to happen," she said. She began to cry. "I knew it!"

Mark gathered her in his arms. "I really think we made some progress," he said.

"Progress!" Laura pushed him at arm's length. She wiped her tears. "Don't you see what they're trying to do to you? They're deliberately goading you into setting yourself against them."

"I have to do what's right," Mark said stubbornly.

"What's right for you or what's right for the church?"

"Who's side are you on, Laura?"

Laura gave him a quick hug. "Dear, I'm on your side. You know that. I promised you I wouldn't interfere and I won't. But getting the elders angry won't help."

"The trouble with a lot of churches," Mark said, "is they're too complacent. That's why we have all this bitterness and hatred against Negroes. The churches should lead."

"Be careful," Laura warned. "You will split the church."

Mark threw up his hands. "All I want to do is to help a few poor unfortunate Negroes."

Laura continued to wipe her teary eyes. "I can't argue with you about that. I was looking forward to a quiet peaceful summer." She took his hand and looked up at him. "Let's go back to Springport. I like it there."

It was a tempting idea. Uncle John's will had been read. He had left the Stoddard house and property to Martha and himself jointly.

"I love Springport too, Laura. But I can't leave now. Not yet. Let's wait and see what happens."

"I'm not opposed to you, Mark. You know that. As far as Negroes are concerned, you knew what I was like when you married me."

"Are you saying I'm trying to change you?"

"Aren't you?" asked Laura.

"I'm going to bed."

"Chicken!" she said. Mark playfully slapped her bottom. "Do that once more and you'll be sorry." And he did. Laura flew at him. While he held her away she kicked his shins. She collapsed into his arms. "You're impossible," she said.

Chapter Twenty-Seven

A few minutes before the Sunday service, Mark came down from his study and glanced around the narthex looking for Buck. He doubted that Buck would come. It was too much to ask of the man. Mark greeted Orson and Duane, who were all frowns. He went through the swinging doors into the sanctuary. Descending a side aisle he nodded to Harry Ironwood, Mrs. Garson and Howie Mason. He did not see Buck until he mounted the platform and opened the guilt-edged lectern Bible. He glanced up and there was Buck sitting beside Steve Roberts in the third pew. Buck grinned triumphantly, closed fist held high. Mark sat down on the throne-like high-backed chair, known, of course, as the Pastor Seat. He bowed his head and said Alleluia. Mrs. Trane, at the organ behind him, boomed a trumpet call. Mark went to the lectern and, after words of greeting, announced the first hymn. The congregation, which occupied about half the sanctuary's seating capacity, stood up to sing *The Church's One Foundation*.

Buck and Steve were sharing a hymnal as they sang the printed words. Buck's deep bass carried throughout the sanctuary. Mark was absorbed in the sight of, perhaps, the first Negro ever to attend a service here. He saw Buck suddenly turn his head to perceive the sound of a commotion in the rear pews. Slowly, to Mark's disbelieving eyes, one by one, the elders left their pews and went to the back of the church. Wives and children followed. They gathered behind the last pew, silent, immobile. Fred Lewis looked around, saw what was happening and left his place. Others followed. Sarah Shamley, the school teacher, was the first woman after the elders' wives. Then Lemuel Orduff and Marian, those gray-haired saints, and after them Mrs. Orson, followed by Blinco

Crowly. At last there remained only Laura, head bowed, Ruth Neeby and several of the young people: Ted Gore, Cray Browne, Alice Roberts and Cincy, Bob and Jenny Glen and a few others. Steve Roberts remained steadfast in his place, until, looking around, he moved to the aisle. Mark felt the blood draining from his face. Steve walked slowly back to his father, Duane, said something to him, and returned quickly to resume his place beside Buck.

The choir, consisting of four women and one man, kept singing. All looked to Mrs. Crane, who signaled to them to "hold the fort," as she later told Mark. She also told him that, since her back was turned, she could not see what was going on.

As if on signal, as the final verse of the hymn began, those standing at the back filed out of the church into the brilliant morning sunshine. Duane Roberts was the last to leave as the choir sang:

> *O happy ones and holy!*
> *Lord give us grace that we,*
> *Like them, the meek and lowly,*
> *On high may dwell with Thee.*

Head bowed, Mark read the invocation from his Service Book. His voice rang out vigorously. Glancing up, he saw Laura's face, blanched and eyes brimming. Mark nodded to the choir. Jenny Glen, mirroring his questioning look, sat down with the others in the choir: Lucille Mason, Cindy Zenkorski, Creighton Browne, and Mrs. Clarissa Crowley, Blinko's mother. Mrs. Crane watched what remained of the congregation in the mirror above the organ keys. Mrs. Crowley made a move as if to leave. Mrs. Lane said "Sit down!" Mrs. Crowley, her lined face livid, obeyed. The faithful Young People's Society remained. They came from throughout the church, gathered together in three pews down front. They gave Mark an affirmative thumbs-up. Buck was still standing. He appeared to be quite amused by the goings-on of the white folks. Steve patted his shoulder and grinned as they sat down. Laura moved from her usual place across the central aisle and sat down beside Buck. She smiled courageously at him. She waved to Mark.

Mark asked the choir and Mrs. Crane to "join our guest" in the pews behind Buck. Mrs. Crane led the way. Mark stood behind the pulpit. He led the surviving members of his congregation in prayer. He gripped the edges of the pulpit for support. He preached.

"I suppose," he said, "you are wondering why this happened. The answer is simple. Often, in a strange situation, we allow our fear to get the best of us. We are prisoners of our fear." He looked down at Laura, who smiled bravely. "It has been my experience that we get out of life what we put into it. If we put in fear, then we will be afraid. If we put in love, then we shall have love. Perfect love casts out fear. If there is trouble in Castle Rock it is because we are afraid to love. You who have remained have permitted love to conquer fear. I do not need to preach to you. But I would say this: let us go from this place more determined to love than ever before, for love is strength and power and joy, all of these and more. In the end love conquers all, even death."

Buck, arms folded, was unreadable. Steve was all smiles.

"In a sense," Mark continued, "the sermon has already been preached. Now our ministry, that road along which God leads us, begins. And that is at it should be. One more thing and I will close. Whatever lies ahead, I thank all of you, and all of them--" He pointed toward the street. "For the witness you, and they, have borne this day. May God keep us all and guide us in His way."

Mark pronounced the benediction, one hand raised in blessing. He stepped down from the pulpit and made his way, leading his silent people, to the narthex and the porch. One by one he shook their hands. On the sidewalk those who had walked out gathered by twos and threes. They looked up at him. They had nothing to say.

When Buck came out Mark gripped his hand. He witnessed understanding in Buck's eyes. Head high, shoulders back, Buck passed among the people, who turned aside to let him pass. He walked along the sidewalk to where it ended and then took to the highway. The people watched him go, and then the people on the sidewalk, who had been joined by those who had stayed behind, began walking toward the open church door. Sam Bryson was the first to reach Mark.

"The service is over," Mark told him.

Turning around, Sam raised his hand. "You might as well go home, folks," he said. "The service is over."

"Don't you go, Sam," Mark said. " I want to see you."

In his study, Mark stood by the bell's rope. He gave it a yank. The bell sang dully. Its echo hovered over Castle Rock.

"What's the idea?" Sam asked. He was flushed from standing in the hot sun. He was also slightly out of breath.

Mark looked out the window. Several of his people on the sidewalk were obviously arguing. A sudden weariness overcame Mark's limbs. He slumped into his swivel chair. "Sam, you can't stop the integration of the church."

Sam loosened his tie and removed his jacket. "I didn't organize that walkout. I didn't have to. People just naturally don't want to go to church with Negroes, and that's the plain truth. Soon's you realize that."

"Next Sunday" said Mark coolly, "there will be more of them in church."

"Then I won't be here, and hardly anybody else. And you had better give a thought to where your paycheck comes from."

"I've thought about it. If I have to I'll get a part-time job."

Sam smiled. "You can't go against the people forever, Mark. And I don't think you want this to be taken to Presbytery."

"Do what you have to do, Sam."

Sam stood up, raised himself to his full height, but Mark was still two inches taller. "You've forgotten who owns this church."

"I haven't forgotten, Sam. Actually this building is owned by The Presbyterian Church in America, remember."

"I know that," Sam said sourly.

Mark spent the afternoon with the migrants. They listened intently to his sermon, calling out "Amen," and laughing at his jokes. Then he spent an hour with three of his young people---Alice Roberts, Cincy Zenkorski and Jenny Glen, who were the only ones to show up that evening for the meeting of the Young Peoples Society. Mark led a discussion on race relations. The girls were weakly in favor of it theoretically, but were embarrassed when Mark pressed the point about integrating the church. At last he called it off and after the three had left crossed the street to the manse.

Seeing him coming, Laura hurried to turn on the parlor lights. She switched on the television set and sat down on the sofa. When he came in she continued to concentrate on the TV screen, as if she had been long absorbed. "Hi, honey!" Mark cried cheerfully. He sat down beside her. "What's happening?" he asked.

Laura placed a finger on her lips. She leaned forward, gripping her hands. The scene faded into a commercial. "Oh darn," she said, "just when it was getting exciting!"

"I don't know how you can watch that drivel."

"Every night I thank God for television."

"Don't you have anything to read?"

"Trouble is," she said with a knowing smile, "Kierkegaard gets too solemn and Bultmann too deep. I've been thinking of doing Tillich, then dip into Buber."

"Stop kidding me," Mark retorted. "They're my books. I take it you're bored. Not enough excitement today?"

"Oh no. Oh no. Oh no. With all those great minds---And especially what happened in church this morning. And, by the way, how did it go with the migrants?"

"Fine, just fine. Buck was hysterical. He made a lot of jokes."

"I feel sorry for them all. It was a cruel thing you did, Mark."

"What cruel thing?" Mark asked.

"Think of what he must have been feeling. He must have hated it."

"Buck told me it was a hoot. He was thankful no one spit on him."

"I've been thinking about going away for a bit, Mark," Laura said.

"Sure, maybe we can take a week or so. Maybe Echo Lake."

"Mark, listen to me. Mother and Dad are taking a trip to the Bahamas. Dad says we can stay at the mansion as long as we like."

"Out of the question, Laura. I've got too much to do here."

"Well then, you can manage by yourself. I'm tired, Mark. Please?"

Shadows of fatigue did, indeed, loop her eyes. Their onset had been gradual and he had not really noticed how deep the shadows were until this moment. Her lips, her cheeks, even her hair, had lost their luster. Of course Laura shut herself up too much in the hot manse, going into the yard only to hang out the washing. It was a wonder, she being three months pregnant, she had not been sick, especially the way she stayed up to all hours watching television.

"I'll have Nancy to take care of me," Laura said. "And Doctor Abengraph says I've got to be careful."

"When do you want to go?" Mark asked.

Laura kissed him. "Tomorrow."

"That's too soon! There will be talk. After this morning—"

"I'm not asking permission," Laura said. "I've made up my mind."

"It's too soon."

"Mark, please understand. I must go. You don't know what it's been like, being locked up in this—this glass house! With everybody spying on me all the time."

"Spying on you?"

"You didn't see Duane Roberts out there just now. He was there all the time you were in the church with the young people. And he's done it before. Often." She paused. "By the way, how many did you have tonight?"

"Just three girls."

Laura laughed. "Three girls! That's why."

"Why what?"

Laura grasped his hand. She issued a generous smile. "Oh Mark. A grown man, and so naïve. Don't you see? Was Alice Roberts there?"

Mark sank his head into his cupped hands. "Good God! Duane's daughter! You think that's why—"

"Exactly. He's done it before. I didn't tell you because I didn't want to worry you. Listen to me. Think of all the times you've been in your study counseling women of the church."

"So? That's my job."

"You've been alone with them, and in their homes. Don't you get it? Duane's been watching you. Mark, while I'm away I want you to be extra careful."

He put his arms around her. "Please, Laura, I need you."

"Mark, I've got to go. I just don't know who I am here in Castle Rock. I've got to get away to find myself. I've been at everyone's beck and call. You don't know how many women come knocking on the door. The women! They come in by the dozen wanting to talk. They think that's my job to listen to them. Why, Alice Roberts comes in a lot. Did you know Alice has a crush on you?"

Mark let out a long guffaw.

Laura ignored him. "I want to go home, Mark. And that has nothing to do with what happened today."

"Of course not, " Mark said bitterly. "It's just a coincidence."

"It did bring things to a head. I can't see myself in a practically empty church Sunday after Sunday, not with everything else I have to put up with."

"Laura, I've got to go through with it, you know that."

She moved away from him to a corner of the sofa. She felt a darkness coming over her. "Why? Tell me why."

"Because it's right," Mark said stubbornly.

"And I'm wrong, is that it?"

"The ministry—"

"Negroes!" Laura corrected him. "You don't think of them as anything but Negroes. You're so full of civil righteousness that you can't see what you're doing to the church, what you've already done. And will you be doing anything to help the Negroes in the long run?"

"Maybe not," he said. He felt a tiredness taking possession of his body. "But it will do something for the church, Laura. The people will come to see they can't live in isolation."

"I know a lot about Negroes too," Laura replied. She smiled through incipient tears. "I'm sorry, Mark. Nancy could make me cry just by raising her voice. She's very nice, the nicest Negro I've every known. Until I met you, Mark, there wasn't a day in my life that I wasn't—"

"Waited upon by Negroes, is that what you intend to say?"

"No I wasn't, smarty! I love you Mark, but sometimes you can be so infuriatingly opinionated." Mark shriveled. "I respected our Negro servants, especially Nancy. She's a sweet-natured girl. She scarcely ever makes any trouble. She's a loveable light-hearted girl. She's a perfect servant. Mother taught me always to treat the Negro with courtesy and respect. Never call a Negro nigger. She insisted upon that. Always obey the Golden Rule with them. That's what Mother said. And, of course, Daddy too."

Despite his intent to sympathize, Mark asked: "Surely you were angry with Nancy sometime, Laura. After all, it's only natural. We're all human."

Laura was silent. She refrained from telling Mark the truth. The only occasion she could remember when she did not treat Nancy with courtesy and respect was the weekend Nancy whipped Earl, son of Sam, the Negro gardener. She was twelve at the time. Earl was helping her to mount her horse when his hand slipped, as she later told Nancy, "right on the seat of my pants." Laura had lashed out in fury, slapping poor Earl's face with her riding crop. The boy, who was about the same age as Laura, hollered in rage. He yanked Laura off the horse onto the tile stable floor. Laura knocked Earl down. They wrestled for a few minutes. Laura was the victor. That was when Nancy came upon them. She snatched up the fallen crop and laid a few strokes on Earl's back. Laura kicked Nancy's legs. She called Nancy names. She had to admit she did not treat Earl or Nancy with courtesy and respect.

"And that's all they mean to you," Mark said. "Just servants."

"Go away," Laura cried. "Leave me alone."

He tried to hold her, to comfort her, but she would not be comforted. "Laura, I don't mind if you go home to your parents. I really don't. You're tired. You need a rest. I've been unfair. Let's pack your suitcase. I'll take you there in the Buick."

"No, I'll take my own car. I'll need it."

Laura dabbed her eyes. "You better not see so much of Ruth Neeby," she said.

"I'll be careful. But if they're going to talk there's not much I can do about it." He laughed nervously. "You're jealous, Laura."

She slapped his face, but only a tap. "You're a fool. You know that, don't you?"

"I know that. The Lord's fool."

"That's just like you, Mark. Just give, give, give. You're going to get hurt."

"Nothing from outside can hurt you," he said, quoting scripture.

"I know. Mark, you have already been hurt from the outside."

"Goes with the territory. It's not being hurt, it's being disciplined."

Laura laughed. "Sometimes I wonder about you, Mark. You're just too good to be true." She shook her head. "I suppose if you weren't I couldn't love you as much as I do." She held his hand. "I really don't want to leave you, but I must." She patted her stomach. "If only for the baby's sake. Let's go to bed."

"You go first," he said. "I want to jot down a few notes about today's happenings. I'll need them when Presbytery opens its inquisition."

"Oh, my God!" she burst out as she clung to him closely. "Heaven forbid."

He went out to the porch. The moon shone brightly on the lawn. Across the street, in front of his church, the maple tree rose strongly from the earth and was unshaken in the night's deep stillness.

Chapter Twenty-Eight

Day after day the thermometer rose to a hundred and stayed there. Day after day a new record was established. The constant sun burned the grass crisp brown. Tar ran in rivulets on Castle Rock Road. In town, the dry wind chased cats under porches. Air conditioners whirred and broke down. Johnny Merritt closed his Esso station and went home to get a shower. Even Fred Lewis shut and locked his grocery. On Sunday the church was unbearable but Mark conducted the service for Buck, Beulah, Lonny, Steve, Cincy Zenkorski, Claudia Crowley and a few others. Mrs. Crane played the organ. There was no choir.

Two days later Mark rose at six o'clock and by seven was in an Xenophon field far back of Sam Bryson's house. It was already hot, about eighty degrees. A parched west wind drove the dust in whorls about his feet. Bending, sometimes straddling a potato plant, he picked the bugs off shriveled leaves one by one. He moved down the endless row, as the baking sun rose higher. He followed Lonny, the skinny young man who had taught him how to pluck the bugs without breaking his gut. Far across the field other migrants labored in long lines. Another kid named Mose, about eleven years old, stretched occasionally. Beulah, recognizable by her gray hair, gratefully accepted a drink of water from a bucket that her pregnant daughter, Naomi, carried from one worker to the next. At noon the workers trailed from the field to the shade of an alder grove by a stream. There, in their midst, Mark shared his sandwiches with Buck and Lonny. When they were finished eating they lay on their backs, looking up through the trees to the emerald sky. The earth, strong and unmovable, cooled them.

Mark remembered the long days on Grandmother Goddard's farm in Springport. He thought of the way his slender shadow bent away from him and danced across the field as he swung his scythe. He heard again the soft low swish of the blade. "You're as good as any man," his grandmother used to say. "You isn't nothin' but a slip of a lad, but you got gumption, boy." And afterward, when he entered the cool dark storage cut into the bank of earth beyond the barn, he used to dream of voyages upon the sea, where Grandfather Goddard sailed in spring to haul cod on the Georges Bank. And he remembered Saturdays when he went fishing on the bay, casting his line, dragging for sea bass. Or on the pond back of the farm, where trout lingered half an hour around the hook and then swam warily away. And he thought of Sundays running with Helen through pine woods green with lichen, then entering their secret glade, where, enfolded by cathedral pines, they lay side by side on new moss, gazing at clouds making maps of faraway lands.

His reverie was broken by Buck's deep voice. "You feeling alright?"

"Sure, I'm fine," Mark said.

"You aren't used to this kind of work."

"Give me another few days."

Buck raised himself on one elbow. His brow, even in the shade, was very wet. The dust that coated his skin was streaked where the sweat ran in rivulets. "You sure are a strange one," Buck said.

"That's the trouble with you niggers. You're prejudiced."

Buck laughed ."Guess we are. Just don't seem right, you working here with us."

"I told you I need the money."

"Because you've been fired."

"Why can't you believe me? I haven't been fired."

"Then why are you here?"

"I love farming."

"Your white folks, they don't need pastoring?"

"Oh, shut up."

Buck lay back. He chuckled. "You aren't fooling me none. Sun's touched you in the head."

That afternoon Steve joined him in the field. Mark taught him how to pick bugs. For a while they worked together and then Steve drifted down the row ahead of him. His hands grew red from the blood of potato bugs. Sometimes the bugs flew into his face, and constantly the dust rose from the dry furrows, filling his eyes, his nose, stopping his ears. And all the while the constant sun beat down in fury. His back felt stiff, immobile. His hands were coated with slime from the potato leaves. The heat enveloped him. He tried facing his shadow, but there was no relief in that. Sweat poured from his hair and forehead into his eyes. Rubbing his eyes with the edge of his hand coated his eyelashes with dust. He wrapped his handkerchief around his head, knotting it in the back. His ankles throbbed. He felt as if he had lost all contact with his toes. He would not rise to stretch. He followed far behind Steve down the endless row.

All week Mark and Steve labored by the side of the migrants. They shared their sparse food. At night they found places on hard bunks. Mark slept dreamlessly, awoke at the first sound of movement and nudged Steve in the bunk below. At suppertime on Saturday Buck went to Sam Bryson's house to present his time sheets and came back with the payroll in cash. The migrants queued in the camp yard to receive their pay, which Buck doled out from the top of an upended crate. Mark received twenty dollars, Steve ten. When all had been paid Buck shouted to everyone to gather around.

"Now all of you listen to me," he said. "I've got orders from Mr. Bryson that we've got to let six of you go."

A murmur of dissension rose.

Buck raised his hand. "There's nothing can be done about it. I already decided how to do it. I put an X on six of the dollar bills that's gone to the men, so I don't know who's got them. Same as you draw lots. So you all look at your money and, if you got a marked bill, you step forward."

Neither Mark or Steve had marked bills. Five men stepped forward. "Who's the other one," Buck roared. He looked fiercely around, hands clenched. "I'm going to search every damn one of you 'less the sixth man comes up. Now!"

Lonny came out of the crowd. He held up a dollar bill. "Just noticed it, Buck."

So fast was Buck's slashing attack that Mark did not see the first blow. Lonny went down and lay still.

Steve stepped forward. Mark grasped his arm. "Don't interfere," Mark said.

"You men," said Buck smoothly. "You leave tomorrow. If you're married, you leave your wife and kids if you want. But you be gone tomorrow by sundown." The migrants drifted away. Buck called Lonny up. The boy shook his head. Buck gave him a grudging grin and joined the others around the fire.

"Big fella," Steve said bitterly.

"He's the boss," Mark said.

Buck came over. "You two staying tonight?"

"Not me," said Steve. "I'm on vacation from my real job at Neeby's, remember? I've got a date."

As Steve was turning to leave, Buck grabbed his arm. "Just you remember no one's to know you're here."

"Sure thing," Steve said. "See you tomorrow." He went behind the barn to get his concealed car.

Mark waved toward Steve's departing figure. "Buck, let Lonny stay. Fire me. If I don't go it's like I'm taking his job."

"You could have got a marked dollar just as much as Lonny. Anyway, what's the difference? There'll be more firings next week."

"Buck, there aren't enough workers now."

"Way Mr. Bryson's got it figured the heat's going to ruin half the crop, so there will be enough of us."

"Not if we get enough rain," Mark protested.

"I've got enough to worry about," Buck said. "What Mr. Bryson wants, Mr. Bryson gets. Anyway, if I was Mr. Bryson I wouldn't hire you."

"Why not? If boys and girls can debug potato plants, why shouldn't I?"

Buck shook his head. "Because you're no good at it."

"I suppose I am out of shape. But the more work I do the stronger I'll get."

Buck laughed. "You won't be here long enough. Mr. Bryson told me. You asked him for the job. You told him you wanted to learn what it's like to be a migrant worker."

"That's right, I did. It takes more than a day."

"For us it takes a lifetime," Buck said solemnly. "You start when you're born, living in trash shacks and bunkhouses, down south or up here. Makes no difference. We can't go to town, except to buy stuff. But one day—" His voice trailed off. "We'll be free one day. Then you will see."

That evening Mark drove the Buick to the church where Russ Neeby was waiting for him. In his study he thanked Russ for his promise to hire the fired migrants. "And I'll thank Sam Bryson," Russ said. "Neeby Foods needs them. They have patience and strength, what it takes to work assembly lines. Just what we need for all the fruit and corn that's coming in." He paused to take a good look at Mark. "My God, Mark, what happened to you? You look terrible."

"My first day working for Sam, on the Xenophon."

"What do you mean?"

"I worked the fields, killing potato bugs. And I will do the same thing as long as Sam lets me."

Russ stared at him in disbelief. "What for?"

"For the experience, Russ. How can I minister to the migrants unless I know what it's like to work all day in a field when it's a hundred degrees?"

"I'll never understand you," Russ said in dismay.

"Russ, how did you get your start in the foods business?"

"I see what you're getting at. Okay, my first job was on the assembly line."

"One of the men you will be hiring this week is named Lonny. Do you think he has a chance of becoming Neeby's president some day."

"No, he probably doesn't have the education." Russ meditated thoughtfully. "And he's black."

"Exactly," Mark said. "Do you think that's right? What if he had the education? What then.?"

"As the way things are now, not a chance. That's the way things are. I'm going to be frank with you, Mark. I agreed with the elders that we should cut your pay to stop you in this---this foolishness. You working with the blacks is just too much. Not so much personal as for the sake of the church."

"Always the church!" Mark cried out. He was trying to control his rising anger. "I want to tell you, Russ, the church will be here long after I'm gone. It's been here a hundred and fifty years and what I'm doing isn't going to make a difference."

"Then why are you doing it?"

"Because I must, despite you, despite the elders, despite everyone."

"Even in spite of Laura leaving you?"

"She hasn't left me. She needed a rest."

"Have it your way. How much longer you going to be working on the farm?"

"The rest of the summer if I'm able, until my classes start. I wish you were on my side."

"Mark, I am on your side. I'm trying to protect you, but a lot of church people don't trust you. If you quit this rebellion you're getting into---"

"No deal, Russ."

"It will go to Presbytery."

"Fine. I'll make my case there. Thanks for hiring the migrants."

"You can thank Ruth and Steve too."

"That's what I figured," Mark said.

He smiled to himself as he crossed the street to the manse. But immediately upon opening the door he missed Laura. Always she had been there to greet him with a smile and a kiss. Now the manse was a hollow shell without her. He picked a clean pair of jeans and drove back to the migrant camp. He joined Buck and his people singing around the fire.

The days passed. There was no letup in the heat wave. And there was no rain. More of the migrants were let go and were employed by Neeby Foods. Mark continued Sunday services. Gradually the number attending increased slightly. He continued visiting his people in the evenings, after working all day in the fields. They were nights of deep loneliness when, aching from his field labor, he tossed sleepless, wanting Laura. They spoke to each other frequently on the phone. Her voice, so close and yet so far away, deepened his loneliness and his wanting. "I want you to come home," he said. "I need you." Laura said she was ready to return. As the Bible said, he rejoiced and was exceeding glad.

Two days later she arrived. Mark was tempted to run off the potato field, to race home to greet her but he labored until quitting time. When he opened the manse door, there she was, beaming a welcoming smile, a long hug. "You may not believe me, Mark, but I missed Castle Rock. I missed you terribly. I also missed our people, Ruth and Steve, Larry and John, Darl and, yes, even Claudia Crowley!" She looked up at him with clear, determined eyes. "I'll never leave you again, Mark. Never, never, never!"

Chapter Twenty-Nine

He was pushing the speed limit along Castle Rock Road when the rain came. The sky had been overcast and the air muggy all week long. Each day his people prayed that the long-awaited rain would fall. Gradually the air became thick and soggy. Without announcing itself with scattered tentative raindrops, the storm came suddenly, slashing the horizon with spiked lightning and audacious thunder. Mark switched the headlights on. The rain fell with sudden solemnity, crashing down, mixed with smashing hail. Mark slowed down. The wipers could not cope with the deluge. He pulled into a Burger King lot. He was on his way to the migrant camp. Buck had telephoned him for help. Naomi was in labor.

Ten minutes passed. Mark drove the Buick toward the highway. He waited patiently for a break in the traffic and eased into a long line waiting for a light to turn green. It took another ten minutes before he was able to turn into the dirt road toward the camp. Naomi lay in a lower bunk, her eyes fixed upon a crack in the ceiling that dripped splashing drops of rain on the blanket that covered her. She smiled at Mark. She stifled an impending scream. Buck stood over her. He looked pale and stunned. Mark had parked the Buick close to the bunkhouse door. He led the way out as Buck easily cradled Naomi in his arms. As mark held the car's rear door open. Buck laid Naomi inside and sat down beside her. Head cradled in Buck's lap, Naomi moaned.

There was no letup in the rain. Mark leaned on the wheel, peering through the raucous swipes of the windshield wipers. At Chesterton Hospital he stopped under the canopied emergency entrance. He hurried into the foyer, where a nurse stood behind a counter. Mark knew her. "Emergency, Miss Markey," he said. "Baby on the way."

"Pastor Christopher," she cried. She pointed in the general direction of Buck. Naomi clung tightly to her husband, arms around his neck. "You know we can't admit—*her*!" She came out from behind the counter and attempted to whisper something in Mark's ear.

"Out of my way, Miss Markey," Mark shouted as he beckoned to Buck to follow him to the elevator. Mark knew his way around. He had visited his people here many times.

"This isn't right," Buck said as the elevator rose toward the maternity ward.

"What's not right?"

"Bringing Naomi here. They aren't going to like this."

"Let me worry about that," Mark said as the doors slipped open. He led the way as Buck bore Naomi toward a vacant bed. New mothers in the ward's other beds watched them with astonishment.

Mark quickly went outside the ward to the nurses station, where a young intern, stethoscope dangling around his neck, asked "Sir, are you responsible for this?"

"I'm afraid I am." He anticipated the worst.

The intern smiled and put out his hand. He had a serious dark face and sorrowing eyes. "Congratulations, sir," he said. Mark shook his hand vigorously. "You've just admitted the first Negro resident patient in the history of Chesterton Hospital."

Mark was on the hospital's list of accredited pastors and so he was permitted to stay for a brief time to lead Naomi and Buck in prayer. The intern came in to examine his new patient. Led by an attending nurse, the other women applauded. "Ladies," the nurse announced. "This is Naomi and her husband, Buck." They applauded again. "He's a little nervous so he'll say goodbye for now." Buck blew a kiss to Naomi. The nurse asked Mark to escort Buck to the room set aside for expectant fathers.

As he drove through Chesterton he noticed that Chesterton Fairgrounds was highly illuminated. He had attended the annual County Fair in the past. His church always had a tent in which the Presbyterian Women's Association served hot meals. In fact, Laura was there now as the ladies prepared for the fair's opening. The rainstorm had dissipated. He drove slowly through the thinning rain. He kept seeing the look on Naomi's face. It had been easy, almost too easy. How often he had been told how difficult, how impossible, it would be to bring about integration---of anything. And yet in a few months he had seen the integration of Neeby's labor force and its union. And of the Lewis Grocery and other stores along Main street in Castle Rock, and of the bus that ran between Chesterton and Castle Rock. Even Ruth Neeby's tavern was now open to Negroes.

Ruth had been one of the first to drop the color bar, and that was because he had simply asked her to drop it. One afternoon, on a visit to her apartment, he suggested that she permit Buck Washington to enter and to serve him. She was outraged at first, but later, when her father began employing the migrants that Sam Bryson had discharged, she relented and told Mark to inform Buck that he was welcome anytime. Soon after, Beulah stopped by Lewis grocery and bought some fruit from Fred. She did not go into the store, it's true, but she stood on the sidewalk as she made her selections from Fred's oudoor stands. After Mary Lewis died Fred invited her to enter the store. Since then Beulah had done all her grocery shopping there.

The integration of the hospital was a major achievement. This was a breakthrough he had not sought. Even if he had, he could never have predicted success. Might as well try to integrate the Chesterton County Fair!

Lightning split the southern sky. The idea was born.

Mark went around a block and drove back toward the fairgrounds. He wheeled the Buick between two high pillars from which paper tigers smiled. He identified himself and was admitted as a concessionaire. He parked the Buick in the employee's lot behind a squat gray frame building that housed the fairground offices. He ran through a Scotch mist to the Presbyterian tent. He leaped two steps, crossed the patio and thrust open the kitchen door..

Laura, Ruth and Steve were there. Ruth said that her bartender was minding the tavern. He took a chair beside them as they sat around a spindle-legged table. Steaming mugs of coffee lay neglected before them on the red checked oilcloth. Steve still had on his dusty jeans and red sport shirt he had worn all day at the farm. Mark told them about taking Naomi to the hospital.

"They admitted her?" Ruth asked. "I can't believe it. Everybody knows it's okay for them to go to emergency, but I never heard that any Negro has ever been admitted before."

"Do you know what that means?" Laura asked. "It means that Mark has just integrated the hospital."

"Who's next, Mark?" Steve asked slyly.

Mark stood up. "Ladies and gentleman," he said. He spoke as if he was a sideshow barker. "I propose we integrate this County Fair."

Steve laughed hilariously. "Why not?"

"Why not?" Mark repeated. "Young man, I hereby appoint you deputy commander of this movement. How many complementary admission tickets can you get?"

"Many as you need," Steve said. He ceremoniously polished his nails with the tail of his red shirt. "Can't we Ruth?"

"You bet," Ruth said. "Concessionaire's get lots of them. Not only for the church but also Neeby Foods. Dad has a booth in Exhibition Hall."

Laura was turning pale. She nervously stroked her forehead. "I don't know, Mark. This means trouble for sure."

Mark rocked back in his chair. "Oh, come on Laura," he said. "What's so startling? All I'm proposing is that we bring the migrants to the fair in a group. Each of them will have a ticket, including the young people and children. They will be peaceful orderly visitors, like everybody else who goes to the fair. They won't cause any trouble, believe me. I know them. I know them all. They're my second congregation."

"That's carrying it a bit too far, Mark," Laura said.

Closing his eyes and striking his fists together in anguish, Steve let out a derisive holler. "Trouble!" he shouted.. "Trouble! My God, man, you'll bring the entire county down on our heads." He looked sheepish. "I exaggerate." He quieted down, relaxed.

"Steve's right," Ruth said. She began to stutter, which was so unlike Ruth that the others looked at her in consternation. "Th-this is foolish. Th-this is utterly ridiculous. "Who-oo would ever have thought of such a thing? No-o. it's quite im-impossible. There will be a riot, a riot for sure, and--and somebody's bound to get hurt."

Laura, who had become increasingly tense with worry through the afternoon as the storm thundered by and came again, and who felt that the twisting and turning of tiny feet and hands within her body was in protest against the onslaught of wind and rain, stood up and walked to the window where water streamed through a rip in the canvas over the patio, while across the vacant flooded square the paper tigers smiled into the wind. In the fair office building a light burned brightly behind a window and a shadow passed in front of the light. She wondered if Sam Bryson, who was chairman of the fair, was there, and what would he say if he knew what they were plotting.

"I agree with Ruth," Laura said. "There's too much at stake. The people of Castle Rock are too much against us already."

"A minority," Mark protested. "Just a few."

"But the right minority!" Laura looked at him with fury in her eyes. "I told you, Mark. There's only so much I can take."

"Laura!" Mark put his arm around her. "Come here, sit down. You've had a terrible day. First the heat and now this storm. It's only a crazy idea I had. I won't go through with it if you don't want me to."

She sat down and looked up at him as tears flowed. "I didn't say I didn't want you to do it."

"It would be too much for you," Mark said. "I can't do it, not the way—the way you are. I can't ask that much of you."

Laura wiped her eyes. "It's not the people of Castle Rock I'm afraid of." She looked at Ruth and Steve, pleading for understanding. "It's Presbytery I'm afraid of, what they will do to you, Mark."

"Presbytery will support me," Mark said firmly. "They will support me because this is the right thing to do."

Ruth touched his hand. "I'm not arguing with you about that, Mark. But is this the time and is this the place? Think of your ministry. Think of your career."

She was perfectly right, Mark thought. A career in the ministry demanded conformity to the rules of Presbytery, especially the rule that a minister was responsible for the *peace and unity* of the church. The trouble was that the church was disunited from the *fellowship of all Christians*, a duty he was pledged to maintain. Furthermore, at what price could the peace of the church be maintained? Sometimes you had to disturb the peace to gain unity.

"I don't know why I was led to become involved with the migrants," he said. "All I know is that I became involved because Buck asked me to. I can't turn my back on Buck and his people. If I do, they'll continue to suffer. My job isn't done. Maybe when it is finished we'll have to leave Castle Rock. I don't know. I do know I can't leave until something is done to help the migrants."

Steve clapped his hands. "Good for you, Mark," he said. "That's the first time I've heard you say plainly what your intentions are. We've been working in the fields together, sometimes spending nights in that rotten bunkhouse, and I thought we were just a nutty pair of welfare workers. Boy, was I wrong! Now I see what you want. You want to lead a movement, an integration movement." He pounded the table. "Well, count me out! Helping the migrants at the camp is one thing, even letting them attend our church and buy stuff at our stores. But it's another thing to try to integrate the fair. It can't be done." He looked toward Ruth for support. "I'm not going to get involved, and that's that." Ruth and Laura were silent. Steve turned his attention to Mark, who had a faraway look in his eyes. "Mark, that's always been your plan, isn't it?"

"No, no," Mark said slowly. "Not exactly. I only wanted to help, and one thing led to another. Let me ask you a question, Steve. Isn't it possible that God had something to do with it? I don't have a plan, Steve. It's something better than a plan. Lord knows I didn't want it to come to this. But hardness of hearts—"

"People around here have been that way all their lives," Ruth said. "Nothing you do can change them."

"I've changed. And so have you, Ruth. Steve has changed—"

"And I've changed too!" Laura exclaimed. "O Lord, Mark, I have, I have! While I was away. I talked and talked with Nancy and Bromley and Earl and Sam and other servants. At the university I talked with my Negro friends. Oh, Mark, they opened my eyes, and my heart too. All along I thought I was a good Christian. But I was blind. Now, as the song goes, I see!"

"Let's pray together, shall we?" Mark said. They stood together and clasped hands, forming a bonding circle. Mark led them in a brief prayer for guidance.

"What if the migrants don't want to go to the fair?" Steve asked. "What if Buck tells them there's danger they'll get hurt?"

"I'll ask them tonight," Mark said.

"I can't wish you luck," Steve said.

In the Buick on the way to the manse Mark said "I won't go ahead with it if you don't want me to, Laura."

She leaned her head on his shoulder. "I want you to go ahead," Mark. "I won't say I'm not afraid, because I am. I know it's wrong the way the Negroes are treated. While I was away I wished you hadn't gotten involved with them. If you had only said no to Buck when he came to the manse to ask you to preach—" She paused and smiled. "Of course you could never have refused, could you?"

Mark saw her safely into the manse and turned back into the rain, which had settled into a steady drizzle. The wind had died down. He found his way without difficulty to the migrant camp. No one was in sight. He walked through the rain-soaked yard to the bunkhouse and opened the door. About an inch of water flowed out. He stepped inside. The place was dark. No light shone from the cubicles. The bunkhouse was empty. Water covered the floor.

He found hem all in the potato barn. Women and children, covered by blankets, huddled in the bins to keep warm. The men were seated on boxes around a tall oil drum from which flames spurted brightly. Surprisingly, Buck was there, dropping sticks of kindling wood into the fire.

"Hello everyone," Mark called out cheerfully. "Buck, what are you doing here?"

"Nothing's going to happen until tomorrow," he said. "I'll go back early."

For an hour he debated with Buck about integrating the fair. "I've always wanted to go there," Buck admitted. "Since years ago. It wasn't a legal matter. Negroes know they weren't welcome there, just like they weren't welcome in most places run by white folks. Things are getting better now, but the fair? That's something else. Tell you what, Mark, I'm willing and I'll put it to the men right now. You come back tomorrow morning, okay? Nobody will be working. Fields are flooded."

The next morning Buck told Mark that the majority of the migrants agreed to go to the fair. Few thought there was a chance they would get in.

Two days later, in the light of early evening, just as the sun was going down, the fanged tigers smiled down from the posters. The space between the two tigers was more than twenty feet. To Mark, as he approached the fairgrounds gate, the space seemed narrow indeed.

He was at the head of a straggly column of migrants. He wished Buck was beside him. But Buck was at the hospital, still waiting for his child to be born. While he was flanked by Lonny and Steve, he felt very much alone. It was impossible, he mused, but he thought he could hear every soft fall of his footsteps upon the black pavement of North Avenue. The gate seemed far away, and yet close, like a dream he could not quite remember. Even the tigers seemed real. But perhaps that was because they copied, in a strange way, the smiling faces and obstinate stance of Sheriff Delaney and his four deputies who, elbow to elbow, barred the gate.

Mark looked neither to the right nor the left. He tried to focus upon the sheriff, who, arms crossed, thrust forward the full weight of his authority. His stiff lips worked furiously. Mark knew the sheriff must be calling to him, but his words were lost among the slobbering jeers and fist-high threats of white fairgoers.

A Bible verse thrust itself suddenly upon his mind. *No man, having set his hand to the plow, and looking back, is worthy of the Kingdom of God.* He would not look back. He would force one leaden foot ahead of the other until he came face to face with the evil force.

He did not want violence. All day he had told himself that. At the migrant camp that afternoon, as he handed out the complementary fair tickets, he voiced his plea: "Whatever happens, don't fight back. Lay down. Cover your head with your hands. Lie limp. If they pick you up and carry you away, let their will be done." He had paused, as if in prayer. "God knows," he had told them, "we will overcome."

Overcome what? The song had no answer. Fear, perhaps. Yes, that was the enemy. Fear in the face of the tiger. Mark forced himself to take one more step. He was face to face with Sheriff Delaney.

"In the name of the law," the sheriff proclaimed sternly, addressing Mark. He thrust his wide-jawed face close to Mark's. "I order you to disperse. Go back to your camp."

Mark looked the sheriff directly with blinking eyes. He felt a quaver in his throat. "We have tickets to enter the fairgrounds," he said. "We intend to use them."

"This is an illegal march," the sheriff said firmly. In his hand his club quivered. "Disperse in the name of the people!"

"People!" This from Steve, who came abreast of Mark. "We demand justice!"

Mark attempted to wave Steve away, but to no avail.

The sheriff maintained his face-to-face encounter with Mark. "Pastor Christopher," he said, "take these damn niggers back to their camp where they belong. That's an order!" He backed away a step. "These people have no right on the street. This is an illegal protest. They're blocking traffic."

"We're coming through," Mark said evenly. He glanced over his shoulder. The migrants stood quietly. A few children whispered to one another. Their elders quietly linked arms, their faces placid, patient. Mark stepped forward. Sheriff Delaney, quicker than a tiger, swung his club. The white faces around them gaped and let out feline screams

The blow fell on Steve's shoulder. He, quicker than the sheriff, had imposed his body under the club, at the same time thrusting Mark aside, an action so much unexpected that Mark staggered. Steve collapsed onto the pavement before Mark could catch him.

Mark bent down to enfold Steve's stricken body. With what malevolence then did the sheriff rain down upon them both the full fury of his frustration—yes, and weakness too. Not even the sheriff's torrent of vocal abuse caused Mark to refrain from his task of raising Steve from the dark road's surface. He cried "Steve, oh Steve" out of pity, perhaps out of his own weakness and despair. For had not Steve taken upon himself the violence of the sheriff's blow?

Sheriff Delaney backed away. Lonny led the way as the entire group of migrants marched between the tigers and entered the fairgrounds. They waved their complementary passes triumphantly as they presented them to the ticket tenders.

Within minutes thick meaty hands thrust Mark and Steve into the back seat of a police car. Sheriff Delaney opened the siren wide. Mark was helping Steve sit up when Steve asked the bitter question: "Are we going to jail?"

"I suppose," Mark said. A finger to his lips, Mark cautioned Steve to whisper. He gestured toward Sheriff Delaney and the driver in the front seat, which was separated from them by a glass shield.

"Did they all get in?" Steve asked.

"Yes," Mark said. "We won."

"Who else got arrested?"

"I don't know. Only us, I hope."

Steve slid into a corner as the car tilted. "We did what you wanted, didn't we?"

"We sure did, Steve. I'm sorry you got hurt."

"That's all right. I can take it. How about you?"

"I have a lump or two."

Steve twisted in pain. "We did integrate the fair, didn't we?"

"I don't know. Lonny was leading everybody though the gate, last I saw."

"O God," Steve moaned.

"Don't talk like that, Steve. It doesn't help."

"I think we're going to jail."

Sheriff Delaney, in the front seat beside the driver, slid open the glass shield. "I heard that! Steve, I know your name now. Yes, that's where you're going, county jail. Not you, Pastor."

"Thank you sheriff, but I'll take my chances," Mark replied.

"Bill," he said to the driver, "stop at the corner."

The car pulled to the corner, outside the Times building on Chesterton Avenue.

"Get out, Pastor," the sheriff ordered. Mark opened the door on the traffic side. On the curb he waved to Steve, who, deserted, waved back feebly.

There had been no chance to explain and, even if there had been, what was there to explain? Mark was up against it now. In the security of his study he might have said, "Tell me about it," and induce the therapy of counseling technique to work its mysterious wonders. But this was no time for works of wonder. The time for action had, at last, arrived. Illogical as it seemed the time cried out for a demonstration which he did not want but which was inevitable. Perhaps that was the meaning of Christ's words from the Cross: *Not my will but thine be done.* The time for thinking-through, mulling over, careful dodging of the issue, was past. Now was the time to put his body on the line.

Mark walked with leaden pace up Main Street toward North Avenue. Not many people were on the street, but the few who were there hurried past him. No doubt, he thought, they were on their way to the fair with visions of dancing lights and tambourines signaling intercession. Strange that his Gethsemane should be Main Street. At Church Street, across from the Chesterton National Bank, he faced a red light. How good it was to pause, to try to think, to clear his blurred vision for a moment. Don't walk! Run perhaps? Walk! Straight ahead, north toward the fair, the fun house in the garden, the intercession for men's dreams. But reality too. Like standing on the stone porch after church and greeting his people one by one and knowing the tearing sense of failure as all the while the kindly voices said, "Fine sermon, Pastor."

You sleep and dream, he thought, and hurry to your work and home again, to sleep and dream again. You mouth foolish urgings, regurgitating ancient precepts, verses from the Book of Proverbs. You visit and you counsel, while not seeming to counsel, touch upon the very core of people's lives, and yet do not touch them, not really where they live. You edged, sometimes, close to the life of your people, but always a certain distance separates you from them.

Now the distance was closing. The midway lights lit the twilight sky. Hurdy-gurdy and carousel. Looking back, he saw people following after him, all hurrying to the pleasure of the County Fair. Each face was fully concentrated upon that goal, that dream. They bent their heads and carried themselves forward with eagerness and anticipation of the pleasure of the night. Yes, and forgetfulness too. But he could not forget. Ahead the tigers smiled.

The gate was clear. He showed his pass to the boy on guard, walked through toward the square, then across to the midway arch, and under the arch. There they were: his people, the Negroes queued before Wonders of the World, all together, in a group waiting for tickets. Quietly, the patience and the wisdom of centuries upon them, they waited until white people presented their money. Then they presented theirs and received their tickets and went in behind the white people, not saying anything, not laughing, but quietly until they vanished into the tent.

All except Lonny, who turned at the last moment and saw Mark gazing at him. Lonny hesitated, as if wondering if he ought to wait, then waved to Mark, turned and went inside.

Mark wandered in search of the deputies who might seize him and take him away. Here and there a fairgrounds cop paced placidly. No one paid attention to him. He returned to the parking lot, started the Buick and headed down North Avenue toward the Chesterton County jail.

Chapter Thirty

Doctor Abengraph was in a rage. She strode around the manse bedroom shaking a thermometer she had just removed from Mark's mouth.

"That Roach," she exclaimed. "That horse doctor! He treats an animal better than he treated you." She held the thermometer up to a window, then looked at Mark with reproach. "You didn't leave it in long enough," she said. She thrust the tiny glass rod into his mouth. "And you, Pastor Christopher, you've no better sense. What sort of a fool stays in jail when he doesn't have to? Preachers! Hah! And don't touch that thermometer." Her large face with its homespun features flamed with indignation. She removed the thermometer again and read it. "Hundred one," she said. "That Roach. Hah!"

Mark twisted and turned. The double bed, minus Laura, felt infirm. He rolled over on his side to get a better look at his busy doctor. "I suppose this is one of your easy days," he said. He threw off the sheet and blanket that covered him. He made a painful attempt to get out of bed. His injured hands could not manage to push his body high enough.

"You lay down, mister," the doctor ordered. He slumped back on the cushion.

"Not another soul in Castle Rock is sick today?" Mark asked.

"Hah!" Doctor Abengraph stomped from the room. Mark laughed, despite his painful wounds, as he heard her mumbling to herself while descending the stairs. She called out "Laura, where are you? Maybe you can do something with that stubborn man."

Laura had taken him from the jail to Chesterton Hospital. An emergency doctor bound up his open wounds, including his damaged hands. Mark insisted on visiting Naomi, who had given birth to a boy.

Buck was there too. The migrant camp was closing. The county health department had condemned the bunkhouse. Buck had arranged a merger of his migrant unit with a Chesterton group. A caravan would take them all to Illinois for the September harvest. Steve was let go without charge. Sheriff Delaney was placed on indefinite leave, with pay. The fair had its highest attendance in many years. The news of what happened at the fair was on the front page of Friday's *Chesterton Times.* Steve told Mark that the fact they were both "jailbirds" was "the talk of the town." The elders had asked Laura to preach. On Sunday the church was packed. Few said they missed Buck Washington.

By the end of the following week Mark's temperature was normal. Doctor Abengraph told him he could be "up and about." He insisted he was ready to preach.

Sunday morning dawned. Laura held Mark's arm as they crossed the street to enter the sanctuary. Every pew was filled. Everyone stood up. No one spoke.

Mark preached, without notes, about Christ in the desert and how beautiful it must have been there. When he raised his bandaged hands his people gasped. They were quiet and attentive to his message. They nodded in assent as he prayed for tolerance and understanding of others. He prayed for forgiveness of prejudice and hate. He gave thanks for new life and healing for the suffering. He confessed weakness and confusion. He looked out over the bowed heads of his people. He saw that Orson Coffey was still worried about his still-ailing cow; that Margaret Gore, clasping and unclasping her hands, wondered what to do about her rebellious son, Ted; that Fred Lewis was asking for strength to carry on after the death of his wife, Mary; that Harry Ironwood was worn out from overwork, and that is why he dozed; that Ruth shared with Steve, by whose side she sat, the hope of a love rewarded; that Howie Mason's face was somber because he knew he would never walk again after a fall from a ladder at Neeby's; that Mrs. Lincoln was prepared for death; that Blinko and Claudia Crowley were on the road to independence and responsibility now that Blinko was working his farm; and that Laura was worried, not for herself, but for him.

Following the benediction Mark sat down. The high-backed chair creaked. He bowed his head in prayer and waited for the people to leave the sanctuary. They would understand, he thought, why he could not shake their hands today. Only gradually did he become aware that Mrs. Trane, at the organ, had failed to begin the postlude. The people were silent. They remained seated. No shuffling feet broke the silence. He looked up and met the gaze of Russ Neeby, who was sitting in the second row. His people were waiting for him. Always his people waited for him to march up the center aisle, all the way to the narthex, before they would rise to follow him. He knew then that they would not leave unless he asked them to leave, or else do what he had always done: thank them for their attendance by walking among them, as Christ walked among his people, acknowledging their oneness, the bonding of their lives in mutual fellowship.

Mark returned to the pulpit. "Friends—"

Suddenly he knew, suddenly he was aware. These were the saints, as imperfect as himself. These were the Fellowship, of which he was now one. How this happened he did not know. He did know that they had been strangers to him before. Now they were his friends. Could he be one of their's?

How he had mocked them in their hour of need. Tell me about it. What had he really known about their lives, their trials? They had asked for bread and he had given them stones.

He stepped down and walked among his people toward the narthex. His people followed him out to the porch. Neil Adams, the sexton, said "Enjoyed your sermon, Pastor." Neil stooped to hook the open door.

Then they all came: Lillian Ironwood, handing him his check in front of everybody, and smiling about it too, as if it was the most natural thing in the world; Fred Lewis gave his arm an extra squeeze and said his invention was coming along just fine; Blinco Crowley passed by on the other side, waving a swift greeting, but Claudia spoke a soft word and hurried her children, Alvin and Mavis, down the steps; Orson Coffey said Nance was feeling a mite poorly and that's why she couldn't come; Lucius Levoning shuffled by and replied to Mark's question that everything was fine at the bank; Harry Ironwood whacked his shoulder; Doctor Abengraph told him to drop by her office to have some bandages removed; Marian Orduff wiped a tear with a gloved hand; Abner Zenkorski, who had not been in church since Easter, forgot himself and squeezed Mark's hand. Mark grimaced in pain.

The young people, who had held back in a group, came forward. Cray and Cincy held hands; the Lewis girls; Lester Ironwood; Ted Gore; and Jenny Glen. They all talked at once: "What was it like in jail?" And," Did they beat you with a rubber hose?" and "Will Steve Roberts have to go to jail again?"

Then came Steve and Ruth, with Ruth taking strong hold of Steve's arm. Steve examined Mark's hands. "I forgot to bring my Purple Heart," he said.

Ruth said "I didn't know you had one, Steve."

"It's Mark who deserves one now," Steve said seriously.

"Maybe I've won a battle," Mark said, "but I may have lost the war."

"At least you got your congregation back," Steve said.

That afternoon, while Laura was napping upstairs, Pastor Fleming came to the manse to inform Mark that Attumwa Presbytery had appointed a commission to investigate charges laid against him by the church's elders. The charges were general but the evidence was specific. Duane Roberts, Lucius Levoning and Orson Coffey made it plain at a hearing. They believed that Mark had "consorted," as their charge put it, with Ruth Neeby and other female members of the church. In addition, they stated, Mark had gone against the desire of the elders by inviting Negroes to the church's worship services. Mr. Coffey had also testified that, despite repeated warnings, Mark had refused to stop associating with unsavory, but unidentified, characters.

"Meanwhile," Pastor Fleming said, "according to the elders, good people with bonafide spiritual needs have been neglected, attendance at services has fallen off to the point of disappearance, collections have declined, pledges have gone unpaid, and parents have refused to send their children to Sunday school and the youth society. In a nutshell, Mark, the charge is that you have neglected your duties as pastor by spending an inordinate amount of time counseling a certain number of individuals, some of whom are not members of the church, including migrants, and resulting in your spending a night in jail."

"What happens next?" Mark asked.

Pastor Fleming looked very tired. "I hate having to do this, Mark. It's the most painful thing I've ever had to do." He glanced at Mark's bandaged hands. "O my God, Mark. What happened?'

Mark told him the entire story about that Saturday night at the Chesterton County Fair.

"What happens now?" Mark asked.

"A trial before Presbytery. The Commission recommends it. There is no other way to clear yourself. Even if you succeed, the stigma remains. I advise you to resign."

"The church, you mean."

"That would be automatic. I mean your candidacy for the ministry."

Mark leaped up. He threw down the paper that recited the charges against him.

"Never, never!" he said firmly. "I have another two semesters to go at Divinity Hall."

"There are other churches, Mark." Pastor Fleming paused. "In other presbyteries, of course."

Mark stiffened to control his anger. "I have half a mind to go back to being a Baptist." He laughed. "Maybe a Methodist."

"Seriously, Mark. I don't think you have much choice. The hearing is not a trial. It's not a matter of finding you guilty or innocent." Pastor Fleming visibly squirmed. "To tell you the truth, Mark, this kind of case, excuse the word, is simply a way our denomination has of keeping a congregation happy. Pastors shift from one congregation to another because they wear out their welcome, they just don't fit in, so to speak. A few elders or rich members think that changing ministers is good for business. It's a burden we pastors must bear."

"Then no pastor is safe," Mark said curtly.

"We all walk a tightrope," Pastor Fleming said. "But that's part of the deal we pastors have to make. Let's just say you have been careless, Mark. You haven't taken the proper precautions. This is only your second pastoral experience. Go somewhere else. Plenty of churches would give anything to have a young, active minister like you. California, for example. You've had it as far as Castle Rock and Attumwa Presbytery are concerned."

Later that afternoon Mark and Laura drove out to their Shangri-La, a hidden valley brimming with marsh grass and cattails. They had discovered the valley the previous fall while exploring the countryside. Because Mark's hands were bandaged and sore, Laura was driving. She turned the Buick sharply into a state forest preserve and entered a narrow dirt fire road. Down a slow descent through heavy brush there it was: their private place, silent and secure, grayed over with hill mist. Grotesque stumps peppered the swamp. It was said that a fire long ago had swept the valley, leaving the blackened maples as its monument. A legend alleged that, after the fire, the valley floor sank and the stream which clove the basin overshot its bank. Now, blackbirds possessed the valley. At times fog rolled off the high forbidding cliffs to form a solid gray cap.

Laura parked near a plank bridge that crossed the algae-green creek. Far away a bullfrog bellowed. Along the banks the dogwoods burst in glowing red and white salute to nature's glory. From the stream's shore Laura skipped flat stones across the still water.

Mark told her the message that Pastor Fleming had given him. "Should I quit?" he asked.

Laura bent low and, with a long curving swing, let loose a stone. It strode, with ever shortening pace, over the stream. "If I weren't so big," Laura said, "I could do a lot better than that."

"You're not that big, Laura. Just wait a little while longer."

"A lot you know about it." She felt her enlarged "bump."

"Feel anything?"

"Not now. Maybe later. It's sleeping."

"I hope it's a boy," Mark said.

"Okay by me," Laura said with an appealing smile. "I think it's a girl." She was silent for a moment, listening to the raucous calls of unseen crows. "You really don't want to quit, do you?"

"No, but we have to ask ourselves, what good can we do here, if so many elders are against us?"

"The people aren't against us, Mark. That's just so much rubbish concocted by Duane Roberts. You have to take his kind for what it's worth." Laura hurled a stone far down the stream. "There isn't any law that says pastors have to love everybody." Orange and black butterflies sprayed from the marsh grass. Along the stream adult cattails shed their furry flowers.

August lingered under the summer sun. Mark returned to Divinity Hall as the countryside turned the color of old gold. With insatiable appetite he read Kierkeguard clear through, returned to Bultmann, staggered over Calvin and Tillich. Each day marched with leaden step. Saturdays found him with nothing to preach and thus the evening light grew dim and faded on unmarked pages. And yet, when he mounted the pulpit, and met the eager eyes of his people, he felt the grip of a renewed passion. His people continued to crown him with the ultimate glory: fixed eyes for his serious points, thoughtful brows for his rhetorical questions, easy laughter for his quiet jokes.

But, back in his study, which became his habit after each service, he prayed continuously, as all the while the absent voices of Duane and Lucius and Orson and Russ and Sam accused him from the witness box.

As for Laura, she held her peace, at least as long as she could. But there were occasions when, her patience pushed to its limit, she permitted her pent-up exasperation to pour forth.

"What are you trying to do to yourself?" she cried. "Where is all this going to get you? Dinner's cold again and it's no good reheating it. And I thought you wanted to go to Shangri-La. I don't know what's come over you lately. You don't pay me any mind in the slightest. If it's the baby, why don't you tell me?" She placed her hand on her abdomen. "I'm ugly, is that it? You don't care for me anymore! You can't stand the sight of me."

All he seemed to be able to do on those occasions was to stand back and look at her, knowing he was looking slightly bemused, but unable to change his expression. This was all so temporary, he thought. Laura became child-like, not only in her speech but also in her silly behavior. She was not content to walk up the three steps from the sidewalk to the manse porch, she had to leap. She could not rest contented against a tree, she had to pretend she was going to climb it. She could not serve him fruit cocktail out of a can, she had to heap a bowl overflowing with every imaginable kind of fresh fruit: honeydew, apples, peaches, strawberries and succulent pears. Everything she did was done in excess, from her words to every action. It was as if, not content to be a child-bearer, she had to be child-like.

Laura welcomed him into her arms at night and then rose at midnight to sack the refrigerator. Before dawn she was in the yard hanging out wash, and breakfast was not served until she scrubbed the kitchen floor. Her mania for cleanliness caused her to tidy the two top drawers of his bureau, which meant he was forever upset about missing shoestrings, nail clippers, tie clips and other sundries. The last straw was when she washed his electric razor, motor case and all.

"You've ruined it!" he shouted. "What am I to do? Do you want me to go behind the pulpit looking like a Trade Smith cough drop?"

September's eloquent Sundays, it's tranquil Saturdays, fled. October, like a masked thief, chased the fallen leaves in tiptoed silence and ushered in the sad long days of Indian Summer. The time for his trial drew near.

The trial was scheduled to be held in First Church of Chesterton. The location was supposed to be fair, since it would give defenders and accusers alike greater opportunity to attend. Besides, Darby Persimmon, an elder of First Church who was a member of the Commission, insisted, for the excellent reason that he had to keep in close touch with his law office down the street.

As chairman of the Commission, Reverend Keith Conaway had the unpleasant task of introducing the evidence, which he gave in the way of a report on the Commission's findings. These consisted generally of a summary of charges made by witnesses who had appeared in secret before the Commission. Pastor Conaway recommended that the charges be reduced to a single offense: that Mr. Christopher had failed to *maintain the peace and unity of the church,* as he had pledged when he was assigned to be Student Pastor of the First Presbyterian Church of Castle Rock.

"In other words," said Mr. Persimmon in his opening remarks, Mark had "willfully and consciously acted in such a manner and engaged in such activities as to split his congregation into two camps, doing nothing whatsoever to heal the breach for which he was responsible." Standing before the representatives of the Presbytery's member churches, Mr. Persimmon stretched himself to the full dignity of his height. "I leave aside all manner of moral turpitude and laxity which have been charged before the Commission, but which in the context of the charge being considered here aided and abetted the deplorable condition into which this congregation has been led."

The facts themselves were well known: the Commission's report contained a sufficient number of sworn statements to indicate that the congregation was indeed split. While many had flocked to Mr. Christopher's banner following integration of the Chesterton County Fair, a significant minority had refused to attend worship services and had threatened to withdraw their financial support. Among the latter was Sam Bryson, who provided a fifth of the church's income.

"Matters have come to such a pass," Mr. Persimmon said, "That if it were not for reserves carefully built up by the church's trustees, the congregation would not be able to pay Mr. Christopher's salary. Needless to say this contractual obligation has been met, after some delay, but the Presbytery tax upon the church, to say nothing of the Synod and General Assembly payments have not. Where would our great church be if we continued to permit this to happen?"

Mr. Persimmon took silence as support and continued: "Means are provided in the Constitution of our church whereby Presbytery may, after serious deliberation, remove a pastor from his charge. Fathers and brethren, as we are given authority, let us proceed to act in a manner commensurate with the gravity of the matter."

Mark was called to the front of the church to answer the charge laid against him. He sat down on a spindly chair which had been provided. It was set in the middle of the chancel, where he was between the Presbytery's moderator and Stated Clerk on one hand and Commission members on the other. Congregational laymen and clergy were scattered in the first few rows of pews.

"We are waiting, Mr. Christopher," Pastor Conaway said, his voice warmly encouraging, which resulted in a serious frown from Mr. Persimmon.

Mark looked to his left to observe the Commissioners. They were a very serious lot, he noticed. He looked around the sanctuary, gazed toward the ceiling, from which dark shaded chandeliers dangled from chains. This is a great church, he told himself. The ceiling's high vault lifted a weight from his spirit. Great stone blocks, fluted from the floor to the ceiling, bore time upward to infinity. Through purple and crimson stained glass windows the sun was transformed to a million strands of colored light. A world was hushed, monument to faith. Stone; glass; silence; death!

"I have nothing to say." Mark uttered those words deliberately, conscientiously, permanently. There was silence in the church. Somewhere outside a siren sounded, loudly, close at first, then faded away.

"Do you deny the charge?" Mr. Persimmon asked sharply.

"How can I deny it?"

"Then you admit it?"

"I neither deny it or admit it. The charge is a fraud."

Pastor Conaway shook his head. "Mark, this is a serious charge."

"I deny that it is serious."

"Are you," said Mr. Persimmon thickly, his bulk rising slowly, "challenging the rights of Presbytery?"

"That is for you to say, sir. I am only a meek and mild student."

"Be careful, young man."

"Oh, yes. Be careful." Mark rose to his feet. He started down the steps that led to the sanctuary's floor.

Mr. Persimmon appeared to be about to dash after him. "Where are you going?" he shouted.

Mark kept going. He turned around. "You have the charge, Mr. Persimmon," he said clearly, so that all in the church could hear him. "You certainly don't need me. If I were a politician, I would say, let the record speak for itself. But I am not a politician. I do not run for the office of minister, to be elected to it by popular vote. Either you take my word for what I am doing or you do not. That is your choice. As for me, I choose to go back to my people where I can do some good."

At this, Mark quickly turned. "I will be obedient to my Lord!" With that he walked quickly up the central aisle and out into the sun.

Church Street was lined with the cars of the Presbytery people. You always knew where Presbytery was meeting by the cars. Was that all he could think about? He laughed aloud. His mind was like ice. He felt girdled by thick stone. It chilled his stomach, then his bowels, reaching to his groin. Only once before had he experienced this feeling of frigid isolation That was when Pastor Fleming's committee reviewed his application for a scholarship. He had been cast out of the meeting while the committee members debated among themselves whether he was worthy of their support. He was left alone, pacing a dark damp hallway. He remembered a frozen moment of silence from the sanctuary beyond the closed forbidding doors, then Pastor Fleming summoning him to hear the dreadful news that he was being cast off, condemned.

Now, as the sun-stroked white concrete pavement, blinding as snow, lifted and fell like a hazy tide, he felt his blood thrash like rock-spring water and his flesh quiver as if pricked by itchy icicles. He returned to the purple and crimson gloom of the sanctuary.

At first he was not noticed. He sat down in a rear pew to listen, but not to hear, a report by Pastor Donald Campbell, chairman of the Missions Committee. Suddenly there was an explosive cough. Two pews ahead, Duane Roberts turned his head and caught Mark's eye. Their mutual stare held a long time. Mark suppressed a dry smile. He had caught his enemy unawares. Slowly Duane rose to his feet. "Mister Moderator!" he cried out.

In mid-sentence, Pastor Campbell stuttered into silence. Reverend Howard Nichols, the moderator, asked: "Point of order, Mr. Roberts?"

Out in the aisle, almost running, Duane headed for the chancel. He mounted the steps and whispered into the moderator's ear. "Mr. Christopher has returned," he announced triumphantly. As all heads turned and a babble broke the sanctuary's peace, the moderator banged his gavel several times. When silence returned, he shielded his eyes against the light. "I must ask you, Mr. Christopher, to come forward."

Chapter Thirty-One

Driving back to Castle Rock, Mark searched for words to announce his fate to Laura. How often, near morning, had words come to his mind which would shake men's minds and sear their souls. But those words had come in dreams and had flown forgotten at dawn's first breaking. They were the words of the priest too sensitive to his calling. They were not those of the man. How far from humanity he had moved! Take seriously the charge of dedication: You are God's man—and you lose flesh and blood, become hollow bones prattling and whistling in the breeze. God's man! We—I—are all God's men. To be set apart is to be God's man no more. Even in spirit it was not right for any man to be separated from his fellow-man.

There was more freedom in the fields. Bending his back alongside Buck, he felt the dignity of free choice. At a furrow's end he was just beginning to feel equal and had leveled himself to be what a pastor ought to be: free to associate with whom he chose for the sake of others. Yes, not even for God's sake, for evil can be committed in the Name of God.

But this was preaching to himself again. Not a good sign. This was rationalizing. He was making excuses for himself. Mark glanced at the speedometer and slowed down, just in time, as the turn into Castle Rock road came up fast. Around the bend, Harry Ironwood's house on the hill shone golden in the slanting light of the western sun. To the right, the meadows slid into the valley's shadow.

Main Street was quiet. Not a soul stirred along its wide three blocks. On the right, the manse stood helpless and alone, naked to the street, vulnerable. Mark inched the Buick into the driveway, cut the ignition and leaned heavily on the steering wheel. The clock ticked away the time. The distance from the garage to the kitchen looked immense. Laura would have dinner ready. I've been dismissed, he would tell her. Choose other words. We've got to move. No, be gentle. Tell her you have decided to look for another church. Don't tell her what Presbytery did. She could not bear knowing. Remember the baby!

Mark eased out of the car. He was at the kitchen door in a flash of time, and there she was standing by the stove, not doing anything, just standing there with one hand on her hip while steam hissed from the pressure cooker and time stopped.

"Hello," she said, not looking up. "How did it go?" Steam spurted from the cooker. Laura took the pot to the sink, turned the faucet and placed the pot beneath the gushing water. "Well?" she said.

"I've been dismissed."

"Did you spit in their eye?"

"I imagine I did."

"When do we leave?"

"As soon as we can."

"Oh, okay." Laura said. "You'll never guess what happened today."

Mark put his arm around her and she curved her back to fit in his embrace.

"Don't you want to know?" Mark asked her.

"About you, yes. About them, no. Don't you want to know what happened here?"

"Laura, I just can't get over you. I was scared to have to tell you about the Presbytery's action. But you take it as if it didn't mean anything. Let me look at you." He turned her around. Her fair skin glowed with health and her red hair shone like sunset in the sun. Only the slightest trembling of her lips, as if she was about to say something, betrayed the thinness of the thread by which her courage was suspended. "Darling." He held her tightly. "Sweetheart." He enfolded her softly, as the pain of what had happened struck like hot iron.

"None of that," Laura said. She pushed him away.

He helped her set the table. When they were seated and he had said the blessing, he asked her what had happened that day that was such an important event.

"Pastor Fleming telephoned." Laura said. "Isn't that wonderful?"

"What's wonderful about it?" Mark asked glumly. "I wish he had attended the trial. Might have done me some good."

"He wants to see you."

"That's nice. I'm in no shape to see him."

"He wants to come here, Mark. He wants to help us. Be reasonable."

Laura took it upon herself to make the call. And so it was that Pastor Fleming came to the rescue. He arrived the next day. Laura was frantically busy in the kitchen preparing coffee and sandwiches when the doorbell rang. She thanked him profusely for coming. "I should have come long ago," he said.

They gathered in the parlor. Pastor Fleming told them he had received a full report on the trial. "Travesty, a travesty!" he said. He hugged Laura and did the same to Mark. When they were all seated comfortably in the parlor, Laura and Mark on the sofa and Pastor Fleming in a lounge chair opposite them, he leaned forward, clasping his hand as if in prayer. "I'm embarrassed by the charge," he said. "I wish I had been there, but, you see, trials are conducted in privacy. Only those whose presence is pertinent to the trial are, shall I say, invited. Mark, my church is your sponsor. Every member of our church is committed to support you in your goal of being ordained to the ministry. I'm sorry to say that we have let you down. We have let you both down. But being sorry isn't enough. Time for action, you two."

He explained that, as the official interim moderator of Mark's church, he could call a meeting of the church's Session or a meeting of the congregation for a special purpose. "If it's okay with you both I will call for a congregational meeting to be held after next Sunday's service."

"What for?" Mark asked.

"To tell them what happened at the trial, of course."

"What good will that do?"

"Well, in the first place, they have to be told about the trial. That's required. But I have something else on my mind. Don't worry. I'm on your side." He smiled broadly.

"Oh, I'm going to enjoy this." Laura joined in the laughter. "Moreover, Mark, I will have the pleasure of hearing you preach. They tell me you are quite a zinger."

Laura wondered who would take care of Pastor Fleming's church in Attumwa while he was gone. "I've given myself a Sunday off, so my assistant will fill in for me. Before I go, Mark, I would like to hear, from you, what happened at the trial."

"I hardly know where to begin," Mark said. "I was out on the street when the vote was taken and I went back in just long enough to hear the verdict. All there was before that was the Commission's report, which made me out to be a disturber of the status quo. At least that's my opinion of it. The exact charge was disturbing the peace, a misdemeanor if you're a layman but practically a criminal one if you're a student pastor, I suppose. Oh, you should have heard Darby Persimmon. I mean 'Are you challenging the rights of Presbytery?' he asks. That was after I told him the charge was a fraud."

"Good for you!" Pastor Woods cried, clapping his hands.

"Then I took off. I mean, really, I walked out. The issue wasn't integration. It was that I was supposed to have split the congregation. Peace and unity of the church and all that. Behind it all was the fact that giving has gone down. Nothing speaks louder than money."

"Was there anything else?" Laura asked. She looked at him evenly. "You know what I mean---"

Pastor Fleming interrupted her. "Is this something personal? If so---"

"Not at all," Mark said. "The charge implicated that I was spending too much time counseling some women in private."

"Good heavens!" Pastor Fleming said. "All pastors do, or should do."

"One of my elders had something to do with that, I think. He was there."

"You walked out?" Pastor Woods asked.

"I'd had it," Mark said. "I thought, well, what's the use? I had all sorts of speeches prepared, if I had the opportunity. I was going to call them blind leaders of the blind, that sort of thing. But when I was up there, near the pulpit, like a condemned man, I thought that this was a dead place. Everyone was so gloomy. It didn't seem real. I could imagine this happening to somebody else, but I found it hard to believe it was happening to me. I'm not a crusader. I thought the ministry was a nice glove into which I would fit comfortably. I mean, I had no intention that what happened at the Fair should happen. It just happened." Mark looked at Laura and Pastor Fleming for understanding because he could not understand it himself. He heaved a sigh. Despite his determination to control himself, he felt tearful. Laura held his hand.

Pastor Fleming shook his head. "If it's too much for you, Mark—"

Mark took a deep breath. "I'm okay," he said. "I appreciate your kindness, Pastor Fleming. I want to tell you. I was told the result of the vote. It was unanimous. There were a few abstentions."

"Cowards," Laura said loudly. "Cowards!" She turned to Pastor Fleming. "What are we going to do?" she asked him. "Will we have to move?"

"I don't know, dear," the minister said. "I will do the best I can for you, I promise. Let's pray about it, shall we?"

Laura cried as Pastor Fleming's prayer flowed by her. She heard his voice but not his words. She tightened her grip on Mark's hand. "My God! My God!" was all she could say.

Later, after Pastor Fleming had left and they were alone together on the sofa, she said "We'll go back to Attumwa. You can finish your studies. Then you can be find a real church and be ordained."

"Laura, please. You're not thinking. I've been found guilty. That can't be undone. The stigma will follow me the rest of my life. What's done can't be undone. There's no hope, Laura."

"We'll go home to Attumwa," she said. "Daddy will understand. We can live with him and Mother until you get your degree. I'll get a job. You'll see, Mark. You'll see. I'm a Duquesne. They can't do this to us. They can't! They can't!"

Mark held her as she sobbed in his arms. He helped her lay down on the sofa. She was quiet. She closed her eyes. Mark covered her with an afghan blanket.

He went to a window overlooking the street. A slate-gray mist descended over his church. Laura found her voice again. It was a monolog. She said, as if to herself alone: "I don't know what to think. It would make more sense if I could only think. Can this be happening to us? Am I dreaming? Is this the latter half of the twentieth century? To ask a man to give up his ministry? And for what? Well, they can have their precious church. If that's the way they treat a fine man like you."

Mark tried his best to understand. He ought to look at the situation from the Presbytery's point of view, to sympathize realistically with circumstances, be calm and rational. Think of the distress of clergy and elders who had to bow to tradition and legal authority in order to get the job done. What job? To please the people with sermons they can *enjoy*? To maintain old churches that are too large for decreasing memberships? To turn a blind eye to sickness and homelessness in their midst? To ignore the evil of segregation?

Laura called. "Mark, come here. I've just thought of something." He sat beside her. "You saw Duane Roberts at the trial, right?"

"Yes, he was in a back pew. I don't know if he had been called as a witness."

Laura looked sharply at Mark. "We both know the real reason for your dismissal, don't we?"

"Yes," Mark said hesitantly.

"And we both know that there is absolutely no reason for suspicion?"

"Yes."

"You never touched one of them?"

"No."

"And yet," she said, still speaking in a tone of pure reason, "the Presbytery acted on the premise that the cause of the split among the members of the church was the fact that you led the march of the Negroes into the fairgrounds. That was the basic cause, wasn't it?" She searched his face for the hoped-for, necessary and all-important confirmation.

"I suppose," he said without conviction. "And don't forget my night in jail."

"That was explained. Anyone with half an eye could see the reason for that."

"Laura, I don't know what you want me to say. I have been judged by the Presbytery and found wanting. Lord knows, I've judged myself more harshly. I'm not bitter about it. I think that, in the long run, Presbytery did me a service." He took her hand. "Let me tell you something." He sat close to her. Only an ocher light from a nearby lamp enclosed them. They were hidden from the world. "I'm not sure I want to be a minister," he said. Laura tried to interrupt. "Let me finish. It's not because of the trial. That is incidental. I'm not discounting its importance. I have to ask myself, why do I want to be a minister? Is it because I felt I was chosen, that I had no other choice? Or was it because it was flattering my ego? Guys I know in Divinity School are there for a lot of different reasons. I thought I had a reason. Now I doubt that it was a real call. I think I'm a misfit. I simply can't do the things that a lot of ministers do to simply keep afloat. I believe in helping people, that's all. Not convert them, not making them members of the church. You see, that's what is expected of me, and that is why I've failed. I'm thinking I would be better off in some other kind of work."

"Whatever you would be happiest doing," Laura said impatiently.

Mark was alarmed. "I can't do anything without your respect, Laura."

"That's a silly thing to say. Of course I respect you."

"And your trust?"

"Dear, I love you. You know that," Laura said cautiously. "What's really bothering you, Mark?"

"I don't want to end up being only a social worker."

"Oh, you!" Laura nudged him and kissed his cheek. "Is it that terrible what they've done to you? " She sat up to find a comfortable position. Mark noted that she did that a lot for the past month. Laura called it her baby bounce. "You could go for a doctorate. Daddy would get you a scholarship."

"I won't take anything from your father," he said stubbornly. "It's something more important to talk about right now. What about the people of Castle Rock, of the church? What's going to happen to them.? It's not that I think I'm indispensable. I owe them something."

"What, for example?"

"I'd like to see Steve and Ruth get married and settle down. I'd like to preach to the migrants again next year. I could be of more help to the Masons and Margaret Gore and Harry Ironwood and all the rest. How can I leave them now? Just when I thought I was getting somewhere with them, simply helping them. That's the hard part, Laura. They're my friends now, every one of them, even Duane Roberts. How much I thought I knew about them, and how little I really know! What's happened to me isn't important compared with what can happen to them. Laura, I need them! They need me!"

"They will get another pastor." She looked around the shadowed parlor. "I've come to love this cosy little manse with its small rooms, even its location in the heart of town. When our baby is born I will like the house even more, I've put a good bit of myself into the manse and sometimes I feel its part of me. To leave this house would be almost as hard as leaving our church people. Castle Rock's a quiet pace and now the people don't seem to be as staid nor quite as cold as they once did. After all we never expected to stay here forever."

"I wouldn't mind," Mark said, surprising himself, now that it was all about to end. "I could have had as good a ministry here as anywhere. Perhaps we are being led. Another town, another church, who knows? The main thing is, Laura, apart from knowing that I failed in some ways, I can't blame myself for the division of the church. Not entirely."

Laura shifted a brief distance away from him. "Mark I have something on my mind. Now, don't get mad." She paused to hear his objection, but he was silent. "Tell me honestly, was there ever, ever anything between you and Ruth?"

We all live, of course, on many levels: the rational, which concerns the present; the memory, which concerns the past; and the dream, which concerns the future. Mark told himself that to answer Laura's question truthfully would require an exposition of his particular view of life. But that view was irrational. Besides, it was personal. Putting it into words made it sound childish. Are we not children all our lives? Even in age we look back on childhood and youth but as yesterday? For Ruth was not merely Ruth today but Ruth in third grade. Perhaps even Helen laughing under the pines. Love plays strange tricks, but seldom leaves us laughing at ourselves. If he had failed to help Ruth because he didn't love her, then why did he help her? Or anyone? But that was generalizing. Each person was a special case.

"What are you thinking about?" Laura asked.

"About your question."

"I'm sorry," Laura said. "It wasn't fair."

"Maybe," Mark said. He felt as if he was standing outside himself taking a good look at himself, perhaps for the first time. "Maybe it was wanting to be ordained, being set apart, that was my mistake. For me, anyway. What do you think?"

"I like being a pastor's wife," Laura said. "Some days it's been so boring I can't stand it, but there are compensations. The women of the church seem to look up to me as some sort of paragon. Why, I'll never understand. They seem to think a pastor's wife was made in heaven. How was I to know that's the way it would be in Castle Rock? Anyway, I don't think this town is everything. Everyone knows, even the people here admit it, that Castle Rock is a fractured town. It's a sick little American town. Why, these people don't know they're alive sometimes, the way they act. They act as if they never heard of the state, let alone Washington, D.C. I'm almost ashamed to mention Attumwa, because they've probably never been there. To tell you the truth, I'll be glad, in a way, to leave."

And so for hours they talked about Castle Rock and its inhabitants, their secrets and their idiosyncrasies, until they became quite giddy with laughter and recollection. At last they went to bed together, and the truth that had once divided them, like a coiled snake, had departed. In his morning dream Mark preached fire and damnation. When he awoke he felt triumphant.

Chapter Thirty-Two

Laura had put all thought of change behind her after she had deserted Mark and fled to her parents' mansion. She was able to accept Castle Rock and its restrictions for Mark's sake, knowing that she had chosen this life, or had been chosen for it, and this was the rock upon which she could lean. Now everything was coming loose. The rock was crumbling, turning to sand beneath her. She had to hold on just the same or else lose her balance and be torn away by the rising, dangerous flood of opposition that awaited them,

In mustering her strength for the ordeal of what might be the final worship service, Laura found herself praying seriously. When she had finished praying she was considerably surprised, especially since her words seemed to have come to her easily and fluidly. She was not fully conscious that many of the words and phrases she had spoken had come from Mark's pastoral prayers. But she did have the passing thought that Mark had taught her, indirectly, how to pray. Most of her words expressed thanksgiving, and her present attitudes, she knew, had been adopted from Mark's.

Strangely, as she sat by their bedroom window gazing at the dun color of the yard, she felt no regret. Now she was eager to have the day done with, to have the whole business end so that they could get on with the next phase of their lives, whatever that was to involve. Prayer seemed to have given her a sense of divine direction. She felt that God's will had been obscurely expressed, but that there had been much good come out of Mark's ministry in Castle Rock, and surely something even better would be built upon that. Laura had a theory that no life experience is without meaning.

Thus, when the time came for her to cross the street to the church, she was surprised to find herself much calmer than she had expected. She walked with a smile, greeting the people who stood on the stone porch as if this worship service would be no different than any other Sunday. Mrs. Orduff and Mrs. Coffey were the first to welcome her as she came up the steps. Each extended a friendly hand.

"You look lovely, my dear," Mrs. Orduff said. "What a lovely dress."

Mrs. Coffey asked why a congregational meeting was to follow the service. "I suppose you know about that, Laura."

"Yes," Laura said calmly. "I understand the elders notified everybody so let's see what happens."

In the sanctuary, which was already half full, the two women accompanied Laura to her usual pew close to the pulpit. They entered first and Laura followed. They bowed their heads in silent prayer. Ten minutes later there was hardly an empty pew. Mrs. Trane sounded the organ. Choir and congregation stood up in unison. Laura turned to watch Mark and Pastor Fleming come down the center aisle side by side. She noticed that a few people stopped singing as they were obviously wondering who Pastor Fleming was. From the pulpit Mark introduced the visiting pastor, who appealed to members to remain in church following the service. "This congregational meeting will be crucial for the life of your church," he said.

Throughout the first half of the service Mark made no reference to the nature of the meeting. As usual, he announced coming events, read Scripture, prayed, disbursed offering plates and called out the numbers of hymns to be sung.

Only when Mark began his sermon did Laura note the unusual intensity of his delivery.

"Have any of you seen a desert?" he asked. To begin a sermon with a question was a recent innovation for Mark. He had told Laura that this was a valuable "hook" to gain the congregation's attention. Laura told herself to pay attention to his meaning and not to concentrate upon making critical mental notes. That afternoon, after lunch, would he would question her, point-by-point, on the thoroughness of his exposition, on the effectiveness of his gestures, on the impact of his inflections?

"…Going into the desert was Jesus' own idea," Mark was saying. As he talked he looked toward a window as if he was gazing at a formidable desert. "Jesus must have thought about going on that journey for a long time. He didn't go there on the spur of the moment. He went there to get away from it all, to give Himself time to think through His future ministry, think it through to the bitter end."

For five minutes Mark painted a picture of that desert: "Fearsome place—nothing, nothing at all, to eat—gnawing pain of hunger—forty days!"

"Of course He didn't know He would be tempted," Mark went on. He surveyed the rapt faces of the congregation, and once met Laura's glance, which she hoped was filled with courage for him, although she felt a trembling in her hands. "We never know that we are going to be tempted either---I mean where or when. I reject the idea that He went into the desert in order to be tempted, to subject Himself to temptation. That is proved by one of the very temptations that He rejected. It is a temptation itself to think of our temptations as a form of trial, like Joan of Arc's. Saint Joan's temptation was to denounce her voices. That would have been easy. The temptation was subtle, reasonable. Some say that in rejecting the temptation she found the strength to suffer the stake. But that is a wrong interpretation. The stake was suffering and torment, even as was the Cross, made no less easy by her rejection of temptation. In the same way, Christ's temptations and His rejection of them no more prepared Him, by strengthening Him, for the future, than Saint Joan's temptations prepared her. Jesus was being true to Himself. He was human as we are and was tempted as we are. He succeeded in rejecting the temptation even as we can have the power to reject our temptations. In a sense He had already rejected the temptations by going into the desert."

As Mark went into the first of his three points, the exposition of Jesus' temptation to turn a stone into bread, Laura felt a strong desire to stand up and tell him to stop. His preaching was akin to wandering in the desert. He was being repetitive, often incoherent. She was afraid. This was not Mark as he usually preached: simply, practically, enthusiastically, dramatically, understandably. And yet it was his bold self-assurance, a strength of will, which seemed to renew and reassert itself, that filled her with purpose. She felt strong enough to conquer anything. All at once she felt as if she was coming out of darkness into light.

Following the closing hymn and benediction, Mark asked Pastor Fleming to open the congregational meeting. Here and there a person stood and left the sanctuary, including Duane Roberts and Russ Neeby. The remainder appeared to Mark to be anxious and attentive.

Pastor Fleming briefly summarized the Commission's hearing and action. Mark would have to abandon his position as their Student Pastor. "You have read all about it in the newspapers," he said. "The question is: do you want to retain Mark as your pastor? I need a firm response. A positive response. If possible a total Yes. Please understand. This is crucial, if too many of you say No then my hands would be tied. Mark needs to appeal the decision of the Commission to a higher court, that of our state Synod. Without an overwhelming Yes vote, Mark doesn't have a chance. So, what I want you to do, is to think this over prayerfully. We will have a simple yes or no secret vote. Each of you will be given a paper ballot." He laughed. "Democratic, don't you think? You have fifteen minutes." Mark's people were silent. Two elders stood ready to distribute the ballots.

Suddenly Steve stood up. He was in a back pew. "We don't need a ballot," he shouted. "Everybody has been talking about Pastor Mark ever since he integrated the County Fair. Pastor Mark took my place in jail. Look at his hands! He laid his life on the line. He suffered a beating for us all."

Laura stood up, then Mrs. Orduff and Mrs. Coffey. The choir rose together. Mrs. Crane sounded a chord of trumpets. Pew by pew Mark's people stood up. They applauded noisily, in unison. They roared "Yes! Yes! Yes!" They sang *For he's a jolly good fellow*. They hollered "Pastor Mark, Pastor Mark." Mark came down from the pulpit. Laura left the pew to join him. They walked down the central aisle hand in hand. Their people followed. They left the church together and poured into the street. Steve and Ruth joined hands with others, forming a circle. They danced around Laura and Mark, singing *Jesus loves me this I know*.

Chapter Thirty-Three

Later that afternoon Laura joined Mark and Pastor Fleming in the manse parlor. Their discussion lingered on the question of what to do next. After a time Laura excused herself. "I'm feeling a little tired," she said. She went upstairs and was soon lying down on the wide bed, She told herself she ought to sleep, but she could not. She had hoped that at least one of the church members would have visited her. But no one came. No one phoned. She was alone. A silence seemed to have settled like a mantle over Castle Rock.

She must have been asleep for she remembered waking to the sound of thunder. But it was only her heart. She made her way to the bathroom, managed to open the medicine cabinet and found a bottle of pills. She swallowed the one that she should have taken that morning but had forgotten. During the next half hour, as she lay gasping, she told herself she felt much better. Still, the thunder uttered its full-throated roar. A quaver from the baby, then another, then twisting thwarted pain. She knew the time of her travail had arrived.

"Not yet!" she cried aloud. "Oh God, not yet!"

Two days later Mark paid his second visit as a first-time father to Chesterton County Hospital. He parked the Buick in a wide parking lot and walked slowly along the rotted brick sidewalks of Church Street, sloshing through leaf-strewn puddles. The sidewalk ran on endlessly ahead of him like a sluggish red river. He bent into the stiff northerly wind, tightened the collar of his dark blue trench coat and plunged toward the hospital's iron gates.

He hesitated before going in. Looking up, he could see many windows blinking in the light of the sinking western sun. These were the rooms in which he had ministered to the injured, the sick and the dying. There, encircled by ivy, was Darla Clark's room. And there, inside, ablaze with light, was the room in which Lem Orduff died. Over there was that the room in which Larry Bainbridge had lain for many days following an automobile accident. Beyond was the maternity ward where Naomi had nursed her newborn son. Higher up was the room in which Sandy MacDonald passed away. There, now, to the right, was the room in which Laura waited for him.

By the time he reached her room the sun had set. Evening criss-cross ripples of light dappled the floor. A dark slab of shadow, laid down by the window's heavy dark drape, fell across the bed. Laura's bare left arm dangled at her side. Her eyes were closed. She looked deathly pale. A deep moaning cry rose in Mark's throat. "Oh God!" But this could not be! He was by her side in a moment. He raised her in his arms. Laura smiled to give him courage.

"Are you alright?" he asked.

"Of course I'm alright," she said, but her voice was weak. "I didn't hear you come in, that's all. I guess I was sleeping."

"Darling! Darling!" He cradled her. He did not like looking into her failing eyes nor upon her opaque (and thankfully, not transparent) skin. He wanted to remember her as she had been when she was in the garden and her hair shone golden in the sun. He held her as he had held her once on the promontory above the River that golden afternoon long ago when their smiles pledged each to the other and the River ran faultlessly from the hills. Now, with the sun down, the room dim and colorless, and her so faded, this body that he held was like a stranger to him, uttering silence like a cold xenophobic stone. (Not like the stones of Springport Bay, which lay softly one on the other down to the sea's edge.) He caressed her hair, once glossy red and with life of its own, but now driven into clotted ribbons. He pressed her fingers to his cheek. How strangely warm!

But I am cold, he thought. Somehow he seemed to have been wrung dry of all emotion. Was that what the ministry did to a man? Had he expended so much emotion on others that he had none left for his wife? The room was cold. Everything about the room, the spare metal bed, the steel cabinet, the upright single-pole lamp, even the shadowed flowers, was cold. Somewhere in the distance, perhaps close by in the street, a dog barked peevishly and insanely. There was no peace in this room. He wondered whether he could take Laura home, if he could think of the manse as a home anymore. At least he could have Laura by his side. That is what he missed--being by her warm contenting side. Since she had been in the hospital the manse had lost every emotion of being a home. It was as cold and cheerless as this hospital room. He had gone about visiting, even though he was no longer officially the pastor, because the elders had become sympathetic for him at last (cold sympathy!) and had permitted him to remain.

"Are you alright?" Laura asked.

"Yes, I'm fine." How marvelous she was to think about him, and her so weak!

"Have you been eating enough?" she asked,

"Sure, Do you think I can't cook?".

"Ruth has been coming in, hasn't she?"

"When she can. I don't like bothering her."

"You've got to take care of yourself, Mark. That's an order."

"Alright. You're the boss."

"And don't you forget it!" She was a strong-willed as ever but her voice betrayed her weakness. Soft like a whisper, her voice had a newly-acquired huskiness which he rather liked. Gone was the stridency she sometimes put on when she became annoyed with his continual absences and his late hours. She appeared content, in good humor even, despite her weakness. Somehow she seemed stronger than he was. Yes, although having the baby had made her weak, she was actually giving him strength!

"Did you see Junior today?" he asked.

"I asked, but they won't bring him to me. He's a good boy, isn't he?'

"A very good, a very fine boy," Mark said. "He looks like you."

"He does not! The nurse told me. He's your spitting image."

"You know what he did? When I first saw him through the glass? He yawned in my face! Bored already. I wish they would bring him to you."

"I want to nurse him," Laura said. "But that young intern, he says I can't. Not yet." She reached up and turned on the lamp. She covered her eyes. 'Oh, that's too bright." Mark blanched at the sudden revelation of her bleached and drawn face. He quickly turned off the lamp. "Do you love me?" she asked suddenly, lending the question a coy twist. While he nodded affirmatively, she said "I feel like a sack of mush. See what I mean." She guided his hand. "No muscles." A pliant softness had indeed supplanted all those hard smooth surfaces fashioned by years of riding and tennis. "It'll be months before I'm any use," she said. "I won't be good for anything."

"That's not you talking."

"Mark, you haven't been through what I've been through. You don't know what it's like."

"Another few days, dear. That's all. You'll be home."

Laura heaved upon an elbow. "We'll go back to Attumwa. You promised."

"Of course we'll go." Mark looked away from her. "Where else is there to go?"

Laura lay back painfully. "I'll be strong again soon, you'll see. It won't take me long, not at the mansion. Won't it be fun to go riding together, like we used to? I've come to one decision. I've decided the only place for us to live is Attumwa. It's no life for us being so far from home."

"Attumwa is your home. It was never mine."

"What do you mean? You lived there all your life, practically."

"You know what I mean. You have your parents."

"Who should mean an awful lot more to you."

"I can take them for a few days at a time but not as a steady diet." Mark held Laura's hand. "Now don't get angry. I promised we'll go back to Attumwa and we will. It's only—"

"What is there to keep us here?" Laura asked sharply. "Haven't we been hurt enough?"

"Yes, I suppose. But it's so—so incomplete. I haven't finished—" He hesitated, searching for the words to express the conclusion he had already reached. He wondered if this was the time to tell her. She needed more time to regain her strength. It would be better to hold back. "I just wondered what you would say if I told you I've been thinking about staying in Castle Rock?"

Laura sank back onto the pillow. She looked at him incredulously and then began to laugh. "Oh, you've had some wild ideas in the past,

Mark Christopher, but this is the wildest. Stay in Castle Rock? Are you?—but that's impossible. Be serious. You've been tossed out by Presbytery, for heavens sake. I know most of the members demonstrated their support, thank goodness. They are your people, but they don't have the power to save you."

"Pastor Fleming said the people want me to stay. Steve says that there is a way while my appeal goes to Synod."

"Good Lord!" Laura turned her face away from him. "Now really. And go through all that again?" She laughed with such derision that she began to gasp for breath. "Why not take it all the way to General Assembly? Why do you think anyone will listen? You're not an ordained minister, only a student."

"I was an accepted candidate."

"No, no, no. I won't stand for it. I'll leave you, Mark. Believe me, I'll leave you. For good. I won't go through the hell you've put me through, not again, not for anything. Believe me, Mark!" She hugged him to her. "You're such a fool! An utter stupid fool. How could you even think of staying here? Anyway, will they pay you? How are we going to live?"

"I'll get a job. As long as they will let me preach. That's all I want."

"They'll kill you. It's the system."

"There's something more important than the system," Mark said.

"I want to go home. That's all I want." Laura turned her face into the pillow.

On the way out Mark stopped at the nursery to see his son again. A short dark-haired nurse raised Mark Junior from his crib and held him up. Mark's son struggled in the nurse's hands as the window light struck his eyes. The baby opened his eyes and squinted. He sees me, Mark thought. Mark Junior had lost the reddish complexion that had perturbed Mark the day before. Now he noticed with greater accuracy that the baby had no hair. He wondered, as he waved a crooked finger, whether something was wrong with the boy.

Mark came back early the next morning. It was before regular visiting hours but he showed his admission card at the nurses desk. He was admitted to the maternity ward. Laura was sitting up, eating breakfast, among the other beds occupied by new mothers. Mark kissed her. He opened a package he had brought her. He took out a blue wool sweater. He helped her put it on. "It's adorable," she said. "Did you see the baby?"

"He's bald, not a single hair on his head."

"So? His hair will grow soon enough."

"I hope. I have so much to tell you, Laura."

"What news could there possibly be?"

"I've reconsidered. I have no right to ask you to go through a risky appeal to Synod. I talked on the phone with Pastor Fleming again. He says it would probably be a tough fight."

Laura was silent. She concentrated on her breakfast . "Mark, please answer this question truthfully: If it weren't for me you wouldn't have given it a second thought, would you? You'd have gone right ahead with your appeal."

"It was an impossible idea."

"Listen to me, Mark. Daddy used to tell me I had a lot of spunk. Lately I haven't been so sure. A minister shouldn't have a wife who's a coward. Are you sorry you married me?"

"It was the best thing I ever did in my life. If you'd rather not talk about it—"

Laura asked a passing nurse's aide to remove her breakfast tray. "We're going to talk about it, Mark," she said firmly. "I suppose I could be like Ruth in the Bible and say whithersoever thou goest I will go, because a minister's wife is believed to be part of the deal when a minister is called to be a church's pastor. I'm sorry, I'm not like that. The only one I've made a deal with is you. And that means if there is to be a fight, then I will fight beside you." She held is hand. "I live my own life, Mark. The church doesn't own me. So I've made my decision independent of the church and independent of you." She was silent as she caught her breath. "It's what I want to do, me alone. It's not for your sake, but for mine. I've never been a quitter and I won't quit now. This is my fight as well as yours."

Laura was actually laughing. "So there," she said. "Put that in your pipe and smoke it."

"I don't have a pipe."

"I'll buy you one. Daddy always says that."

"Then we'll stay?"

"As long as it takes," Laura replied.

He gave her a hug. "I talked with Keith Conaway. He's the Synod executive. He says he will help. We'll spit in their eyes, won't we?"

"You bet," Laura said. "We'll spit in their eyes." She leaned over and kissed him. "I love you, Mark. I love my husband. I love Mark Junior. Let's go to Shangri-La, Mark. I bet I can throw a stone farther than you."

On Church Street the wind whisked the elm trees bare. The sun came out and the sky was clear. Yesterday's chill was gone, replaced by a calm warmth, the forerunner of silent snow.

The End

Printed in the United States
By Bookmasters